I0691512

Also by Mykel Hawke

The Quick and Dirty Guide to Learning Languages Fast
(as A.G. Hawke)

Hawke's Green Beret Survival Manual

Hawke's Special Forces Survival Handbook

KIM MARTIN
MYKEL HAWKE

IN THE DARK OF THE SUN

A JAKE TYLER NOVEL

PIXEL DRAGON PRRESS

In the Dark of the Sun is a work of fiction. Names, characters, places, and incidents either are products of the authors' creation or are used fictitiously. Certain real persons, places, and things are used by permission.

For information email:martinandhawke@gmail.com.

First Pixel Dragon Press US trade edition August 2010

Published and printed in the United States.

Book Design by Kim Martin

www.martinandhawke.com

ISBN: 978-0-9829316-0-8

ACKNOWLEDGMENTS

IN THE DARK OF THE SUN has been dawning for quite a few years, and there are more than a few people who played a role in helping it see the light.

The authors would like to thank Phillip Gonzales, who provided the first push and much of the grist that launched the story—also an amazing Amazonian adventure.

Paul Jimenez and Jack Ewing for their generosity in sharing not only their indigenous knowledge of Colombia and Costa Rica, but also themselves; reading, offering invaluable suggestions, and so much more. Special thanks to *Hacienda Barú*.

Cesar Franco and his colleagues at the *Franco Consulting Group* for their technical expertise and other insights.

For helping to guide us in the skies: H. Jay Brown, US Army MW4 (retired), President and Executive Director, *Combat Helicopter Pilots Association*; Rhea Rippey, US Army Captain (retired) and founding board member of the *Combat Helicopter Pilots Association;* John Fore, US Army CW3 (retired).

In Costa Rica: Bruce Blevins for lending himself and *Banana Bay Marina*. Many thanks to the people and places of Costa Rica: William Cook and the *Pacuare Lodge*; Marco Montoya and the *Hotel Grano de Oro*; Victor Esquivel Chaverri and the *Tabacón Resort*; Orlando Albisetti of *Lynch Travel* in Quepos; the *Hemingway Inn*; Joel Burgess and *Anywhere Costa Rica*; Sean Flynn; Glen Love for the generous use of *Villa Mango* and *Casa Amigo*. The ever-enchanting Dominical.

In Colombia: Jorge Sanjines, Peruvian Air Force Major (retired); Fernando Cadena Duque for his oversight of diving and Cartagena; John Fox of the *Red Lion*; Tim and Becky McKeown for their gracious and memorable hospitality; Jim Carrender for an unforgettable evening in Bogotá.

In the Bahamas: Bill and Susan Little for the Caribbean, sailing, and *Hawk's Nest*. Also for being enthusiastic first readers. Additional help from Anton, JR, and Randy of *Hawk's Nest*, Nathaniel "Top Cat" Gilbert and family, and Susan Murphy of *Tango Beach Cottages*. Special thanks to the Bahamas' *Ministry of Tourism and Film Commission*, particularly Craig

Woods and Angela Archer.

Trevor Perfect for flying, Zak Matten and Bob Anslow for *Millennium* and high-octane sailing, Helena Wescombe-Down and Rosalind Koepke for *Shark Shield*.

There are quite a few others whose help, information, and knowledge was key but who, for security reasons, asked to remain anonymous—they know who they are and for their contributions, we are extremely grateful.

Adrienne Dennis for not only reading, but cheerleading, motivating, and believing.

A band of brothers who, in one way or another, lent their spirit.

Finally, we thank our friends and families for their love and support.

IN THE DARK OF THE SUN

PIXEL DRAGON PRESS
2010

PART ONE

A PLACE CALLED VERTIGO

1

THEY WERE ON THE last mission of the day, skittering swiftly across the jungle canopy in lengthening shadows of the sun's final glare, when the plane in front of them just dropped out of the sky. One moment the Thrush was making a smooth sweep over a large field of coca and in the next, as it rose and began its upward arc over the trees beyond, it lurched, dipped, and was swallowed whole by the jungle.

Perched in the open door of a Bell 212, strapped in but mostly hanging out, Jake Tyler saw it happen and swept his 7.62mm Galil back and forth, looking for telltale signs of a ground-to-air assault. But the only things that seemed to be stirring as their helicopter passed overhead were the treetops, giant prehistoric-looking evergreens whose dense crowns undulated in the aerial downdraft.

"Son of a bitch!" the pilot barked into his headset. "Son of a bitch!" he screamed again, leaning forward over the instrument panel to scan the jungle terrain below, as were the other six occupants from their various vantage points in the chopper. The pilot spent the next several minutes trying to establish radio contact with the Thrush. He got nothing but dead air.

"Shit," Jake muttered, hesitating only a second. "Okay, let's go. Take her down now," he said, raising a fist in the air and hooking a thumb toward the floorboards.

The man seated beside him said, "Not so fast, Jake. We need to get some intel, see what's down there."

"No, Alberto," Jake responded. "We don't have time to wait on intel. I'm going down. Get my medical bag and gear."

Alberto Hernandez, a former Special Forces vet from the Vietnam era, cast him a tight look, but Jake was already reaching for his gear, additional weapons and ammunition. Hernandez knew him well enough to know it was futile to dissuade Jake once his mind was made up. And truthfully, by the time they got any solid intelligence radioed from their base, the embassy, army, or police, it would be too late. They all knew it could already be too late.

Behind Hernandez, their mission commander spoke up. He, too, was former Special Forces with a similar background as that of Hernandez, the only difference being in his rank and stature; where Hernandez was slim and slight of build with short dark hair and a trim mustache, Lieutenant Colonel Paul Traynor was a tall and husky man with a full head of silver hair and beard to match. "Okay, Jake," Traynor responded, "but one of us is coming with you."

"No, let me go," Jake said, glancing dubiously at the *junglas* aboard. "I'll let you know the situation as soon as I get down there."

While the pilot, Haskell Delaney, made circuitous sweeps over the area where the plane had gone down, the co-pilot radioed the search and rescue in to their base commander and Hernandez helped Jake prepare for his drop. The *junglas*, a pair of Colombians manning the opposite door, were armed with slightly heavier firepower—an M60 machine gun and M79 grenade launcher between them—and Traynor took Jake's place with an M4. The co-pilot could be heard communicating with the Huey gunships in their fleet.

"Reaper One, Two, Three, this is Rescue. We have a flyboy down...I say again, flyboy down. SAR medic going in. Take overwatch positions and standby for further, over."

Delaney had maneuvered the Bell to a semi-cleared spot near the tree line, hovering about seventy-five feet over a thatch of brush to provide Jake some cover.

Moments later, Jake flexed his knees and sprung backward from the helicopter, tethered by the rope running smoothly and swiftly through his hands as he descended to the ground five to ten feet at a time. While the maneuver was as effortless and fundamental to him as zipping up a jacket or twisting off a bottle cap, the dexterity and precision with which it was executed could only be mastered by many dozens of drills and even more actual operations. His feet were together, legs straight, body bent at the waist in perfect L formation. The second his boots touched the ground, he unclipped the snap link and disengaged, flipped the safety off his rifle, and radioed back to the crew.

He stood stock-still for several moments, watching and listening as the helicopter pulled up to about two hundred feet, backing off just enough to allow him to hear but hovering close enough to lay down suppressive fire if necessary. Clad in camouflage fatigues, a faded khaki head wrap worn like a do-rag, and sunglasses, Jake easily blended with the bush as he moved toward the tree line. He was composed and clear-headed, characteristics that served him well during special ops, but he could also feel the undercurrent of adrenaline beginning a steady drum-line from his heart. His movements fell in cadence with his pulse, slower but on beat, eyes constantly moving as his mind worked the possible scenarios. Removing his Wiley X shades, he slipped further into the shadowy jungle rim.

This was strange, he thought. Earlier, they had swept the area thoroughly, which was part of what they did on these missions, and declared it secure. But he knew with the number of guerrilla forces in the area that could change very quickly. He'd been doing counternarcotics work in Colombia for several months now as part of a private government contract, and today's five flights were the last scheduled for his current stint. As one of the more experienced Special Forces operatives, Jake had been recruited to work CSAR—combat search and rescue—in a dual security and medical role. This was not his first time working counternarcotics; he'd completed a contract years ago, vowing at the time it was not something he would be doing again. Funny how life had a way of boomeranging on you—there had been a lot of things he said he'd never do again. Like stalking through a Colombian jungle in narcoguerrilla territory.

Not more than an hour ago their Bell, as part of a four-chopper escort team for a pair of Turbo Thrushes, had taken the lead in securing the area to be sprayed. Normally, as the SAR bird, they would be hovering high overhead and above it all, out of play, but they were training the

Colombians and therefore leading by example. Flying low and fast at treetop level, they were close enough to spot any movement below and if, after several passes, they had not drawn any ground fire, the Thrushes would begin their dive-and-dump of herbicide. The four choppers then lined up at the corners of the field and began an intricate do-si-do, nearly rotor tip to rotor tip, one pair flying high and the other low, alternating positions. They would make a continual circuit until the planes had completed overlapping swaths and roared off, returning to base.

But something had obviously gone wrong here. Whether from a mechanical malfunction or a guerrilla strike, one plane would not be returning tonight. Jake just hoped its pilot would be.

THIRTY-FIVE MINUTES INTO his search, dark smoke and the distinctively alcoholic vapors of burnt or burning JP4 drew Jake to the downed plane—or what was left of it. It lay smoldering in its own heat, seared and twisted metal in a pit of severed tree limbs, stripped bare and disfigured by a combination of the crash and human pillage. Either natives of a nearby village had gone foraging or, more likely, guerrillas had. Checking a handheld GPS, Jake verified his position and radioed the coordinates to his team. Then, after a quick look in all directions, listening for any movement around him, he picked through the wreckage. Several yards from the debris field, he found the pilot.

He felt a knot of emotion in his throat as he looked down at the skinny middle-aged man, clad in an olive drab flight suit with a University of Iowa t-shirt visible beneath. Wayne Gilby was a crop duster, as were most of the civilian pilots recruited for counternarcotic eradication missions; they had the specialized flying skills needed for coca fumigation. Jake knew this had been Gilby's last pass on the last day of his last mission, and it was a job the man had never wanted. From a conversation he'd had with Gilby, Jake learned that the Iowan had accepted the contract as a last resort because jobs were scarce in the farm belt. He had a wife and five children to provide for, and in taking the counternarcotics contract he had been given assurances that the next non-combat job would be his. Earlier today, Jake had seen him high-five one of his fellow pilots, probably already thinking about a fishing trip with his kids or catching a movie with his wife, looking forward to going home.

A cursory inspection revealed that, like the plane, Gilby had been stripped of his equipment: weapons, radio, survival gear. It was impossible to tell if he'd been alive after the crash, but from the pulverized body parts, Jake doubted it. At least he hoped the crash had killed Gilby, and quick; the pilot's throat gaped open from the slash of a broad blade, the gelatinous glob of blood still sticky. Now, gazing down at the gruesome remains of Wayne Gilby, Jake's thoughts turned to getting his body back to the chopper.

Surveying the dense woods around him, listening even more intently now that he knew others had been here, Jake could hear the distant drone of the helicopters but little else. From indeterminate depths of the jungle, branches creaked and palm fronds swished with the play of monkeys and other small creatures. That was a good sign as it gave indications of nature undisturbed. But then he picked up something from another direction that tripped the hair-trigger on his internal warning system, something that simultaneously sent a bevy of large-winged birds fluttering noisily off toward a skylight in the tree canopy. That deep green ceiling had darkened appreciably since he'd last looked up; day was tilting toward dusk, and in the Amazon the sun could show its dark side with jarringly sudden stealth. Like the outline of an assassin caught in a passing shadow. Now he could clearly hear sounds he recognized, a mashing of spongy bog alternated with crunching thatch— boots marching across and through brush, many pairs of boots.

Boots. Here, where he was, boots meant guerrillas or paramilitaries.

Glancing back at Gilby, Jake weighed whether to take him now or come back later with reinforcements. "Oh fuck it," he murmured. "Got to get you outta this shithole, buddy."

Hefting Gilby's body over his shoulder, Jake struck out in the opposite direction, sweating and breathing heavier with the additional cargo and his quickening pace. Though slight of build at five-foot-ten, 165 pounds, he was hard-bodied and well-accustomed to hauling a weighty rucksack, medical kit, weapons and ammo, but he was grateful Gilby was a little guy. Even as the latent sun receded, its darkening heat sweltered through the jungle canopy and Jake could feel his perspiration spreading, plastering clothing to skin. Flies and mosquitoes buzzed around his face, drawn by the stench of death draped over his shoulder. Behind him, the jungle had become ominously quiet. There were different kinds of quiet, and this was not the good kind.

He had gone about a hundred paces when he came to a savanna of grasses that ranged from ankle- to shin-high. In the opening above, the sky was mockingly blue, a last seduction to the escaping day. The shadows below, around him, seemed to momentarily disappear as the atmospheric balance shifted. The grasses seemed impossibly green. He crossed to the far side of the small field and propped Gilby's stiffening body against the broad base of a tree, and spoke into the tiny boom mic that curved around his jaw.

"Reaper Rescue, come in...requesting—" Jake's transmission was abruptly cut off by a rattling from within the trees. Now brush crackled and popped around him, dust kicking up at his feet as thudding objects pocked the ground. Bullets. He raised the Galil and pivoted, right then left, then right again. And saw the guerrillas, about a hundred or more, closing in from the periphery. He was about to be ambushed.

"Reaper Rescue, do you read me?" he called again, more emphatically, "Reaper Rescue, I have company!"

His radio stuttered, but the eruption of gunfire all around him obliterated the communication. Jake emptied a clip from his Galil as he scrambled around the tree, bark flying off in chunks as bullets struck the buttress. A large limb cracked overhead and thumped down beside him. By the time he snapped another clip in the gun, automatic fire was raining down from the choppers, driving most of the guerrilla force back beyond the tree line. A few troops continued to dart forward until Jake's fire repelled them, but a determined pair managed to slip behind a pocket of trees adjacent to him.

Risking quick exposure, Jake swung around the front of the tree and came up behind the pair, unsheathing his Glock 17 and firing two rounds into the backs of their heads before they even knew he had moved. They fell forward into the brush with a soft thud.

"*Reaper Rescue to Medic,*" he heard in his earpiece. Paul Traynor's voice. "*Advise with status, over.*"

"Ready for exfil if you are," Jake called back. "Recovery is DOA and in custody, over."

Just then he heard the Bell 212 lowering to the clearing, the Hueys still firing steadily into the trees. Jake shouldered Gilby's body once more and made a dash for the chopper, pushing into the vortex created by its spinning rotors. Several pairs of arms reached out to assist him, taking Gilby. He hoisted himself into the Bell as bullets pocked its titanium skin. Seconds later, it sped off in a cyclone of dust and smoke.

Watching as clusters of guerrillas reemerged and swarmed through the swaying grasses below, Jake guzzled a bottle of water in one big gulp, wiped his mouth with a sweat-drenched sleeve, and said grimly, "Another day at the office, boys." Unfortunately not one of the better ones, he thought, as he gazed at the now-covered body of the fallen pilot whose wife was a new widow of war—another kind of war, but war nevertheless.

DUSK WAS FINALLY DROPPING her heavy lids on the day as the Bell 212 headed back to base camp. It was located near the juncture of the Colombian departments of Caquetá, Putumayo, and Amazonas, within a small counternarcotics police outpost surrounded by grasslands and jungle. Except for a rural town and military compound about ten kilometers to the east, the base camp was pretty well isolated from everything but *narcotraficante* activity and conflicts between the armed forces, paramilitaries, and guerrillas. The evening sky was cloudless and already sprinkled with stars, but as the helicopter began its descent, stars were not the only thing twinkling.

They were flying at less than a thousand feet when the ground below lit up with a profusion of flashes, and within seconds the armored floor plating began to vibrate as bullets struck. Jake could feel the sensation through the soles of his boots, causing his feet to actually itch. "A little too close for comfort, bro!" he remarked to the cockpit. With their lower altitude, slower speed, and open-door exposure, they were most vulnerable; their best asset now was upward mobility.

Haskell Delaney gave him a thumbs-up in acknowledgment and lifted the Bell to the safety of higher altitudes, where the temperature immediately dropped a good twenty degrees. Jake tugged on his night vision goggles and stuck his head into the chilled air to survey the scope of activity. Through the NVGs, the artillery seemed to float weightlessly through the atmosphere like bright green blips on a radar screen.

Relaying reports from his satcom radio communications, Alberto Hernandez said, "There is a front of about five hundred troops just outside of the base. Apparently they knew our schedule and approach path and figured out about where we would come into firing range."

"That's an awfully tall order for our gunships," Paul Traynor replied. "How are we doing on fuel? Think we can bypass and make it to the forward base?"

"We're light," Delaney said from the cockpit, "but it's within range." But under his breath, he muttered, "Fuck. Fuck, fuck, fuck."

After they'd been circling the base camp for thirty minutes, Jake heard the co-pilot, a young Puerto Rican named Juan Castro, nervously tell Delaney that the low fuel light had flashed on, indicating about twenty minutes of fuel left.

"Shit," Delaney sputtered. "Okay, listen up boys and girls...I gotta put this bird down, so smoke 'em if you see 'em!"

Everyone else on board anchored themselves into position with their weapons and prepared to fire as necessary. With the Huey gunships leading the way, the Bell once again began its descent. Below, the ground was still alight with gunfire, but now it appeared to be moving away from the compound.

Hernandez was grinning. "Looks like the Colombians rallied their troops and are pushing them—"

The rest of Hernandez's sentence was lost in a screechy cough from the Lycomings just before the chopper hit the ground with a jolt that caused it to teeter sideways on one skid. When it reeled down on the other skid, Delaney jerked himself out of his harness and vaulted from the pilot's seat.

Jake turned to congratulate his friend for making the landing, but Delaney was already gone.

WHEN JAKE TYLER HAD stepped off the aircraft that March evening years before, the suffocating heat hit him like a sledgehammer. The next thing to hit him was a gurney with a soldier missing half of his chest, another right behind him with pulverized bone and hunks of muscle protruding from a hemorrhaging arm. "Got your medical bag?" he was asked. "Need you to fix these two first, and there are more waiting. Come on, let's go!"

That had been his initial welcome to Colombia, when he'd flown in from Bogotá on a small plane, wearing a black wool turtleneck and slacks—clothing suited for the mountain cool of Bogotá but nothing short of ridiculous for the tropical Amazonian climate. He had been recruited by Alberto Hernandez to sign on with the Virginia-based defense contractor for what had been described as "a lucrative but short-term counternarcotics gig." As it turned out, the lucrative part was truthful enough; short-termed it was not. But that, he conceded, was partly his own fault.

The infamous Drug War that raged and ravaged Colombia had seemed to turn the corner at the break of the millennium, with significant crop reduction by eradication efforts, a dramatic increase in combat-ready Colombian troops trained by the US military, hundreds of tons of cocaine seized and labs destroyed, thousands of guerrillas and paramilitaries captured and again as many arms confiscated. But after 9/11, Colombia's problems became a forgotten fly lazily circling the remains of a freshly stripped rack of ribs, searching for just one fissure with a dangling piece of meat. It wasn't long before eggs were laid, maggots hatched, and new outcrops of flies emerged. Consequently, as the world order began to re-brick into its defensive wall against terrorism, a new "Plan Colombia" was hastily and half-heartedly drawn, renamed the Andean Counterdrug Initiative. After years of renewed efforts—despite recent setbacks to the enemy—cocaine production had spiked and now there was military intelligence of a new guerrilla offensive dubbed *Plan Renacer* or "Plan Rebirth." The new counternarcotics ops would start by picking up where the last left off, resuming eradication and interdiction operations but on a much smaller scale. Once again, the call went out to special operatives for hire, and once again Alberto Hernandez had placed a call to Jake Tyler.

Once again, he'd said yes.

When Hernandez initially contacted him, Jake was just out of the military, but—as was the case with so many combat veterans—quickly discovered the military machine was not quite ready to let him go and the military mindset was not quite ready to leave him. The counternarcotics gig seemed to be a good transition, or so he'd thought at the time. Unlike Jake, Hernandez had found his niche in life and was happily living it, working in Colombia for close to twenty years and dividing his time between inspired medical missions, a thriving emerald business, and working counternarcotics. A rather odd mix on the surface, but Hernandez knew everybody on both sides of the fence, which made him the perfect point man for staging operations of all kinds in this volatile theater.

Now, as Jake hopped off the Bell 212 and looked around for Delaney, the irony of the unfolding scenario struck him like those gurneys; the heat was still oppressive, and he was being approached by several Colombian soldiers on the run, shouting, *"Medico! Medico!"*

He drew in a tight breath, checked his weapons, resettled his gear, and trotted briskly toward them. *"Qué? Dónde?"* he asked.

In a fusillade of Spanish, the soldiers directed him to a triage area inside the compound where the wounded had been brought. Weapons and ammunition lay scattered like abandoned toys, the acrid smell of urine, body fluids, vomit, and sweat was pervasively sour. Hernandez was already making assessments on the half-dozen men sitting or lying on the blood-smeared floor. He gestured to Jake with one hand. "Here, this one first. A couple of guys were patrolling the perimeter and got hit by a command-detonated claymore."

Jake knew immediately why this man had been pegged first priority when he glanced down and saw Hernandez's other hand clamped over splayed leg flesh, a nearly severed femoral artery spurting blood as red as rubies. Jake quickly dropped his rucksack and medical bag, rolled up his sleeves, and hunkered down across from Hernandez. He snapped on a pair of latex gloves and began to dig wads and rolls of gauze from his medical bag, lots of it. The two of them labored to staunch the bright red flow while also treating the soldier for shock. Numerous times, they thought they had lost him. Blood gurgled and geysered, but finally slowed to a manageable ooze. When he got to a point where he could leave the man to Hernandez, Jake sought the next most serious injury. Spotting the soldier grasping at his chest and hissing with every breath, he pegged him for number two. Possible tension pneumo, he gauged, and knelt before the soldier. *"Relajese, hombre,"* he said calmly, *"Me hare cargo de usted."*

The man nodded dimly and slumped forward. Jake propped him back up, listening through his stethoscope to the rapidly decreasing breath sounds. A needle thoracentesis was going to be necessary, more likely a chest tube. He snapped a BP cuff on, moved the head of the stethoscope to the man's bicep, and confirmed what he already suspected—blood pressure dropping. In Spanish, he addressed a couple of soldiers who had been hovering anxiously, giving them instructions. When they scurried off to do and get what he'd asked, he began to select items from his bag. Pleural decompression needle, tubing, Lidocaine, Betadine, spreaders, Kelly clamp, scalpel, suture kit, dressings. It was going to be late in the evening before his head hit the pillow, pitiful lump of fabric that it was.

Palpating his patient's chest to find the second rib space for the needle insertion, Jake again surveyed the triage area. Pilots, mechanics, technicians, soldiers, and police came and went. *Where the hell was Haskell?*

IT TOOK SIX EXHAUSTING hours to dispense with all the medical emergencies, the latter part of which Alberto Hernandez spent arguing heatedly with the Colombian commander of the compound. The two most seriously wounded they had treated were still fighting for their lives and needed to be medevaced to a hospital, the nearest being some three hours away by flight. The Colombian commander, Major Ramón Grajales, insisted that they were police and as such had no authority to make the flight; they would have to wait until the military could make the arrangements, which would be sometime the next morning—*later* in the morning, as it already was.

"These men will be dead by then!" Jake protested angrily.

Major Grajales shook his head ruefully. "I am sorry. Really. But no, I just cannot allow—" He stopped abruptly as the muzzle of Hernandez's pistol touched his temple.

"Hágalo. Haga que sucede," Hernandez spat. Do it. Make it happen.

The major authorized the flight.

Hernandez muttered a surly goodnight to Jake and departed for his bunk. Jake stood for several moments, exhaustion rolling over him in an almost nauseating wave, torn between collapsing on his bed and looking for Delaney. It was not like Delaney to just disappear, particularly when there was a critical need for his help. Granted, Delaney's role here was not a medical one, but he had never shirked assisting Jake with anything. Not here, not ever. So what the hell was going on? Jake knew Delaney was upset about the landing, but in the bigger assessment of their gauntlets here, it was nothing more than a minor mishap.

Stifling a yawn against the back of his hand, Jake decided he would sort things out with Delaney in a few hours. And in a few hours, they would be packing up for their last break from this mission, a two-week respite before completing the contract.

Then what? he wondered.

As he trudged over to the corner of his clinic and began to peel off his clothing, indifferent to the stench of sweat and blood now coagulating in the fibers, all he could think about was leaving here for two weeks. Two weeks and then, after the final month, done. Finished. Over. The light of that promise flickered in his mind and flashed a brief rush of reverie that quickly faded with the reality of sheer exhaustion.

He pulled on a pair of running shorts and a t-shirt and dropped onto his cot with a weary moan that seemed to resonate in his bones. The fingers of his right hand slid sleepily through his hair, those of his left absently touched the insignia on his shorts. *De Oppresso Liber.* To liberate the oppressed. To liberate…to free. His lids twitched and images of past such liberations exploded against his irises. Then sleep crooked an enticing finger and blew titillatingly in his ear. With one final sigh, he let sleep lead him to her lair.

So he never saw Haskell Delaney's shadow pause, then pass, the clinic entrance. And he did not hear Delaney just outside the clinic's window, telling someone, "I'll fucking be there." And: "No, he doesn't know—and he won't."

Outside the window, somewhere beyond the base camp, the sun was tricking the imminent heat with a cold, flat light that spilled over the great river and sat like an oily slick. In those prescient moments before dawn, the pulses of life quivered. Then stilled. Then beat again.

The sun broke, and lay dawn bare and vulnerable.

2

HE FOUND DELANEY SEATED in the mess hall, drinking the sludge that passed for coffee. Jake poured himself a cup, scowling at the first bitter swallow as it coursed down his throat and lay like hot tar in his belly. Eyes fixed on the back of Delaney's clean-shaven head, he approached slowly, giving his thoughts a chance to elucidate; he found that irritation still biased them.

Straddling the bench next to Delaney, he asked dryly, "What the hell happened to you last night?"

Delaney half-turned and, seeing Jake, flashed him one of his patent hundred-watt smiles. "Hey, bro!" A plate speckled with small lumps of what might have been eggs dragged through ketchup sat on the table in front of him. They looked like regurgitated blood clots.

"So?" Jake repeated, swallowing the rest of his coffee like a shot. It was easier that way.

Delaney laughed—an anemic titter than sounded like a comic's last-ditch grasp on a dying joke—but didn't look at Jake. The egg curds on his plate seemed to hold more interest. He rearranged them aimlessly with his fork, scraping the tin plate. "So what? Nothing, man. I was just pissed. I took a walk."

"For the rest of the evening? I could have used you. We had a lot of wounded." Reproach bit into his words, leaving a nastier aftertaste in his mouth than the coffee.

"Hey, I'm sorry," Delaney replied, his voice curiously unremorseful.

"I didn't know it was that bad. Straight up. Like I said, I took a walk." When Jake didn't say anything, he added, "If I'd known you needed me, I would have been there. You know that." Twisting toward Jake, he bared teeth that would have drawn the awe of any Hollywood dentist— big, blazingly white, lined up like fence pickets. He laughed again, this one more his typical nasal snort. "C'mon. We got some R&R coming up!"

Jake surveyed the mess area, taking in the activity. Despite the inauspicious events of the past twenty-four hours, the collective mood of the coffee klatch was upbeat. And why not? Jake thought, watching the cooks passing out plates, the men waving forks and metal cups in the air as they chatted. They were alive, and in another few hours would be either spending some time with their wives and girlfriends or, more likely, fleshy Colombian surrogates.

His gaze drifted back to Delaney who had immersed himself in an animated exchange with his co-pilot, Juan Castro. The young Puerto Rican was hiccupping with laughter, slapping his leg as Delaney recounted one of his many manic misadventures. Jake stared at the back of Delaney's head, smooth as polished river rock, bobbing as Delaney plunged into another story, this one—whether by random selection from his seemingly limitless story bank or by a subtle attempt to make atonement—included Jake.

"...and in El Sal you run into a lot of black market medical middlemen," Delaney was saying. "So Jake and me, we're in this clinic—at least we were told it was a clinic—and we're supposed to be dispensing these medical supplies. Mostly drugs. Only we find out that half the stuff is legit and half is shit. Not only counterfeit, but not even drugs."

Castro was leaning in, rapt, and now a handful of others had gathered behind him to listen.

Delaney continued. "So these really bad-ass guys come in and they're armed to the teeth, of course. They tell us they want the goods. And they're looking everything over very thoroughly. One of their guys knew a little something about medicine and tips them off, tells them some of the stuff is shit. Now they think we're trying to screw them. Weapons are drawn. So Jake says, 'Hey, look here, my man...this lot comes from the private stock of an African shaman. It's over a thousand years old and was cached in a diamond mine until we recently confiscated it. There have been some limited trials since and it's...well, it's *potent*.' At this point, Jake lowers his voice and gestures for them to come closer. Then he says, 'Word is, this medicine has some extra benefits...like, shall we say, *sexual* benefits.' Needless to say, they took it all and we got the hell outta there!"

Jake grinned in spite of his annoyance.

If Jake Tyler had a best friend, Haskell Delaney was it, though the designation was hard bought. Jake had made many friends during his adult years, through both the military and his extensive travels, but none of them really knew him. Delaney, who he'd met during at Fort Bragg, came the closest.

After spending four years in the US Marine Corps, Delaney had moved on to the army, and his career ever since ran a near parallel to Jake's. When they'd both been sprung from active duty and were looking for a way to earn a living by putting their elite skills to use, SpecOps had been the result. They spent the next few years recruiting individuals from all branches of military, with an emphasis on diversity of specialties. Their company was marketed as an adventure travel service that also offered customized consulting and contracting; they arranged edgy junkets for thrill-seekers and provided medical and security personnel for individuals and companies. Since the launch of SpecOps, they had packaged and run numerous trips—mostly in Costa Rica, which they had selected as their base of operations—and worked as expert advisors, docs, and bodyguards for business executives, civilian and government contractors, and even filmmakers. Their venture had its highs and lows, but for the most part, was a success. More importantly, it gave them the independence needed to accommodate their renegade lives.

And that's what they were in Jake's view. Renegades. Military was all about structure and discipline, but the lifestyle it designed for its special operatives was one of nonconformity, where walking an electrically charged high wire would always prevail over riding a clearly marked highway from one pre-destined point to another.

One of the cooks had put a plate in front of him. The eggs looked no more appetizing just scooped from the pan, nor did the charred sliver of meat next to them. Jake ignored the plate and rose from the bench. To

Delaney, he said, "All right, bro. Catch you later. Noon, right?"

Delaney stood, facing him. There were gray smudges beneath his eyes, which looked dull and drawn. He held Jake's gaze for a fraction of a second before glancing off, unwilling to endure their laser penetration. "Uh, actually, I won't be leaving just yet."

"What?"

"I told Alberto I'd stick around another day or so to give him a hand with a mercy mission."

"I didn't know Alberto had another one planned," Jake replied skeptically. "Usually he tells me, especially if it's going to involve medical aid. Is it?"

"No," Delaney said, a little too quickly. "There's just another shipment of food and supplies that needs to be distributed, that's all. I'll head out after that."

Jake considered Delaney's response for several moments, something not quite settling, but decided to let it go. "Okay," he said finally, extending his hand for Delaney to clasp, which he did after a hesitation long enough to be awkward but brief enough to overlook. Their eyes met again, and this time Delaney's held on.

Jake said, "See you in CR."

"See you in CR," Delaney repeated, releasing Jake's hand and watching him stride from the mess. He half expected an over-the-shoulder glance back from Jake, but he didn't get it. It was something he would think about the rest of the day.

THE FLIGHT ABOARD THE Cessna Caravan 208 was much later than the scheduled noon departure, but it took little over an hour to reach San José del Guaviare, one of a few forward armament airbases designated for counternarcotics traffic. When Jake stepped off the light utility plane, it was late afternoon and the heat radiating from the concrete shimmered visibly in the sunlight. He hefted his duffels and strode to the hangar, checking in with a police lieutenant before heading for the cafeteria in search of something to quench his thirst.

What he found along the way made him temporarily forget his thirst, but reminded him very quickly how hungry he was.

As he crossed the grass to the small building, he spotted a woman standing in the shade of a tree cluster. Undoubtedly she had seen the Cessna land, had seen him emerge from it, had seen him stride past the hangar. Undoubtedly she had expected him to head that way. For refreshment.

He halted, a little stupefied, and drank in her silhouette.

Elena Torres García continued to gaze toward the revetment, her focus still on the small planes and helicopters parked there. Tall and slender, she wore a full denim skirt with a matching sleeveless halter top, both of which buttoned up the front and both of which were generously filled by the rounds of breast and hip. Her waist was cinched by a wide brown leather belt on which Jake became momentarily fixated, imaging the wicked things he'd like to do with it. She turned then, long locks of hair blowing in the breeze. It was the rich, dark color of Godiva chocolate with glints of cinnamon.

She sauntered over with the lope of a bored feline, and by the time she reached him, he was nearly salivating. A sudden throb in his groin caused him to suck in a big breath.

"Well now," Jake rasped.

"*Hola,*" she responded simply, one hand on her hip, the other swirling a strand of hair around a slender finger. The deep red of a ruby glittered from one of her knuckles.

"What are you doing here?" he asked when command reasserted his voice.

"I am on an assignment," she said, her voice lightly accented.

His brows lifted. "On assignment *here?*"

"Yes." She shrugged a shoulder in the general direction of the command post where, Jake knew, the base commander and his lieutenants took up rank. "For *Semana,*" she added.

"About?"

"I imagine you know."

"The fact that you're here, yes, I imagine I do." He shook his head, feeling a mix of bewilderment and skepticism even as his libido was less inclined to ambivalence. "I find the timing a bit uncanny. Did you know I was coming in here?"

She flicked her lashes, a slow smile spreading her lips to reveal a brief glisten of tongue and teeth. "I guess you could say I had inside information." Taking in his light beard and hair-growth—the lick that tended to curve across his forehead and the ends that curled at his neck—she remarked, "Been in the bush for a bit."

"Uh-huh." Jake's eyes dropped to the wide brown belt again, noticing for the first time that half of the buttons on the skirt below it were undone, providing some mighty enticing views of mocha-tanned leg, even if limited by the portions covered by brown suede boots.

Elena was looking around with the expectant expression of someone waiting for another arrival. She said, "Where is Haskell? Is he not with you?"

"Uh, no," Jake said curtly.

"Oh, I just thought—"

"I was about to get something cold to drink," Jake said distractedly, thinking he needed a lot more than a cold drink. "Care to join me?" In response, she checked her watch. "Got an appointment?" he asked.

"Actually, yes, but I have time."

As they strolled into the cafeteria, Jake asked, "So who is this appointment with? Anybody I know?"

She laughed, a throaty, almost masculine laugh, and replied, "Most intimately."

He gave her a broad, lustful grin, but it quickly deflated when she said, "A helicopter. They are taking me up in a helicopter, after dark."

"Whatever the hell for?"

"Because I asked them to."

JAKE HAD MET ELENA while cooling his heels in Bogotá, on hiatus from his first counternarcotics assignment. She was from Spain but had lived in the Virgin Islands before coming to Colombia. As a freelance journalist, her primary beat was Central and South American politics, something about which she was articulately outspoken. They had become acquainted over drinks in a popular nightspot, and then carried on a marathon political debate that ended in volcanic sexual fusion. In the years since, he had seen her a few times—sharing several long and passionate weekends in various locales—and, on this stint, after his initial arrival in Bogotá a month ago.

Jake watched her swigging from a bottle of Cristal, her full sienna lips encircling the nozzle. As she tipped it up, tilting her head back, water drizzled from the corners of her mouth and he watched the streaks slide down the sides of her jaws to her neck, past her collarbone, disappearing in the deep crease between the mounds that strained against the denim top. His eyes lingered on a single droplet that clung to the cleft.

"Jake."

His head bobbed up. "What?"

"I have to go."

They'd been talking for an hour or so, and now Jake realized that dusk had slipped in and begun to snuff out the sun. Outside, the sky was fanning the embers of brilliant colors and peeling back the first layer of stars, faint points of light scattered like fireflies.

Jake stood, took their empty water bottles, and sunk them into a trashcan with a thunk. Gathering his gear, he said, "Come on."

"I told you, I have to go. They are expecting me."

"Tell me again why you want to go up in a helicopter now?"

"I want to see what it looks like at night, for background."

"You do know there's a very real risk of being shot at," he warned, his expression stern. "This ain't Bogotá."

"And this is not the first time I have been at the frontlines," she replied, a flinty edge to her voice.

"Okay, as long as you've already been cleared to go up, let me see what the plan is. Wait here." He left her in the cafeteria and sought the lieutenant at the command post. Finding him engaged with the helicopter pilot, he had a brief discussion and returned to Elena.

"Are they ready for me?" she asked.

"Yeah, let's go."

"You are going, too? I thought you had a plane to catch."

"I do. Later."

Jake led Elena back out to the helo revetment, to a Bell 212 just like the one he had flown in less than twenty-four hours ago. The pilot and co-pilot had preceded them and were already well underway with the pre-flight check. Before Jake could help her into the cabin, Elena had hiked up her skirt, lifted a booted foot to the doorway, and pulled herself inside. He followed her and spent the next few minutes getting them settled in. The rotors were spinning, the engines whining, and the pilot was radioing his final takeoff data. Jake and Elena were alone in the cabin.

When the chopper lifted from the airstrip, dusk was only a glowing reminder rimming the ground below, a saffron ring dissolving into the deep sapphire of early evening. The stars were more defined and drawing closer together on the deep blue that was moving swifter and swifter beyond them. Tonight the skies were silent but for the steady rumble-and-chop of the Bell as it climbed higher above the Sabanas de la Fuga, a swath of low jungle carved up by the Guaviare River to the north and flanked by the peaks of the Serranía de la Macarena much farther to the west.

They were quiet for a while, watching the landscape grow darker and darker until the deep blue gave way to near black. The helicopter was cruising comfortably at about 120 knots, somewhere around three hundred feet, when Jake reached over and unstrapped her. Leaning close to her, he said, "Come see what it really looks like."

He yanked on the chopper's door handle and slit the rushing night open, pulling a gust of chilled air into the cabin. Elena's hair blew back from her face and he could feel the warmth of her breath on his skin as she said, "Let me see it."

So he did.

First, he lassoed her waist with one of the straps. Then, fitting her with night vision goggles, he positioned her near the door, holding her by the waist as she leaned out and looked down. "Oh my God," she exclaimed. *"Eso es increíble!"*

He had slipped his own NVGs on and was looking down with her, the landscape now visible through iridescent green. He pulled her back inside the cabin and felt her head drop to his lap, fingers tugging his zipper down and slipping inside his cargo pants. An erection that had been rather uncomfortably constrained for the past couple of hours sprang to life in her hands and, just as quickly, in the wet suction of her mouth. He moaned, clutching a fistful of her hair as she worked up and down, alternately licking then nibbling. She managed to fully encompass him, and the sensation of touching the back of her throat nearly drove him mad. His head banged back against the rim of the door and he felt the wind's icy teeth sink into his hair.

Just as he felt his release coming, he lifted her from him and slung her roughly down on the floor plate. She groaned and pulled him to her, their mouths joining in a furious tango of lips and tongues. With nimble fingers, he released the buttons on her top and rubbed his thumbs across the nipples of her breasts. They were as hard and round as small pebbles. He leaned down and nipped them with his teeth, eliciting a yelp of pleasure from her. Abruptly, he rose up, parted her skirt, wrenched the thin strip of thong aside, and pushed inside her. The two of them had moved further over the door edge and now, through the NVGs, he could see the Colombian terrain flowing in a green jet stream below.

He was thrusting hard and fast, one hand on the door and the other on the floor. At their culmination they had edged past the opening, and Jake had to maneuver his weight to keep from pushing her out. Nothing under their necks and shoulders but rushing air and, hundreds of feet below, the Colombian jungle. The surge of blood to their heads was nearly as intoxicating as their climax, but Jake quickly jerked them back in the cabin.

Several minutes later, seated and fully strapped in again as the chopper began its descent, Elena leaned close and said, "So this is what it looks like from up here at night."

"Yeah," Jake replied, his hand closing around her breast with a firm squeeze. "What do you think?"

"I think I have some good background for my article."

"Is that all?"

"No, that is not all," she said with a cryptic smile. "But all for now."

THE INSTANT THE BELL touched down, Jake was sprinting for the Cessna. Elena stood on the asphalt, shrouded by darkness, the slowly unwinding rotors blowing her hair all around. He looked back once but could not see her; she had already been woven into the all-encompassing cape of night. His groin tingled, but the gravity of emotional distance was already pulling him away. The cabin of the Caravan, by contrast with the Bell 212, was light and cozy. He sank down in his seat, closed his eyes, and waited for takeoff.

NINETY MINUTES LATER JAKE was making his way through the chaos that always gnarled the El Dorado Airport just outside Bogotá. His military identification got him through the security checkpoints with relative ease, and he had a little time before his TACA flight to San José departed, so he went in search of a snack. Suddenly, he was starving.

He was backing away from the counter at Presto, taking a generous bite of a roast beef sandwich, when he bumped into someone. He turned to offer a quick apology to the man, who was bent over a large duffel bag that had long seen better days. Jake would have recognized the top of the man's head anywhere, even with the weathered khaki cap covering it.

Alberto Hernandez.

Over the terminal din, he heard the first boarding call for his flight.

3

FOR THE FOURTH TIME that day, Jake tapped one of the programmed speed-dials on his cell phone, and for the fourth time he got voicemail. He'd already left a message—two, in fact—and sent a text. Delaney had not responded.

He thought: *Haskell, what the fuck are you doing?*

The previous evening, Jake had only a couple of minutes to talk to Alberto Hernandez before sprinting to catch his flight out of Bogotá, and all he'd learned was that there had been no additional mercy mission and Hernandez had no idea why Delaney remained behind.

"Damn," he said out loud, and set the BlackBerry down beside him. He was seated on a concrete bench near the edge of the Plaza de la Cultura in downtown San José, a busy and colorful square off Avenida Central. He had spent most of the day reconnecting with his provisional life; dropping by the bank and the post office, checking his email, making phone calls. One, repeatedly.

Sipping from a container of iced tea, he fanned through a stack of opened mail, a mix of aging bills, business and commercial correspondence. Very little of a personal nature—his provisional life. Over the years, returning from a military deployment or a mission had become something of a rote of passage, a narrow window for reassessment and recalibration. Sometimes, while passing through that window, he felt the faint breeze of yearning for something he could not define, something he could sense but not quite see or hear, something he could feel but not quite touch...and so he never reached. When the window closed, the breeze snuffed out, he would turn back into the wild wind he had always known. But somewhere, distantly, intimately, the breeze whispered in the delicate tinkle of chimes.

It was approaching dusk as he worked his way through the mail and returned phone calls, idly watching the activity that swarmed around him. It had been a bracingly beautiful day, the temperature topping out around eighty degrees, sun buttering a sky of popcorn clouds in a blue only a photographer's Polaroid filter could create. A dozen or so yards away, the pedestrian mall of the *avenida* streamed with people, and tourists were still crossing back and forth between the shops and hotels, the baroque grandeur of Teatro Nacional looming in the rear. Mimes and magicians performed, street vendors hawked, children tossed peanuts into clusters of pigeons. A roving clown was juggling a fistful of balloons and an endless strip of colorful handkerchiefs.

He was talking on his cell phone with a local SpecOps associate when something else caught his eye. Across the *avenida* a pretty little blond was drawing a great deal of attention from the male *Ticos,* something that obviously made her uncomfortable. They were leering and whistling as she walked tentatively along the mall, occasionally glancing at what might have been a map or, perhaps, something with an address as she was also peering incomprehensibly up at storefronts and street signs in search of mostly non-existent numbers. With her fair skin and pale blond hair, she could not have been a more conspicuous *gringa* in this Latino capitol. She wore a white voile sundress, shirred at the top and ruffled at the bottom, the hem of which was low enough to preserve modesty, but high enough to invite lingering appraisals of her slender legs.

As Jake continued talking and listening on his cell phone, he watched her with the kind of abstract interest a butterfly might garner—something remote and pretty fluttering at the periphery of his vision. But her growing anxiety was evident, and he found himself watching her more intently as his conversation began to fade in and out like a radio station not quite holding the signal.

"—a few interesting inquiries that I think you might want to pursue if—"

"What?" Jake asked, his attention shifting back to the voice on his cell phone. He looked down at some notes he had scratched on the back of an envelope.

"I was saying, there are some good potential gigs if you want to—"

But Jake was only half-listening now, as he saw something happening that galvanized his attention in an instant.

CALLIE KANE STOOD IN front of a shop selling native art and handicrafts, puzzling over the ambiguous directions written on a piece of notepaper clipped to a small map of the city. The directions were penned in her own handwriting, transposed from an email sent by the man she was supposed to meet somewhere, as near as she could determine, along Avenida Central at the Plaza de la Cultura. At least that's what she thought his directions meant, but now she wasn't so sure. The email she had received less than forty-eight hours ago instructed her to look for a Latino man, mid-thirties, of average height and build wearing tan slacks and a white shirt. It occurred to her just how vague and generic the description was; she had, in fact, passed several men during the course of the day that categorically qualified. At this moment, as she looked up and down the busy pedestrian mall and across to the square, she spotted several "average" men wearing some combination of tan-and-white. And many of them looked pointedly back at her, as had others everywhere she'd been, but their interest seemed disconcertingly salacious.

Over the past few hours she had been enjoying the day, a little nervous but exhilarated with the sense of adventure; now she was beginning to feel somewhat overwhelmed.

Shortly before noon, Callie had deplaned from an American Airlines flight, taken a taxi to the hotel she'd booked, dropped her luggage, and set out to get a sampling of the city before the appointed meeting time. From the Hemingway Inn, a charming and historic bed-and-breakfast, she walked down the hill to the Museo de Jade where she marveled at the breathtaking eleventh-floor view of the mountain-capped city. Next, she crossed the street to the Parque España with its towering trees full of chattering birds. Strolling around the pretty green park, she took in the statue of Juan Vásquez de Coronado, Costa Rica's Spanish founder, commanding in bronze from the center of an elevated fountain. She was struck with the realization that she was standing on grounds steeped in Spanish history, tales of Indians and pirates and conquistadors. Leaving the park, she passed Escuela Metálica, a century-old metal-sided schoolhouse that had been shipped in pieces from Belgium. A harried pair of teachers was trying without much success to pose a rambunctious group of children to have their picture taken in front. Callie smiled as a couple of the dark-haired youngsters waved vigorously at her and called out *hola*. She gave them a wave back and continued, crossing over to the larger Parque Morazán through a small Japanese garden and on to the center of the park, which was dominated by a dome-roofed structure called Templo de la Música. Gazing at the tall neo-classical columns supporting the big cupola, she imagined a band of musicians serenading couples by moonlight.

Heading south on Calle 5, she had then traversed a few more blocks to Avenida Central, turned right, and begun her search for a man wearing tan and white who would be meeting her at 5:30 PM between Calles 3 and 5 of the pedestrian mall. He had given her some distances for the exact spot—so many meters past this or that—but she had no idea if she was even in the vicinity.

It was now nearing 5:45 and she had been wandering the length of the strip from corner to corner, expecting an accented voice she'd heard only twice on the phone to say, *"Hola...Dino DeMarco—"*

"—You must be Callie."

She wheeled around to face a Latino man in his mid-thirties clad, as indicated, in tan slacks and a white guayabera shirt. He was also wearing a white Panama hat and very dark sunglasses, a lot of gold jewelry, and white Toschi loafers without socks. He carried a leather satchel and smelled faintly of rum, atomized with mint breath spray and a citrus-based cologne.

"Yes," she replied, wariness slowly giving way to relief. Sunlight was rapidly draining from the sky and she was suddenly, glaringly aware that she was alone in a big city, a good many blocks from her hotel, talking to a man who was essentially a stranger.

"I apologize for being late," he said, showing her his teeth in a wide, ingratiating grin. "Did you have any trouble finding your way?"

"Only a little. I enjoyed the sightseeing."

"Good, good," he replied hastily, glimpsing over his shoulder, back toward a bank of phones where shadows were drifting over the cement. "I am happy to meet you, *Señorita*. I think you will be pleased with what I have arranged for you." He paused, assessing her with an appreciative nod. "You are *muy hermosa, Señorita...muy hermosa.*"

"What does that mean?"

"I am saying that you are very beautiful. You were wise to hire me as your guide. You will attract much attention here, not all of it desirable."

Callie clutched her purse, a woven white bag hanging from a macramé strap, tighter to her side. "Mr....*Señor* DeMarco, did you bring the agreement?"

"Yes. Yes, of course. You have the fee?"

"Yes."

"I hope you understand why I require cash up front." When she didn't answer right away, he said, "As I told you, in order for me to customize this kind of itinerary, I will have to pay on demand and generously."

"Okay," she said, but for the first time she was wondering if this was such a good idea.

As if he could read her reluctance, he asked, "Did you check the references I supplied?"

"Yes, I did." In truth, she had only checked a few, and now regretted not delving further. Even so, what she'd heard seemed solid enough even if her research on the Internet was inconclusive.

Dino DeMarco gave her another toothy grin and clasped his hands together. A thick gold chain linked his left wrist, a Rolex banded his right. He said, "Okay, then."

Hands shaking slightly, Callie reached into her purse for the envelope containing a hundred US dollar bills. A hundred *fifty*-dollar bills. Inhaled deeply. And took the envelope out, gripping it in her right hand.

At that moment, a man came barreling from beyond the bank of phones, a sudden disembodiment from the shroud of shadows enveloping that corner of the square. Pigeons squawked and scattered in a scurry of flapping wings. Callie felt the force of impact before she even registered the propulsion toward her. She was wrenched around, slammed into a cement pillar, and hit in the face with what felt like a boulder. A cracking sound reverberated through her teeth and jaws. Her face was on fire, buzzing and burning with a pain that went from white-hot to near numb almost instantly. The bitter taste of blood seeped into her sinuses, causing her to gag. Images were at once stark and omnipotent and then, just as quickly, a collision of sound and shadow and then, darkness.

ACROSS THE MALL, JAKE looked up from his notes.

4

JAKE SCOOPED HIS MAIL up and sprang from the bench. Sprinting across the *avenida*, he had to dodge couples and families that continued to traverse the pavement oblivious to the commotion taking place beyond them. Dusk was deepening with increasing swiftness and some of the light globes overhead were glowing on. Even so, it was that time of day wherein light and dark meet each other in a hazy impasse, squaring off one final time before their next conciliatory dance at dawn. Most of the pedestrians that filled the mall at this hour were squinting into that haze with the momentary blindness of a night owl negotiating past the first light-infused layers of darkness. But for Jake, who was accustomed to maneuvering in virtually all elements and conditions, the shadowy action was not unlike the spectral images he routinely viewed through night vision, and his mind was already spooling reactionary options.

When he reached the other side of the mall, the only figure remaining was that of the young woman. The man in tan and white had dissolved into the gloom-obscured crowd and her assailant had fled in the opposite direction, darting into a narrow side street. Jake thought he might catch up with one of the two if he took off in pursuit now, but a quick glance down at the blond crumpled against a column made his choice.

Squatting in front of her, he reached for her wrist with one hand and lifted her chin with the other; her pulse was erratic and she was blinking back to semi-consciousness. "Hey," he said, "can you hear me?" He got a weak nod. "Talk to me."

His voice was deep and authoritative, distant then startlingly close. Her lips moved soundlessly and her eyelashes fluttered.

He was cupping her head in his hand now, leaning in as he gently thumbed her eyelids and studied the pupils of both eyes. They were a very dark brown, pupils all but indistinguishable. His assessment was significantly limited in the filtered light offered by the streetlamps, but her responses seemed to be improving slowly.

"Okay, just let me check you out. You got pretty banged up."

She winced as his fingers moved around her face and neck, bruising and swelling already underway. Trickles of blood were oozing from her mouth and nose, as well as from several scrapes and lacerations. He glanced around, noticing for the first time that he had a few onlookers, though more curious than concerned. Of course, there were no police anywhere to be seen.

"*Alguien tiene un pañuelo?*" he inquired of those watching.

A matronly woman with two small children clinging to her dress stepped forward and handed him a handkerchief.

"*Muchas gracias, Señora,*" Jake said, and turned back to the young woman who was stirring a little more. "Easy," he told her, dabbing at the blood. Checking her pulse again, he said, "I think you need to get to a hospital. The closest are several blocks from here, so—"

"No...no, please," she said weakly, trying to raise up.

He put a hand on her shoulder to stop her. "What's your name?"

The question seemed to stump her for a few seconds before she answered, "Callie."

"Callie, I'm Jake. Jake Tyler." He gave her a reassuring but fleeting smile that was replaced with a look of concern. "I saw what happened and you took an ugly hit. I'm medically trained but I can't tell much out here. It's getting too dark. I do know you need further evaluation and care, and it shouldn't wait."

"Please," she implored, "no hospital. I just got here today and I...and I..." Her voice faltered and the words fell off into a fuzzy void.

"Okay. Here's what we'll do. I've got a place nearby. I'll take you there and sort things out further." He briefly considered calling the police but decided there was little they could or would do tonight. The two men that had fled the scene were, without a doubt, long gone.

Carefully, Jake helped her up and slipped an arm around her waist, supporting her as they walked slowly to the corner of Calle 5. With a sharp whistle, he summoned a taxi.

THE PLACE WAS A modest condominium about thirty minutes away in Rohrmoser, a quiet residential burg just northwest of the city. It belonged to a friend who gave Jake access whenever he was in town. The friend was currently away on a business trip. Jake flipped the light switch, illuminating the interior décor of an owner whose presence was probably occasional at best; the furniture was comfortable but lacking in flair, the accents placed to fill empty pockets rather than define any particular style. The walls were stucco, the floors hardwood and tile with neutral-colored area rugs, the ceilings high. A kitchen and dining area was visible over an open bar alcove.

During the short taxi ride to the condo Callie had barely moved, but as Jake led her to a couch she began to tremble. Seeing her for the first time in good light, he noted how pale she was, and scuffed up. In addition to the cuts and bruises from the assault, rough contact with the cement column had scraped her flesh. Blood spattered her white sundress and smeared her face, arms, and legs. But his most immediate concern was twofold: the onset of shock or concussion.

"Okay," he said softly, easing her onto the couch, "I'm going to get my medical bag." Her eyes widened, following him out of the room. When he returned, she was shaking more visibly. Sitting beside her, he said, "So tell me what that was all about." He wanted to get her talking, as that was one of the best and quickest ways to start an injury evaluation.

"What...that...?" she murmured, still dazed and now distracted by his examination. He flashed a penlight in her eyes, his confidence and concentration total. She flinched as his hands slipped around her neck, palpating beneath her skull, the back of her head, around her ears, up to her temples, down the jaw line, along her cheekbones. Her face prickled, felt hot, then cold, then prickly again.

In the low husky voice she'd first heard on regaining consciousness, he began to methodically ask questions as he continued his examination. Though at times his voice had a gentle quality, there was an abiding firmness and probing intensity that compelled response. Did her head hurt? Her stomach? Was her vision blurred? Was she dizzy? Did she feel nauseated? Did she feel any tingling or numbness? Her answer to most of his inquiries was *a little.*

When he began dabbing the cuts and scrapes with antiseptic, she recoiled with a moan. "Sorry, hon," he said, stroking a gash on her cheek with a cotton swab. "I know it stings. Almost done."

Finally, he said again, "Tell me what that was about."

Her own voice hoarse and shaky, she stammered, "I was meeting a man…I hired him as a guide and I…and I didn't know…I didn't know him. I—" She broke off as a sob snatched the last from her breath and tears came, trailing across streaks and smudges of dried blood. Thin rivulets of red drizzled down her cheeks.

"Callie, just tell me what happened."

"I was supposed to give him the fee for—" She gasped, looking around the room in a sudden rush of panic. "My purse! Oh, no…did he…?"

"I'm sorry, it's gone. The guy who attacked you got it. I might have caught him if I had taken chase, but my first concern had to be you considering the shape you were in."

Callie's head drooped, sobs climbing up her throat.

Jake reached under her chin and drew her head back up, looking into her eyes. They were the color of espresso. Tears pooled the surface, and overflowed. He brushed them lightly with his fingertip.

"It's okay, Callie. It will be okay."

But she was shaking more intensely now, her arms clutched across her chest. Her jaw trembled and her teeth chattered. Despite the warm evening, she seemed to be cold.

He found a wool blanket in a linen closet and draped it around her. Then he went into the kitchen in search of something that would warm her on the inside. Reasonably satisfied that her head injury was not serious, his focus turned to getting her comfortable. Among his friend's liquor stock, he found a bottle of brandy. Some good stuff, Courvoisier cognac. He poured a small amount in two glasses and handed one to her. She looked up at him uncertainly, but took a small sip, and shivered. Felt the heat swell from her throat down to her chest. Took another sip, then another. Warmth spread and her muscles relaxed. Shaking abated.

"You said earlier that you just got here?" Jake prompted.

"Yes, this morning."

"Are you staying somewhere?"

Her face registered distress and she almost dropped her glass. Jake grabbed it before it hit her lap. Haltingly, she said, "The Hemingway Inn. I have to go...see what..."

"No worries. I know the folks who run the place. I'll give them a call. You need to stay put tonight." Rising from the couch, Jake plucked his BlackBerry from the clip on his pants and punched 1-1-3 for directory assistance. Less than a minute later he was cordially conversing with the manager of The Hemingway.

After completing the call, Jake turned back to Callie and found that sleep had shut her down.

He lifted her up in his arms, carried her to one of the condo's two bedrooms, and carefully laid her on the bed. He untied the pair of canvas espadrilles on her feet and removed them, then pulled the bed's comforter over her slender form. His questions would have to wait until morning. For several moments, he stood over her, watching her slip beneath the cover of slumber.

SHE CAME AWAKE WITH a start, disoriented at first and then increasingly aware of discomfort and soreness. There was a heaviness of body that made her feel almost inert, as if a she were floating under a sheet of lead. She pulled herself up in the bed with agonizing stiffness, wincing at the jabs of pain and the caustic sensation of fabric dragging against torn skin. Melon-colored light was filtering in through a small set of windows dressed in gauzy curtains. The room was compact and tidy, detachedly cheerful. A Roberto Escalante print, rich in primary colors, hung over the bed celebrating a single tree, full and green against a bright blue sky. An arrangement of tropical heliconias in pinks and reds brightened the dresser.

As she slid slowly from the bed and gingerly inched her frame into a standing position, she was momentarily horrified by the splatters of dried blood on her dress. It took several disconcerting minutes for most of the pieces from yesterday to surface, but when they did she began to recall what had happened. Before she could fully assimilate where she was now, the morning after, she heard a vaguely familiar voice coming from the next room. A deep, masculine voice. She moved shyly toward it, a funny tingle under her skin.

When she reached the doorway, she saw the owner of the voice, and remembered.

Jake stood with his back to her, shirtless and barefoot, wearing only a pair of stonewashed jeans. Now clean-shaven, his hair was trimmed shorter but still naturally thick, nearly the color of charcoal. Tanned and muscular, his torso tapered in a trim V to his waist. A tattoo that looked like a braided band with a feather was visible on his right bicep.

Sensing her presence, Jake finished his phone conversation and turned toward her. He gave her a broad smile, transforming his face from stern to handsome, something that sent queasy little ripples through her stomach. The sight of his smooth bare chest jolted her heart like an electric current. Something small and shiny at one of his nipples caught her eye. She quickly looked away.

"Morning," he greeted pleasantly. "How are you feeling?"

"Pretty sore," she answered and, with a flush of embarrassment, "dirty." She didn't even want to imagine what she must look like, wanting instead to somehow peel out of herself. Grit clung to her skin in a fine dust, sealed by perspiration.

"The sore will take a while, but I think I can help with the rest."

She felt a jittery wave pulse through her, not sure what he meant by *help with the rest*, and then she noticed her luggage by the bathroom door.

In response to her surprised look, he said, "I had your things sent over." He paused, adding, "If you want to take a shower, the bathroom's all yours. Then we'll talk. Okay?"

"Okay." She tried to give him a smile, but her face hurt so much that just lifting the corners of her mouth was an effort. She retreated to the shower and attempted to wash away the ugliness of yesterday; the grit and grime dissolved with soap and water, the defilement of the assault proved a lot more difficult.

WHEN SHE EMERGED FROM the bathroom thirty minutes later, Callie was wearing a coral print dress that clung loosely to her waist and hips. Lavender butterflies frolicked across the light material. Her pale blond hair hung in ringlets that coiled past her shoulders. She had made a painful attempt at makeup, finally giving up near tears; her eyes were too swollen, her cheeks too bruised, her lips too tender.

"Feel better?" Jake asked, emerging from the kitchen with two steaming mugs of coffee. He had put on a t-shirt, starkly white against the bronze of his skin. He set the mugs on the bar, took a seat, and patted the one next to him. When she sat, he caught a whiff of floral-scented soap.

"Yes, much better," she said, "but I look awful."

"Hardly," he scoffed, thinking that she looked strikingly pretty in spite of the wash of blues and purples that touched her face here and there. Her skin was otherwise as fair and silky as French cream. And no amount of bruising or swelling could detract from those eyes. Slightly almond in shape with long thin lashes, they gave her an exotic look, particularly with hair the color of the palest sauvignon. No wonder she turned heads, here especially. He sipped from his mug, savoring the rich flavor of the Costa Rican java, dark and aromatic and among the best in the world, and watched as she added sugar and cream to hers. Setting his coffee on the counter, he said, "Okay, let's talk. First and foremost, your passport. Was it in your purse?"

Her eyes dropped to her lap. "Yes."

"You have a copy?" he asked expectantly.

"No," she said in a small voice.

Mildly reproachful, he said, "You should always keep copies of everything. What about credit cards and cash?"

She shook her head forlornly.

"All gone?" His eyes widened. "Everything was in your purse?"

Callie felt her face growing hot, tears stinging the corners of her eyes.

Jake touched her arm. "Let's back up, talk about what happened. Tell me who the slick asshole was."

"His name is Dino DeMarco and I was supposed to meet him there to pay his fee."

"His fee? For what?"

"Well, a few weeks ago I was looking to hire a guide. Not a tour operator with a tour package, but an individual guide."

"Okay, I'm with you so far. How did you find this guy?"

"I was posting on an Internet travel message board and he emailed me to say that he was interested. He said he was well connected and could put together just about anything I wanted."

"And what was it you wanted exactly?"

"I wasn't really sure. I've just started researching for a book I'm writing. A novel that I want to set against the backdrop of Central and possibly South America. I've never been here or there and wanted to be exposed to it."

"You're a writer?" Jake asked, his interest piqued.

"Working at it," she replied modestly.

"So what was the deal you struck with this DeMarco?"

"He told me if I had a couple of weeks, he could take me all over the peninsula, including some very remote places. The only condition was that I would have to pay up front and it would have to be in cash. I was leery of that, but he said he had good references. They appeared to check out. You think he was part of what happened?"

"Possibly. He could have enlisted a thug with the intention of coming off as part victim instead of victimizer. That way he would get all of the cash less whatever he gave the mugger—no responsibility to you and no fees paid out in tour expenses. Why did he ask you to meet him there?"

"He told me he lived outside of San José and would make it easy on me by meeting me in the city."

"At sundown," Jake said wryly.

"How could I be so foolish?" she lamented, shaking her head and feeling utterly humiliated.

Jake gave her arm a squeeze. "Hey, it's okay."

"I guess I should have known better with the cash-only up front stipulation."

"Not necessarily. Actually, I run an adventure tour company with some buddies and we require payment up front. We do take credit cards, though. This guy presenting himself as an individual, it would be logical to assume he would have to ask for cash. And he could have easily pre-fabricated those references." Jake smacked his hands on his thighs, stood up and said, "*You* need some breakfast, missy. We'll grab a bite and stop by the embassy."

Callie followed him to the front door, which he held open for her passage. As she stepped into the brilliant Costa Rican sunshine and stood next to the handsome man who had so valiantly come to her aid the night before, her heart was crushed with despair.

"Jake," she said softly. "I have no money."

He slipped his arm around her waist, guiding her to the stone walk that lined the narrow street. Facing her, his dark eyes focused intently on hers, he said, "We'll work something out."

AFTER A LIGHT BREAKFAST at a neighborhood cafe, they went downtown by taxi to the Organismo de Investigacion Judicial, otherwise known as the OIJ or judicial police. Here, Jake related the incident, in Spanish, to the senior officer on duty and then helped Callie file a report. He didn't tell her it was most likely a futile formality. The next stop was the offices of American Express and Visa/MasterCard, with more re-ports filed and forms filled out. Finally, they headed out of the city, traveling along Pavas Boulevard to the US Embassy. The west-south-west suburbs of San José are often referred to as "gringo gulch," evidenced by the strip malls and plazas populated with the likes of McDonald's and Kentucky Fried Chicken. As they approached the em-bassy, commercial zones were interspersed with vast complexes of palatial estates and residential towers. Compact cars and weathered SUVs gave way to sleek sedans with diplomatic tags.

Inside the embassy, they were directed to the American Citizen Ser-vices where Callie worked her way through what was, by far, the most daunting amount of paperwork in the process.

By the time they returned to the condo, Callie was completely de-jected and exhausted and Jake wanted to hunt down Dino DeMarco and rip his gonads out. While she napped, Jake made some phone calls to see if he could unearth any information on DeMarco but found nothing useful. The contact number Callie had been given was no longer in service, nor was the email address. DeMarco apparently existed but had managed to cover his trail well.

THE HOTEL GRANO DE Oro is a lovely converted Victorian mansion just off the Paseo Colón, tucked in a quiet side street and surrounded by pretty green gardens. The restaurant inside the hotel was one of Jake's favorites for breakfast, but he'd never experienced their more elegant dinner fare; while he enjoyed a gourmet meal every now and then, his culinary tastes tended to run toward the more grounded. But after what he knew had been a demoralizing day for Callie, Jake decided dinner here would be a good way to push past the pall of misfortune.

Earlier, when Callie had awakened from her nap, it was dark and she had an unsettling feeling of déjà vu. She'd dozed fitfully in vaguely miserable positions with distinctly miserable dreams. After splashing water on her face, she had managed to sparingly apply some makeup—a touch of blush, mascara, and lipstick—and put on a crinkled lace peasant dress the color of raspberry ice cream. When she emerged from the bedroom, she saw that Jake had switched from jeans and t-shirt to sand-colored Dockers and a black polo shirt open at the neck and tucked in at the waist.

Now, as they sat across from each other in the courtyard of the restaurant, she was taking in the tropical foliage that surrounded them and he was looking at her. A bottle of Chilean merlot was open, and they had been sipping some from their glasses while waiting on the food. Meeting his intense gaze, Callie flushed and reached for her wineglass, unable to stifle the tremor in her hand.

"This is nice," she said, ducking her head and brushing self-consciously at her face. Even though the swelling had gone down, the coloring of bruised places had deepened and the cuts were beginning to darken as healing began.

"Yes," he replied, his gaze unbroken.

Callie peered down at her silverware. When she looked up again, his focus had shifted momentarily to the waiter who had brought bread and salads, but just as quickly his eyes were back on her.

"So," Jake said, "Callie is short for Caledonia."

"Yes, it is. I guess you saw that on all those forms."

"Nice...and suits you." He speared a piece of asparagus and slipped it into his mouth, nodding his satisfaction. "Caledonia," he pronounced with a sensual roll of his tongue. "Sounds Greek."

"It does, but I'm not sure. My mother told me she came across it in a book and loved it. Ironically, a few years after I was born there was a song by that name, by Robin Trower. I really like the song, too."

Jake smiled. "I'll have to give that a listen sometime. So, Miss Caledonia, where are you from?"

"Savannah, Georgia."

"Your accent is subtle. Move around a lot growing up?"

His quick perception surprised her. "Yes, I did. My father was in the navy."

Jake concealed a small smile with another bite of salad. "Do your parents live in Savannah?"

Callie shook her head slowly. "No. My parents...died a few years ago, in a car accident. "

"I'm sorry." After a measured pause, he said, "You have other family?"

She shook her head but did not reply.

"Boyfriend?"

She shook her head again, but this time there was a noticeable wave of unease as she shifted in her chair.

"You ever been married?"

"No," she said, but something seemed to snag on that, like a piece of bread that wouldn't quite go down.

"But?"

His inquiry hung in the air like a hummingbird intent on extracting nectar from a flower whose petals were folding. "Nothing," she said, recovering. "No."

He was weighing his next question when Callie asked, "Where are *you* from?"

With a little laugh, Jake said, "I am from all over."

When he didn't elaborate, she asked, "Do you live here now?"

"No. Technically I'm homeless. I guess you could say I'm in a constant state of transition. Must be the Indian in me."

"Indian?"

He nodded. "I'm half-Greek, half-Chiricahua. That's southwestern Apache."

Callie stole a shy glance at his face, found herself locked into his eyes again—deep, dark, formidably mysterious—noted his naturally swarthy skin tone, the luster in his dark hair. His eyes bore into hers, forcing her to look away.

Prodding some lettuce on her salad plate, she said, "Your name doesn't sound Indian...or Greek?"

"That's a story for another time," he replied a little distantly.

The waiter interrupted with their entrees, a filet mignon for Jake and shrimp for Callie. The food arranged on their china plates looked like works of art, each piece in perfect symmetry with sauces drizzled and accents fanned around the sides. They spent a few minutes enjoying their meal in the cool evening air that wafted through the courtyard. The bright reds and yellows of heliconias and ginger plants glowed in the soft lantern lighting. Dinner conversation among the other patrons was intimately muted.

With a little hitch in her voice, Callie said, "Jake, I don't know how to thank you for taking care of everything. I don't know what I would have done. I still don't know what I'm going to do."

"I've been thinking about that," he mused, hands encircling the base of his wineglass, fingertips touching. "Tell me about this book you're writing."

"It's going to be action-adventure, set here and in South America."

"Costa Rica is a perfect place for that genre, the whole place is filled with adventure. Why South America?"

"To tie in dangerous elements," she replied, adding, "and the lead character is former military who—"

Jake snorted around a swallow of merlot. In response to her look of bewilderment, he just shook his head with a crooked grin and said, "Nothing. Go on."

"That's it, really. I need background material to breathe life into the story."

"And the character?" he asked, still grinning.

"Yes."

"So you came down here, alone, with the idea of having a guide—someone intimately familiar with this territory—take you to key locales and activities."

"Yes. But I guess maybe it wasn't such a good idea after all."

"Oh, on the contrary. I think it's a very good idea. And an uncanny one."

"Uncanny?"

Jake only smiled cryptically in response.

Presently, he said, "I was planning to leave San José tomorrow."

Callie looked up from her plate, her appetite waning.

"Why don't you come with me? As I told you, I have an adventure travel company and we offer the very services you were seeking. I have about a week free, so I could show you around the country. Maybe provide you with a bit of background info. Besides, it will give me a chance to catch up with some of the people and places we work with for the tours."

Her heart fluttered, suffused first with relief, then with anxiety. "Really? But, the money…?" she began, her voice trailing off uncertainly.

"No worries. If you want to come, I'll work it out." He took another bite of steak and sighed. "God, this is good." He mopped the last piece of steak through mushroom sauce and popped it in his mouth, chewed and savored. Then, pushing his plate aside, he leaned over the table on his forearms. "So," he said, "ready for some adventure?"

JAKE PULLED HIS SHIRT off, dropping it into a chair next to the bed. He padded over to the window and stood gazing thoughtfully into the night holding court on the other side, a stir of breeze tickling his chest. Something else was stirring inside him, something he could not identify. It felt both pleasant and unsettling. Instinctively, he was warding it off until he could evaluate it and understand it. And yet, there was another feeling developing, one that was not responding to his instincts.

The breeze blew softly against his chest.

He unbuttoned his Dockers, unzipped, hooked his fingers in the waistband, and then stopped. Reaching for his cell and sat phones, he unclipped them. Placed the satellite phone on the dresser. Then the BlackBerry. The LED was blinking.

He picked it up and looked at the log. *Missed call.* He recognized the number. *Haskell.*

"Son of a bitch," he muttered, and tossed the phone to the bed.

5

WITH ESSENTIALLY NO SUMMER or winter, spring in Costa Rica is more the transition from dry season to wet. As the apricot yoke of dawn broke over the environs of San José that segue was ever apparent in the warm mist clinging to the lush green hills and valleys that rose and fell along the Interamericana. Jake smiled to himself as he bumpily navigated the jeep along the highway, content in the knowledge that this was going to be a near-ideal day in Costa Rica.

Beside him, Callie sleepily watched the panorama unfold in gradually lightening layers of morning. Already dressed in cargo pants, t-shirt, and Pitkin trail shoes, Jake had roused her a little before five, and while she showered and dressed, he made some calls. The first, to Delaney, went unanswered—unsurprisingly. The next few were to make some arrangements and to find a vehicle he could use for the week. He lucked out with an acquaintance in the city that was willing to loan his Jeep Cherokee. Four-wheel drive was virtually a prerequisite on the country's roads, the best of which were inconsistently paved and all of which were harshly graded. On the way out of town, Jake had stopped for breakfast, prodding Callie through a plate of *gallo pinto* with eggs and tortillas.

"Trust me," he said, "you're going to need every bit of that later."

Then they were on the road, traveling west and north between the Golfo de Nicoya and the Cordillera de Tilarán. While Jake concentrated on his driving, he managed to cast periodic sidelong glances at Callie, enjoying the slide-show of wonder playing over her face as the lovely scenery rolled by her window. She was wearing pale blue slacks and a poplin blouse unbuttoned over a white cotton camisole. A smile curved into her pretty mouth as they passed a pair of white Brahma cattle lounging beneath the majestic umbrella of a Guanacaste tree. Further back from the road, a *sabañero* was attempting to corral the rest of his herd. The terrain became increasingly steep as hills thickened with tracts of giant evergreens and arching palms. The ride, now traversing more dirt and gravel than asphalt, was becoming bone-jarringly rough.

"Where are we going today?" she asked.

He smiled happily. "Where the clouds are green."

MONTEVERDE WAS A QUAKER farming community before it became known as one of the most celebrated cloud forest reserves in the country. The small group of Quakers—originally draft opponents from the States who settled there in the early fifties—began dairy farming that eventually led to the establishment of a cheese factory. Today it remains one of the focal points of interest in the area, producing thousands of pounds of cheese daily. The Quakers themselves are less ubiquitous and leave the tourist attractions to the locals, preferring the privacy of their farms. Spread across the Continental Divide at nearly six thousand feet, Monteverde brings together the provinces of Puntarenas, Guanacaste, and Alajuela in the north, about four hours from San José.

From the dusty road taken out of a Latino city congested with people, street noise, and greasy diesel fumes, Callie could not have imagined being immersed in a place like the one he was about to take her—and a day's activities that would set the tone for the remaining week.

While the whole reserve covered some thirty thousand acres, Jake was instinctively adept in selecting the trails that best captured the essence of the place. He led Callie down the first one and watched awe take her like a dandelion seed on the wind. Suddenly surrounded by a mist-enshrouded netherworld of emerald, she stood with lips parted, eyes wide and roving, adrift in the unspeakable magnificence of the cloud forest.

Jake smiled broadly. "Beautiful, isn't it?"

She tried to say something, found words inadequate. So for a while, they just walked. Watched. Listened. Saw, felt, and heard nature communing in a way so primitive and primal that it seemed to blend the senses into one permeable sensory that simply absorbed it all.

As they made their way along the narrow trails, the musk of dark, rich earth rose with each step and mist swirled through the air like a fleet of lazy ghosts. Higher up, the forest ceiling was textured with a veil of palest green—clouds formed by moist trade winds sweeping in from the Atlantic and crossing over the Continental Divide—sustenance for the living things that comprised this beautiful and complex eco-system. Very faint dripping, steady as an IV, could be heard against the backdrop of the alternately quiet and clamorous soundtrack. Sometimes a lone wail or whisper or warble would pine through the mist, other times a cacophony of shrieks, howls, cackles, and strident symphonies would rattle across the branches overhead. Most passages were thick with ferns and palms and trees fringed with lichen. Moss draped from branches like leftover garland from some ancient Christmas in a Dickens' living room.

But punctuating the deep, shadowy green were hallucinatory flashes of brilliant color: turquoise, scarlet, tangerine, teal, violet, chartreuse, canary. The unexpected appearances of orchids as delicate as Oriental porcelain and butterflies and hummingbirds so light they barely stirred the mist contrasted with the brash intrusion of birds and monkeys, the vivid red-and-green resplendent quetzal and howler monkey being among the most frequent. Big toucans as colorful as a kindergartner's finger-painting called across the canopy, warbling *tweedle-de-doo...tweedle-de-doo.*

Callie was squinting into the high branches of a strangler fig, the bright purple of a flower catching her eye, when she felt something light drop beside her neck. She emitted a high-pitched gasp.

A few steps ahead, Jake quickly looked around to find her frozen in consternation, her head twisted at an odd angle toward her shoulder. Crossing to her, he saw the cause of her alarm and let out a light-hearted guffaw.

"Relax," he chided, reaching over and touching her shoulder with an outstretched finger, prodding a spindly creature the size of a cloverleaf. "This little critter," he said, transferring the eight-legged buff-colored spider to the palm of his hand, "is just your typical forest inhabitant. Nothing to get excited about."

Callie watched as Jake carefully set the spider on an outstretched tree limb, but it took several minutes of walking before she could shake the crawly feeling.

WHEN HE STOPPED AT a sign directing them to something called SKY TREK, she felt a premonitory spike of anxiety.

"Jake? What is this?"

He gave her a confident smile. "Something you'll never forget."

"But...what is it?"

He extended his hand. "Come on, you'll see."

Taking his hand, she walked with him toward a small yellow building with the SKY TREK logo, waiting outside as he suggested. A few minutes later he emerged, accompanied by a pair of young men carrying white helmets and harnesses. They greeted her with enthusiasm and continued chatting animatedly with Jake in both English and Spanish. Reaching for her hand again, Jake gave her another smile and tugged her gently up a pathway toward another expanse of forest that at once rose and fell and spread in every direction. It seemed to be limitless in depth and height.

And then they were in a metal mesh lift, ascending through the greens, skyward. The lift stopped with a jerky clank and they stepped onto a platform. Treetops were now below them with long cables stretched high above. Sky spanned weightlessly around the platform.

Callie looked at Jake, wide-eyed with trepidation, enlightenment as vivid as the vista around her. "No," she said softly, her voice almost a whisper. "No, Jake, I can't."

"Sure you can," he said with assurance, already taking a helmet and Petzl harness from one of the operators. "You'll see."

"No," she repeated desperately, peering down at the treetops that seemed surrealistically small as compared to those that had towered over her just a little while ago.

He came close, gave her hand a reassuring squeeze, and looked her squarely in the eyes. "Trust me, Callie. It's not as scary as it looks. I promise. It's called zip line and it's perfectly safe. They harness you in and then you're clipped to sturdy pulleys that slide across the cables." He eyed her hopefully, but she was still looking down, shaking her head.

"No, Jake. I can't...I'm sorry."

He heaved a sigh heavy with regret and shrugged toward the two operators, handing over the helmet and harness. "It's okay," he told Callie, but his voice betrayed disappointment. Another thought occurred to him as they retreated. "Will you try something else for me?" he asked.

Instantly wary, she wasn't sure how to respond. Before she could, Jake held up a finger and went back over to the pair of operators. After a brief conversation, he returned and led her a short distance to another staging area with another platform. Stretched from this one was a long suspension bridge, maybe five or six hundred feet in length. It swayed gently in the breeze, sun reflecting brightly off its metal railings and mesh. Below, a canyon plunged.

"I don't know, Jake," she said, but watching a couple stroll from the opposite side, stopping only to aim binoculars, gave her pause.

Sensing her equivocation, he took her hand, held it firmly, and started across.

As it turned out, he was right. It was something she would never forget. But Jake was still disappointed that he'd not been able to get her on the zip line, not so much for the activity as for the step it would have been beyond her comfort zone.

"See?" he said when they had made it to the other side. "Nothing to it."

AFTER A LIGHT LUNCH of *arreglados*, they were back on an even rougher road heading west out of Santa Elena. The Jeep Cherokee bounced over a minefield of ruts and ridges for close to two hours, and despite being secured by seatbelt, Callie braced herself against the dashboard or the door almost the entire time. Jake proved extraordinarily adept in road navigation that, with its blind curves and Jacuzzi-sized potholes, lent itself more to stunt-driving. As their route wound north, the road became slightly less combative but the wind picked up and began to push against the vehicle. Callie looked ahead and blinked in utter wonderment as the silvery expanse of Laguna de Arenal first came into view. It rippled in the afternoon sunshine, sprawled as far as she could see. Arenal Volcano rose like a gray giant reclining on the far shore, lips puckered to blow wisps of clouds against a sky the color of a baby's blanket. They veered west again and the grade steepened, cresting with a field of huge white windmills spinning along the ridge. From there the route turned eastward and began to descend, with the lake view widening on their right.

Lake Arenal, covering thirty-three square miles, is the largest body of water in Costa Rica and forms the basin for the hydroelectric project producing 70 percent of the country's electricity. The Caribbean winds that course through the northern mountains blow across the lake and often meet with a strong northeasterly flow from the Gulf of Mexico, which has made it one of the world's premiere spots for windsurfing. Today, the western end of the lake was filled with enthusiasts bouncing around the waves on boards, working tall sails or tethered to kites. As the road looped south, the wind slacked off to a moderate breeze and the lake's waters became less crowded. Vegetation was thick along the road, alternately obscuring the lake, and monkeys could be seen playing in the treetops.

Soon they were crossing the Instituto Costaricense de Electricidad dam—otherwise known as ICE—built for the power company, then over a small bridge and uphill. Finally, Jake turned into a stone-bricked drive surrounded by palms and dense foliage. A framed wooden sign with brass lettering read: TABACÓN GRAND SPA THERMAL RESORT. They got out of the Jeep Cherokee and strolled up to the entrance for a collection of brightly painted gold buildings trimmed in burnished wood and covered by rust-colored stucco.

"Time for a bit of indulgence," Jake said, "and this is just the ticket."

A few minutes later they were in a beautiful balconied suite with a queen-size bed and a Jacuzzi with a spectacular view of the volcano. The floors were ceramic tile, the colors rich earth tones, and there were orchids on the pillows.

Before she could say anything, Jake said, "I'll take the sofa bed. If you're not comfortable with this, I can probably get an extra room. This is what they had for me."

"Oh no, no," Callie said quickly, but her eyes were wide and riveted on the beds. "This is fine. More than fine. I just can't believe you arranged this. It must be very expensive...it's really okay?"

Jake smiled. "Yes, it's really okay. Now, what do you say we freshen up and get some dinner? The food here is incredible."

AND IT WAS. THEY got a table in Los Tucanes, overlooking the pool's cascading waterfall. While they had showered and dressed for dinner, evening pulled the switch on day and filled in around the lights of night, cloaking the mountain against a deep purple sky and dropping random shadows over the bright aqua pool below the restaurant.

Callie looked utterly feminine again, wearing a sheer slip dress that dropped to her calves, her blond mane pulled back in a clip and sporting one of the lilac-colored orchids. It matched her dress. It no longer matched her bruises—they had faded below her creamy skin.

Jake wore black.

They were talking about Arenal and what Jake had in mind for tomorrow, when his cell phone vibrated. Checking the display, he saw Delaney's number and tersely told Callie, "I need to take this." Rising briskly from his seat, he left the restaurant and stepped outside.

"Haskell?"

"Jake—" The rest was unintelligibly frayed by static.

"Where the hell are you?" The signal wavered and Jake could only hear fractional syllables. "Haskell?"

"—hear me? Damn sat phone...Jake?" The transmission broke in bits like a rat was gnawing at the waves. "—I just—really it's only—so I—you—Jake, do you hear me?"

"Shit, no, I can't hear you," Jake snapped in frustration. He moved further along the stone path toward the pool deck. Briefly, in one crystal moment of clarity as the satellites seemed to line up in perfect symmetry somewhere in the universe above, he heard the voice of his friend as plainly as if he were standing next to him.

Delaney said, "Look, I know you're probably really pissed at me right now, but I'll explain everything later. Okay? Okay, Jake?"

Jake was ready to grab hold of that, reel him in, pull words through, when another burst of static filled his ear. Random particles of Delaney's voice continued to fade in and out, drowned in a wash of telephonic wasps.

Then the connection was lost.

He was walking back to the table when his cell phone vibrated again. Coming right on the heels of the broken sat call, it was improbable that Delaney would be in a situation where he could turn right around and communicate by cell, but Jake checked the caller ID anyway. Normally he let most calls go to voicemail, but this one—coming from the Tabacón's Caña Brava Bar—he was taking. He answered, spoke briefly, and sought the maitre d'. With an assurance that Callie would be taken care of in his absence, Jake headed across the grounds toward the lobby bar.

The man he met there was leaning against the counter drinking a beer, eyes on the entrance. Seeing Jake, he nodded and brought his Imperial bottle over to a table away from the groupings of people watching sports on a large screen TV. They clasped hands in greeting.

Jake said, "Thanks for making the trek, man."

"No problem. Buy you a drink?"

"I'm good."

Their eyes met and an unspoken communication passed in the way it often does between brethren joined by cause or circumstance. The man was tall and fit, close-shaven, clad in navy blue sweats. His jacket sleeves were pushed back, one forearm showing a Trident tattoo. Wordlessly, he reached into the canvas pouch fitted around his waist and handed its contents to Jake.

"Any issues?" Jake asked.

"For me? Nah. Him? Depends on how long it takes public works to inspect the sewer near his place…you know how underfunded they are. Beyond that"—he shrugged—"he'll need to find a new line of work that doesn't require good motor skills."

Jake couldn't help a smirk. "Thanks, well done." He stood, extracted his wallet and took out several bills. Placed them firmly in the man's hand and made eye contact again. They exchanged a final nod and parted company.

✳ ✳ ✳ ✳ ✳

CALLIE SWIRLED A BITE of shrimp cannelloni through tomato sauce, gazing out at the floodlit pool. It shimmered through misty layers of blue and green. She slipped the pillow of pasta into her mouth, following it with a tiny sip of Chardonnay, and watched as couples huddled romantically at the swim-up bar and frolicked around the waterfall. Inside the restaurant, the lighting was warm but subdued beneath the exposed wood beam ceiling, tables draped in starched gold linen. Crystal and china clinked lightly, conversations were intimate and cordial, but she was beginning to feel overwhelmed as the activities of the past few days spun through her mind. And now she was in a world-class resort, about to share a room with a man she'd just met and then take off together on a jaunt around a country she'd never been in. But she'd been about to do much the same thing with Dino DeMarco. Just not with this level of intimacy. She shuddered at the thought of the hustler in San José.

Jake's low voice coming from behind startled her. "My apologies," he said, touching her shoulder as he passed. He took his seat and placed something in his lap. A waiter appeared and refilled their wineglasses. When they were alone again, Jake reached beneath the table edge and produced a bulky manila envelope. He put it by her plate.

"What's this?" Callie asked.

"Open it."

She touched the envelope cautiously. It was about two inches thick.

Jake chuckled. "It's not radioactive…go ahead, open it."

When she did, her mouth parted in surprise. "Is this…?"

"Your money, yes, ma'am. Sorry it's in *colones*, so a lot of bills."

"The police found him?"

Jake sipped his Chardonnay, let a few moments pass. "Not exactly."

Confused, Callie blinked at him, not quite making the connection.

"Things have a way of working out," he said.

"How did…? Did you—"

"Let's just say that's need to know."

Callie looked at him, perplexed.

Jake looked down at his plate. "Military term. Just means you *don't* need to know."

She felt a funny little flutter in her stomach. "You're in the military?"

He did not respond right away, but when he did it was with an air of casualty that belied the pride he actually felt. "Army Special Forces," he replied, then qualified, "*Was* in the army."

"You're not anymore?"

"Well, yeah. Am, was, who knows anymore." Seeing the questions building in her eyes, he elaborated. "I have learned that once Uncle gets his hooks in you, your soul is bought and paid for. I signed on with the army at seventeen, did several tours, and got out after ten years. After seven conflicts and something like eighty engagements. Thought I could then find a nice little niche in life, be a regular Joe with a nine-to-five, a mortgage on a nice little house, a yard with a dog that barked enough to annoy the neighbors, a wife, kids maybe. But it never quite happened. So I picked up missions here and there. Private and government contract work everywhere you can imagine, some pretty intense."

She had been listening intently, her face was as solemn as a cemetery. "Oh, Jake."

He said nothing and after a long moment, her eyes dropped to the envelope of money. Before she could say or ask anything else, Jake reached over and put his hand over hers. "Hey, let's go relax."

BACK IN THEIR SUITE, Jake stood pacing by the window. "Come on out here, missy," he called, his voice inflected with jeer.

Callie emerged from the bathroom wearing one of the fluffy robes they'd been provided. Jake stood watching her with his hands on his hips. He was bare-chested, wearing dark blue swim trunks.

"Come on, let's see it," he chided.

Bashfully, she said, "I found a bathing suit in one of the gift shops, but it's really skimpy."

"Well, that's what you get for not bringing a bathing suit to Costa Rica," he chuckled. "And, you know, that's kind of the way bathing suits are supposed to be. So let's see it."

Slowly, she unwrapped the robe and let it fall open, revealing a trim bikini covered with bright tropical flowers in pink, purple, and orange.

Jake wasn't paying much attention to the flowers. Her skin, though pale, was smooth and taut over a form that was in no way voluptuous. Even so, the curves were there and their narrowness held another kind of allure—the kind a mysterious cave might promise when a kayak edges through its tight mouth and finds a glorious sun-worshipped grotto on the other side. He closed the space between them, eying her appreciatively.

A lingering look, a measured smile, and he took her hand. They left the suite, heading for the thermal pools. On the way, they passed through the Tabacón's exquisitely landscaped gardens, during which Jake's mind seemed to have drifted somewhere else. During the walk, they heard an occasional rumble, caught an occasional glimpse of the volcano's flare through the lush foliage. As further portent, off to one side a large wooden sign engraved with bright yellow letters warned: PELIGRO ZONA DE ALTO RIESGO VOLCANICO PROHIBIDO EL PASO. Danger. Area of high volcanic activity. No trespassing.

As they sank down into the hot, gushing water, Jake groaned and Callie sighed deeply. The hours of road-abuse and physical exertion in Monteverde began to dissolve. They sipped tall, frosty fruit drinks and languished contentedly. Alternately, they wandered through the many churning streams and waterfalls, reveling in the volcanically heated mineral waters. They wound up in a secluded pool under a canopy of stars that sparkled like a billion-dollar diamond heist spread across a swath of black velvet. For Jake, it was the first time since he had left Colombia that he could actually feel a sense of release. For Callie, it was the first time since she had arrived in Costa Rica that she felt herself beginning to open to it. Orchid petals fell from overhead, dropping onto the water surface and floating around them in the warm mist, their fragrance a sweet sachet of the delicate and exotic.

Jake and Callie's skin touched below the water.

Not so far away, Arenal Volcano exploded into the diamond-studded darkness. Fire painted the night sky in bursts and lava streamed deep from its pit, red and hot and hungry.

6

IN THE DAYS THAT followed, Jake's personalized itinerary took them hiking through breathtaking trails, first exploring the rolling hills below the volcano by foot and horseback and then moving north toward the Nicaraguan border. There, he showed her around the river-veined natural park that was Rincón de la Vieja, the centerpiece of which was also a volcano, though not as active as Arenal. A two-hour drive southwest took them to the Costa Rican gold coast, where they spent a day and a half in and around the sun-swept, palm-lined beaches of Playa Grande. Coastal road took them to the southern tip of the immense Peninsula de Nicoya with its spectacular views of the vast blue Pacific from one sugarcoated *playa* to the next, each with its own unique seaside signature. They ferried across the Golfo de Nicoya to Puntarenas and traveled eastward, back through San José, headed toward the Caribbean coast.

Driving through first, the verdant hillsides that rose on either side of the Parque Nacional Braulio Carrillo along the Limón highway, then past a handful of small towns sprawling toward the Caribbean lowlands, and finally a boisterous twenty-mile stretch of road that plundered through enticing snatches of rainforest, they arrived at the Río Pacuare just as the sun was easing below the trees. They camped by the river and awoke to arias of birdsong sweet as a Mozart minuet. Watching Callie's eyes fill with light as the sun rose on another day, Jake felt a bubble of buoyancy in his heart that caught him strangely off guard.

After Pacuare, Jake took the southern route below Braulio Carrillo, one that passed through plantations of bananas and coffee and macadamias. When he hit the main highway out of Cartago, he skirted the entire length of the Reserva Forestal Río Macho, another natural reserve covering tens of thousands of acres, where the road climbed steadily up and over the Cerro de la Muerte. Here, from ten thousand feet above sea level, there is a spot where, on a perfectly clear day—something considerably rare at that altitude—one can literally see from sea to sea, the Pacific Ocean to the west and the Caribbean to the east. This was not the case today, as a more typical mountain mist clung loosely to the peaks like celestial dust bunnies, restricting visibility to a few miles in all directions. After descending into San Isidro and veering off the Interamericana, it was up and down another 3800 feet over Tinamastes Ridge. About twenty minutes later, he arrived at what had been his original destination on arrival from Colombia.

Haskell Delaney's beach house near Dominical.

A tiny town of perhaps a hundred and fifty full-time residents and a thousand more during the tourist season, Dominical is one of the lesser-known surfer havens. As such, it has retained much of its natural charm and domestic dignity with only a main street comprising a few small restaurants and businesses and a scattering of hotels and other rentals on the outskirts. Beyond the little town, rainforest climbs a slope that overlooks its slices of beach, north and east of which runs the Barú River and, farther south, a few private villas built to maximize varying vistas.

It was to one of these villas that Jake drove, turning down a short gravel access road that led to another shorter drive, this one ending in a mixture of crushed gravel, shells, and sand.

Jake made the drive in about six hours, during most of which he let Callie doze. Her night in the Pacuare wilderness had been one of restless tossing, and when he woke her just before dawn she'd still looked tired. Traveling with him had been a steep learning curve for her; his lifestyle was one of heady freefall, always seeking the deeper, the higher, the farther, the faster, the rougher. All in all, quite a jolt to Callie's comfort zone. She was stirring now, blinking in the bright sun that blazed through the Jeep's windshield.

"We're here?" she asked, straightening in her seat and squinting into the sunshine. From her passenger-side window, the Pacific spanned limitlessly across the horizon, the sky and ocean fiercely competing for the more vivid blue. The sand was the color of oatmeal, framed by rainforest, palms, and sea grass. With the exception of spindly-legged birds pecking and prancing around in the waves there wasn't a soul on the beach.

Callie gasped.

Jake smiled, and felt it radiate somewhere inside him. He went around to open the door for her. "Nice, isn't it?" he said. "The locals say *pura vida*. That means pure life."

Wordlessly, she slid from her seat and stood staring. Aware of Jake unloading the Jeep, she snapped out of her reverie and turned to see him toting their bags to the front porch of a stucco villa, white with a red tile roof. A pair of macramé hammocks were strung on one side, a cane loveseat swayed ever so slightly on the other. Hanging baskets overflowed with bougainvillea the color of pink nail polish and potted palms sat by the door.

"This is...?" she started, shaking her head in disbelief.

"This is my bud's place, my partner in the tour company." Saying that, he felt a pang of dismay, and sighed deeply. He opened the door, revealing more white stucco with dark post-and-beam accents, big cane ceiling fans, and Italian tile floor the color of baked clay. The living and dining rooms flowed together, with the kitchen separated only by a wide alcove. The main room was open to the second floor, which was railed with ornamental black iron. Prints and furniture fabric were bright and festive in design.

Leaning into Callie's ear, he said, "Slip into that *skimpy* bikini and you'll see how nice it really is here."

THEY PLAYED IN THE waves until the sun began its descent, casting a golden glaze over the sand and turning the ocean the color of topaz. After showering and dressing, they drove a few miles farther south to a restaurant on a bluff with a spectacular vista. Members of La Parcela's staff greeted Jake with warmth and familiarity as they were seated.

They settled in, watching waves crash over the rocks below.

"Your friend's place is incredible," Callie remarked.

Jake chuckled. "He's not a millionaire, in case you wondered. He paid for the place with an insurance settlement and some gambling winnings. Still, Costa Rican living is very inexpensive, and peaceful."

"Is that why you're here?" she asked.

He didn't respond, gazing pensively over the balcony beside their table, his eyes on the blood-red sun hovering very near the edge of ocean. In a matter of moments its fire would spread across the sky in an oil slick of oranges, from hot to sultry to scorched.

After their order was taken, Jake turned back to study her. She was wearing a strapless dress that sheathed her slender form in pastel pink, watercolor sailboats adding a touch of green and darker rose. Her hair was pulled up, tendrils of champagne-colored curls hanging in spirals around her face, which was now sun-kissed to a peachy radiance. He noticed for the first time how long her eyelashes were.

Flushing when she caught his look, Callie said, "This week has been incredible. Jake, I don't know how to thank you, for everything. Obviously, the money is all yours, but that hardly seems equitable. Your time…I'm sure you had more important things to do."

He reached over the table and squeezed her hand. "Did you enjoy it?"

"Oh yes," she said, with emphasis.

"Did it provide the start that you need for your book?"

"Yes."

He beamed. "Okay then. That's the way it was meant and thanks enough for me."

The waiter set plates of red snapper and steamed vegetables in front of them and while Jake began to eat, Callie hesitated. Chewing, he asked, "What are you thinking about?"

"Just…not sure what I'm going to do now."

He sipped some wine, thinking. "Why don't you stay here for a while? It's up to you, of course, but you can stay at the villa for as long as you'd like. Certainly couldn't have a more relaxing and inspiring place in which to create. What do you do back in Savannah? You have a job there?"

She shook her head, looked away. The sun's radiance had drained from her face as a shadow seemed to cross an unpleasant chamber in her mind.

He let a few ponderous moments pass. "Callie, you know I'll be leaving tomorrow afternoon," he said soberly.

"Where are you going?"

"Colombia."

"Colombia? *South America*? What are you doing there?"

He stiffened. "I'd rather not say, hon."

She processed his revelation for a moment, then asked, "Jake, is there any way I can go? I guess I could use my credit cards to cover the expense. I could get so much there, for the book."

"God, no," he said without hesitation. "*That* Colombia is one of the most dangerous places on the face of the earth. You would literally be eaten alive. No way. Believe me, I wouldn't be going if I didn't have to. And it will be the last time, I assure you," he said emphatically. Softening, he said, "Listen, here's an idea. If you're still here when I return a month from now, maybe I can work with you a little more on the book."

"I'd like that," she replied hopefully.

He speared a piece of fish and popped it in his mouth. "I have a job lined up here when I return. Through the tour company, I also work with media. Provide medical, security, and linguistic services for remote locations and international productions. Also in high-threat areas such as war zones and under primitive working conditions. There's a couple of guys planning a new television show—a reality thing, I think—and we'll be working with them. Perhaps I can get you something there, writing-related."

"That sounds promising," she said, but the earlier lightness of her mood had dimmed, along with her appetite. Most of the succulent snapper remained untouched on her plate.

THEY WERE SEATED ON the patio that extended behind and to one side of the villa, in cushioned wicker chairs angled toward each other. A beveled glass table between them held two tall glasses stacked with ice and filled with Tanqueray and tonic, wedges of lime floating on top. A bean-shaped pool glowed in aqua fluorescence a few feet away, surrounded on one side by flowering tropical plants that tumbled from a landscaped slope and a crescent of ocean view on the other.

Callie could not imagine anything more beautiful and, this moment, more desolate. The air was thick with the perfume of blooming flowers, jasmine and ginger mixing to make an intoxicating spice. A soothing rumble of waves underscored the twinkle of chimes around the villa, a random bird called out forlornly. Somewhere, from down the coastal road, a motorcycle buzzed.

Jake sipped his gin and tonic, cooling the side of his face with the frosty glass. Callie watched him silently, her heart beating a little faster. He placed his glass back on the table with a light clink and inhaled the fragrant night air, gazing intently at the moon above. It was not quite full, the color of a candle flame.

He watched as Callie rose from her seat and strolled to the patio's edge, peering down at the ocean. As he approached her from behind, he saw her shoulders hitch slightly and put his hands on them. She raised a hand to her face and appeared to be wiping her eyes.

"Hey, no being sad, okay?"

She sniffled faintly. "I'm sorry. I just…the time just went by so fast."

"Yes. Yes, it did. And I enjoyed it very much."

He turned her around, looked directly into her eyes. They were still moist with the tears she was trying to suppress. He drew her closer, feeling her tense as the front of his body pressed against hers. The soft, feminine feel of her was warming him inside, warming and stirring a hunger he did not expect. For several torturous moments he fought it, warning himself this was probably not a good idea. Not a good idea at all. But holding this sweet creature in his arms, feeling the flutter of her heart against his chest as he pulled her even closer, feeling the feathery brush of her breath on his neck, was too much. Tilting her face up with his finger, he pressed his lips to hers. They felt like rose petals. The soft, moist sensation and ambrosial taste swelled inside him like hot honey. So soft, so warm, so hot.

A warning voice was echoing *No, no, no…not a good idea…stop.*

But he wasn't stopping, and as her mouth parted in awe, his kiss expanded, craving the honey. His tongue slid between the petal-soft lips, nudged inside the wet, warm hollow. Sweet, hot honey. Cradling her in one arm, his other hand cupped the back of her neck as he continued kissing her, slower, longer, deeper, hungrier.

He heard a little whimper from her, felt the beginning of a tremor, and whispered in her ear, "It's okay, Callie."

Was it?

His hands slid down her dress, tracing the slim curves of her waist and hips. She murmured his name, almost inaudible, and he could feel her trembling now.

"Don't be afraid of me."

She looked up at him, as if to assess his honesty, her beautiful brown eyes wide and plaintive, and he felt his heart flip. Gazing into those eyes, desire leapt up inside him with the ferocity of a fire stoked by a gust of pure oxygen. His pulse was racing, pounding like surf in his head.

And then, from somewhere in the villa, another pounding, followed by a thump and a crash. Someone had just entered from the front, forcibly.

7

JAKE'S ADRENALINE ALREADY PUMPING, he moved quickly, pulling Callie to the shadows of the villa's overhang. "Stay right here," he whispered firmly. Through the French doors that opened next to the kitchen, Jake saw a man rummaging through the drawers of a teak desk by the staircase. Some lights were on inside the villa, so Jake waited until the guy made a move to go up the stairs, his back momentarily to the patio doors. Popping the latch on the door, Jake flipped the wall switch just inside, putting his side of the first floor in semi-darkness. The intruder swung around with his arm raised, and fired two shots from a semi-automatic handgun. Before the man made the turn, Jake had pivoted away, so the shots went wide. One torpedoed into the stucco and sent particles crumbling, the other pelted one of the French doors and shattered glass.

Crouched low and shielding himself with the furniture, Jake made his way closer to the shooter. Catching a glimpse of the man between a sofa and chair, he saw a longhaired Anglo wearing all black and carrying a Beretta. He was big and hulking, muscles bulging through a tank top, legs packed into jeans. His hair, pulled untidily into a ponytail, was the color of old rope, his skin that of a man who spends a copious amount of time on a surfboard. Jake's eyes followed the man and he moved accordingly, keeping his target in front of him. When the shooter had circled to the end of the sofa and was facing the French doors, Jake sprung up behind him and went straight for his neck. Jake's left arm collared the guy in a quick choke, while his right seized control of the gunhand wrist. The Beretta went clattering across the tile floor.

The shooter, now without his gun, aimed what—depending on his level and range of combative skills—was possibly a much more lethal weapon: his body. He managed to free his wrist from Jake's grasp and wheeled around, bringing a thick arm upside Jake's head, the muscles corded like a reptile's tail. Jake side-stepped the swing and moved into the man's body, but before he could complete the maneuver, his opponent's other arm—with a closed fist that looked like a beef knucklebone—grazed the side of his face, something hard scraping against his skin. The longhaired thug was stoked now and pummeled Jake's chest and upper arms in a rapid series of one-twos. As they jockeyed around, knickknacks went flying from polished wood and glass surfaces, shattering as they hit the floor. Jake and his opponent stumbled into a sofa table and sent a lamp rocketing into the air before it crashed into the wall, sparking on impact.

With black belts in multiple martial arts, Jake could have—and normally would have—taken his opponent out swiftly and with very little effort, but he needed to find out who the guy was and why he had broken into Delaney's place. Jake refreshed his focus and energy quickly, executing a wrist-and-finger twist as his opponent thrust an open hand toward his face. This time when Jake had his wrist, he got a better hold, pushing it acutely inward.

The man responded by backpedaling, which relaxed the pressure on his wrist and allowed Jake to make his next move, stepping in front and extending the man's hand out to the side. Despite his size, which bettered Jake's by nearly a foot and a good forty to forty-five pounds, the intruder's balance went off-kilter, and Jake completed the move by rotating his shoulder at the end of the bicep. Moving with the momentum, Jake was able to put his weight effortlessly behind the rotation, spiraling the man to the ground. Keeping the man's shoulder down and his hand pinned, Jake kneeled over the fallen intruder with his knee planted firmly in the middle of his back.

"Okay, motherfucker," Jake growled, "start talking."

The only sound uttered from the intruder was an agonized grunt.

Jake was pretty sure he'd ripped the man's arm out of its socket; most likely, it was broken.

"Look," Jake said, his voice low and even but full of menace, "we can do this one of two ways. I think you know what those two ways are."

Stupidly, the intruder muttered, "Fuck you."

"That's not the way I would have suggested," said Jake, and pressed his fingers into the point of dislocation, causing him to howl in pain. "Second chance, asshole." Maintaining the pin, he used his free hand to grab the man's hair by the ponytail and twist his head around which, in turn, increased the torque on the incapacitated arm. Jake could see beads of sweat gathering along the man's hairline, his lips gnarled into a grimace.

But the man said nothing.

Jake let go of the man's hair and reached around, shoving his hand into the right rear pocket of the man's jeans and coming out with a slim black leather wallet. He flipped it open, thumbed out a driver's license, and scanned the information. It was Costa Rican, with a photo that more or less matched the man pinned beneath him, height and weight about right, but the name was highly dubious. *Diego Vizcaya.* This guy looked about as much like a Diego Vizcaya as Carlos Santana looked like Kenny Chesney.

"Okay, *Diego*," Jake snarled, his voice laden with sarcasm, "why don't we start with you telling me what the fuck you're doing breaking in here and shooting up the place." When his quarry still said nothing, Jake applied more pressure to his wrist. "Tough guy, huh? Okay, here's the deal. Either you can talk to me and get your ass booted out the door or I can put your lights out and let the cops collect you. Your choice."

"I ain't lookin' for you, asshole," the intruder murmured insolently, a slight twang of indeterminate origin in his voice.

"Now see, I knew *Diego* just didn't suit you. So who are you?"

"I don't particularly think you need to know that."

"And I don't think you're in a position to tell me what I need to know," Jake said, increasing the pull on the man's arm, eliciting another painful groan. "Who the fuck are you?" he demanded.

"Name's Duster," the man grimaced.

Jake harrumphed. "Okay, *Duster*, who *are* you looking for?" he asked, but he already knew the likely answer.

"Delaney. I'm lookin' for Delaney."

"Yeah? And what do you want with him?"

"None of your goddamned business, pal."

"Since you saw fit to come calling on my watch, you've made it my fucking business, Duster. So I'm going to ask again, nicely. What do you want with him?"

"That's between him and me."

"Okay, now you're beginning to piss me off," Jake said, tightening his left-hand grip and once again yanking the man's head up by the hair. "What the fuck do you want with him?"

Through teeth clenched in pain, the man who claimed to be Duster said, "Between him and me. And that's all I'm sayin' so you can just toss my ass out now."

With that, Jake chopped his hand in an *atemi* strike at the nape of the man's neck. It was quick, precise, and relatively light, but it put him out instantly. To the unconscious man, he said, "I'm usually an honorable man, Duster...but I lied," and went to call an acquaintance he had with the local police.

NOT MORE THAN TWENTY minutes later, Jake stood talking to Pablo Luis Ayala, a young cop he had met on his first visit to Dominical. A native *Tico*, Ayala had been very helpful during the initial founding of SpecOps and had been a friend of Jake and Delaney ever since. He wasn't on duty tonight, so he had brought a pair of fellow officers who were. The two policemen managed to rouse the unconscious intruder long enough to get him into an upright position. It took both of them to drag the big man outside.

"So what do you think happened here?" Ayala asked, carefully picking around the bullet that was wedged in stucco. The round that had smashed into the French door was already in an evidence bag. The young Costa Rican was small but athletic looking with close-cropped black hair and animated eyes that clearly found Jake fascinating.

Hands on his hips, Jake shrugged. "Who the hell knows, Luis. Haskell's obviously gotten himself on somebody's shit list. I think this guy was either a messenger, a collector, or an enforcer—maybe all of the above."

"I did not recognize him," Ayala said, plucking the bullet from the wall and holding it up for inspection.

"Obviously, the driver's license is a fake. Might be former military, had some good moves."

Ayala grinned. "Not so good as yours, *mi amigo*. How *did* you take down a man that big? With a gun no less?" he inquired, his expression manifesting the respect he obviously felt for Jake.

Jake didn't reply.

"Special Forces stuff, yes? Okay, well, we will certainly do our best to find out who is this man and why he comes here."

The two police officers that had accompanied Ayala burst through the front door, both breathing heavily and sputtering in Spanish. Out of their excited babble, Jake heard the word *escapado* and muttered, "Shit." Duster or Vizcaya, or whoever the hell he was, had gotten away.

"*Cómo?*" asked Ayala, to which the officers in unison replied, "*Motocicleta.*"

The motorcycle heard earlier, down the coastal road. *Shit.* The guy had driven it to a point and stashed it, just far enough away to prevent drawing Jake's attention.

"*Vaya! Ahora!*" Ayala shouted, and ran after them, throwing a hand up to Jake on the way out.

Closing the door behind Ayala, Jake ascended the stairs and padded to the bedroom where he had secured Callie as soon as he'd disabled the intruder.

She was sitting on the bed, very still, feet together on the floor, arms crossed over her chest, hands tightly clenched. In a calm voice, he said, "Everything's all right now, Callie. The cops will handle it."

Her eyes widened in alarm as she noticed the blood on his face and arms. "Jake, you're hurt!"

He swiped absently at the gash on his face, looked disinterestedly at the blood smear on the back of his hand. "I'm okay. Just a couple of scrapes, nothing serious."

Crossing to her, he slipped an arm around her shoulders and drew her against him. He stroked her hair softly until her breathing slowed;

long before that, his own quickened as a latent internal aching began to distract him from the soreness in the rest of his body.

Sighing deeply, he released her, and kissed her gently on the forehead. He gazed into her eyes, felt his lips tingle. Pressing them together, he touched her cheek and said, "Get some sleep, okay?"

JAKE'S BARE FEET POUNDED against the sand, leaving imprints that the surf washed and ironed out minutes after he'd passed. The ocean whispered waves into the thinning night, rolling them out and pulling them back in. A wafer of moon the color of antique linen followed him, holding solemn vigil on the final hour. Running along the Pacific in the isolation of pre-dawn, the world seemed small and remote. The beat of his heart, the weight of emotion inside, was rolling in his head like the tide. As he ran, he tried to flush out thoughts and images of Delaney, but the heaviness of dread held them there like a weighted trunk. They had shared so much, been through so much. He loved him like a brother. He knew him so well. And now, he was beginning to realize maybe he didn't know Haskell Delaney at all.

He thought about the mission before him instead, his final commitment to the Colombia contract, and found his mind clearing. But the emotion in his heart was not so easily purged. He wondered if it was something other than his conflicted feelings about Delaney.

He stopped, dropped to the sand and sat with his knees drawn up. Distantly, the ocean and sky slowly delineated as a pale glow stretched and widened across the dark horizon. It was gold, then almost white, then amber. The sun broke and floated lazily over the water, blinding the surface in a shimmering disco dazzle of dawn. In the sky, reds and pinks bled out until blue was all that remained. Blue on the bottom and blue on the top...just miles and miles of blue.

AFTER BREAKFAST WITH CALLIE at the Soda Nanyoa, a small local restaurant, Jake had stopped by the police station for an update from Pablo Luis Ayala. Regretfully, there wasn't much to report. Ayala informed him that the thug's motorcycle had been found, abandoned several miles from Delaney's villa, but so far it could not be traced—as had been the case of the Beretta. And so far there was nothing coming back associated with the names Diego Vizcaya or Duster.

Jake spent the rest of his morning and early afternoon in industrious isolation, trying to distance himself from the freshly generated emotions he could not allow himself to feel now as he prepared for his return trip to Colombia. It took a significant mental effort to keep Delaney off his mind; for reasons he still could not fathom, it took even more effort to keep from thinking about Callie.

But as the morning flipped to afternoon and the hour of his departure drew near, his military discipline kicked in and he found the metal jacket he needed to insulate himself from emotional and mental distractions. By the time he returned to the villa, his mind was on Colombia and only Colombia. He gathered his gear, repacked his bags, made phone calls. Twice he spoke to the middle-aged *Tica* housekeeper, giving her detailed instructions in Spanish. Each time, the woman glanced at Callie and nodded vigorously.

Callie watched Jake from her chair in the living room. The broken lamp and other accessories from the previous night's encounter between Jake and the intruder had been removed with expeditious care. A pretty glass dolphin she had admired was missing, as were quite a few other table ornaments. But the only remaining evidence of the violence that had taken place was the starburst of fractured glass in the French door. Callie found her eyes returning to it repeatedly, staring at the bullet hole in the middle.

"Hey."

She turned to see Jake standing in front of her, freshly showered and groomed, dressed in crisp khaki slacks and collared shirt. Both his cellular and satellite phones were clipped to his belt, a carry-on duffel slung over his shoulder. A quick glance to the front door, where the rest of his bags were assembled, confirmed his imminent departure. Callie tried to say something, but a knot had formed in her throat.

He perched on the arm of the chair, placed his hand tenderly on her shoulder. "Don't worry about last night," he said. "Luis is working on it. Stay here at the villa as long as you like, it's perfectly safe. Luis and his men will be keeping a close eye out. Camilla will make sure you're comfortable and have everything you need. Okay?"

In a shaky voice, she asked, "Are you sure your friend won't mind?"

"Not at all."

"Jake..." she began, and could not finish.

"Whatever you decide to do will be good. No worries." He stood, smacked his hands on his thighs, and said, "Okay, then. Got to get going." He turned toward the door.

Callie stood, feeling a desperate torrent of emotion rush through her. "Jake..."

He glanced back over his shoulder, his head canted.

"Thank you."

Smiling, he replied, "My pleasure."

"Jake?"

He glanced back again, but his face was clouding now with a sternness she'd not seen before.

"Be careful."

"Always." He strode to the door, turning one last time. "Okay, take care, Callie." His hand was on the doorknob, but he paused and looked back at her one last time. One more time than he should have. She stood, looking small and docile and pretty in the same white sundress she'd been wearing the day he had come to her aid in San José. "Remember," he said, "to write about life, you have to live it."

And then he collected his bags and went through the door.

Tears welled in Callie's eyes.

Outside, Jake stood on the porch and took a deep breath. His meticulously constructed wall of resolve crumbled then, and the emotions he'd been holding tightly in check tumbled recklessly over the top.

He felt a cavern of frustration and disappointment for having failed to open Callie up, to find out who she really was, why she was so fearful. There was something there, and he wanted to know what it was. But, no. She was not his type—not his type at all. She was nothing like the kind of women he found himself attracted to, involved with and ultimately, he conceded, parted from. He was attracted to strong women, women with fire and passion, even anger. Aggressive women who knew what they wanted and went after it. Unlike Callie who, though beautiful and intelligent was shy and sensitive, was as delicate and fragile as a china teacup, and the idea of handling something so breakable was deeply troubling.

Which is why it totally stupefied him that he thought he might be falling in love…for the first time in his life.

He slid behind the wheel of the Jeep Cherokee and slipped the key into the ignition. Just before turning the engine over, he heard the porch chimes lightly chinking. Strange, he thought idly. There was no breeze.

CALLIE WALKED ALONG THE beach for what seemed like hours, just listening to the soothing rhythm of the ocean. The waves were calm, the sky an excruciating blue with clouds as light as whipped meringue. The sand felt like sugar between her toes.

Shortly after Jake left, she'd sat for a long while in the villa's lovely living room and felt the stale, penetrating silence. The past week in Costa Rica had changed her life, and now that she was alone with it she had no idea what to do. The catalyst for the change—Jake—was gone, and his electric intensity had vaporized the moment he disappeared through the door. The absence of Jake was crushing. Inside, she quivered with a longing she had never felt before.

Now, as she strolled across the sand, wandering in and out of the warm, clear water that caressed the shores, she wondered what had really happened during that week. When she had come to Costa Rica, she wasn't quite sure what she expected to happen. She had certainly not expected any of this. Because of Jake, she had seen and done things she never really knew about, things she would never have considered doing even if she had. Jake had a way that was both reassuring and unsettling, understanding and demanding, and even after being with him for a week, she still found herself a little afraid of him. But she also felt something else, something she'd never felt before.

Desire. And now, loss.

IN HER BEDROOM AT the villa, she began to unzip the sundress, heading toward the bathroom to take a shower. She stopped as she reached the edge of the bed. It was king-size, with an engraved bamboo-and-cane headboard and footboard, comforter and linens in alternating rich and muted shades of terra cotta and teal. There was an orchid on her pillow. It was white with a pale pink center. She smiled wanly. Camilla, the housekeeper, must have put it there when she made the bed this morning. Her fingertips brushed it, gingerly closing around the stem. She lifted it to her face.

Then she saw a folded piece of paper attached to it. Her heart prickled. She slipped it off the orchid, tremulously opened it.

It read: *Until we meet again...J*

Callie wondered if they would.

8

THE CHANGE IN TEMPERATURE between San José and the spot where he now stood was marginal, but the humidity was a mind-numbing 90 percent—a heat index equivalent of 120 to 130 degrees Fahrenheit. The sun was high but looked so close it blended shapelessly into the sky, making hollandaise out of its blueness. It was hot. *Welcome back to the real deal*, Jake thought grimly.

After checking into base camp little over an hour ago, his first order of business had been to inquire on Delaney's whereabouts. He was told that Delaney had made a supply run to Bogotá the day before and was probably still unloading. Though no one he asked seemed to know exactly where that was, Jake had a pretty good idea and set off on foot into the bush surrounding their compound. He had hiked approximately two miles when he came to the clearing. He stopped, plucked a bottle of Manantial mineral water from his rucksack, took a healthy swig, and wiped his brow. The sweat-faded head wrap was already soaked.

The plane—an ancient DC-3—sat at the end of a dirt strip, perhaps fifteen hundred feet in length, wedged in a pocket of brush and draped with a camouflage net. It looked like a giant olive-colored wasp caught in a spider's lair. A bullet-pocked and wear-rutted Toyota Land Cruiser was parked next to the plane, roof rack already loaded down with boxes and shrink-wrapped packages. As Jake got closer to the plane's open rear hatch, he could hear the metallic thunk of someone moving around inside. He was about to pound on the side of the aircraft and announce his presence when Delaney's stocky figure appeared in the opening.

"Fuck!" he exclaimed, startled by Jake and nearly dropping the armful of supplies he was carrying as a result. Recovering his balance and composure, he sputtered, "Make me shit my pants why don'tcha?" When Jake said nothing, Delaney tossed the packages onto the ground, following them with an easy hop. Composing a tenuous smile, he wheezed a nervous laugh. "So, Wildman, you just get in?"

Dryly, Jake said, "Yeah. You?"

"Uh, yeah, about that..." Delaney began, slapping dust from his hands onto his pants.

Before he could continue, Jake snapped, "Yeah, tell me about that. Haskell, what the fuck is going on?"

Another nervous twitter from Delaney, who reached over and took Jake's water bottle, helping himself to several noisy gulps. "Hey, chill out, bro. Nothing's *going on*. Okay? I just decided to stick around here until we're done, that's all. Went up to Bogie with a couple of the guys, had me some decent chow, some zealous libation, and as much tail as I could handle." A mischievous gleam appeared in his eyes. "Actually, one very hot Colombian tail." He stuck his tongue out, panting lewdly.

"You sure you didn't stay behind to avoid anyone in Costa Rica?" Jake asked, unsmiling, eying him narrowly.

Hoisting the supplies he had offloaded from the plane, Delaney carried them to the Land Cruiser and set them just inside the back. With his head in the rear of the vehicle as he rearranged the cargo, he asked, "What do you mean?"

"Know a guy named Diego Vizcaya?"

Delaney's head popped out, his expression lacking any sign of recognition. "Should I?" he asked.

"Called himself *Duster*," Jake added, and thought he detected the slightest twitch at the corner of Delaney's eye. Watched as Delaney wiped more sweat from his brow.

"No, never heard of anybody by that name. Why?" Once again, he busied himself moving the contents of the vehicle around.

"He paid me a visit in Dominical, looking for you."

Delaney shrugged. "Maybe we met somewhere. You know me, I collect drinking buddies like fruit collects flies."

"If he was a drinking buddy, you must owe him a lot more than a bar tab, my friend," Jake said tightly.

Delaney straightened up and cast Jake a vaguely troubled look. Small creases appeared in his forehead and he licked his lips. "Why? What did he say, this guy?"

"Well, after I helped him redecorate your living room, he didn't say much. Except that his business was with you. Must be pretty serious business considering he was armed. Dumped a few of his bullets in the house before I took him down."

The creases in Delaney's brow became furrows, rivulets of sweat running through them. His clean-shaven head glistened. "What did you do with him?"

"Got Luis and the police to come, but the son of a bitch got away." Jake found it odd that Delaney actually seemed relieved by that outcome. He waited until Delaney was looking at him and asked pointedly, "Haskell, are you tapped again?"

Over the course of their friendship, Jake had watched as Delaney's casual forays into casinos became first an enthralling hobby and then a gambling obsession, everything from high stake poker to sporting bets to staggering double-or-nothing wagers. Ultimately, it defined his life in stark black-and-white flashpoints. When he was up, his world was a genie in the bottle with an abundance of light and an endless array of treasures. When he was down, the genie turned dark and demonic, dancing in the dungeon and daring him to come back to the light. After one too many trips to the dungeon, Delaney had sworn off hardcore gambling for good, even though Jake had long suspected his friend still occasionally indulged. He'd just deduced that Delaney had managed to stay in the genie's good graces. He now suspected he had been wrong about that.

"Hey, bubba," Delaney said with a smile that would have sautéed mushrooms, "not to worry. How about giving me a hand with this stuff? Lots of good shit here...water purification kits, hygiene products, meds, oh and got your candy and toys for the kids!"

"Good." Surveying the dirt strip and the dense bush surrounding, Jake said, "Why the hell did you pick this spot to land? It's out of our secured AO."

There was a brief pause before Delaney responded, "Some of the last shipment I brought in disappeared and was never accounted for."

"Really? You report that to Paul?"

He shook his head. "Nah, figured the less I said the better. Didn't want to stir up a stink with the Colombians."

"Okay," Jake replied, glancing at his watch, "we need to get back to base. Briefing is at fourteen-hundred."

SEATED IN THE COMPOUND'S briefing room—a relatively spacious but otherwise dismal area blocked in by concrete walls and outfitted with plastic patio-style chairs—were members of the Colombian police, select *junglas*, and the US team. Their chief, Paul Traynor, stood with Major Ramón Grajales, the Colombian base commander. Alberto Hernandez sat just to the side of Traynor next to a table covered with computer printouts. Satellite imagery and topographical and tactical maps papered the wall behind them.

They began with an overview of mission accomplishments to date and a quick run-through of ongoing issues. They made several references to the maps, using colored pushpins to show the latest FARC fronts and paramilitary activity. Since its establishment in the sixties, the Revolutionary Armed Forces of Colombia—Fuerzas Armadas Revolucionarias de Colombia—known as FARC, has been the largest guerrilla faction governing an area of southern Colombia roughly the size of Switzerland. While most NATO nations consider al-Qaeda, the Taliban, and Hezbollah the greatest threats among terrorist organizations and therefore highest priority, the FARC—still numbering in the tens of thousands despite losing about half their force in recent years—remains one of the most ruthless in the world, financed by kidnapping and ransom, extortion, and narcotics trafficking. And now there was a whole new dimension developing, shadowy splinter groups muscling into gaps forged by the successful government campaigns against the rightwing militias and the leftist guerrillas; as a result, production was on the increase and more supply routes were opening up.

"Now then," Paul Traynor said, scanning the assembled group, "here is the latest directive from the embassy, as channeled by NAS and DEA.

For our final phase of the mission we will focus on taking out labs. We have some new intel but will need additional recon to nail our targets. Needless to say, with their string of recent setbacks, the guerrillas have been making a concerted effort to reassert their strength. Last week, they bombed the Occidental oil pipeline near here, killed several workers, and took others hostage. What's old is new again."

That it is, thought Jake, *that it is*. And nothing much had changed since his earlier counternarcotics work. The US was still deluding itself that their eradication programs were making a difference, but what they were doing was nothing more than putting dime-sized chinks in an infrastructure as resilient as a colony of fire ants. Knock down one anthill, a bigger one emerges a week later, expanding at an even faster rate. Wipe out one peasant farmer's coca field, six more would replace it months later. At least by finding and taking out the labs, they were hitting the narcos a little closer to the jugular. What they really needed to do was have the balls to go after the top guys. Then when other *narcotraficantes* stepped into their shoes, they could be taken out before they were able to establish power. This would force the cartels to disperse and operate in smaller cells that were easier to track and eliminate. Instead, even years later under the Andean Counterdrug Initiative with its ambitious *new* agenda, they were still taking pages out of the original game book. Much like the army.

Jake was just glad that, for him, it would be over for good in a few weeks.

Leaning forward, he said, "The pipeline hostages, have they become a K&R yet?" What he referred to was known as kidnap and ransom, a multi-million dollar industry fortified by specialized insurance policies underwritten to cover the staggering ransom demands made by terrorists who abducted individuals working for high profile companies. When a K&R was made known, special operatives were almost always employed and Jake had run several of these missions.

Traynor shook his head. "Not so far. Occidental has taken so many hits, my guess is they have the takers on speed-dial and are probably already in negotiations. I'm sure they have a substantial K&R policy."

When the briefing concluded and the group began to file out, Traynor snagged Jake and Delaney. Alberto Hernandez had remained by his side. "I didn't want to address this to the entire group," Traynor began, "but before we start on the labs, I need you guys to go with Alberto to a village about twenty klicks from here. The last coca fields we wiped out were their primary stipend and the narcos have stripped them raw. Haskell, how are the supplies?"

"Good, very good. I have everything we should need."

"Great. Tomorrow morning Alberto will take the two of you, with assistance from a couple of locals, to Afortunado."

IRONICALLY, AFORTUNADO TRANSLATED AS 'fortunate.' And this place, this tiny town on the banks of the Río Putumayo, was anything but. A hodgepodge of huts and shacks constructed with whatever raw materials were available—scrap wood, tree branches, thatch, mud—made up the shantytown. From all appearances it looked like it had been knocked down and put back together again more than a few times. Children wandered dusty roads with mongrel dogs and chickens, the look of the lost tattooed on their small faces, while adults shuffled aimlessly back and forth. It was a ghost town where bodies still dwelled but their spirits had long since departed.

As was their routine with relief missions, they set up a base of operation in the center of town. Typically, this was either a church or, as was the case here, a *bodega*. The small grocery had been stripped of everything but the wood planks, the only clue to its former identity a single hand-woven basket of rotting fruit. Flies swarmed deliriously over the sour pulp of yellow, green, red, and orange. Tossing the mess aside, Delaney set up a bank of food and supplies while Jake and Hernandez began medical triage. The locals who accompanied them, young boys named Manuel and Emilio, had prepared the villagers for *ayuda de los gringos*—help from the gringos—so the reception they got, though initially wary, was one of welcome.

Delaney spent his time distributing grain, flour, oil, milk powder, sugar, bottled water, high-energy biscuits, and vitamins, discussing logistics for future food sources, most of which had been depleted by the guerrillas. He also dispensed their special cache of candy and toys to the children. They giggled in delight as he entertained them with a colorful repertoire of animal sounds, later captivating them with stories he effortlessly fabricated.

Assisted by Hernandez, Jake immersed himself in medical examinations and treatments. He listened intently to heartbeats, breathing, pulses and, when they trusted him, the natives themselves. He palpated a multitude of body parts, filled a box with used hypodermic needles and empty ampoules, tirelessly swabbed, bandaged, and wrapped. Besides the usual maladies, there were many shrapnel-related injuries, some of which required painful procedures. To Jake's ceaseless admiration, the majority of these victims sat or lay stoically silent as he cut, extracted, repaired, and stitched. This, followed by a grave and sincere *Muchas gracias, Doctor.*

As the grateful *campesinos* began to discreetly disperse to their respective abodes, Delaney packed up for the day and set up for the night. Since they typically remained until the most immediate and urgent needs were identified and fulfilled, this usually meant at least one overnight stay. From the Land Cruiser he unpacked their gear, which included high-power binoculars, night vision goggles, Jake's Nikon digital camera, high-beam flashlights, lanterns, and multi-purpose utility tools. For sleeping, they carried hammocks, mosquito nets, light blankets, and ponchos. When he finished bringing everything inside the *bodega*, he took a walk. He glanced briefly over his shoulder, watching his friend and partner at work.

Jake was cajoling a frightened little girl of about six whose leg was badly lacerated by shrapnel and beginning to show signs of infection. *"Tranquila, chiquita...todo está bien,"* he soothed, carefully probing her wounds. When he applied antiseptic to the raw, weeping flesh she shrieked and kicked, almost coming off the gurney he was using as an examining table. Working nearby, Alberto Hernandez took a tentative step forward to lend his assistance and then stopped, watching as Jake calmly continued. The small girl's shrieks and kicks persisted, but Jake managed to finish irrigating and dressing the wound with sterile gauze, followed by a painful injection in a little arm not much bigger than a broomstick. He pulled off his bloody latex gloves with a snap, dropped them into a tin can full of discards, and reached into the box of toys. The sight of a soft, caramel-colored teddy bear won him a tearful smile and, after the briefest hesitation, a hug.

He humbly accepted the mother's effusive thanks and began his cleanup, heavily lathering his hands and arms in anti-bacterial soap. He scrubbed vigorously for a few minutes and rinsed with bottled water. On his knees in the shack he leaned back and squeezed his eyes shut, rubbing the corners, red and irritated from the dust and hot sun. He was about to lift the near-empty gallon jug to his parched lips and let the few swallows of water drain into his mouth when he heard Hernandez say, "Buy you a cold one, *amigo*."

Jake chuckled hoarsely. "Don't I wish."

"Your wish is my command," Hernandez said, placing an icy plastic water bottle against Jake's sweat-coated neck.

Emitting a small yip of surprise, Jake asked, "Where'd *this* come from?"

"The cooler Haskell brought from the plane."

Jake guzzled the Manantial, emptying it with a couple of long swallows. He noticed that Delaney had already strung up their hammocks. Delaney had also apparently brought sandwiches from his magic cooler, which Jake and Hernandez wolfed down hungrily. Some kind of meat and cheese that tasted merely like bread with something in the middle. It might have been human spleen or goat guts, but neither of them cared. Out here food and water was simple sustenance that became epicurean ecstasy in whatever form it took.

"Hey, where is Haskell?" Jake asked, suddenly realizing that he had not seen Delaney for the past hour or so.

Hernandez shrugged. "I saw him walking outside, probably just stretching his legs."

Jake frowned. "Alberto, have you noticed anything odd with Haskell's behavior lately?" He sucked down more of the cold water. It felt like steel on his parched throat.

"Odd? Like what? You mean, like saying he was going to assist me in an aid run that I had not planned?"

"Well, yeah, like that...but anything else?"

Hernandez shook his head. "Not really, but I do not work as closely with him as you do."

"Lately *I* don't work as close with him as I do."

Jake removed his kit vest and ammo pouches but left the Glock inside his waistband. He swallowed the last of his water and stripped off his shirt, dropping the bloody garment on the ground. Pulling on a clean t-shirt, he flopped into a hammock with a sigh as heavy as the night. And his concerns about Delaney.

Moments later, Delaney stepped inside the *bodega*. Before Jake could question him, he said, "While you guys were finishing, I took a little walk around, talked to some of the locals. They've had it pretty rough lately. Been pillaged twice in the past two weeks, but nothing as extreme as this." He grabbed a bottle of water and a sandwich. "Alberto, you heard anything about bounties? One of the farmers said something about rumors of some of the new players issuing bounties on the territory narcos? Have you heard that?"

"Nothing officially," Hernandez remarked cautiously. "But unofficially, yes. I would not get any ideas, if I were you."

Delaney laughed. "Like arming myself to the teeth and going on a one-man kingpin hunt? No thanks."

From his hammock, Jake cast him a long, ponderous look.

Without looking back, Delaney reached for his H&K Mark 23, checked the magazine, and announced, "I'll take first sentry."

SLIMED IN BLOOD AND lathered in sweat, Jake cradled the tiny lifeless form in his hands and numbed himself to the sobs of the woman whose legs were spread immodestly before him. Beside her, the young father stood listless and silent, his hand on her damp head. He had been watching Jake work, honed anxiously on his face for some clue, but as soon as he had seen the dark bloody mass emerge from the woman's body, he knew.

"*Lo siento,*" Jake said solemnly, carefully wrapping the dead infant in some towels. As fluent as he was in Spanish and as accustomed as he'd become to death over the years, having to tell someone he was sorry for it never became any easier.

The young man, who was still a teenager, nodded sadly and spoke soothingly to the woman. Jake estimated the mother to be no more than fifteen or sixteen herself.

Hours earlier, her hysterical screams had catapulted him from a ragged layer of sleep. He had been disconcerted to discover daylight already present and Delaney gone again. By the time he had scrambled into pants and boots, collected his essential medical gear and located the woman, she was well into labor. He could tell immediately by the amount of blood that mother and baby were in trouble. After a quick examination of both, he knew his efforts would be wasted on the child. He had delivered enough babies to recognize the symptoms of stillbirth, and even though it was not a one hundred percent certainty until the baby was fully out and could be checked more closely, without the resources of a hospital or an evac vehicle, a choice had to be made. He could not palpate a pulse or detect a heartbeat from the infant, so he concentrated on controlling the mother's bleeding. She had lost a good bit of blood and he could only hope it was not enough to be life threatening because a radio distress call to the Red Cross or the nearest missionary clinic would not be quick enough.

After over an hour of steady improvement by the mother he felt reasonably sure she would be all right. In Spanish, he gave the father instructions for her care, indicating he would return later to monitor her progress. He noticed that a pair of women—the village midwives most likely—had unceremoniously removed the infant's body, for which he was grateful.

Still wondering where Delaney was, he returned to the *bodega* to clean up—a disposable plastic smock had managed to keep most but not all of the blood off his clothes—and get a bite to eat. After gobbling down two bananas with a protein bar and drinking some Gatorade, he tried to raise Delaney on the radio with no response.

He made a brief circuit around the village, checking on those he had treated the day before and stopping to tend to new situations. During the night a roving trio of young boys had apparently startled and, in turn, been bitten by bats, and there had been one snakebite. He cleaned and bandaged the bloody lacerations caused by the bats and injected antivenom for the snakebite. As he made his rounds, he inquired about other pregnant women—he had not seen the girl, whose name was Marielos, during their triage last night—and was relieved to find no evidence of potential problems among the few others he encountered. He looked in again on Marielos and found her sleeping peacefully under the vigilant supervision of the midwives. Finally satisfied that all was reasonably under control, he set out to find his errant partner.

HE FOUND HASKELL NEAR the river, rigging a well.

Jake had hiked across an open savanna where the *campesinos* were working to establish a new settlement and poked his way through a corridor of tree ferns and palms, emerging at the river edge. There, along with Delaney, he found a hive of activity. Women were washing clothes and utensils, children were splashing each other while being bathed, men and boys were fishing. Judging from the stockpile of fish, they'd been at it since pre-dawn. There would be good eating for them tonight. A small boy was jubilantly showing off a fat, wriggling catfish nearly as big as he was. A cluster of little girls were pointing and giggling at something downstream—the animated play of otters.

South American river life was an endless source of awe and fascination to Jake, a predatory theater teeming with thousands of exotic birds, fish, reptiles, and mammals. And these resourceful natives, ever resilient, were adapting to their circumstances with remarkable ease, embracing the river with all of its challenges and rewards. He watched, enthralled, as fathers and sons stood on the riverbank or waded through its current, using a variety of fish-catching methods. Some used spears and blowguns, while others used more traditional casting nets and crudely made wooden fishing poles. Their catches consisted of mostly catfish, with some varieties of tucanaré, pacu, arawana, and piranha. Farther down the river others had ventured out in canoes and were making much of a just-speared pirarucu—one of the largest freshwater fish in the world, some of which exceed six-foot lengths and several hundred pounds. This one was a healthy-looking specimen of perhaps seventy-five pounds. Fishing in South American waters was heady adventure, the size of the fish only outdone by their athletic ability. There were species that could leap several feet out of the water to snatch birds from low-hanging tree branches, and piranhas were not the only carnivorous fish with mouthfuls of teeth. Then there were the frogs, turtles, lizards, snakes, reptiles, and rodents. While the frogs were primarily nocturnal and could be heard gutturally harmonizing with the birds and monkeys, iguanas and boa constrictors seemed to perch perennially on tree limbs as eels and anacondas slithered through the water alongside the alligators and caimans. Capybara, rodents as large as pigs, shared the river with packs of stout-bodied tapirs resembling small rhinos. Scattered across the llanos were opossums, sloths, anteaters, armadillos, deer, raccoons, weasels, coati, kinkajous, and olingos. Pumas, ocelots, and jaguars stealthily traversed the denser jungle areas, often emerging riverside for a drink or to track prey. Set against the exquisite canvas of brightly colored butterflies, birds, and flowering fauna, this primitive and predatory eat-or-be-eaten tropical world was a living masterpiece.

"Decided to join the worker bees? Must have finished your morning coffee and newspaper," Delaney remarked jauntily without looking up, using a trowel to apply and smooth cement around the well's platform. Despite the bandanna covering his head, sweat was dripping steadily down his tanned face. The installation of a fresh water well using a hand pump and incorporating a simple water purification system was always one of their prime objectives in a relief scenario. Providing healthy water for drinking, washing, and bathing would save many more lives than their aid or provisions ever could.

Brushing the dust of drying cement from his fatigues, Delaney followed Jake to the spot where the Land Cruiser was parked, shaded and almost obscured by palm leaves. "I got up pretty early—wasn't even light—because I wanted to ride back and check on the plane. Which is why I took the truck." Wiping sweat from his forehead with a dusty arm, he reached for a bottle of water and emptied it in a series of hearty gulps.

The explanation, while reasonable enough, did not satisfy Jake. Delaney, who was an electronic genius, had the DC-3 rigged with more security systems than a Porsche dealership, and rarely in the past had he given it a second thought once he'd landed it somewhere. Sure, some attempts to hijack or sabotage had occurred at different times, but short of blowing it up Jake could not imagine anyone succeeding. With his back turned to Delaney, Jake blew sharply into the mic of his radio headset. Behind him, Delaney grimaced.

"What'd you do that for, you little prick?"

"Testing," Jake replied laconically.

"Obviously, it works fine," Delaney retorted, touching the earpiece curled around his lobe.

Turning to face him, Jake asked, "Why haven't you been responding then?"

"I didn't hear you if you tried to raise me this morning, but then I've been drilling a well."

Jake sighed, shaking his head. "Sorry, my day didn't start very well."

"I let you sleep, I figured you needed it," Delaney remarked, his gaze fixed on a spot somewhere behind Jake's head.

"Well, I didn't get much sleep. One of the young girls, someone we didn't even see last night, went into labor. She was already bleeding profusely and—"

The machete was whisked out so swiftly that Jake only heard and felt the whistle of air as it sliced over his head. Ducking instinctively, he barely avoided the blade. "Jesus Christ, Haskell, what are you—" He stopped, seeing the severed remains of a deadly fer-de-lance at his feet. A bite from this snake could cause hypotension, renal failure, or even intra-cranial hemorrhage.

Without missing a beat, Delaney said, "So you delivered the baby?" He was indifferently tossing hunks of snake into the brush as if it were an old garden hose, now a delicacy for some lucky predator.

Recovering his composure, Jake said, "Yes, but it was stillborn. I think the girl will be okay. Some midwives are taking care of her."

They strolled back toward the well to check the finished product. The hot midday sun had baked it almost dry, which was fortunate because the daily afternoon rain showers would be commencing soon. "I want to work on a few more boats and huts," Delaney said. "Several groups just returned from a market downriver so they've got more building supplies."

"Good. Well, I'm going to take the truck back to town."

As Jake strolled toward the 4x4, he heard Delaney begin to serenade his hapless audience of well diggers with a chorus of "Wild Thing." Jake could not stop the slow smile tugging at the corners of his mouth as Delaney wailed, *"Wild tha-ang, you make my heart sa-ang...Wild tha-ang, you make everytha-ang...ga-ro-oovy...Wild tha-ang, I tha-ank I lo-ooove you..."*

Driving back to town, Jake thought about the war-debilitated *campes-inos* whose lives had been reinvigorated by them, if only for a while, and felt a surge of pride. As he drove the path Delaney had forged with the Land Cruiser's bull bar, his senses reveled in the sound and texture and beauty of the countryside. Admired the fuchsia and scarlet bromeliad plants burgeoning from tree limbs and roots and the tall canopy of evergreens that secreted the tropical world from an ethereal sky beyond. Inhaled the rich loamy smell of the undergrowth. He emerged from the forest and headed back across the savanna toward the town called Afortunado, almost riding into a harem of fluorescently colored hummingbirds pollinating a meadow of flowers that rivaled their beauty. And, marveling at them, he nearly hit a lazy anteater the size of a large dog lumbering through the pampas. In spite of the inauspicious start to his day and his mounting suspicions about Delaney's behavior, he was beginning to feel pretty good.

He stopped just short of the village and surveyed the diorama of activity there. Delaney had been right about the acquisition of new supplies. The shacks had been outfitted with hammocks and wooden shades made from rough-hewn *tablas*, and there was fresh meat being prepared for the cooking pit—a large crater lined with layers of branches, stone, and banana leaves. Baskets of fruit and nuts had been collected for more trade, while some of the older women had contributed weavings. Chickens scurried around, chased by cackling children, many of which had been crying last night. This, Jake thought, was what it was all about. He had done more dangerous or adventurous things in his life—lunged out of airplanes, scaled and plummeted off the sides of mountains, dove into the ocean depths and swam amidst sharks—but nothing made him feel more vital and alive than helping those in need. And these people, it appeared, would be all right for now. They'd had their immediate food and medical needs addressed, tapped a river for a new water source from which a purifying well had been installed, and fortified the structures of their thatched housing.

Still, as much as he tried, Jake could not shake the uneasy feeling that something was just not right with Delaney. On impulse, he drove back toward the jungle edge, searching for the covert turnoff—a matted tangle of ferns framed by a towering pair of Brazil nut trees—that led to the dirt airstrip. He was thinking that maybe he should check on the plane, too.

BY THE TIME JAKE pulled up to the airstrip a light rain had started, cooling the temperature, but the sun was not ready to relinquish its presence, sifting in and out of the clouds like a guest reluctant to leave the reception. Raindrops cooled his hot skin as he climbed out of the vehicle and walked stiffly over to the plane, aware of a vague tingling in his spine.

Immediately he felt, rather than saw, that something was different about the plane. Was it the position? Had it been *moved*? Or had someone been on board? He could not put his finger on what it was, but something just didn't seem right. He felt as if he'd returned to a room where something, maybe just one thing, had been touched or picked up and put back in the wrong place, a framed photo tilted an opposite angle, a wrinkle in a bedspread, a door left ajar. The camouflage net did not seem to be draped in the way he remembered. He could have sworn the nose of the DC-3 had barely poked out from beneath, but perhaps Delaney had noticed when he was here earlier and pulled it over the exposed tip. Surely, Jake told himself, Delaney would have said something if he had found anything amiss. Maybe Delaney had been on board himself. Of course, he reasoned, that was probably it. Delaney had gone on board to check out the cabin, the remaining cargo. Or maybe the plane was exactly the way Delaney had left it, untouched and in exactly the same spot.

Walking around the plane to inspect the rest of it before returning to town, Jake was startled by Delaney's strident voice crackling through his radio earpiece for the first time since they had arrived. He was singing, again. Jake groaned, but his smile was quick and genuine. This time it was Tom Petty, the ups and downs of life-flying.

Feeling a little ashamed of his distrust, Jake tried to speak, but Delaney continued his warbling. Distracted by Delaney's singing, Jake didn't hear the click directly behind him, but seconds later he did feel the barrel of the gun as it was jammed behind his ear.

9

"QUÉ PASA?" JAKE ASKED the man holding the gun to his head. But he already had a pretty good idea what was going on.

The response was quick and uninspiredly brutal. The butt of the weapon was slammed into the base of his skull, just behind the ear, and Jake was momentarily incapacitated with an excruciating burst of pain that seared from one side of his head to the other, like laser tag. He put his fingers to the place where a knot was already forming, touching oozing stickiness that he knew was blood. It trickled lazily down the back of his neck into the collar of his shirt.

He was surrounded by about a dozen men, all wearing a mix of military garb and overtly hostile expressions, substantially armed with an assortment of M16 and AK47 assault rifles, M60 machine guns, and M79 grenade launchers—the full picnic basket. With the bread-and-butter array of handguns. He was reasonably certain they were FARC, but it hardly mattered. Whether FARC or ELN or any of the many other extremist paramilitary groups, they were on the wrong side of the minefield.

A man who appeared to be the leader of the cadre stepped forward and glared at Jake for several moments before addressing him. No more than twenty, he wore a dark t-shirt and leather ammo vest, camouflage pants tucked into black rubber boots, and a bandanna tied around his arm with the colors of the Colombian flag. In reasonably good English, he asked, "Who are you and what is your business here?"

When Jake said nothing, he nodded pointedly to one of his men who swiftly stripped Jake of his radio headset and, after a rough pat-down, the Glock from inside his pants. The man holding the gun to Jake's head had not moved since striking him.

"I asked, who are you and what is your business here?" he demanded again, this time with an acidic edge to his voice.

"Jake Tyler," Jake answered, managing to keep his voice steady. Of course, he was not about to say *I am here as part of a US counternarcotics team taking out your coca fields and labs*, opting instead for the less inflammatory humanitarian angle. He began, "The plane belongs to me and my partner, Haskell Delaney. We are here to—"

His explanation was clipped by the sharp toe of a boot spiking the back of his knee, at the vulnerable bend, followed by a fist jab in the kidney, and he fought to maintain his balance. Solid conditioning saved him that humiliation. He clamped down on his lip, struggling to repress an overwhelming desire to spin around and unify his tormentor with the atomic structure of the universe—something he was unequivocally capable of, but which he knew would be wasted valor in the spray of automatic gunfire that would send him to the same place instants later.

Clearly not interested in hearing any supplementary information, the guerrilla leader said crisply, "You will come with us, *Señor* Tyler."

The man with the gun pointed at Jake's head gave him a rough push toward the Land Cruiser.

"*Entré!*" the gunman commanded, opening the passenger-side door and shoving Jake into the seat. He kept his handgun, a military-issue Colt, trained on Jake while one of his comrades climbed into the driver's seat, holding an Uzi casually in his lap. A jeep had pulled in front of them while two more drove up behind. Jake's mind had fuzzily begun to assemble pieces of possible escape scenarios when he was struck again, hard, sweeping his senses into a vacuum that pulled all rational thought and feeling out of him like the last swirl of water sucked down by a drain. He was vacuously aware of the remaining men piling into the military vehicles, their movements blurred and slithery to him—lizards climbing onto rolling rocks. The caravan trundled down a pocked dirt road headed, undoubtedly, for another village inhabited by the guerrillas.

Helplessly drifting, Jake heard Delaney's pitiful singing sinking down the drain with him, his own voice echoing hollowly...*in some deep shit now*...as he finally lost consciousness.

WHEN HE CAME TO, he was in the corner of a sealed room, sitting on a dirt floor. The walls were stone and stucco, primitive but very solid. There was a door and a single window. Jake sat still for several minutes, becoming oriented, willing himself to ignore the fierce throbbing in his head and concentrate on his environment, consider his options. There didn't seem to be many at this point. Faintly remembering the radio exchange he'd been having with Delaney when the guerrillas had appeared, he wondered how long it would be before Delaney suspected foul play and came looking for him. Then, culling back over his friend's recent behavior, he wondered if that thought would even occur to him.

He got up stiffly, coughing as dust stirred in the dampness, coating his lungs. His skin was damp, his fatigues were damp, his throat and eyes as dry and grainy as burlap. And his mind was already taking him back down that torturous mental path where a secret cache of life-altering atrocities was stored. The place where the skeletons of indignity, impotence, and incapacitation hung like a necklace of shark's teeth; the place that housed the shelf of brokenness, broken pride, broken faith, broken hope, broken spirit; the place where the inconceivable evils of humanity were burrowed. It was a dark, dark place, one that Jake fought to keep tightly locked and sealed. But as he sat on the dusty floor that was not unlike the other dusty floors—or bare grounds—he could hear the skeletons rattling in the darkness. Visions from the infernal trunk of time spent in those places floated before him like mist rising from a very deep lake. El Salvador, Azerbaijan, Bosnia, Sierra Leone.

At least he wasn't shackled, or bound, or hanging. Yet.

He squeezed his eyes tightly shut, shook his head as if the mere act of shaking could dislodge the images. It didn't work.

Pacing restlessly back and forth for an indeterminable stretch of time, his mind transitioned, as it had the other times, through the basic trinity of emotions evoked by captivity: fear of the unknown, anger for allowing himself to be taken, and finally, readiness to evade death or accept it. He hoped the torture would be minimal—he never expected the minimum, but he always hoped which strengthened the resolve to overcome.

Waiting for the inevitable was almost worse than the torture itself, and a mentally exhausting exercise of repression against memories of the past; the last thing you wanted was to allow them a place to roost where they gave validation to fear. He knew only too well that was something you needed to move quickly past as it clouded the disciplines of self-preservation and survival. Even so, as he waited, now the sights and sounds and smells rattled from within that trunk, seeming both deeply buried in the past and close beneath the lid—just an emotional click away from spilling blood-splattered mud and hot-pepper singed flesh and the eyes, so many eyes.

He was peering through an essentially viewless window when the door opened, framing a pair of armed guerrilla soldiers. One of them tossed Jake's medical bag into the room where it dropped heavily on the dirt floor, sending up another musty cloud. Jake put a hand to his mouth and nose, but not quickly enough to avoid inhaling. Coughing again, he reached for the bag, watching the guerrillas guardedly.

"*Vamos!*" one of them barked, stepping into the room behind Jake, poking him with the barrel of an M16 assault rifle. "*Vamos andando!*" he repeated with a more insistent jab.

Following the other soldier, Jake was led outside, now understanding what was expected of him. The FARC obviously had wounded in need of medical treatment. The question was, would he be released as payback for his services or would they simply discard his corpse by the side of the road like a butchered carcass? Human life held no moralistic or consequential value to them whatsoever. And since the recent release of the FARC's last known foreign hostage, the capture of an American—especially one in the military—would no doubt be hailed as a real coup.

His alertness rallying, Jake marched stoically through what had once been a village but now resembled more of a military compound. Barracks and bunkers had been set up in several outlying locations—one of which was a terrorist's fantasy come true, a small-nation-sized arsenal of weapons, ammunition by the caseload, grenade- and rocket-launchers, missiles, and explosives—while the housing was primarily occupied by families of the guerrillas and the *campesinos* under their control. The afternoon rain had pounded down then passed over, and when the sun returned it waxed anemic, hanging lower in the sky. There were some women moving about, but the population was predominantly male and blatantly militaristic. As Jake was escorted to the barracks, he noticed some small children of both sexes playing, seemingly oblivious to their inimical environment. One of the little boys gave him a jaunty wave, chanting, *"Guapo gringo! Guapo gringo!"* Jake smiled indulgently at the little boy who had, with his exclamation, been admiring Jake's American handsomeness, but when he realized what the boy and other small children were doing, the pleasantry instantly disintegrated and a sick feeling dredged his stomach. The little boy had a handgun that Jake could only pray was either dysfunctional or unloaded, and he was aggressively soldiering his small playmates into various submissive tasks. *God*, Jake thought despondently, *they're just babies*. They would be indoctrinated before they knew any other way. It was the same in dozens of other cities and countries he'd operated in.

Jake had looked away, shifted his attention back to the direction he was being steered, when a gunshot fired behind him. He flinched and felt sourness of the inevitable in his gut. *No, God no...* But when he peered around, the children were all there, giggling now as they stood over something flopping in the dust. A *chicken*—the boy had shot a chicken.

Jake faced forward again and kept pace with his armed escorts.

As he had suspected, one section of the barracks contained dozens of wounded guerrilla soldiers, along with some injured and sick villagers. Jake's sentimental inclination would have been to treat the *campesinos* first, but he knew better. He wondered if he would be allowed to treat them at all.

Jake was led to a man with generously gelled hair, cologned skin, and gold jewelry that could have paid a month's lease on a New York Fifth Avenue apartment. He was flanked by a quartet of men Jake assumed were the designated medical assistants. The gel in the man's hair gleamed like the oily feathers on a crow's back. Extending his hand to Jake, he said, "I am Máximo Castillo, *commandante* of the base." Indicating the medical bag slung over Jake's shoulder, he remarked, "You are a doctor, yes?"

Jake nodded. "A medic."

"*Señor* Tyler, I can expect your total cooperation?" Without waiting for an answer, he continued, "These men will be at your disposal to utilize in any way you find necessary. What are your needs?"

The only supplies Jake had were in this extra medical bag he kept in the Land Cruiser for emergencies, and without even assessing the type of casualties sustained by the group, he knew he was ill-equipped to treat the majority of them. And he was about to explain this to Castillo when he saw a covered flatbed truck backing up to an open side. Moments later it was being energetically unloaded, its contents being sorted and stocked on a long table. He watched in stunned silence as the appointed assistants haphazardly set up IV stands with glucose, saline, and plasma that had been taken off the truck. Additionally, there was a surprisingly complete selection of medicines, bandages, even medical instruments. In answer to the *commandante's* question, all Jake could say was, "I'll just have to see what we've got here and do the best that I can."

"Be sure that you do," Castillo replied icily as he departed. And with those few words, the tacit edict had been signed; Jake's success or failure would determine the probability—or improbability—of his own survival.

JAKE WORKED FOR SEVERAL hours, into dusk, tending to the most critical cases during the first forty-five minutes. Fortunately, there were only a handful of bad ones. One soldier had caught a grenade in the chest and another had driven over a mine. Probably, Jake thought disdainfully, one of their own. To his grim dismay, they both became immediate fatalities. He had mentally moved beyond the potential repercussions, concentrating instead on the relative success he was having otherwise. After treating all the combat-related injuries, several of which required extensive work and careful monitoring, he was relieved to be allowed a small block of time for the villagers. Their medical problems were more of the common or chronic variety—sprains, broken bones, infections, and sicknesses—so he remedied what he could and provided meager comfort to the rest.

Jake was taking a break, mentally inventorying the unused medical supplies as he applied some antiseptic to his own head wound, when he heard something that arrested his attention. Delaney—at least it *sounded* like Delaney—outside the barracks, twenty or thirty yards away, conversing in Spanish with Castillo. From this distance, Jake could not see them clearly in the dusk or hear what they were saying, but it was the posturing between the two figures that interested him. The guerrilla commander did not appear to be the least bit defensive, despite the fact that he stood alone with Delaney. *If* it was Delaney. Jake just couldn't be sure. Whoever the other man was, he seemed to be agitated, evident in his pacing and gestures, but in control of the conversation. Jake kept staring until finally he felt certain that the man with the *commandante* was, in fact, his partner.

Choosing his moment carefully, checking the positions of armed men and the activities of others around him, Jake made a move toward the outside. And might have succeeded had it not been for something totally unexpected. Just as he reached the entrance to the barracks, an elderly woman collapsed at his feet. For a fleeting instant he wavered indecisively, a look of determination focused on the spot where the *commandante* and Delaney were—or had been—standing. But the instant passed, and he knelt down beside the elderly woman, checking first to see if she was breathing.

In the moments that followed, Jake immersed himself in the now all-encompassing task of performing CPR. Thoughts and images of the guerrillas, the two dead soldiers, Castillo, and Delaney were completely overtaken by his resuscitation, mouth-to-mouth breathing and chest compressions. When he finally got a pulse and a heartbeat, he allowed those assisting him to step in and participate in stabilizing the woman, instructing them on proper IV applications.

He was checking the woman's pupils when he felt a tap on his shoulder. Straightening up, he was mildly surprised to find Castillo standing behind him. He had been so absorbed in the life-saving efforts for this woman he had momentarily lost cognizance of his situation. Now, locked in the guerrilla leader's stern gaze, Jake sullenly realized it must be his time of reckoning. The fact that he had saved this perceptually worthless peasant woman's life would, in the eyes of the FARC commander, be unconditionally invalidated by the loss of the militarily vital lives of the two guerrilla soldiers.

"*Señor* Tyler," the colonel said unemotionally, "a word with you, please." He turned away and strolled almost casually past the bodies of the two dead soldiers, as if they might have been dead alley cats instead.

"That woman needs—"

The *commandante* put his hand up, silencing Jake with a stony look. "We will see that she is transported to a hospital. Now"—he turned and looked indirectly at the two corpses, then back at Jake—"tell me about the men."

In what he hoped was an authoritative but condolent voice, Jake related the injuries in detail explaining that, essentially, both deaths were the result of massive internal trauma and blood loss, emphasizing that even given better facilities and faster reaction, the damage to vital organs would have been much too extensive to repair. Castillo listened without expression, arms folded across his chest. When Jake was finished with his account, the *commandante* nodded silently and stood stroking his mustache for several moments. Finally, he looked squarely at Jake and said simply, "Your services are no longer required. You are free to go, *Señor* Tyler." With that, he turned sharply on heel and strode briskly away.

Jake watched in disbelief as the FARC commander left the barracks, chortling robustly as he conversed on his cell phone. Then he suddenly remembered Delaney, wondering if his partner was somewhere in the village compound. He peered around in the gathering darkness for Castillo, but before he could look any further, he was addressed by one of the guerrillas.

"*Estas de buenas, gringo doc,*" he remarked in a voice dripping with sarcasm. "You are permitted to leave." He sneered, stepping aside with a mock flourish, clearing the way to the idling Land Cruiser. Noting the blank expression on Jake's face, he said, "Your lucky day, yes? If the *commandante's* mother had not almost died so you could save her, we might be fighting over your tight-ass gringo *calzoncillos* about now."

Jake brushed past him without saying a word. He climbed into the Land Cruiser, fixed a steely look on the guerrilla soldier, and drove off in search of Delaney.

* * * * *

AS IT TURNED OUT, Delaney was not in the village compound, or at least not at the time of Jake's release. After driving a circuitous route through the militarized areas, Jake headed back to Afortunado, passing the airstrip on the way. He gave it a hard look but did not stop.

During the short drive, following the bouncing moon illuminating the road, he inhaled deeply from the night air, thinking that the stars seemed somehow brighter and the air fresher, everything sharper. But thinking about Delaney, his mind was a blur of turmoil as he tried to deal with the maelstrom of conflicting emotions. He felt relief for having survived another captivity; concern for not yet knowing if he would actually find Delaney waiting for him or if the FARC guerrillas had taken him hostage, too; suspicion he still could not satisfy; frustration for his inability to read or reach Delaney; and sadness at the deficit of trust. And if Delaney *was* there and had not been imprisoned, then why had he been gone when Jake was released? He also thought about the bitter irony of the start and end of his day: the loss of a young, innocent life while he had been forced to treat possibly the same guerrillas that had raided the parents' village, the trauma of which had likely contributed to the stillbirth...and then saving the life of an elderly woman who had given birth to the man who commanded those guerrillas and who had intended to kill him.

His mind was still reeling with the jumble of emotion, mental as well as physical exhaustion taking hold, when he drove the Land Cruiser into the settlement. The moon stopped bouncing overhead, glowing like a beacon to nowhere. He flipped the headlights off and sat motionlessly for several minutes, his arms and head bowed over the steering wheel. The night folded around him, the air warm and lightly humid. A compost of decaying matter, burnt wood, and animal secretions wafted up from the ground.

"God, Jake. Where the hell have you been?"

Jake's head snapped up so abruptly he bumped it against the steering wheel, causing him to wince at the renewed pain in his skull. Rubbing his temple, he clambering out of the vehicle and found himself blinking up at Delaney. Blearily, he said, "What do you mean where have I been? You were there…where did you go, why did you leave without me?"

"Hey, come on, bubba," Delaney said soothingly, "let's get you something to drink. Looks like you've had a rough time." As they walked to their quarters in the *bodega*, he added, "You worried the shit outta me."

Jake sat on his hammock, staring at Delaney in disbelief. "You were there," he said again. "I *heard* you."

Delaney had turned his back to Jake, reaching into the cooler for a beer. "What are you talking about, bro? What happened to you anyway?" Facing Jake with his most winsome smile, he offered a bottle of Costeña.

Jake shook his head. "Just some water. That's all I want." Glaring at Delaney now as he dug into the cooler for a bottle of water, he said, "I went by the plane and these guys—narcoguerrillas—grabbed me. It was like…" Suddenly, a theory filled in one of the many blanks that continued to populate in his mind. "It was like they were *watching* the plane."

Delaney tossed him the bottle of Manantial, his eyebrows arched in surprise. "Really?"

"Yeah. So they knocked me out and took me back to a militarized village." His tone was flat, eyes glazed as he wearily recited what had happened to him.

When he was done Delaney remarked, "Jesus Christ, Jake, I just thought you were involved in a medical complication or something around here."

"Haskell," Jake pressed, clenching his teeth, "I *heard* you, talking to the commander." Despite his affirmation, for the first time Jake wondered if he could have been mistaken.

"Wasn't me, bubba," Delaney replied, a little too lightly, grinning a little too largely. "I've been right here, shoring up the huts. If it had been me, I would have had your ass outta there."

Jake sighed, suddenly too tired to launch a challenge. "Okay, I just want some rack. My head is killing me." He lay down in his hammock, too exhausted to remove his bloodied, sweat-dampened and dust-soiled clothing. He could feel the afternoon's heaviness settle within him and then levitate from his body. Sleep was tugging at the edge of his battered brain, the night embracing him again. But before he could let go, his head turned, his eyes flicked open for just an instant. Just an instant was all it took—to see his Glock and radio headset, confiscated by his guerrilla captors, sitting on top of his personal medical bag.

10

THE EXPLANATION GIVEN WAS simple and, on the surface, credible enough. But as much as Jake wanted to believe Delaney, desperately needed to believe Delaney, he could not.

On waking early the next morning, following Jake's involuntary services to the FARC guerrillas, an uncomfortable silence had replaced the usual light banter between them as they collected and packed their supplies. Humming inanimately to himself as he took down and rolled up the hammocks, Delaney attempted to manifest unimpeached integrity, but there was a flatness in his eyes that conceded ownership of deception. When Jake had questioned him about the mysterious "return" of his weapon and radio, Delaney's response had been that he'd simply found them in the Land Cruiser buried amidst Jake's medical gear, suggesting the guerrillas had haphazardly tossed it all in there upon his release. Jake wanted to have it out with Delaney right then, blast apart the tension that had been steadily building, but he knew their energies needed to be focused on the next leg of their mission and, once again, let it go. There would be time later.

Now, as they finished loading up, the sun was shining with unrestrained yellow brilliance over the newly established settlement, a place more closely resembling the town it had once been—a tiny collateral victory piered in the larger harbor of defeats. Throngs of grateful *campesinos* trailed after them as they departed in the Land Cruiser, a jubilant conga line of children waving and cheering. Among them, the little girl whose shrapnel wound Jake had treated. Her name was Rosita. He smiled and gave her a wave.

ON RETURN TO THE base compound, they were met with orders to commence recon missions immediately. After a quick mission briefing that included latest intelligence, proposed targets, flight routes and times, radio frequencies, and an inventory of weapons and ammunitions, the teams were dispatched. Delaney's co-pilot, Juan Castro, a pair of Colombian gunners, one additional *jungla*, and two of their own operatives joined Jake and Delaney in the SAR helicopter. Leading the outgoing aircraft, they were Team Alpha.

Flying weather this day was about as good as it got, skies with minimal clouds at a ceiling of several thousand feet, visibility between ten and twelve kilometers. Jake's team was upbeat, feeling the cowboy lust for a little trigger time, even though this initial mission was primarily to scout locations that intel had turned up. As always, their objective in this mode was to fire only if fired upon. That was rarely ever the case.

Twenty minutes into the flight, they spotted one of the coca labs. It was in the usual place, on a riverbank surrounded by dense jungle with a small landing strip. After a couple of passes, decreasing altitude each time, the place appeared to be empty. Jake knew that more often than not, this was an invitation for ambush, and his defensive radar flared.

From the cockpit, Delaney said, "Your call, Chief. Want to go in?"

"I say we do," Jake called back, "but let's go in and expect the unexpected. *Me entienden, Señores?*"

Heads nodded around the cabin and thumbs went up.

"Okay, then." Jake had full confidence in the abilities of his own operators but had yet to be convinced their Colombian counterparts were anywhere close to that level of competency. Mostly for their benefit and in Spanish, he said, "You know how this goes down, just like we've trained. Buddy teams. Survey the site, keep eyes on the target, watch for ambush. Any contact, go hot."

Again, all heads nodded their understanding.

Delaney took the helicopter down and held it in hover about four feet off the ground until the team disembarked. When their chopper was clear, a second banked in and dropped off Team Bravo. The remaining teams stayed in the air to provide firepower, should it be necessary. Alpha and Bravo detachments fell into their preconfigured formation and advanced slowly through the jungle toward the clearing by the river where the lab was.

It appeared to be abandoned, which immediately made Jake suspicious. He radioed this information to Delaney who, in turn, would relay it to the other teams and to base command. With sentries posted, the two ground teams swept through the lab compound with quick and thorough efficiency, reporting their findings by radio and photographing the contents. A fairly large facility, it was subdivided into areas for eating and sleeping with a communications station wired with satellite, various radios, and scanners. There were three gasoline generators, several microwaves, and filtering and drying equipment. Storage areas were packed with chemicals—vats and jugs and drums of ethyl ether, hydrochloric acid, potassium permanganate, sulfuric acid, toluene, sodium carbonate, acetone, kerosene, ammonia—but no cocaine. A milky residue lined the *pozo*, a large plastic-covered pit near the river where the coca leaves were converted to paste, but it, too, was empty.

Jake thought: *They've either been tipped off and bugged out, or we're about to become sitting ducks.* The small hairs at the back of his neck tingled with premonitory foreboding. Something didn't wash.

And with that thought came an onslaught of automatic fire, from both sides of the river. Around them, the jungle lit up like flashing Christmas tree lights. Jake estimated two dozen guerrillas or more. His teams took defensive positions, returning fire and moving forward in staccato sprints. The guerrillas were resistant, but the teams continued to move in and the barrage began to fall off, finally reduced to sporadic stutters. And then, nothing. The guerrillas had retreated. For now.

"*Vamanos!*" Jake yelled. "Let's get the hell out of here!" He made a quick check of his teams and was amazed to find only a couple of flesh wounds. Several of the guerrillas hadn't been so lucky. They came across three dead, all of them young men. One was only a teenager. Jake instructed the team to dispose of the bodies in the compound's garbage dump, and radioed Delaney to request extraction.

Minutes later they were back on board the helicopters, pulling out.

From below, a parting barrage of gunfire exploded just beyond the jungle edge, a few miles from the lab. Bullets popped and rattled the bottom and sides of the Bell, shell casings jittering across the floor before tumbling out the door. The gunships banked in to respond, laying suppressive fire over a large riverside ranch. Open flatland stretched beyond it on the other side, ending at the next expanse of jungle. As they descended to treetop level to check it out, an impressive looking hacienda came into view. With a satellite dish mounted on top. A wood fence stitched a tidy perimeter around the ranch, and as they drew closer, Jake saw five men perched along it like a gaggle of blackbirds. They all wore ironed blue jeans and clean, wrinkleless white shirts, shined cowboy boots. With silver toes. They were all clutching M16s.

"Whoa Nelly," Jake muttered, looking down at the five men sitting neatly on their tidy wood fence. "Holy shit, we just hit a drug lord's house. Something tells me they're not gonna take it sitting down."

He proved to be right. Within seconds, the air was alive with a new assault, this one up close and very personal.

"Shit!" one of his operatives exclaimed, scurrying away from the chopper's door. "They've got better aim than that whole troop of guerrillas."

"You got that right," Delaney said. "I'm gettin' the hell out of Dodge."

The radio crackled and Jake heard hysterical Spanish from one of the gunships. *"Medico! Medico!"*

He moved up to the cockpit and responded into the radio, "Okay, calm down. Is somebody hit? Who's hit?"

The Colombian pilots were nearly shrieking. *"The gunner! The gunner is hit! He is bleeding—oh my God, he is bleeding everywhere! We are putting down right here, right now—Madre de Dios!—you must come get him now!"*

"No, no," Jake said emphatically. "Do not—I say again—*do not* land now. We have hostiles down there. Proceed to LZ North-Two—*Norte Dos*—and I'll take care of him there. Copy?"

Whether they heard him or not, they were landing, right here, right now. Not more than five hundred meters from the men whose bullet or bullets had scored. *Shit, fuck, piss be damned, we're all gonna die,* thought Jake. And directed Delaney to set down about fifty meters from the gunship. When he got out, two *junglas* were waiting to take him to the wounded gunner, frantically waving their arms. *Why didn't they bring him to me?* Jake wondered.

He knelt down beside the young Colombian who had, from the look of it, pumped a significant amount of blood from a severed brachial artery. No wonder the pilots had been freaking out, he'd probably drenched them in the cockpit. On examination, Jake found that the man's hand had been punctured by a round through-and-through which then passed into his chest, right over the rim of his chicken plate—the protective body armor worn by gunners—skirting the inside of his chest cavity along the ribs, exiting his shoulder region and shattering the humeral head. Next to him, he heard urgent calls for a stretcher.

"Oh no," Jake said, applying direct pressure to the gunner's arm. "No time for that. We've got to get out of here!" He jerked his head toward the five men from the ranch on the run toward them, less than a few hundred meters away. Their M16s were aimed, and they now began shooting. To the injured gunner, Jake asked, "Your legs are okay?"

He nodded weakly.

"Then get up on them and let's move!"

The gunner hopped up and ran to the helicopter, arterial blood spraying like a hydrant opened onto a hot summer sidewalk. Jake lunged after him, plugging the hole in the gunner's arm with his finger as they bundled into the Huey, already lifting off the ground. Behind them, the five men were close, firing relentlessly. He could feel the heat and the sting of bullets whizzing past, some impacting millimeters behind him.

Jake worked earnestly on the gunner as they whirled away. Minutes later, the fleet of helicopters rose into a seamless blue sky as calm and quiet as a Midwest cornfield.

THE FOLLOWING DAY, THEY blew up the lab. And a few more in other places just like it. And so it went like that, most days not so eventful, other days even more so.

Jake was restocking his clinic and medical bags from a new shipment of supplies on what was taking the guise of one of those less eventful days when Alberto Hernandez poked his head inside the door and announced, "There is someone outside who wants to speak to you."

Looking up, Jake asked, "Who is it?"

"I am not sure, but I think it is one of the villagers from Afortunado. He says he will only speak to you."

"Well, okay," Jake said, and followed Hernandez out of the clinic. When they reached the front of the base camp, Jake saw a small man who looked vaguely familiar. The man was clearly nervous and kept glancing furtively around as if he expected a squadron of commandoes to close in on him at any moment.

"*Hola, Señor,*" Jake greeted, extending his hand to the man who accepted it readily, still looking over his shoulder. In Spanish, Jake said, "Why don't we come just inside here. Okay?"

That suggestion seemed to make the man even more uneasy, but he followed Jake past a bunkered area into a small anteroom just inside the building compound. When Jake gestured, the man sat in a plastic chair opposite him. "So, what is it that you need or what can I do for you?"

In a nervous jumble of Spanish, the man introduced himself as Felipe Cadeña, Rosita's father. Jake nodded his remembrance, smiling. Encouraged, the man rambled on without stopping. He explained that he had been a coca farmer until recently when his crops had been eradicated by the counternarcotics operations. Prior to growing coca, he had farmed many other products but was constantly pressured by the local narco-guerrillas to make the switch. Increasingly worried about the repercussions of his resistance, Cadeña had finally given in, but now that his fields had been sprayed it would take time to regenerate—the narcos would insist that he replant—and ever since their village had been ravaged, they were struggling to survive. At this point, he thanked Jake profusely for taking care of his daughter and for the help given their town in recovery.

His voice quavering, Felipe Cadeña bent closer to Jake and said, in English, "I know where iss the narcos. I know where iss...*el jefe.*"

Jake's eyes widened and now he, too, glanced around to see who else might be within earshot. He knew there was always the possibility of information being compromised, even within their ranks. "*Señor* Cadeña, I understand and appreciate the risk you are taking here. Are you sure you want to give me this information?" he asked.

Cadeña sighed, and nodded. Reverting to Spanish, he said, "Yes. These are bad people. This is a bad man. Very bad. Even when we do what he says, we are threatened and often punished. Very bad punishments. We want to live in peace again. I do not know if it is possible."

"This narco," Jake said cautiously, "how do you know his identity and how did you come to find out where he is?"

"My daughter was playing with some other children by the river yesterday," Cadeña said, squeezing his bony hands together. "They went a little too far down and heard some of the bad men, so they hid. After they left, she came back and told me what she heard. From what I could understand, one of the men was talking about a party he was going to attend at the narco's house. The other men did not believe him, so he told them where the house is. We have heard some talk of this place before, so I believe it is true."

"Okay," Jake said. "Who is this guy and where can we find him?"

PAUL TRAYNOR AND ALBERTO Hernandez listened, incredulous, as Jake recounted the information he had received from Felipe Cadeña—incredulous because Traynor had already heard the name come up in his embassy briefings. The "narco bad man" Cadeña had heroically given up was a kingpin in possibly the most powerful new cartel in Colombia. His actual name was not publicized by the DEA and NAS, but his nom de guerre—*La Víbora*—was widely known.

"Goddamn, Jake," Traynor remarked, shaking his head in disbelief. "On the Richter Scale of informant tips, I'd say this is about a forty. But Jesus, what a position it puts me in." He raked his big fingers through the thick mesh of silver on his chin, deep creases grooving his forehead.

"What do you mean?" Jake asked. "Why? Isn't this what we live for? Getting this kind of information? We can whack this *jefe* and, just like that, take down a cartel that's probably supplying half or more of the product coming out of Colombia right now."

"It is not as easy as that," Hernandez replied. "And you know the embassy's position on going after the top level."

"Yeah," Jake said with disgust, "but it's bullshit. Taking out the top guys is the only way to really make a lasting difference. This shit we're doing now, killing the weed and hitting a few labs here and there, is just pissing in their soup and we know it. Even the Colombian government finally wised up and put bounties on these guys."

Traynor said, "But like it or not, Jake, we're here working in alliance with the embassy directives and within the guidelines of our contract. Nothing more. Look, I will pass the information on to—"

"No, that's not good enough." His eyes blazed with determination. "Opportunities like this are few and far between. You know that. We have to act on this now." He thought for a minute, then offered, "How about this? If we're out on a mission and we happen to find this guy in the process...what would they expect us to do? Just tuck our tails, turn around, and return to base?"

"What they would expect is for you to stand down and pass along the intel. Besides, you know good and well that you can't just take a team and drop in on a guy of this caliber."

Jake said nothing, but Hernandez surprised both of them by saying, "Stranger things have happened."

Traynor's head swiveled to him, eyes widening. "What?"

Hernandez only shrugged.

Turning his attention back to Jake, Traynor said, "Don't do this. You don't have much longer on the contract. Just do your thing until time is up, let me see what I can do with this information."

"With all due respect, Paul," Jake said evenly, "and you know I have the utmost respect for you—I can act on this and possibly pull it off. You can't. The worst that can happen to me is I get spanked. It would be much worse for you."

Traynor sighed in exasperation and stared down at the floor for several long moments, hands on his hips. Finally, he said, "Whatever you do with this, I don't want to know." To Hernandez, he snapped, "And you're going with him, but I don't know that, either."

IT TOOK A NUMBER of passes to locate the estate of La Víbora, as it was within a highly secluded enclave that, by all appearances, could have been a nature preserve or wilderness resort. It was about 150 kilometers from the base camp along a river near the Ecuadorian border. Not surprising since covert border passage was a major requisite for the brokerage of deals involving drugs, arms, and money laundering. Prime *narcotraficante* real estate if you could find it, and that he had.

Jake's teams began their surveillance in a Cessna Caravan, staggering their flyovers and going lower only at night. They had to rely primarily on their own intel, but Hernandez had pulled some strings and managed to obtain satellite imagery that he hoped had not drawn any interest from the embassy. After two days and one night of reconnaissance, Jake was ready to take a couple of teams in.

On the second night, as the sun slid below tree level, the helicopters inserted Alpha and Bravo into a partially wooded area several kilometers downriver from the enclave. There, they set up camp, dug in, and discussed the plan.

Seated by a fire where the team members had just chowed on meatloaf MREs, Jake and Hernandez drank bitter coffee and reviewed their data. "Okay, Jake," Hernandez said, "what do you want to do?"

"Well, first we need to get as close to the estate as we can to make sure this is what it is. Also make sure the *jefe* is in the house."

"Yes, most definitely."

"What we need to do is then get him out of the house, maybe spook him so he goes on the run. Then we can take him out." Jake knew that going after the house itself was too big of a risk; law dictated that if they fired on any civilian who turned out to be innocent, it was an automatic ten-year prison sentence without parole. Not to mention the fact that, tactically, they'd need an operation much larger in manpower and scope to take on the kingpin's security force.

"That could work," Hernandez said. "Certainly worth a try."

Turning to address the men assembled around the fire, Jake said, "Here's the plan. We move in around the estate and set up surveillance in the teams we discussed. Each team will radio any activity until we have a clear picture of who's there, their comings and goings and—most importantly—where the big fish is. Once we can confirm he's there, we'll retreat and link up with the birds. The next phase will be to smoke him out. To do this, we will set up our own little firefight just outside the estate. When he leaves the premises—most likely in the company of his bodyguards and in a bulletproof vehicle—we'll have a roadblock in place. I've made arrangements with some paramilitaries I know to help us stage this. When we have him out of the car, the bodyguards will be isolated and contained while we apprehend La Víbora. Everybody clear?"

One of the men, a former Army Ranger by the name of Brennan, said, "What are we going to do with him once we have him?"

"Now that," Jake quipped, "is a good question."

AFTER TWO DAYS OF ground reconnaissance with no sighting of the target coming from or going to the premises, Jake made the decision to move in closer. They had assessed and analyzed the security elements which, in addition to the armed phalanx, included a fairly formidable electronic fence and microwave sensors. The house itself was a two-story stone dwelling with a red-tiled roof and a curving cobblestone driveway. A pool large enough to entertain a synchronized swimming team or, alternately, swallow a helicopter or two, glimmered serenely in back.

On the second evening, Jake and Hernandez, with a pair of men covering them, set up outside the rear of the property and continued surveillance with night vision. They had already determined that the best time for a breach was a block of time between seven and eight-thirty, apparently both dinnertime and shift change for the armed patrol. So, at precisely 7:00 PM, Jake and Hernandez approached the fence. It was constructed of high-tensile wire, stretched in eight-foot sections between concrete-anchored metal posts. Intruders who touched it—whether by climbing or cutting—would be juiced with somewhere between 3500 and 15,000 volts at 3 or 4 joules, not lethal but extremely painful and incapacitating. More importantly, any contact would trigger an alarm. While there were more complex ways to get past it, such as rerouting the current to allow for cutting of the wire, the easiest and quickest way—not to mention one that would leave no trace of a breach—was to go over it without making any contact. For that, they had brought a tactical ladder which was extracted from its backpack harness, configured to the needed height and doubled over. Once Jake and

Hernandez had climbed, with their gear, up and over the ladder, they moved very slowly and deliberately in a narrow zone they had identified to infiltrate. In a well-designed and maintained security perimeter there are virtually no so-called dead zones, but on this property they had managed to find one in the form of a metal trash bin. Metal reflects microwave signals, so allowances must be made or some other form of surveillance added to compensate; in this case, an infrared field. But it was one they could see through their night vision and therefore avoid with careful maneuvering. To further aid in their cover, they wore new, unwashed dark camo suits, which were also light-reflective.

Staying low in the zone, they watched and waited.

It was shortly after eight o'clock, a time when, on both previous nights, a figure thought to be that of the man had come out on the deck smoking what was probably an after-dinner cigar. While Hernandez continually swept the entire visual area, Jake's only focus was the side of the house some fifty meters away. After making some initial adjustments to his night vision monocular, he set up a tripod and attached a high-definition Canon camcorder. Looking through the viewfinder, he zoomed in on the deck which extended about ten feet over a small garden.

At 8:20 PM, a figure emerged from the house and stepped onto the deck. Strolled to the railing, glass tumbler in one hand and cigar in the other. Peered out into the darkness, at one point looking right in their direction. If the man on the deck heard or saw anything, his demeanor did not reflect it. He remained in place for approximately fifteen minutes, drinking and smoking, and then, extinguishing the cigar in an ashcan near the door, the man went back inside.

Hernandez joined Jake to review the footage he'd recorded. The images, while surprisingly distinct, would need some digital manipulation and, with lights dimming inside the house, it appeared this was all they would get tonight. They packed up their gear, backtracked the way they'd come, and climbed back over the ladder. From there it was a short hike through the woods to a staging area where the rest of this team had been on standby, followed by the longer trek back to camp.

Jake and Hernandez worked through the night, drinking coffee as they hunched over Toughbook laptops, running the video through various software applications until they achieved maximum enhancement on their subject. Layer by layer, shadows were lifted, distortions cleaned up, lines and dimensions defined. Now they were looking at a colorized enlargement with enough detail to show the brand of cigar the man was smoking, a Cuban Cohiba.

"Is it him?" Jake asked Hernandez.

Hernandez nodded. "I will put in the call for the choppers."

THEIR MOCK FIREFIGHT WAS a simple matter of strategically placed charges that were rigged to fire in sporadic intervals. They were spaced and set back far enough in the bush to give the appearance of approaching troops. The entire setup was on a timer. About three hundred meters down the access road, the paramilitary group, led by a man named Raúl Aguilar, was in position at the roadblock. Jake met Aguilar during his first counternarcotics contract when Aguilar had sent his group to their aid during a particularly hairy—and personal—ground battle. They had become friends, but to this day Jake could not be sure on which side of the political or military fence Aguilar stood. But he always responded when Jake had a need. As he did today.

Shortly after 8:00 AM, the charges were detonated. Less than five minutes into the blasting, several men armed with M16s came running from the house. Realizing that the artillery was coming from the trees, they went back inside. And, just as Jake had predicted, a few minutes later a car emerged from the garage, occupants concealed behind tinted glass. Waxed to a sheen that made it impossible to tell the exact color, the vehicle accelerated to the main gate, which automatically swung open. The car then sped down the road.

WHEN AGUILAR'S MEN STOPPED the car, the driver-side window slid down revealing a man wearing a suit and dark glasses. He was firmly ordered to turn the car's engine off and unlock all the doors so the vehicle could be inspected. The driver wanted to know the purpose of the roadblock and vehicle search, so Aguilar's men pointed to the estate of La Víbora. In unison they said, *"El Hombre."*

"*Qué?*" The chauffeur laughed and, without thinking, said, "*Imposible! El hombre está aquí.*" And instantly regretted his mistake.

With his AK47 pointed at the chauffeur's head, the man on the driver's side reached in and pushed the lock release while other men yanked open the car's rear doors.

A pair of helicopters roared overhead, all but drowning out the charges still detonating and sending a dust storm eddying over the road. They landed just beyond the blockade. Jake sprang out on a trot and went straight for the man being extracted from the rear of the car.

La Víbora was tall and slender, a distinguished looking man in his early fifties with short, gray-flecked dark hair and sideburns and the bemused expression of someone who was waiting for a camera crew from a reality show to emerge. He was obviously aware of his anonymity and prepared to play it to the hilt. Clad in a custom-tailored Italian suit and polished Ferragamo loafers, he could have been a corporate banker or an oil executive. Eyes gravitating to Jake who stood before him in fatigues and dark glasses, armed with his Galil, the narco kingpin said, "Is there a problem?" The tone of his voice was as casual as a man asking for another cup of coffee at the breakfast table.

"That depends, *Señor*," Jake said.

"On what?"

"On whether you will go nicely into the helicopter right here."

For the first time, the man's expression went flat, and cold. He stared into the dark lenses of Jake's Wiley X shades as if he could see right through. "I will go," he said. "But you are making a big mistake."

THE RIGHT THING TO do, Jake knew, would have been to turn the captured kingpin in to the CNP commander at the base. That would, of course, have set off a political firestorm at the embassy and launch a media feeding frenzy the likes of which hadn't been seen since the capture of North of the Valley cartel boss, Don Diego Montoya. Publicly, Jake and all involved might be hailed as heroes, but privately they'd be lucky to emerge with their hides intact.

So it was a surreal but oddly comfortable decision to do the better thing.

Standing next to La Víbora, Jake made a point of looking up as another pair of helicopters flew overhead, but these opened fire. Tracers pelted down around them, causing Aguilar's men to scramble for cover while they returned fire. Jake made a dash for his chopper, leaving the *narcotraficante* standing in the middle of the road with a look of total disorientation on his face. His bodyguards grabbed him and hastily shoved him into the car. Then they began firing back at the helicopters.

By now Aguilar and his men had withdrawn to the jungle, and the car carrying La Víbora was the only thing remaining on the road.

Until something whistled down from one of the choppers and blew it into a mass of fire and billowing black smoke.

WATCHING THE EXPLOSION FROM his helicopter, Jake radioed the Charlie and Delta teams. "Good job, gents. Good job."

From the cockpit Delaney said, "I really don't think that was a good idea, bubba."

"I think it worked," said Jake. "As far as we're concerned, we got a tip, we checked it out. We were going to apprehend the guy and take him in. Then, what do you know, out of the blue we get fired on. We fire back, we retreat, and the *jefe* is on his own. He might have made it, too…but even bulletproof cars can't withstand explosives. So unknown unfriendlies conveniently took care of La Víbora for us."

"Conveniently," Delaney echoed sardonically. "And you don't think this can be traced to us?"

"Why would it be? A narco gets blown up by a car bomb?"

"Not just any narco. What if somebody on one of the teams breaks code and says something?"

"Guess that's the risk," Jake said. Below, the black smoke that obliterated the roadblock was reduced to a tiny puff as their altitude and distance increased. Soon, it was totally out of view.

11

NEXT TO THE LAST day of Jake's contracted time with counternarcotics in Colombia, Alberto Hernandez approached him with the dour look of bad news.

Jake glanced up from his packing. "What is it, Alberto?"

"The embassy just called. They want us to return to Afortunado. Apparently, there was another guerrilla attack. They may need more medical aid and supplies."

Jake sighed leadenly. Stared at his feet. Met Hernandez's eyes. They were as dismal and gray and ominous as an overcast afternoon. "Okay," Jake said. "Let's go."

THE MOMENT THEY MADE the final turn into Afortunado, they knew.

The stench of death and decay was everywhere. The stillness, the silence, the sad serenity, hung like a shroud of mourning. It was another brutally hot day, the sun blazing overhead with the gluttonous eye of an insatiable vulture. Everything it touched was baking in its own rancid grease, and the air was heavy with the fetor of rotting flesh.

Jake's stomach lurched as he took the dreadful walk toward the *bodega*, passing the decayed and unrecognizable remains of animals, mostly bones and dried blood. The *bodega* had again been stripped bare, but this time there were bodies inside—a pile of them—and Jake had to turn his head, gagging at both the sight and smell. His stomach heaved. Behind him, Hernandez and Delaney coughed. They had all seen it, many times. But there was no immunity for dealing with death.

Slipping off his head wrap, Jake used it to cover his mouth and nose, slowly moving closer to the bodies. These, he now saw, were all women. Some were half-clothed, most were naked. Even from their grotesque positions and advanced decomposition, he ascertained they had been raped and brutalized.

As Jake continued through the settlement with Hernandez and Delaney, none of them spoke. There was no need. They just walked and took it all in.

It had been a massacre, with no survivors.

The village men had been beheaded, their torsos irreverently dumped in an open grave. Following a trail of coagulated blood thick as syrup, they wound up by the river, and found the heads. They had been tossed into the water, undoubtedly gnawed clean by piranhas, and some of the skulls had since washed ashore and lay cluttering the banks like so many conch shells.

The massacre, for Jake, was a mosaic of all the inconceivably horrible bloodbaths, all the cemeteries, all the boneyards, all the killing courts his war-weary eyes had seen over the years. Haiti or Sierra Leone or any of the other places. Blood was blood was blood. You could wash it off, you could cleanse it from your body—most times, after a while, you could even clear it from your mind—but it never left your soul. Never. And every war-torn hellhole in which he'd served had managed to find a more ghastly and depraved way to humiliate, torture, and butcher human beings, images that were forever embedded in those dark places in his heart and mind.

He turned away and trudged back to the village center, walking numbly past the carnage. More huts with bodies, more brutality and desecration. He forced himself to look, because they were people—just people who had been caught in the middle of the dirty little war that festered in a forgotten continent—and he began to recognize some of the natives, the ones he'd helped.

He found the body of Felipe Cadeña hanging from a tree. Despite the badly decomposing flesh, it was obvious Cadeña had been tortured. His jaw was grotesquely widened around something that protruded. It looked like it might have been a small animal of some kind, tuffs of fur and part of a tail still visible. Cadeña's feet had been chopped off, the ground below damp and dark with the blood mass it had absorbed, big clots sitting on the surface. He turned away, his jaw clenched so tightly he could feel his own blood pulsing at the temples.

And then he saw Rosita.

Her little body lay near that of her half-naked mother, the fingers of their hands almost touching. The dressing he had applied to her shrapnel wound was still intact—but that was all that was. Both mother and daughter had been brutalized like the rest, their clothing in shreds. Flies did drunken eights over their corpses, maggots had become more intimate.

Rosita's other hand clutched the teddy bear Jake had given her. It was matted with her blood. Its head was missing.

Jake dropped to his knees and sucked at the air, fighting fiercely to keep his composure. He bit his lip and closed his eyes tightly.

HE WASN'T SURE HOW much time he stayed beside the little girl, but at some point a hand lightly touched his shoulder. It was Delaney. He rose, and without a word, followed his friend back to the Land Cruiser where Hernandez was waiting behind the wheel.

He turned his back to them for one last look. It was not a look for remembrance, not even a look for condolences. It was a look for deliverance. He hoped they had finally found it. He stood for what seemed like a long time, just listening to the beating of his own heart, willing the images to dissipate along with the feelings of profound sorrow.

At that moment, he wanted to think of life, feel life, be alive.

He thought of Callie.

Climbing into the Land Cruiser, he said, "Get me the hell out of here."

12

HE WAS HIKING IN the highlands of the Cordillera Oriental, climbing steep slopes and descending beautiful emerald gorges that sparkled with crystal lakes and rushing waterfalls, but his thoughts wandered inexorably back to the troubled territory of Haskell Delaney.

Jake stopped along a ridge overlooking a valley of silver and gold *frailejones* plants, with their rosette-shaped down-covered leaves. A waterfall gurgled noisily into a lake just below. The sun's rays hit the undulating water like hundreds of popping flashbulbs, soft diamond brilliance against the deep blue-green. Above, the sky was as dramatically bright as the waters below were dark, bold with lavender-edged cumulonimbus clouds; there would be rain in a while. But for the present moment, it was as profoundly and heartbreakingly beautiful a day as one could ever behold. So beautiful, so splendidly and pristinely beautiful that Jake felt tears misting his eyes—because the beauty was marred by the heaviness in his heart and the dismay in his soul. He knew, in that jewel-sharp, fiercely penetrating spasm of sorrowful beauty, that he had lost Delaney to something, something unknown and unforgiving. And most frustrating of all, he knew there was absolutely nothing he could do about it.

There had been much to question about Delaney's behavior during their mission, but the time of departure had capped it all.

Jake had risen well before dawn this morning—actually he'd not even slept—and hauled his bags and gear to the Land Cruiser. He had waited on Delaney for nearly an hour before it occurred to him that maybe he was still asleep. Returning to the barracks, he stuck his head in Delaney's quarters. The cot was empty, Delaney's belongings gone. He tried to raise him on his sat phone to no avail. Next, he loaded up the 4x4 and drove to the airstrip where he'd last seen the plane.

It, too, was gone.

Ever since they'd met, Delaney was the closest thing to family Jake had. Together they had enjoyed a balance of life's hits and misses; more significantly, they had navigated the treacherous channels of grief, emerging with a bond that was stronger for it. But as close as they had become over the years, there were sides they camouflaged from each other. And now, mentally reviewing the past few months, Jake realized that Delaney had been gradually building a firewall around himself. Who or what was he concealing? Or protecting?

Pondering that, Jake recalled another time when Delaney's behavior had been deceptively erratic. Doing a stint as a private investigator, Delaney had been hired to perform domestic surveillance on a philandering husband, a typically mundane assignment until he found himself sexually involved with the wife. But even then, he transmitted signals that Jake was able to decode, subtle communication of a need for disclosure. And as fiercely independent as they both were, when the affair had taken an unpredictably nasty turn, with the husband attempting to kill Delaney and the wife trying to strip him of his license, Delaney had sought Jake's help. As he had during another sordid incident while investigating suspected graft within a big-city police force; the guilty parties—all highly respected officers—had cleverly managed to deflect impropriety on Delaney and would have succeeded without Jake's resourceful intervention. Unlike now, as Delaney was obviously going this one—whatever it was—utterly alone.

Jake sat on the edge of a rock jutting out over the lake, inhaling the clean cool air, and took in the stunning panorama—spartan mountain tops towering on the horizon contrasting with the variegated grasses, ferns, and flowers within reach below. He looked imploringly at the infinity of sky with its tall, mushrooming clouds, and watched with rapt fascination as a large hawk sailed serenely overhead. It looped back over the lake, swooped down and emerged with something wriggling in its beak. Not a fish—hawks were carnivorously predatory—maybe a water-dwelling rodent. But then, curiously, he looked again…and thought he was hallucinating. Because now the thing in the hawk's beak looked like a *flower*. Jake focused intently, transfixed, and then saw that he had been mistaken. Of course he had. It was not a flower, after all, and why would it have been? It was a small animal. And yet, as the hawk peeled away, angling toward the gorge, petals were floating down from him. Dark, red petals that looked like drops of blood swallowed by the churning waters below.

ON RETURNING TO BOGOTÁ earlier that morning, Jake had checked into a charming and lovely colonial guesthouse in the southern Candelaria district. As with most places he stayed while traveling, it belonged to someone he'd come to know through the military. Now, returning from his hike, he found that Delaney had still not checked in. It was where they had both stayed before, and he had confirmed the accommodation with Delaney last night. Jake went to his room, dropped his rucksack, and stripped off his clothes. Padding to the shower, a hand touched his bare shoulder.

He spun around, tensed and ready to strike, then stopped.

Standing before him, wearing nothing but her deep mocha tan and a sultry smile, was Elena Torres García.

"My God, woman" he said, exhaling sharply, "don't ever do that. You're lucky I didn't deck you."

"You military guys are so jumpy," she mused, sliding her arms around his trim waist. Her hands went lower, fingertips tracing the crevice of his firm ass.

"How did you know I was here?"

"Darling, you know journalists cannot reveal their sources," she quipped with a wink. "But I *am* here." She was leaning into him, her kohl eyes boring into his, maneuvering him to the shower. When they were both inside, he turned the water on, and as it sprayed over them their bodies welded wetly together. Clenching him tightly around the neck, Elena swung her legs up over his hips and took charge. Consummation came quickly in a series of hard slams against the shower wall.

Out of the shower and onto the bed, copulation resumed with Elena astride him. She leaned over him, long wet strands of her thick, dark hair thrashing across his face as her rhythmic heaving intensified. Her cinnamon-colored fingernails dug fiercely into his flesh, and at the height of her passion as he stiffened beneath her, she bit into his chest with a guttural wail buffered by his body. Elena rolled over with a pleasurable moan. Jake closed his eyes and sighed, physically gratified but feeling strangely unfulfilled. As they lay isolated by their own thoughts, Elena asked about the mission.

Yawning, he said, "I really don't want to talk about it."

Propped up on one elbow, his eyes followed the journey of his fingertips around a breast the size of a grapefruit and devoid of tan lines, down to the slash of navel and the swell of hip. His gaze lingered just inside her right thigh, honed on the nickel-sized tattoo imprinted there. He had two of his own, one on each bicep, both more or less militantly themed. But no matter how many times he saw hers, it remained an enigmatic fascination to him, particularly since Elena offered no story behind the origin, airily dismissing it as simply "whimsy." Her tattoo was brightly colored with an orchid in the foreground, but it was the background that piqued his curiosity the most. Behind the pretty flower was a sinisterly feral pair of eyes. Staring sleepily at the tattoo, he realized Elena was talking. The last thing he remembered before succumbing was an inquiry about Delaney, to which he responded, "...have no idea, no idea at all..."

And then he slept.

WHEN HE AWAKENED HOURS later, the room was thick with evening shadows, and Elena was gone. As he was dressing, slipping into a pair of jeans and a long-sleeved black turtleneck, he found a note she had left on the bureau. In it she indicated that she had been called for an assignment. She was staying at the Hotel Tequendama, as was her custom. Located in the international center, it was the posh address frequented by the media as well as distinguished businesspersons and foreign dignitaries. A telephone number was listed with her suite. Glancing at his watch, he was astonished to see that it was approaching eight o'clock, so he dialed her number thinking she might be through with the assignment by now or could take a break for a late dinner. When he got no answer, he checked with the Tequendama's front desk, only to be succinctly told: "*Señorita* García has left word that she will be returning late and we are to take any messages." When asked if he cared to leave one, Jake politely declined.

His grumbling stomach reminded him that he had only snacked while hiking, so he decided to head for a downtown restaurant. On his way out, he stopped by the front desk of his hotel, inquiring about Delaney. No, he was told apologetically, *Señor* Delaney had not checked in and had not telephoned to leave a message. Not sure whether to be concerned or irritated, Jake checked his cell and sat phones for messages, finding none from Delaney. The lack of communication was truly bewildering. He called Delaney's numbers and got voicemail.

Brooding, Jake climbed onto his rented motorcycle and headed north along the busy commercial Carrera 15 into the Zona Rosa section of the city. The evening was cool and clear, chilled by the ever-present Andean embrace that encircled the altitudinous Colombian city, a dramatic departure from the sweltering jungle that lurked on the outer rim. He sped down the avenue, one of the primary commercial arteries in the city, letting the air slap his face and arrest his thoughts. He stopped at OMA, between Calles 82 and 84, and ate a club sandwich in somber solitude. When he was through, he borrowed a telephone directory and phoned several suburban airports—Delaney typically avoided the city airports in favor of the smaller, less traveled ones—but after trying a half-dozen without success, he gave up. Emerging from the bistro, on an impulse he decided to venture farther north to the Chico sector seeking Molotov's.

The local nightspot known as the Russian House collected a wildly divergent assortment of patrons. At any given time you could find missionaries and priests propositioned by prostitutes and thieves, diplomats and businessmen negotiating with spies, guerrillas gloating amidst mercenaries. An interesting phenomenon about the bars and nightclubs frequented by war zones gladiators was that they tended to be considered neutral ground, an asylum of temporary truce where the good guys and bad guys were often elbow to elbow at play. Each knew they could be sparring the very next day, but for the night, for just a few hours, causes and arms were set aside for drinking and sex. It was all about appetites and priorities.

Molotov's being one of their favorite haunts, Jake half-expected to find Delaney here, surrounded by comrades near the full-wall video screen showing the Playboy Channel or gyrating on the raised dance platform with an attractive, scantily-clad lady. He spent several minutes weaving his way through the packed place, actually running into several of his guys boisterously enjoying themselves. He was at the long, mirrored bar savoring a glass of Warre's and chatting with Alfonso, Molotov's charismatic owner, when he saw Delaney.

He was tucked in a dim corner, and Jake might not have seen him at all had it not been for the person he was with. Even in the hazy lighting he could make out the familiar, exotically sensual features of the woman he had been in bed with only hours ago. Elena Torres García was seated close to Delaney on one of the sofas, smoking a cigarette, something Jake had never observed her doing. She held a drink in her cigarette hand, Delaney's dog tags clutched playfully in the other. Delaney was slouched against her, leering drunkenly, one hand buried in the thick mass of Elena's mahogany hair and the other squeezing one of her ample breasts, clearly visible through a black crochet thigh-high dress that stockinged her body.

What the hell?

Jake was weaving through the bodies cluttering his path, his mind trying to process what he was seeing, when Elena's next move stopped him in his tracks. She helped Delaney up from the sofa, guiding him to the front door and out into the street. Jake continued through the throng of Molotov's patrons, following the two of them. Outside the tavern, Delaney was hanging onto Elena, speaking sleazy-sounding gibberish to her as he continued his hand explorations of her body. She was searching the street as if she were looking for someone, and in a few moments a car as smooth and sleek as a reef shark drew up alongside the curb. Jake quickly got to his motorcycle and strapped his helmet on, watching as Elena pushed Delaney into the backseat of the car. She looked around, stepped in after him, and pulled the door shut. Then the car, a late-model Lexus, peeled off to the north.

As he raced after them, Jake's initial astonishment fused into anger, though he was not quite sure why. Elena's promiscuity was certainly not the issue, nor was Delaney's. But seeing the two of them together like that was yet another behavioral anomaly from Delaney, and somehow, even on the most primal level, it just did not square. If Elena was merely indulging the obviously drunken Delaney, possibly making sure he got safely back to his hotel, they were definitely headed in the wrong direction. In fact, they were headed in the wrong direction if she was taking him back to her hotel. And as the minutes passed, the traffic and buildings thinning into the black void of empty road and open landscape, Jake realized with savage clarity that he was about to find a loose string to the cloak Delaney had been wearing—the seed for a betrayal the depths of which he was only beginning to excavate.

13

AS JAKE TAILED THE car containing Delaney and Elena, riding his motorcycle north along the Bogotá-Tunja road, his mind was scurrying senselessly, as empty of comprehension as it was full of furor. It was fury unchanneled because he didn't know who or what to target, but it fermented just the same. The farther north they went the sparser the traffic, so he was forced to drop back to prevent being spied. The trip seemed to stretch endlessly into the night, the minutes ticking past with the miles, until after about an hour the Lexus veered off the main road and took the first in a series of narrow and winding back roads. From his observations of landmarks and calculation of mileage and direction, Jake deduced that they were somewhere in the vicinity of Suesca. Some eighty kilometers northeast of Bogotá, the small colonial town dated back to the time of the early Spanish conquest and was surrounded by spectacular rocky cliffs and breathtaking gorges. Isolated and terraced high into one of the hills was a multileveled mansion built of stone and stucco.

When the Lexus turned onto the sprawling gravel drive leading up to the iron-gated entrance, Jake pulled his motorcycle off into a thatch of brush, parked it, and cut the engine. He hiked swiftly up the drive, aware of the crunching gravel beneath his shoes. As he reached the entrance to the estate, he trod lightly to minimize the sound. The iron gate had electronically closed behind the car, which drew up to a cobbled circular drive and stopped in front of a triple-arched façade. Angled spotlights swept over the exterior in a wide swath while others crisscrossed the grounds in a tighter, more security-oriented configuration. With the additional overhead illumination of a full moon, the architectural style of the mansion was well defined even from where he stood. It had the look of a Mediterranean villa, the stucco arches half-concealed by palma de cera and draped with flowering bougainvillea vines, adjacent to which was an elevated courtyard featuring a fountain bathed in blue-green light. Just beyond, through a larger arch, colored and lunar lights played over the still turquoise waters of a kidney-shaped swimming pool. A lush expanse of uniformly cropped grass sloped down to the high stone wall interspersed with intricate ironwork.

On closer inspection, Jake was almost certain the wall was electrically wired, possibly charged. In the distance, he could see the car's driver assisting Elena with Delaney, the two of them walking him unsteadily through one of the arches. Thoughts were sprinting through his head like relay runners, each plunging into the next as he tried to process the last, but surging adrenaline took precedence over intellect.

He started looking around for a means to get over the stone-and-iron barrier, and found it in a tall, leaning eucalyptus tree toward the rear of the property. It was every bit of six feet away from the wall, but it would have to do, so he shimmied to the top and evaluated the height and distance. If he failed to get enough momentum, he would go crashing into the stone or else come down on top of it or, worse, impale himself on the spears jutting up from the ironwork. Any of those results would cause injuries, probably serious ones. Going on the assumption he would make the jump, he peered down to judge his landing. When he was ready to go, he rocked his weight in the cluster of branches until he felt that he had sufficient impetus and then catapulted off. He hit the ground hard but went into a perfectly timed tumble and came up standing on the inside of the wall.

As he made his way up the slope, it occurred to him that the estate was also probably equipped with motion sensors. With any luck they had been disengaged for Elena's arrival. And then he wondered: Whose mansion was this? Was she an invited guest? An authorized occupant? Or, incredibly, could she be the *owner*? No, Jake told himself, that certainly could not be. A mansion like this on a journalist's salary? No, she must be a guest. Perhaps, he reasoned, the place belonged to some media mogul for whom she was working. And why had she brought Delaney here? A crazy thought with a distinctly nasty flavor to it had been lobbying relentlessly in his mind ever since he'd left Molotov's, but he continued to push it away.

He surveyed the premises thoroughly, wandering in search of guard dogs or personnel and checking for signs of security systems. As he had suspected, his quest resulted in detection of surveillance equipment, motion sensors, and other types of alarms, but after waiting for several minutes he was convinced that all was quiet—at least for the time being—and methodically began to investigate the interior.

As he went from window to window, he was a little surprised at the absence of occupants. For a mansion this size—he estimated anywhere from five to eight thousand square feet—servants were as much a requisite as the elaborate security. And what had become of the driver? The Lexus was still parked in front, so he had to be somewhere on the premises. Not seeing anyone at all was somewhat unsettling, but it was possible that the servants had separate quarters or had been given the night off. Lighting inside the house was subdued but warm, glowing over the terra cotta tile flooring. The wall surfaces alternated between textured plaster, brick, and stone. The great room was large enough for two fireplaces, with enough pottery distributed about the heavy oak tables to fill a small gallery. Its ceiling was a dome of glass panels, through which moonlight beamed luminously. A window on the back side of the house, located just off yet another terraced garden, revealed the master bedroom suite.

Staying in shadow Jake stole a glance inside, and saw Delaney and Elena. His pulse spiked and he could feel the heat building inside him again.

A massive bed constructed of ornamental black wrought iron was centered in the room. The covering and coordinating pillows were a wash of desert shades, sienna and slate, the area rug below vaguely Aztec. A mural-sized mirror framed to match the bed dominated one of the deep salmon-colored walls, indistinguishable Spanish artwork was spaced over the others. More mirrors beyond reflected the presence of a marble garden tub the size of a wading pool. Moonlight and the flames of a multitude of candles fanned and flickered in a dance of abstract shadows around the room.

Delaney lay outstretched on the bed, naked and lolling drunkenly, eyes closed and mouth contorted into an absurdly lunatic grin. Elena stood in statuesque profile with her tanned back to the window, stripped to a black thong, which she peeled off as she sauntered over to the bed. Her bare ass gleamed, as round in shape and rich in color as a ripe Bosc pear.

Standing outside the window, Jake was torn between the inclination to keep watching and somehow make sense of what he was seeing and the desire to burst into the house and confront them. His emotions were in such dissonance that cool-headed logic was evading him. Aware of the tension in his clamped jaw and clenched fists, he mentally went through some aikido internal breathing exercises to center himself before he looked back through the window.

Inside the bedroom, he saw that Elena had straddled Delaney, who was writhing in submissive reciprocation. Oddly, it appeared that she was talking to him, and when he did not respond she would lean down and pinch his cheek or jiggle his chin. Delaney would grin wider, maybe laugh a little, his closed eyelids fluttering, and his lips would move in a clumsy effort to form words. Elena swiveled her hips, rocked astride him, tossed her head back. Delaney, despite his intoxication, was responding to her, his hands clamped onto her very fine ass. She rocked. He writhed.

After a while, a few minutes that to Jake seemed like hours, he could not watch anymore. Revulsion soured in his stomach and his head throbbed. Mindful of the setting, his wariness returned and he knew he needed to stay alert and focused. He was about to turn away from the window when a tiny flashing light from inside caught his attention. It was coming from a box mounted on a wall near the interior doorway. An alarm monitor. And it was going off, flashing red. Elena was obviously absorbed in the sex and therefore oblivious to it, but Jake was sure that somewhere someone else was reacting to it. At any rate, he had certainly seen more than enough, so he directed his focus to finding a way out before whatever security plan in effect was implemented. If the alarm was dispatched to an off-site security company—highly unlikely in this remote area—he had a parcel of time in which to act, but the residential telephone would soon be ringing, if it wasn't already. And if the alarm was internally monitored, he had no time.

His earlier tour of the grounds had not revealed another tree or high place from which he could vault back over the wall, so he was going to have to come up with an alternative way out. As he set off in this pursuit, the lawn was suddenly flooded with higher beams of light, and the bark of an excited dog blasted the silence like a shotgun volley. His martial arts training had instilled in him the advantage of energy preservation, and without a known means of exit he knew his best strategy would be to let the confrontation come to him.

Standing in the cobblestone driveway, he watched and waited for his attackers.

Poised in the direction of the barking dog, Jake did not see the man coming at him from behind, but he heard the footfalls. Grabbing his assailant by the wrist, Jake stepped off the line of attack and to his rear, twisting the man's arm into a torque that sent him flying. The man, a wiry Latino with a mustache, stared at Jake in dazed agony, then coughed once and passed out. A second man and a dog, a Rottweiler with the miniaturized but no less daunting build of a Pamplona bull, came barreling around the back of the mansion in tandem. Jake gauged the man's speed and timed his move. Stepping smoothly into his second attacker, he applied a single strike to the face with the palm of his hand, forcing nose into cranium, which sent him sprawling backwards. Because of the momentum of the attack, the man's landing knocked him out instantly, helped by the fact that his head cracked on contact with the cobblestone drive. The dog was not as easily deterred.

Facing the animal, Jake focused on a point above and beyond his head. The dog stood quivering and growling, teeth barred, nostrils flaring, apparently trained to attack on command. Without his command, the Rottweiler—a breed renowned for its intelligence—deferred to instinct, and cautiously advanced. When he was close enough to see Jake's face, Jake slowly but deliberately looked away. The dog's head turned in the direction of Jake's gaze, which gave Jake his opening. He applied a measured chop to the canine's neck, striking a vital pressure point. The

Rottweiler dropped to the grass like a sack of cement mix. Jake slipped his fingers into the dog's groin and was glad to detect a weak but steady femoral pulse; he hadn't wanted to kill him.

A quick body search of his fallen attackers turned up a pair of Beretta 9mm handguns, which Jake tossed into one of the gardens, but nothing useful for the electric gate.

Dodging the floodlights, Jake zigzagged his way back to the front entrance and deliberated his options. If he'd had his motorcycle on this side of the gate, he could have simply ridden over the magnetic field for an automatic release, or he could achieve the same results if he found something metal that was heavy enough to roll across it. But locating the control box for the gate, he decided there was a much quicker and more effective way. Using his pocketknife, he popped the cover of the box and examined the cluster of colored wires knotted inside. He selected two, scraped the plastic coating back, and twisted the bare wires together. Then, wedging his hands between the middle rungs of the gate, he was able to push them apart with only a minimum of resistance.

He retrieved his motorcycle from the thatch of brush where he'd left it, straddled it, and roared down the drive spewing gravel in his wake. He hit the Bogotá-Tunja road doing at least eighty.

HIS HEAD SNAPPED UP with the muted bing that preceded the elevator doors *shooshing* open. He watched as she emerged from between them, gracefully pivot, and stride down the hallway in his direction, stiletto-heeled Jimmy Choo sandals making a soft thumping noise on the carpet. By day, she had transformed into the more conservative guises of the *periodista*, hair worn up, designer sunglasses shading her eyes, dressed in a taupe striped suit. But the undertone of sex was as ubiquitous as natural musk under perfume. And then there was the suit, pencil skirt hemmed mere inches below her curvaceous hips, vertical stripes that went diagonally astray just above the short blazer's waist and angled indicatively at the bosom. He slowly drew himself up from the sitting position he'd been crouched in for the past several hours, planted by the door to her Tequendama suite. During that time, his mind had plagued him with perpetual playback of the night's events like a scene stuck in rewind, and he could no more make sense of it now than before.

When Elena saw him there was the slightest waver in her step, but she recovered with cool equanimity. Peering at him over the rims of her sunglasses, she smirked and said, "Well, here is a welcome room service." She opened the door with a swipe of her key card and stepped into the plush suite, dropping her purse and sunglasses on a foyer table as she passed.

Jake quietly closed the door behind them, waiting for her to face him. When she did, she had removed a leopard-printed scarf from her neck and was already beginning to unbutton the low front of her jacket, but one probe into his eyes stopped her on the second button. "Some assignment that was," he said in a tone hard enough to break stone.

Elena gave a nervous little laugh, glancing away from his boring eyes. "Yes, well, it did go on a lot longer than I expected," she murmured. "I am sorry I did not call you, *querido*. There was much more to it, and I got into—"

"Fucking Haskell."

Her jaw dropped, glossed lips forming an O of surprise, and then closed with a snap. "He told you that?" she asked, clearly taken aback.

"No, he didn't," Jake said stiffly. "In fact, he hasn't told me much of anything lately and now I know why."

There was a subtle but significant change in her expression as cognizance clicked, and with it came the swift resurrection of composure. "So," she said coolly, "it was you who put the security men in the hospital. One of them has a broken hip and dislocated shoulder. The other one is in intensive care with a fractured skull and severe head trauma."

"How long has it been going on, Elena?" he demanded, some of the bitterness penetrating his voice.

"There is nothing going on," she replied succinctly, putting some space between them by strolling into the sitting area of the suite. It was luxuriously appointed, decorated in gem shades, a tad too spotless to be occupied. The window afforded an impressive mountain view, below which the city looped its necklaces of roads and beaded strings of buildings.

"No?"

"No," she said firmly. "There is nothing going on between Haskell and I, at least not what you think." Brittleness had crept into her voice. "Jake, I am not a journalist." She paused, giving him a chance to react, but he stood silently glaring at her. She continued, "I work for the DEA, and I have information that Haskell is involved in drug trafficking."

"What?" Jake took several steps, closing the gap between them.

"Yes, I am afraid so. The problem is I cannot prove it. My assignment was to identify his sources and connections."

"You work for the DEA," Jake repeated, his voice flat.

"It is true, *querido*," she said bleakly, crossing back to the foyer to retrieve her purse, some kind of leather Gucci with an intricate chain and bamboo strap. She dug through it and produced a laminated DEA identification. After holding it up briefly for him to see, the gold-and-blue agency emblem all too familiar with its eagle crest, she stuffed it back into her bag. Noticing that her top was still unbuttoned, she cast Jake an ineffectively demure smile as she refastened it. Even buttoned, the top revealed a dimple of tanned cleavage, which she tried to accentuate with some carefully choreographed moves, but he was not taking.

"Haskell's *not* a goddamn drug trafficker," Jake declared, but even as the assertion was made his feelings were sinking into a cesspool of doubt and dread. The missing piece of the puzzle had just flipped over.

Elena kept silent, trying to tap his thoughts by looking deeply into the boiling black of his eyes. But she could read nothing.

"Who do you work for at the DEA?" he asked dubiously.

"That is classified information."

"If you're not a journalist, is anything else you've told me true?"

"Certainly some things are true," she snapped, noticeably offended.

"Then tell me who you work for at DEA," he persisted. "Better yet"— he unhooked his cell phone and held it out to her—"get them on the phone. Now." He shoved the phone in her face.

"I told you, it is classified," she said, turning her head away from the cell phone, her tone clipped and brusque.

He replaced his phone and continued to stare intently at her, hands planted on his hips. Finally, he said, "So you've been using me to get to Haskell."

"No. What we have has nothing to do with him."

Jake said nothing, just glared.

"Really, *querido*. Nothing at all."

"All I want to know is, what were you doing with him last night? What was that about? Whose house is that?"

"That was purely business. I cannot talk to you about that. But I will say this, Jake. If you care about him at all, you will convince him to give me what I want. He is in serious trouble. If he will cooperate now I can get him a deal, maybe even immunity from prosecution."

"How is fucking my best friend purely business? Explain that." His mind fanned over their past trysts, a blur of times and places ending at his hotel bed yesterday afternoon. "And what about me?" he asked. "Was I purely business, too?"

"Of course not," she said sharply, "that had nothing to do with this. Look, I have told you all that I can." Moistening her lips, she released her mahogany hair from its clip, let it fall to her shoulders, and blinked slowly, softening gestures that failed to get any reaction.

"Well, that's fine," Jake said abruptly, "because that's all I care to hear." He turned and stalked toward the door.

Elena made a grab for him which he shook off, spinning her back onto the bed where she landed in a sprawled sitting position, her long bare legs spread to reveal a sliver of thong between her thighs, spiked heel sandals anchored on the carpet.

"Jake," Elena called after him. "Please. Talk to Haskell. And I hope you'll—"

But Jake was already gone, and hope was not something he took with him.

14

ON RETURN TO THE guesthouse, Jake checked at the front desk for messages, already resigned to the probability that there would be nothing from Delaney. And he was right.

There was nothing. Nothing at all. Nothing that filled him with every blackened emotion his mind could imagine. Nothing that made any sense at all. Nothing that eased the weight growing heavier in his heart. Just nothing.

As he let himself into his room, his BlackBerry vibrated. He snatched it from his waist and checked the display, prepared to launch assault. But it was not a live call, only his phone indicating he had a voice message waiting. He pressed the button to retrieve it. The message was dry and terse, Delaney in a monotone, informing him that he was going to take off after refueling. Almost as an afterthought, he gave a mumbled location of the airfield from which he was departing. Jake had never heard of it, but he was going to find it—if he had enough time. He prodded the BlackBerry's touch-screen until he found a fairly detailed navigational map, focusing on the outer environs of Bogotá. Studying it closely, he located the spot. It was easily sixty to eighty kilometers northwest. If he stood a chance of catching Delaney before takeoff, he would have to make the motorcycle fly. And hope there were no roadblocks.

After fueling up the motorcycle Jake took off, and as he left the city and built his speed, thoughts from the back shelf of his mind began to tumble down. Listening to the engine's growl, feeling his body thrum with its vibration as he leaned into the ride, he reflected on the past several weeks.

First, there had been Delaney's evasiveness at base camp, followed by his elusiveness after mysteriously skipping their R&R time in Costa Rica. Then there had been his continued distant demeanor during the village aid, and failure to respond to radio calls. Even more erratic had been his parking of the plane at an obscure and unsecured airstrip instead of the designated one at the compound. Throughout this counternarcotics tour, Delaney had been evasive at practically every turn, both interactively and communicatively. Now Jake wondered if the reason Delaney claimed he never heard the radio calls could be because he was monitoring other frequencies. *Guerrilla frequencies?* Perhaps the reason for his frequent and unexplained disappearances was clandestine meetings—*with the narcoguerrillas?* That was crazy, he told himself, utterly insane. Delaney was *not* a drug trafficker. But Jake felt his heart descend to its abyss, the leaden weight of doubt pulling it down, down, down. He remembered the eerie feeling he'd had on stopping by the airstrip to check on the plane, as if something was out of order, out of sync. The guerrillas that had taken him hostage to treat their wounded had most likely been watching the plane. And strangest of all had been Delaney's appearance—and consequent denial of it—at the guerrilla compound and his confrontation with the colonel. In retrospect, Jake now wondered if Delaney knew the colonel and his soldiers and, on hearing of Jake's abduction, had been expressing his outrage. Without that intervention, Jake concluded that he might have been released in exchange for his services, but not with such passivity. And he would never have seen his supplies returned, certainly not his radio and weapon. Finally there was Delaney's uncharacteristic aversion in going after the *narcotraficante* kingpin.

Which brought him to the abhorrently unthinkable betrayal with Elena. Who had actually betrayed whom? Had Elena seduced Delaney, as she had implied, for the purpose of entrapment? But then it did take two to tango as the inane saying went, and Delaney certainly seemed to be a willing participant...or was he? He had appeared to be heavily inebriated, but now it occurred to Jake that he had failed to consider another theory. He had been so blinded by his rage that he'd dismissed any mitigating factors. Drunk and lascivious behavior was one thing, but what if Delaney had been drugged? Rehashing it all, Jake felt only uncomprehending fury—fury at the deception, fury at the betrayal, fury even at himself for not confronting Delaney when he'd had the chance. Most of all, fury at the unknown.

ABOUT TWENTY MILES FROM the place he was headed, Jake ran smack-dab into a small village in the festive throes of a celebration. Cursing the obstacle, he earnestly searched for a way around it. Knowing he had no time to get off track, he consulted the map he'd saved on his phone and realized the road through the village was the quickest, most direct route. To venture any other direction would add miles he could not afford. Sighing with resignation, he removed his helmet and slowly continued along the dirt road, his speed reduced to just above an idle as he navigated through the exuberant throngs.

The village was called Tocaquira, and apparently the reason for the celebration was the betrothal of a young couple who were being paraded through the streets in the back of a dilapidated white pickup truck. The bride wore a white muslin dress and a circle of bright flowers around her head, the groom, an ill-fitting hand-me-down suit and shined black boots. Roving bands were playing a combination of native Guascarrilera and Ranchera music on guitars, maracas, and wooden scrapers known as *guacharacas*. Celebrants danced and clapped along behind them, punctuating the music with rousing chants and cheers. There did not appear to be a single soul that was not inebriated. Colorful decorations were strung from every building and the piquant aroma of roasting meat permeated the air.

Jake carefully wove the motorcycle through the crowd, smiling and nodding to individuals who greeted him so as not to warrant any extra attention. But as a good-looking stranger, especially a *Norte Americano*, his presence did cause more than a few head turns. He kept his pace steady and avoided direct eye contact. Tables and chairs lining the road were occupied with revelers eating and drinking—mostly drinking—some, Jake noted without surprise, requisitioned by the ever-attendant guerrillas. He watched them distrustfully, his right hand resting against the bulge of the Glock inside his waistband. But they were drinking, too, clinking beer bottles and knocking back shots, laughing bawdily and making vulgar catcalls to the young women who passed.

One pair of guerrillas, segregated from the rest, drew Jake's gaze. The first thing he noticed was their detachment from the crowd; they were seated at the end of a block, just off an alleyway, talking on a handheld radio. They did not appear to be intoxicated. And Jake was certain he recognized one of them. The memory flicked like the ball on a roulette table, bouncing in and out of mental slots before finally rolling into one but not the one where the bet was placed. Had he really seen that guerrilla somewhere before? Given his remote location, that was highly unlikely. And yet, the memory bounced and rolled. But never settled. It troubled him.

Finally, Jake pulled out on the far side of the village and hit open road, accelerating until he was going as fast as the terrain would safely allow. Maybe a little faster. Five more miles fell away, then ten.

As he approached the location Delaney had provided on the voice message, he realized with a start that almost an hour had passed. He hoped he was not too late.

THE AIRSTRIP WAS NOTHING more than a desolate and dusty clearing cut like a swath through a stretch of dense jungle. Jake was mildly surprised to see that there were actually a half dozen hangars and a couple of fuel tankards. It also appeared to be deserted. He skidded to a dust-erupting stop, removed his helmet, and slammed his fist on the handlebar of the motorcycle.

"Goddammit!" he swore out loud to the utterly still, utterly empty air. "Goddammit, Haskell, goddammit!"

He sat slumped and defeated on the motorcycle, head bowed over the helmet cradled in his arms. A voice in the dusty stillness jolted him to a quick and clumsy dismount.

"Jake?"

He followed the voice, a hollow echo that seemed to come from inside a tin drum. The back hangar, partially obstructed by encroaching jungle. Jake cautiously rounded the metal side and almost walked into

Delaney. Emotions, hot and ripe, burst forth at the sight of his partner, and he had to use every lever of self-control he knew to refrain from grabbing him by the throat.

Delaney stood beside the olive-camouflage DC-3, clad in fatigues, safari hat, and aviator sunglasses, looking no more, no less, the same Haskell Delaney that had departed from Costa Rica with him at the onset of this mission. And yet Jake knew in his heart that this was not the same Haskell Delaney—this was an imposter, victim of some vile soul-invader that had eaten away the living core of his old friend and left something contaminated on the inside.

Jake looked at Delaney and exhaled heavily, and the pain he felt was like a layer of razor blades in his chest. "Haskell," was all he could say before his throat constricted.

"Hey, bubba." The big, pearly white-toothed grin, a little wilted but no less radiant. Standing there grinning like somebody's beloved shoe-chewing Golden Retriever.

Gazing at him, Jake's emotions were rushing like whitewater—all the anger, hurt, and confusion swirling around with all the love and friendship he'd felt for this man through the many years—and he could feel his pulse pounding like war drums in his head. Finally, in a voice remarkably steady, he asked, "Were you just going to leave?"

"Eventually," Delaney remarked lightly. "I was waiting for you, figured you'd call me or just show up."

Jake went to stand beside him, leaning back against the plane. Looking out at the arid dirt strip just beyond the hangar, he said, "Why take off from this god-forsaken outpost? Whatever happened to airfields with fueling facilities and mechanics, paved runways with lights? LZs in the field we *have* to do, but there must be dozens of good airfields within a thirty-mile radius of here."

"This is what I call hassle-free flying," Delaney joked. "Easy in, easy out."

"If you don't get picked off by some guerrilla commandos first," Jake said, watching Delaney's reaction from the corner of his eye.

"Well, that *is* one of the drawbacks," he quipped, still grinning easily.

Jake turned abruptly to face Delaney. "What the hell is going on with you?"

Delaney chortled, slapping his thigh. "Shit if I know." He pushed himself away from the plane and began strolling casually around it, ostensibly giving it a final cursory inspection before takeoff. His big hands caressed the innumerable dings and dents in the aircraft's metal with the fond familiarity of a lover.

Jake caught up, grasped him firmly by the shoulder and spun him around. "No, Haskell, I mean it. What's going on?"

Delaney's grin wrinkled into an astonished grimace, only thinly disguising the anguish that had been festering beneath the smile all along. He awkwardly manufactured a bewildered look that quickly dissolved to wan resignation. "I've got a hangover from hell," he confessed abjectly.

"I guess you do," Jake muttered grimly. "How did you and Elena happen?"

He groaned. "Shit...you know about that?"

Jake said nothing.

Delaney massaged his temples, not bothering to conceal his misery since it was now an established fact. Shaking his head dejectedly, he said, "Truthfully, Jake, I don't know. I mean, I *really* don't know. Shit. All I remember is going to Molotov's, having a few drinks, hanging with the guys, just typical macho bullshit, and at some point I noticed that Elena was there. I asked her where you were and she said she'd been with you earlier, but she got called for an assignment. She said she was on her way to rejoin you but thought she'd stop in Molotov's first to see who was around. She asked if she could buy me a drink, then we sat down and had some conversation...and that's all I remember."

"So you don't remember going to the house?"

"Not at all. I only know I woke up there this morning, sick as a fucking dog. I can't figure it out because you know I can drink a fleet of sailors under and still walk a pretty straight line. I hate to say this, Jake, but I think she *drugged* me."

"Yeah, I think maybe she did," Jake said disdainfully. "And you don't have any idea why?"

"Of course not!" Delaney exclaimed, and Jake thought his sense of indignation sounded almost authentic. "She was gone when I came to this morning and some Latino asshole drove me back to the city without any explanations. Just whose house is that? Have you ever been there?"

"Would it help shed any light if I told you she's a DEA agent?"

Even with the sunglasses covering Delaney's eyes, Jake could imagine the bright flecks of light firing off in the gray-green irises as his pupils dilated in shock. "Who told you that?" he sputtered.

"She did. This morning when I confronted her. Since you don't seem to remember what happened last night, I'm going to tell you," Jake said, unable to keep the asperity out of his voice. "I popped in Molotov's, too, looking for you. Since you hadn't bothered to leave a message to let me know you got here in one piece. I hung out for a while and was about to leave when I saw Elena with you. You looked like you were pissed out of your head, and you were all over her. Elena was giving it back. She took you outside, a car drove up, and off the two of you went. I followed the car to this massive estate high up in the hills, somewhere around Suesca. I got over the security fence and took a tour of the grounds. Through the window to the master bedroom I saw you and Elena—"

Delaney was stomping away, hands over his ears. "Stop it, just stop it! I've heard enough!" He turned sharply on his heels and said, "God, Jake, you know I would never do anything to hurt you. If you don't know anything else, surely you know that."

Quietly, Jake said, "Do I? Haskell, last night I was furious beyond words over the betrayal with Elena. But this morning that became as trivial as a wrong turn. When Elena told me she was with the DEA, she also said it was you she was after." Looking squarely at Delaney, his voice grim and uncompromising, he said, "I want to know what the hell you're into. No more secrets, no more lies."

"The bitch must be *on* drugs," Delaney spouted angrily. The anger turned quickly to incredulity as he studied Jake's hardened face. "Surely you don't believe her!"

"I admit I didn't at first, but Haskell I've known something was going on with you since the beginning of the mission." The tension had been building in his voice and now his jaw was clenched again, his breathing thick. "So just tell me, that's all I'm asking. Just tell me."

Delaney's hands were on his hips as he swaggered around, silently stewing in his private hell. After a long time, he stopped and looked up as if he'd suddenly remembered something. Jerking his head toward the DC-3, he said, "Guess I better get this thing started."

"You're not going anywhere until you tell me," Jake said adamantly.

"Jake, don't."

"You can't dodge me anymore."

"Okay, then you know," Delaney snapped bitterly. "There, are you happy? You don't need to know anything else, otherwise you'll be a part of it."

"Don't you understand? Last night, this morning, I became a part of it—whatever the fuck it is—and if it's you, I *am* a part of it." Jake realized his anger was escalating again, and fought to reel in his passion.

"No, Jake," Delaney said forcefully. "You can be mad, you can even hate me, I don't fucking care. But forget this, drop it and forget it *now*. Let's just get back home and do some SpecOps gigs for a while...and just forget. Okay?"

"I'll drop it—for now—if you just tell me why."

Delaney sighed and shook his head in frustration. "You're a goddamn stubborn son of a bitch and it's gonna get you killed one of these days. Sure, I'll give you that. If you think any of it's for me then you really don't know me at all. There's not one fucking dime in it for me."

"So why—"

"Jesus Christ, Jake!" he screamed. "That's it, enough! I'm going to start this plane and fly it the hell out of here."

But Jake's fury was only intensifying. "What's on the plane, Haskell? Where have you got it?"

"Jake."

But Jake could not stop himself, could not let go. "Did they stash it for you or do you take care of that yourself?"

"Jake, don't."

"Tell me, Haskell, how does it feel to possibly be responsible for the massacre of a village, to have the blood on your hands, and—"

Delaney's fist shot out, directed at Jake's jaw, but Jake tucked his head and blocked it with a wrist grab. Immediately, he promised himself that he would not retaliate because his wrath was so strong he feared his moves might not just immobilize Delaney. He released Delaney's wrist and backed off, extending his arms in concession.

"Okay, I shouldn't have said that. But are you so foolish that you didn't realize they were going to kill me simply because I was near *our* plane?"

"I would never—" Delaney began, then cut himself short. Inhaled bracingly. "Look, I'm going to get the Gooney Bird cranked up and wing it home. I'm going to find a beach with some sexy ladies, screw more than a few of them, consume mile-high cheeseburgers and greasy French fries with enough cholesterol to clog the arteries of an entire aerobics class, and catch bass big enough to be in the Prehistoric exhibit of the Smithsonian. I'm going to sleep until I wake up, surf until I wipe out, listen to Tom Petty until I can't get the fucking songs out of my head, and drink beer so cold I have to crack the icicles off my balls. And when you get there, we'll do all that together. Okay? Okay. Now let me get this old whore started."

Delaney gave Jake a lingering look of salvaged indemnity before he wrenched the cockpit door open with a protesting creak. He hoisted himself up and climbed into the airplane.

Jake retreated from the hangar, walking slowly back toward his motorcycle. He stood there watching and listening as Delaney started the DC-3's twin Pratt & Whitneys, his fury-torn thoughts still cut and bleeding out of control in his head. But a soft spot in his heart had intervened, as it always did with Delaney, and even though he could not let *this* go, he was going to have to compromise and let Delaney go. Again, for now.

He felt a sad twinge of nostalgia, thinking back on their first trip to Colombia, before the missions had actually begun. They had been hiking through the jungle when they'd happened on this ancient warplane. The fifty-plus-year-old bird had seen action over the beaches of Normandy and the rice fields of Vietnam, irreverently rewarded for her service by passing into the depraved ranks of the drug traffickers. This particular plane had suffered mechanical failure and been abandoned by dealers, apparently left to decompose in the jungle. With Jake and Delaney's subsequent adoption and renovation—Jake could still remember the sparkle in Delaney's eyes when they'd discovered it—the inception of a new cause that would become a passion embraced, and now, reviled.

Delaney had rolled the plane out onto the dirt strip and was readying for takeoff. The change in engine sound, a low whine, seemed to plead for speed. Unexpectedly, the door at the rear of the plane was opened and Delaney climbed halfway out, one leg on the top step. He stood there for a moment, saying nothing, and somewhere—even above the guttural rumble of the DC-3's engines—primitively and peculiarly, some species of bird could be heard warbling through a singsong scale from within the cover of jungle.

"Look, Jake—" he started.

Jake took a tentative step toward him, but something inexplicably stopped him. Like an invisible hand, something stopped him, and at the same instant the little roulette ball slid into place and stopped rolling.

And then the world was ripped apart.

A deafening roar, an earth-pummeling explosion, a projectile firebomb that threw heat and flames and black smoke into the edge of forever. Jake was lifted up, propelled violently backwards and high—

—blanketed by the shimmering heat, but he found pieces of the sky and with it, the ground. He staggered to his feet, deafened and reeling from the impact, and saw Haskell.

He had been blown out of the plane and lay face down in the dirt, behind him and all around him great orange fireballs bursting into the sky amid billowing black smoke and earth-shaking booms. Jake screamed his name, scrambling to his side, the scorching heat already baking his own skin as the smoke filled and burned his eyes. His ears were ringing so acutely it was as if he'd been standing directly beside a very large and very heavy church bell when it tolled. He struggled with Delaney's limp form, dragging him away from the spreading smoke and flames. Frantically, he coughed to clear his lungs and wiped at his eyes, trying to see through the film of stingy tears. Shook his head in an attempt to quiet the ringing. Carefully, he rolled Delaney onto his side and blearily tried to focus as he groped for a limb, for a pulse. In horror that at once liquefied his bowels and pumped a hot wave of bile into his throat, he dimly realized that he was touching pulp and blood...pieces, great hunks of body were gone, craters and cavities gaping and gushing geysers of blood.

Jake leaned close, diffidently turning Delaney's head and swallowing a nauseating gasp at the shredded and bloody flaps of skin that hung loosely over broiled, eviscerated face. Through the years Jake had seen plenty of gut-wrenching and gruesome atrocities, and even though there was always one that left a sorrowful or sickening aftertaste—like Afortunado—his stoic composure and authoritative command seldom failed him. But it did now, completely, as he looked into the ruin of his beloved friend's face. Miraculously, Delaney was still breathing. Barely. For one fleeting and senseless moment he considered seeking help, and then harsh reality heartlessly mocked him. *You're nowhere, miles from nowhere.*

"Jake..." His voice a ghostly whisper, blood trickling from both sides of his charred and blistered mouth.

Jake gingerly scooped the glutinous mass of Delaney in his arms, trying desperately to somehow contain it against him. But even as he held on he could feel the blood, the breath, and the breadth that remained of Haskell seeping out and fading away. Unable to fight back the tears, he held on tight, gasping in broken sobs.

"Haskell, you bastard...don't you fucking die on me! Do you hear me? Yes, goddammit, I'm mad as hell at you right now, but I'll get over it! Don't you fucking die on me! Oh God, don't you fucking"—he sobbed—"do it..."

Against his face, roasted and slick with perspiration from the heat of the fire, he felt Delaney's blood and soft tissue congealing, and a very faint breath sound. Jake slowly tilted his head back and looked imploringly into the last light of Haskell's placid gray-green eyes.

"Fucked...Jake," Delaney rasped weakly, "sorry...bro."

And then the faintness of breath ceased, the paleness of life drained from his face. "No!" Jake screamed—a scream that echoed deafeningly in his head. And then he just held on, gazing uncomprehendingly into the stone-stillness of the big gray-green eyes vacantly staring up at him, unseeing and unknowing. Maybe. Or maybe seeing and knowing all now.

Jake lay down on top of Delaney, saturated with his blood, and wept.

When he looked up at last, the fire had diminished substantially, smoldering in the incinerated shards of metal plane. An occasional spear of flame would shoot up, crackling briefly as it unearthed something new in the wreckage. He sat in the dirt, caked and red with Delaney's blood, and watched in dazed silence as the remaining fragments of DC-3 disintegrated before him. A plane that had taken them many places, but mostly here—and now nowhere, ever again.

Dimly, he became aware that the sky was no longer blue. It had filled up with thick ashen clouds, and he could hear thunder rumbling distantly, shaking the ground slightly beneath him.

He cast his eyes down on the fallen soldier whose friendship and bravery would endure long beyond and high above the pain and darkness he had so unintentionally invoked. Looking into those now forever eyes and listening to the thunder rolling down the dusty road, Jake thought: *There's one hell of a storm coming.*

A precursory gale whisked across the clearing as raindrops began to fall, and Jake watched numbly as Delaney's safari hat, without so much as a singe, sailed by his face and off into the jungle.

PART TWO

SKY OF LOVE SKY OF TEARS

15

THE BIG BOAT WAS gliding smoothly on a starboard tack between the tips of Little Exuma and Long Island, not quite twenty miles past the Tropic of Cancer. Hitting the deeper waters of Exuma Sound, it reached broadly into an exhilarating 16-knot trade wind. The warm Caribbean waters were a calm and sparkling sapphire blue, lightly dappled with sporadic whitecaps as the breeze picked up. Overhead, the sky was equally tranquil with low and widely scattered thin clouds. Early afternoon in late spring, it was as perfect a sailing day as a sailor could want, but to Jake it was just as flat and dead as each of the others recently preceding.

It was, or had been, Delaney's boat. He had bought the forty-four-foot Beneteau yacht, easily worth quarter of a million dollars, for a song. On a tip from a former marine comrade working for the US Coast Guard, Delaney made an offer before the vessel hit the auction block for narcotics property seizures. Jake suspected the annual mooring fees probably cost more than Delaney's bid on the boat.

Propped against the side of the cockpit in white swim trunks and Docksides, arms crossed over his deeply tanned bare chest, he gazed ponderously up at the billowing blue-and-white genoa nosing jauntily toward the wind. In some ways, the images from those dreadful days at the end of his counternarcotics stint seemed long ago and faraway, dim shadows at the end of a long and narrow hall. But mostly they were sharp and painful, close and suffocating. It took every fiber of will he possessed to force them back down the dark hall, but the boat and the sea—like the plane and the sky—was so much Haskell Delaney, so much his maverick spirit, that the images could only be obscured for brief interludes. Now was not one of them.

Because sailing into the Bahamas was so keenly familiar, a homecoming ritual of sorts and, like walking into an empty house where furniture and life had once been, the vastly beautiful blues of ocean and sky reflecting only the shapes of profound emptiness.

Normally, the DC-3 would be waiting back at the little airstrip on Cat Island, its pilot already a week or so sated by cold beer, salty sea treats, and sandy romps with sun-bronzed ladies. Instead, just over a week ago Jake had loaded what was left of his friend's body onto a military transport plane bound stateside, having failed to convince Delaney's ex-military father that his son would have, under the circumstances, preferred cremation and burial at sea. He was sure Delaney's parents would wage territorial war over funeral arrangements, and he would leave that to them. After all, funerals were not for the dead, they were a commiserating and often selfish indulgence for the living. In the end he was sure Delaney's father, a vain and pedantic man with a distinguished military career of his own, would have his way and there would be the pomp and protocol of a traditional military funeral for a son he had never really known.

Delaney's parents divorced when he was a teenager, forcing him to live with his father who, as a civilian had become an engineer in aerospace technology. Their relationship was fitful at best, a clash of two strong-willed personalities brewed from hostilities established early on. Delaney had even less of a relationship with his mother, once an attractive lounge singer who, it turned out, had absolutely nothing in common with her intellectually superior husband. Years of too much time in the bars and pharmacies had taken their toll on her, and by the time of the divorce she barely resembled the woman Delaney knew as his mother. And neither parent, Jake thought sadly, had a clue what their son had been all about; they knew nothing of his accomplishments, nothing of his personality, nothing of his hopes and dreams—dreams never to be realized. Jake ruminated on some of the darker times they had weathered together, and then the lighter ones. And of the light, oh so much light, all snuffed out in one explosive instant that had blown a hole right through the middle of his soul. More shards for the shelf of brokenness.

In the days that followed Delaney's death Jake had managed to isolate himself from the pain, drifting trancelike through a senseless blur of activity that included embassy and military inquiries and intervention, police procedures and investigation, and the convergence of local comrades flushed from the field by the news of Delaney's death. Alberto Hernandez had come forth in swift and unconditional support, offering to conduct a memorial service, something Jake briefly debated then declined. In another more sobering conversation, Raúl Aguilar subtly implied retaliatory measures but wisely and respectfully opted not to pursue that any further with Jake. Jake had spent an inordinate amount of time in the imposing fortress compound of the US Embassy where the ambassador, consulting with a fleet of attachés, advisors, and deputies, had launched his own investigation, vowing definitive results. The Colombian police and military, after an initial barrage of grating questions, to which Jake responded with stoic reticence, began to detach themselves from the incident. There was the usual speculation of mechanical malfunction and, unsurprisingly, suspicions of guerrilla involvement with the suggestion that the plane had been rigged to explode as an act of violence ostensibly targeted toward the US's renewed involvement in counternarcotics. But in the end it really did not matter—it did not matter who or how—Jake knew *what* had caused it. And that was enough.

Just before he'd left Bogotá, Jake had made some final inquiries of his own, already guessing what the outcome would be. He'd stopped by the Hotel Tequendama and had been told that *Señorita* García had checked out. He took a drive on two separate occasions, one in the daytime and another after dark, to the mansion in the hills near Suesca. The place seemed sterile and deserted.

He should have returned to Costa Rica then, but he just needed some time to himself. Time to be alone with his feelings, and with the shadowy specter of Haskell Delaney.

The capricious wind had decreased slightly and shifted, nudging the boat west toward the more shallow turquoise waters enveloping the cays. Jake decided to bear away, easing the mainsail out allowing the boat to heel windward. When the sails were luffing his speed slowed, and as he steered in the direction of the cays he looked longingly into the crystal-clear water. Unable to pass on its siren call, he proceeded to back the headsail and steered to leeward. Once the boat was hove-to and he'd dropped anchor, he retrieved his snorkel, mask, and fins from the locker in the stern swim platform. Moments later, he dove in.

Gliding through the shallow depths of temperate water, Jake gratefully lost himself in its aquamarine serenity. It was as soothing as it was beautiful, an ephemeral balm for the ache that was starting to penetrate his heart. As he snorkeled and swam along the barrier reefs, he let his mind empty of thought, filling it instead with the visually stunning images of the Caribbean underwater world. Jake held a bachelor's degree in biology which, like his master's in psychology, had been earned by diligent self-study during desultory hours snatched in between missions and deployments, oceanography being a favorite area of study. So he always looked forward to underwater excursions, whether in the form of full-scale dives or more casual snorkeling. He was pleased to see that these reefs along the Exuma Cays appeared to be healthy and thriving. Deterioration of coral reefs and bleaching had become a great concern in recent years; flamingly vivid color blanched to white as their symbiotic algae was destroyed, disease and damage caused by a variety of conditions, most of which were of man's making. Although erratic climatic and environmental changes were a factor, most of the physiological stress could be blamed on sedimentation, pollution, and ecological imbalance: land development, over-fishing, scavenging, and boat anchorages. Beyond the destruction of the reefs, these progressive trends had an adverse effect on the entire marine ecosystem.

But the colors and textures of these reefs, and the flora and fauna within them, were very much alive. Here, he encountered the burnt orange elkhorn with its wide, flattened branches and nubby texture, colonies of the rounded-head star coral, and the yellow, green, and gray finger coral. Mollusk beds were rampant, dispersed among turtles, starfish, anemones, sponges, urchins, and jellyfish. He swam past teeming schools of minnows and a kite-shaped stingray flapping its broad wing like pectoral fins. Flashes of royal blue, streaks of silver, and sunbursts of orange and yellow surrounded him on all sides. Yellow-tailed snapper, speckled gray grouper, gray goatfish with their barbs protruding from the jaw, silvery saw-toothed barracudas, yellow-and-black triggerfish with their white polka-dotted bellies. A pair of shy nurse sharks shadowed him from below before scurrying off in a cloud of white sand. Even a dolphin joined him for a while, guiding him around the barnacled remains of a shipwreck. The effect on his disposition was almost magical; by the time he swam back to the boat's underside, a calmness had stilled his troubled mind and he felt refreshed. When he broke the water's surface, he was mildly surprised to find that the sky's blue had grayed and it was sprinkling rain. Blinking into the droplets dimpling the lightly rolling turquoise waves, he thought, *tears into the ocean...*like dust to dust. And the circle is unbroken.

A FEW HOURS LATER, as Jake approached the harbor of Hawk's Nest at the southern tip of Cat Island, he furled the sails and switched to the power of the yacht's 85-hp Perkins. The twenty-eight-slip marina was relatively empty this time of day as most of the "sporties" were still out on their big fishing boats in zealous pursuit of the monster blue marlin. Even so, Jake preferred to dock under power, particularly when there was an on or offshore wind. The Beneteau cruiser was often a challenge to navigate solo, but he liked the workout. Delaney had it specially fitted with taller rigs, single-handed furling and reefing, self-tacking jib, push-button trimming, electric Lewmar winches, and a number of other configurations to facilitate solo sailing. He steered the boat past the rock jetty and yellow Point House on the left and eased into one of the slips. Then he tidied up, changed into Dockers shorts and a white t-shirt, and prepared to go ashore.

Hawk's Nest, so-named for a giant hawk that had made her nest on the island for several years, is a quaint little resort with a well-appointed marina and excellent amenities. It was a place they had come to consider their unofficial pit stop following the completion of certain missions. And it was the name with which Delaney had christened the Beneteau.

After docking, Jake walked just under a mile north, crossing the resort's private airstrip and continuing to the clubhouse. Though he wasn't really hungry, he went inside and got a bite to eat before heading for the beach. The sun had returned to warm the pink-and-white sands with soft, snowy brilliance for a few more hours before melting into a typically Bahamian sherbet-colored sunset. He settled into an Adirondack beach chair with an audible sigh and sipped from a bottle of water. Watching the waves roll onto the beach and cascade over the sand, he felt the emergence of a reluctant peace.

"Hey, Jake!"

He turned to see one of the island locals, a tall black man with a smile that gleamed like a pearl necklace. Top Cat was one of the resort's guides and a bonefishing legend. Delaney and Jake had met him on their first visit to the island and been casual friends ever since.

"Hey, Top Cat," Jake replied listlessly.

"Anton just told me you were here. When did you get in?" Top Cat asked, dragging another wood-plank chair across the sand and dropping his large frame into it. He took a swig from the bottle of Guinness beer in his hand.

"This morning," Jake replied.

"Where's Delaney? I haven't seen the plane."

Jake's chin dipped and he felt his throat go dry, words missing. After a moment, he simply said, "He's...he's not coming this time." Quickly changing the subject, he nodded toward the water. "I'm surprised you aren't out there in the thick of it."

The big man grinned. "I have been, *mon*. Came in to leave something for the others to catch."

"So, what's going on?" Jake asked.

"Just the usual, you know. Busy with the fishing and charters. Oh, there was one thing. Somebody I didn't recognize was asking around about you, just the other day."

Jake looked back at him with interest. "Really? Was it a woman?"

Top Cat chuckled and poked Jake lightly on the arm. "Women *always* ask about you! But no, this was a guy."

"You say you didn't recognize him?"

"Nope. Never seen him before. Latino dude." He scratched his head, thinking. "He was asking if anyone knew when or if you'd be here."

"When *I'd* be here or when *we'd* be here?" Jake asked, feeling a ripple of wariness.

Top Cat considered the distinction for a moment, then replied, "Now that I think about it, he only mentioned you."

"And you told him...?"

"I just told him I had no idea. You guys blow in and outta here like the wind." He shrugged unconcernedly, sipping his beer.

"Did he have a boat or plane?"

"Not that I remember. Sound like anybody you know?" He chuckled again. "Must have been somebody you ran into south of the border."

Jake frowned, thinking, *Yeah, and somebody who obviously already knew Haskell wouldn't be with me.* He said, "Maybe so. Well, I need to stretch my sea-legs so I'm going to head for the hills." He pulled himself up from the beach chair, reaching over to clasp the fisherman's hand.

"Okay, *mon*," Top Cat beamed. "See you later."

FROM THE TOP OF Mount Alvernia, just over two hundred feet up, the lush and vastly uncultivated beauty of Cat Island could be viewed in a full 360-degree vista. Sixty or more miles of the pale pink and sugar-white beaches; dense forests of guinep, pigeon plum, sapodilla, bread-fruit, sea grape, guava, mangroves, and tamarind trees; crumbling ruins of vine-covered stone walls from ancient cotton plantations; orchards of pineapples and bananas; clearings punctuated by the legendary blue holes. These were limestone-rimmed pools of fresh or salt water, some a mysterious combination of both, ranging in size from a half-mile to almost ten. Many were considered to be bottomless and held in super-stitious awe by islanders, some of whom actually believed in the legends of sea monsters handed down from their ancestors. They were an end-less fascination for divers, quite a few of the pools being linked to the ocean through intricate mazes of subterranean caverns.

Jake sat on the high limestone cliff overlooking the island's pretty panorama, momentarily mesmerized by the alternately blue and green turquoises of the sea. Behind him, the medieval monastery built in the 1930s by a missionary architect named Father Jerome, sat in stony rev-erence. Sacramentally etched above one of the recessed wooden doors was the epitaph: BLESSED ARE THE DEAD WHO DIE IN THE LORD.

He watched the sea birds circling and diving into the waters below.

There were no hawks flying the Caribbean skies today. The sun had begun its slow and deliberate descent, pale heat deepening to ember shades of dying day as it slipped ever closer to the ocean's surface. The reluctant peace was taking hold in the comforting environment of this familiar paradise, but there was an uneasiness stirring in the trade winds.

He clutched the metal chain in his hand, let his fingers feel the imprint on the dangling pieces. Names etched in the metal, names representing life here and life gone. It was time. He knew it was time to let go, to forgive and let go. But he would not—could not—forget. Not just yet. A sweet and mournful refrain of a forgotten tune played through his mind, about working through the sadness of secrets revealed and tending the broken heart in that aftermath.

Again, he felt the quiver of unease. Something, something deeply unsettling. But the circle was coming around. Something ending, something beginning...*the circle is unbroken*. The tips of his fingers rubbed the engraved letters on the dog tags, rubbed them as if they might reveal an answer. Something, something out there waiting for him.

But now, it was time to grieve for a friend.

16

HE HELD THE DOG tags that had been laced to Delaney's boots, looking out across the glistening waters of the Caribbean. He had been sitting on the foredeck of the Beneteau for the past hour watching the sky's celestial brush paint another spectacular Bahamian sunset with coral hues of pink and orange. The boat was hove-to in the middle of Exuma Sound, about thirty miles northwest of Hawk's Nest Point, and he was just letting it drift gently with the light current. Sitting against the trunk of the cabin with his face lifted to the ocean breeze, eyes filled with the florid colors of early evening, heart open to the sounds of infinity's emotions, Jake could almost feel the presence of Delaney.

Almost.

Delaney and his wickedly robust laughter, Delaney and his upbeat songs. Except he could not hear Delaney singing them anymore.

Earlier in the day, closer to Cat Island, he had gone scuba diving again, exploring more reefs and wrecks and some underwater caves, managing to enjoy his ventures despite the heaviness of heart. But as late afternoon approached he had become restless, and his heart began to ache with what he knew was a yearning for acceptance. Acceptance with grief and clarity, forgiveness with love and understanding. But there was no clarity or understanding in this, and he didn't see how there ever could be.

Jake opened his hand and peered down at Delaney's dog tags, nudging them lightly around on his palm, thinking about all the history, all the valor, all of the man they represented. For a moment he hesitated, clutching them tightly in his fist, thinking, *I can't, I can't let go*...but then knowing that he must, knowing it was time. He brought his fist slowly up to his mouth, pressed his lips against the metal, felt the sudden tears burning hotly behind his closed eyelids as his chest heaved.

He drew his arm back and tossed the tags up to the molten evening sky. The instant his hand was empty he felt a piercing in his heart, the intensity of which was greater than that of any bullet he'd ever taken. Briefly, the metal tags caught the tiniest glint of waning light as they turned in the air, and then they were lost until he saw and heard the faint splash in the ocean a few dozen yards away. The heart-piercing pain lifted cleanly, as if the atmosphere had somehow absorbed it, leaving a lofty kind of peace in its wake.

You deserve to be somewhere open and free now, my brother.

And where, Jake wondered, would that be? Was there a place in Heaven for renegades like Delaney and himself? Could the Great Spirit reconcile and balance the good they did with the bad? How dark was too dark?

He wiped his eyes, took a deep centering breath, and headed for the cockpit.

SEATED AT THE WELL-appointed nav station below deck, Jake had switched to autopilot while he studied the Nobeltec charting on a Dell laptop computer. The boat's rich cherry interior had two cabins, one fore and one aft, and a head with shower. The spacious salon featured a large pedestal table with smartly upholstered settee, next to which was the fully equipped galley with stove, refrigerator-freezer, icemaker, dishwasher, and microwave. An abundance of storage was incorporated in shelves along the hull, drawers beneath the berths, cupboards, lockers, and bookshelves. An entertainment center had been built in opposite the nav station, including a TV, DVD and CD stereo system.

Tom Petty was crooning from the speakers now as Jake got up to stretch, his concentration faltering. He tipped a bottle of Evian up to his mouth and, peering through one of the skylights above, saw that it was getting dark. He slid back into his seat at the chart table, finished the

Nobeltec and checked the other navigational instrumentation. Like the rest of the yacht, the nav station was loaded with state-of-the-art technology, electronics from Autohelm, Brookes & Gatehouse, Garmin, Simrad, and Furuno: autopilot, wind instruments, speedometers, logs, depth sounder, digital barometer, electric compass, GPS, loran, radar, direction finders, electronic charts and video displays. Immarsat dominated the communications setup, with the added support of wireless weather, HF, VHF, and SSB radios.

Mindlessly, more out of routine than conscious action, Jake's fingers tapped a few keys on the Dell Inspiron, and several moments later he was looking at the Google screen for Gmail. Inputting his personal login information, he waited for the connection to complete. From his BlackBerry he already knew he had a backlog of email, so seeing all the bolded messages came as no surprise.

As he scanned the contents of his Inbox, he felt a spiky sliver of dread. There were fifty or more messages, some from acquaintances and some spam mail, but there was one that stood out from the rest, one that cinched his chest and quickened his heartbeat.

It was from Delaney, sent over a week ago when he had been in Bogotá—*alive* in Bogotá. How had he missed that?

Jake could feel a twitchy sensation starting in his hand as his fingers rested lightly on the keyboard. His first impulse was to delete it unread, which was what he immediately did to the spam mail. He saved the other emails for later reading, which left Delaney's message bold and isolated on the screen. He sat staring at the subject line.

It said simply: *Mañana.*

He clicked on it and Delaney's words flashed onto the screen in minute 10pt Arial font, his silenced voice now speaking, from cyberspace. Unlike Jake, whose emails were typically succinct, even terse, Delaney had always been flamboyantly verbose in his messages.

Cryptically, this one said only: *Sorry, Bubba. Más Tarde.*

Jake read and reread the words numbly, senselessly. *Sorry? Sorry for what? For whatever the hell he had been involved in? Sorry for getting himself killed?* He wanted to pound the video screen, extract the rest of the message from whatever vault held it hostage—because there had to be more. Where were the words? Where were the answers? Finally, he logged off the computer and strolled across the salon to the cabin.

It was spartanly tidy with a layout that was both functional and comfortable, the beds and other upholstery in matching nautical-patterned blues. It was carpeted and there were a few sailing-themed pictures on the cabin walls. At a glance, there was nothing conspicuously Delaney in view, but as Jake entered he could again feel his friend's presence in the personal effects that he knew were there. Things like the two framed photographs—one of them standing on deck after christening the boat, the other taken at Fort Bragg, the two of them in uniform—both representing big life-defining moments. Looking at the photo from Bragg, he felt a sad sweep of nostalgia, thinking how young they had been then. Before the world had really taken hold and installed its ambushes, booby traps, and complications. He sighed dejectedly as he sifted through Delaney's personal items. Clothing, a ball cap or two, a cache of Bazooka bubblegum, a round of ammo for the H&K pistol, loose coins and wadded paper currency from international travels, an extra pair of sunglasses, a box of condoms. At the bottom of a drawer filled with some t-shirts and underwear, he found the jewel case for an old 38 Special CD, *Resolution*; Delaney's favorite genre of music had been vintage rock. Tucking the clothing neatly back in place, he returned to the salon and was about to search for the missing CD when the jewel case popped open.

There was a key taped inside.

Removing the key from the case, he turned it over in his hand, studying it closely. It appeared to be a key for a bank safe deposit box, but there was nothing on the key or in the CD case to identify the name or location of the bank. He wondered if it was the bank they used in Nassau, but he was not sure he wanted it to be. He put the key on a shelf at the nav station and climbed the companionway steps to the cockpit.

As he prepared for night sailing, changing to a smaller headsail and switching on the navigation lights, the music of Tom Petty drifted up from the speakers below deck. The song about starting over after the secrets, after the heartbreak.

Now, standing at the steering wheel, gazing up at the moon and stars shining like thousands of headlights on a night-darkened highway, he felt no more sadness and no more grief. He felt only anger and conviction.

Resolution, how ironic. Yes, he could be patient, he could wait…but not forever. There were answers out there somewhere, and he would find them.

As the Beneteau cruised through the dark, moving smoothly from a broad reach to a moderate run, Jake thought: *I have a start—I have a key—and I have somewhere to go.*

ON THE AFTERNOON OF the following day, after finding a slip in the crowded Yacht Haven Marina in Nassau harbor and grabbing a few hours' sleep, Jake headed down East Bay Street. As always, it teemed with exuberant tourists set loose from the continuous procession of giant cruise ships. They trundled busily in and out of the restaurants and shops, stopping to snap pictures or converse with other tourists. Walking casually along the street, past the restored colonial buildings painted in pastel seashell colors with their broad white columned fronts, he tried not to think about the task that lay ahead. Instead, at least for a short while, he enjoyed the mild sunshine smiling down on the festival of life in the popular harbor town. When he arrived at the five-story building that housed the Bahamian branch of Banco de Bogotá, he felt his pulse quicken.

The fact that compensation from some of their contract work had been deposited in a Bahamian bank was initially a fortuitous maneuver, but in retrospect it was a move Jake certainly did not regret.

Often referred to as the Zurich of the tropics, the Bahamas have built a dynasty of offshore banking centers with over 200 billion dollars in US assets alone distributed throughout four hundred or more banks. Their popularity in banking and investment thrives on a stable economy and strict enforcement of confidentiality laws. Unfortunately, it is also a haven for money-laundering drug kingpins. The Bahamas have no taxes on income, capital gains, inheritance, or sales, and to engage in offshore banking or establish a trust requires less information than the renewal of a driver's license. Another plus for elicit trade.

Heavy-footed, Jake climbed the steps to the building's entrance, stepped inside, and took the elevator to the bank's top-floor office suite. Inside, he waited until one of the account representatives was available and then took a seat at his desk. The nameplate read Nelson Bonamy. He was a young island native with a courteous manner, and greeted Jake with a ready smile. Jake took out his bankbook and placed it on the clerk's desk.

"Good afternoon, sir," Nelson Bonamy said, his voice accented with the distinctive Bahamian lilt. "Are you making a deposit or withdrawal today?"

"I don't know," Jake said uncertainly, realizing that he had not thought that far ahead. "Can you just tell me what our"—there was a catch in his throat as he corrected—"*my* balance is?"

Still smiling pleasantly, Nelson Bonamy swiveled his chair around to the computer on his side desk and tapped in the account number. When the information appeared on the screen, he copied it onto a piece of notepaper which he peeled from the pad and handed to Jake.

Jake looked at the figure neatly printed on the paper with its yellow bird-like insignia, and was dumbfounded. "Are you sure you pulled up the right account?" he asked the young man. "Can you check it again?"

Bonamy shrugged unconcernedly. "Certainly, it is no problem." Again he input the information, tapping his keyboard until the data had finished processing. This time he sent the information to his printer, plucking the sheet of paper that slid onto the tray. He turned back to Jake, his expression unchanged. "The balance is correct, Mr. Tyler. Here is a copy of your account activity to date. Did you want to make a transaction?"

Jake accepted the computer printout, which he folded and tucked into the bankbook, too overwhelmed to think about it now. "No, but there is something else I hope you can help me with."

"Certainly."

Jake produced the safe deposit box key and handed it to the clerk. He could see by the flash of recognition on Bonamy's face that the key was one of theirs. Before he could ask, the young man stood up from his desk and pointed to another room.

"The safe deposit boxes are in there. Would you like to access yours?"

Jake nodded dumbly and followed Bonamy to the room. About fifteen minutes later, he was walking back down East Bay Street with the contents of the box in the pocket of his navy shorts. There had been two items—a sealed envelope with his name on it, penned in Delaney's haphazardly looping handwriting, and a computer USB flash drive—and Jake had immediately decided to deal with them both later, much later on the boat. After he'd had time to absorb the fact that their bank balance had unaccountably expanded from under seventy-five thousand dollars to well over a million.

JAKE SPENT THE NEXT few hours shopping in town, aimlessly picking up supplies for the boat. He had dinner at a lively harbor side restaurant called The Poop Deck, dining on fresh grouper that he barely tasted, and then returned to the marina. He refueled the boat and worked above deck, industriously inspecting the sails, sheets and lines, spars and riggings, and halyards, until it began to get dark. Before he finished, he did a routine check of the engine, as well as the electrical and water systems. Then, mired in the gloom of recurring dread, he retired below deck for the night.

After showering, he sat at the nav station with the laptop. The bankbook with the updated account activity, the envelope, and the flash drive were spread on the table beside it. He looked first at the account information. The most recent deposits corresponded with their downtime during the counternarcotics contract. There was a deposit six months ago for $50,000, followed by another a month afterward for $100,000. Then the amounts steadily increased. $200,000, $250,000, $300,000. He rubbed his eyes, not believing what he was seeing. He plugged the flash drive in, waited for the operating software to load, and opened a file labeled with a series of letters. The file contained an Excel spreadsheet with a list of numbers in illogical sequences. He stared at them, tried to make some sense of them, implored them to mean something. But they meant nothing. They were just numbers in neatly formatted columns. Next, he opened the envelope, and found a letter. It was dated several weeks ago.

Jake,

If you are reading this now, it means my run has come to an end. I wish

I was telling you this years from now, on a beach in the Caribbean, getting wasted on Cuervo, but reality bites...You are probably pissed as hell with me by now, having discovered the balance in our bank account. I know you'll never understand why I did it—I'm not sure I understand myself—but what's done is done. You know how you were always saying you wanted to do good things, maybe establish camps for troubled and underprivileged kids? Conduct some mercy missions on our own? Well, that's not exactly how it started, but rather what it turned into. I took an opportunity to turn something evil into something good...kind of like Robin Hood, taking from the rich to give to the poor...only this was taking from the bad to give to the good. If only it could have remained that simple—obviously, it did not. Not only do these guys not play by the rules, they make them up as they go along. The deal recently changed into something so mind-blowing and heinous that I've got to get out. The problem is I don't know how. That's the double jeopardy...once you're in, you're in it for the long haul. But I am going to try, after this next run—and I can only hope for God's forgiveness, because I'll never forgive myself. If you're reading this now, obviously I didn't make it. So my challenge to you, Jake, is make it count for something.

See you in the great wide open, my brother.

Haskell

Everything felt so still Jake could hear himself breathing, and suddenly the lights seemed too bright, the silence too loud. Delaney *had* been dealing with the narcotraffickers; in his words, taking from the bad to give to the good. Like Robin Hood. Jake felt a bone-penetrating chill. And what had he meant by *something so mind-blowing and heinous?*

He laid his head on the table and fought to suppress his rage, rage for what, at whom, he wasn't sure.

At some point, night matured and a new day was born, in much the same way good had transformed into bad, but he did not really remember when the transition occurred. It just had.

He was ready to return to Costa Rica.

Needed to.

17

HE STOOD WATCHING HER for what might have been hours, captivated by the way the air swirled by the ceiling fan gently lifted strands of her hair from her face, gently lifted them in the air and then gently let them back down to rest briefly on her smooth skin. Time suspended, the world evolving around the paddles of the ceiling fan overhead, turning, turning, swirling the air, touching and tousling her hair. Drawing him in to that intimate dance of light in the darkness. Her eyelashes flicked ever so slightly. In the moon's pale sigh, her curls looked like some silken blend of silver and gold, so luminous it could have been fairy dust. Her small lips were barely parted, the breath drawn between them so faint yet he could hear every intake and exhale. The cotton pillowcase dimpled with the blow of her breath. A tiny freckle dotted a place below her cheek like a miniscule imperfection in a piece of fine bone china, and he watched as a pale wisp of hair fell over it, then lifted, then fell over it again. The moon loved her, caressed her through the window, traced every nuance of her body, lingered on the place right below her neck and trailed down below the edge of the sheets.

Light in the darkness.

He leaned down and touched his lips to the place the moon caressed, wanted to follow its beams beyond, but pulled back. Reached and brushed his fingertips across the silken strands of hair, let them feel the faint warmth of the breath blowing from her lips onto the pillowcase.

Life. Fragile and complicated, innocent and simple. Beautiful,

beautiful life, drifting in the dreams of sleep. So close, so far, just within reach.

He felt the stillness of the room, the protective vigilance of the moon, the delicate beating of a sleeping heart. He felt the roar of war fade far away as he watched strands of her hair lift and fall in the moonlight. Lift and fall, lift and fall, brushing so lightly against her face.

The moon was smitten with her face.

SHE AWOKE WITH THE sun warming her skin. But just barely. It was early. The room was dim with the same shadows, the same quiet, of the past few weeks. And yet, something was different.

Coffee.

She smelled coffee.

Callie got dressed and cautiously tiptoed down the stairs. Her heart seemed to be beating louder than the foyer clock was ticking. A big and ornate Bulova. She stepped off the last riser and rounded the corner. Caught her breath in her throat.

Jake sat at the kitchen bar, a mug of coffee cupped in one hand, the other resting on his thigh. His eyes were honed on the spot where she now stood. A smile turned the corners of his mouth upward.

He said, "Hello, love." His voice was low and full of affection.

All she could say was, "Jake." Her heart was beating like erratic tribal drums and it filled her head as the Bulova ticked steadily by the stairs.

His smile broadened. "You look well." He stood, patted the seat beside him, watched her as she came over. She was wearing a white cotton tank top trimmed in lace, an eyelet skirt flowing below "Everything been okay?" he asked, reaching over the bar for the coffee and pouring some into a mug for her.

Sitting, she said, "Yes. Yes, it has." She smiled. "I'm glad you're back."

"Me, too." He looked at her. "Me, too."

She took a small sip of coffee, placing the mug back on the bar in front of her. He put his hand on hers. It was warm and firm and the touch sent a tingling sensation through a million tiny nerves.

"You know what I'd like?" he asked. She tilted her head, and he said, "To go for a walk on the beach."

✳   ✳   ✳   ✳   ✳

THEY HAD BEEN STROLLING the beach for a little over an hour, holding hands, wading in and out of the ocean's lick, when Jake's cell phone vibrated. He had Callie talking about the book, so he ignored it. Not even a minute later, it vibrated again.

"Shit," he muttered, then apologized to her and unclipped the phone. The number displayed was local, so this time he answered. "Yes...what, you're here now? Where are you staying?" He heaved a sigh laden with displeasure. "Well, I wasn't expecting you today. I actually just got in, but yes, okay." He glanced at his watch. "I will meet you there at ten-thirty. See you then."

"You have to go somewhere?" Callie asked, her disappointment hanging in the air like mist after a heavy rain.

The expression on her face scraped his heart, and he was aware of a dull ache spreading through him. "Afraid so. Remember those guys I told you about who have contracted with me to help them on a television project? I didn't expect them for another few days, but they arrived early and want to meet. But that's all I'm going to do with them today. When I get done, we'll go out, grab a bite, take a drive, talk. Okay?"

She nodded, they squeezed hands, and he retreated to the house. For the first time, she wondered where Jake's friend was and why he'd not accompanied Jake back from Colombia.

ON FIRST IMPRESSION, JAKE thought that the two television guys could not have made an odder pair. One was an outspoken "Jersey boy" clad in Levi's, chambray shirt, and boots; the other a chatty London East Ender wearing Paul Smith coordinates that were, to Jake's eye, anything but coordinating. Both were about Jake's age; the American had short brown hair worn spiky, the Brit had longish dark blond hair pulled into a ponytail. But the more he listened to them talk over each other, gesturing with their hands and punctuating each other's sentences, he decided they were a strangely compatible fit. They were also quite entertaining and engaging, and despite its quirkiness, their project interested him.

Eddie Falcone and Curran Niles had, literally, just flown into San José's Juan Santamaría International Airport, rented a car, and driven straight to Dominical. They were staying at the Villas Río Mar where they now sat, sipping coffee in the bungalow restaurant.

Falcone took his coffee black; Niles dumped enough cream and sugar in his to make fudge.

"The producers envision a concept of the *Survivor* ilk, but much edgier," Niles was saying, stirring his caffeine confection. He was fair-complected with enough natural color in his lips, cheeks, and eyelashes to fool a makeup artist. A gold loop the size of a dime hung from the lobe of his left ear.

Jake snickered. "Edgier than *Survivor*," he repeated, making no attempt to hide his sarcasm.

"I take it you don't find *Survivor* edgy?"

"Hardly," he scoffed. "But go on."

"Think lost people on a scavenger hunt, being hunted," Niles explained, monitoring Jake's face for reaction. When his face remained neutral, Niles said, "Actually, I liked my idea a lot better. I suggested a kind of international spy game."

"Now that, I like," Jake said, adding, "my company does Spy Games."

"Yeah, well, we've got to do what the producers want," Falcone remarked dryly.

"How would the show start?" Jake asked.

"They're planning to have the contestants flown in to New York first, then to London. Once there, they will attend a ritzy banquet and be given individual itineraries. For the scavenger hunt. Only once they disperse and begin, they will be captured." Niles brightened, noting a flash of curiosity in Jake's expression. "After they're captured, they will be blindfolded and put on another plane."

"Sounds like a pricey production," Jake commented.

"It is," Falcone agreed. "This is the same production team that did *Strike Back LA*." The movie to which Eddie Falcone referred had been an action blockbuster from the previous summer, the plot centering around a counter-terrorism team avenging an assault on Los Angeles.

Motioning the waitress for coffee refills, Curran Niles continued.

"Here's the best part," he said, rubbing his hands together, his big blue eyes filling with the animation of a pinball table. "They are then dropped in the middle of an Amazon jun—"

Jake put his hand up, his jaw tightening. "Hold up there, bro. If you're about to say what I think you are, we might have to stop right now."

Falcone was instantly defensive, color rising in his face. "What the hell are you talking about? You said we could go anywhere on the planet, your exact words. We're depending on you here."

"Yes, I did say anywhere," Jake said tightly, letting out a measured breath. "It just didn't occur to me you'd want to go to the place I just returned from."

"You just returned from the Amazon?" Niles asked.

"I did."

"That is a bloody coincidence, isn't it?"

"That's not what I'd call it," Jake murmured. Straightening his posture and looking them both squarely in the eyes, he said, "Okay, gents, what is it you want me to do for you?"

"Initially, we want to get with you and your team on the action elements of the show. We need your technical expertise. For that, I guess we can work around here," Falcone said with a wide sweep of his arm. "Then, we want to head south of the border, scout locations, see what we've got to contend with. The sooner, the better."

Jake eyed the two of them, saw their eager sincerity and thought, *No big deal, it's what I do.* But somewhere, deep in his gut, dread was setting up camp.

DELANEY'S OLD FOUR-WHEEL drive Toyota pickup was battered but moved with relative ease down the Costanera Sur. As Jake drove south, headed toward the Osa Peninsula, conversation with Callie encompassed the book and the television project. On parting with Falcone and Niles, Jake had promised to start work with them in a day or so, adamantly declining their request to get together again for a dinner session tonight.

He glanced over at Callie whose gaze alternated between him and the boundless blue Pacific as they sped along in the brilliant sunshine.

When their eyes met, a shy smile would appear and a soft flush would bloom in her face. The ache inside him was slowly intensifying.

His destination took close to three hours, going south along the Interamericana, looping west at Palmar Norte, then south again toward the Golfo Dulce. It was mid-afternoon when he brought the pickup to a halt near the water's edge. They had arrived at a small collection of bright yellow buildings trimmed in white.

The Banana Bay Marina in Golfito sits off the edge of yet another beautiful Costa Rican rainforest, nestled in a deep, draft gulf. Its floating docks are typically filled with serious-looking sport yachts, at least one over 125 feet, and the lively Bilge Bar and Grill services a steady stream of tourists and locals as fishing bounties are compared.

When Jake and Callie passed through the gate, she drew keen looks from all who were assembled around the marina area. At Jake's hinting, Callie had worn a lavender slip dress and now, surrounded by locals and tourists—mostly fishing enthusiasts hauling rods and reels and toting buckets of bait—she felt awkwardly out of place.

Jake put an arm around her, waiting as the marina manager approached. Young and tanned with sandy brown hair, he wore a t-shirt with the marina logo and was accompanied by a friendly dog that appeared to be a mix of Boxer and something else. The brown-and-white dog sidled up to Callie, wagging his stub tail. She bent down to pet him as the marina manager said, "His name is Scupper and I think he's in love." To Jake, he said, "You're all set. Stocked, fueled, ready to roll. The end slip."

"Thanks, Bruce. Appreciate everything."

"Anytime." He whistled to the boxer, who reluctantly followed, and retreated to the marina office.

Jake led Callie down to the docks. When it became apparent what he had in mind, her embarrassment gave way to awe as she stared at the forty-six-foot sailboat he was striding toward. She stopped, both hands going to her open mouth. He turned on heel, grinning. "What's wrong?"

"We're going on...*that*?"

"That was the idea. You said you liked boats."

"I do, but..." she stammered.

He backtracked, snatched her hand, and led her to the yacht, a sleek blue Oyster. Jake climbed on board and was eagerly assisted by a young Latino dockhand in helping Callie over the rail. He got her settled in the cockpit and spent the next thirty minutes becoming familiar with the cruiser, navigating northwest down the bay toward the main channel, only raising the sails when they had cleared other boat traffic. Callie watched and listened, her attention rapt as he explained the basics of sailing, pointing out dolphins briskly stitching the ocean surface alongside them.

When the shore was a distant silhouette of palms and rainforest, Jake dropped anchor. The deep water was calm, the sun easing down. The sounds of splashing dolphins and cawing seabirds began to lessen as the light faded, while the chatter of howler monkeys drifted across from shore. Bringing drinks from the galley, Jake sat beside her and sighed contentedly. "How's this?" he asked.

"It's beyond words, Jake," Callie said, momentarily hypnotized by the sun's fire dance on the water.

Sipping from his gin and tonic, he said, "I'm glad you stayed on and really pleased that you've gotten such a good start on the book." He let a few minutes pass, then said, "Now, tell me about you, Callie."

Feeling small and cornered, she asked uncertainly, "What do you mean? We…we've talked about…what do you want to know?" And he could feel the wall going up.

"I want to know about *you*," he said, facing her and taking her hands in his, looking directly into her eyes.

"There's nothing else really," she started, casting her eyes downward to her lap.

He lifted her chin until their eyes connected again. "Yes, there is. Talk to me, love."

"If you mean…"

When she faltered, he nodded. "Yes, that's what I mean."

After taking several steadying breaths, she finally said, "There was a man. Right before I came to Costa Rica." She bit her lip and her eyes moistened. She wanted to stop right there, it was already too much, but she could see he had no intention of letting it go. "He worked with me at a marketing company. He seemed nice and, I don't know, one day he started talking to me. Pretty soon he went out of his way to find reasons to be around me at work. He asked me out and we dated a little. I hadn't really dated anyone before, so I didn't know how it was supposed to go."

"When you say you hadn't really dated before, are you saying no sex?" he asked bluntly, trying to keep incredulity from his expression. She shrank visibly from his candid probe but nodded, almost imperceptibly, her head dropping. Again, he lifted her face back up, forced her to maintain eye contact. More gently, he said, "Go on, love."

"After a while things didn't seem right. His attitude changed and he became intense...in a bad way." She sipped her drink shakily, badly wanting to stop now.

"How so?"

"He got very agitated when anybody else was around me, male or female. He called constantly, wrote notes, sent emails. He wanted to know everything I did, everyone I talked to, everywhere I went. If he called and I didn't answer, he'd come to my house and want to know where I'd been. Sometimes, I'd be driving somewhere and I'd notice him following me. Before long, he was following me everywhere. At one point he was convinced I was seeing someone else and became obsessed with finding out who it was. I wasn't seeing anyone, but he would watch my house, interrogate my neighbors and co-workers.

"It was all so frightening that it got to the point I couldn't concentrate on my job, I couldn't eat or sleep. But I was afraid to break up with him."

"Was he violent?" When she didn't answer, Jake asked, "Did he hurt you, Callie?"

Tears trickled from her eyes and she gave a slow nod. "He completely transformed in just a few weeks, became vicious and vindictive. But he would also have these intervals where he'd be nice again, as if the hostility didn't exist. I was trying to get the courage to break up with him when he told me we were going to get married."

"He said you were going to get married?" Jake repeated.

Wiping the tears, she said, "Yes. And he had it all planned. The next day I asked a neighbor to come over, be with me when I broke up with him."

"And how did he take it?"

There was a long pause and tears sprung anew. Finally, she said, "That's why I left Savannah. And it's another reason I'm here, in Costa

Rica."

She cried quietly, and he held her until the tears stopped.

AS THE RETIRING MELON-colored sun traded places with the paler wedge of moon and the stars strung their lights across an indigo sky, Jake had retreated to the galley to retrieve a tray stacked with fruit, cheese, cold cuts, and bread. After one more question, an all-important one to Jake, the conversation about Callie's past had ended; the question was whether there had been sex. With great reluctance, Callie said yes.

Jake had sensed there was more, maybe even much more, but he knew it had taken a lot for her to tell him what she did. It was a beginning.

Now, as their dinner settled and he brought them fresh drinks— Callie had all but abandoned the first in the painful throes of her story— Jake reached into the pocket of his shorts and came up with a fistful of tiny shells, linked into a necklace and set with a small heart carved from opal. "When I was in Nassau the other day, I saw this and thought you might like it."

Touching it with her fingertips, she said, "Jake, it's beautiful."

"Well, let's put it on." He slipped it around her neck, fastened the catch. Stepping back to admire it, his eyes were admiring her instead. The moon was romancing her again, glowing over her skin and from within her eyes.

"You were in Nassau? The Bahamas?"

Jake inhaled and exhaled, feeling his own defenses harden. Quietly, he said, "Yes. I needed some time. Callie, the friend whose house we're staying in...he died in Colombia."

"He...*died*? Oh, Jake. Oh, Jake, I'm sorry. How...how did it happen?"

"I'd rather not talk about it just now, okay?" Softly, he said, "Come here, love." And reached for her.

Kissed her.

The taste of warm honey filled his mouth again, the sweet ambrosia on her lips and in her mouth flooded his senses, and suddenly every sensual and sexual element of his making seemed to peel away, levitate to another place. Something totally unfamiliar was taking over. On some level, even as he was surrendering to whatever was taking him, he knew he'd never intended for this to happen, had truly doubted physical compatibility with her. Because they were so different. He had done things with women most men could only imagine in their wildest, most erotic fantasies. He'd been with all kinds of women the world over, French, Russian, Oriental, African, even a voodoo priestess. She was not like any of them. And yet, with all the experiences and all the relationships, all he wanted right now was so basic, so simple...so utterly simple.

He wanted to be where the moon had been last night. Where the moon was right now.

He took her hand and led her down the companionway steps, across the gleaming wood floor of the galley, into the master cabin. The lighting was dimmed, moonlight filtering through the Plexiglas panels. The boat swayed in the night's mild currents ever so slightly.

He tugged his shirt off and shucked his shorts. Crossed to her, slipped his hands around her back. Tenderly, he unzipped the sheer lavender slip dress and slid the spaghetti straps from her shoulders. The dress cascaded to the floor. Callie stood, shivering though the air was warm, wearing only the shell necklace and lacy white panties. She crossed her arms modestly over her bare breasts.

Smiling, Jake said, "Don't be shy. You are beautiful." Unfolding her arms, he gazed at her and caught his breath. Though small, her breasts were perfectly shaped, pale pink nipples already budding in texture and color. Below her slim waist and hips, smooth, slender legs. "So beautiful," he murmured.

She was blinking at him, her breath coming rapidly. The muted sound of water lapping against the boat's hull filled the sensually charged quiet.

"Come here, angel," he said gently, drawing her over and into the cabin's big bed. She held back at first, but his grasp was compelling, his dark eyes hypnotic, and she folded into his arms.

He removed his underwear, slid her lacy panties off, his mouth and hands hungrily exploring her. She shuddered and squirmed under his touch, making indiscernible little noises. But when she felt his hardness against her for the first time, fear rose up swift and fierce like a sudden headwind. Feeling her tense, he kissed her more tenderly, saying, "Relax for me, sweetheart...just relax." Rising up, he looked into her anxious face and stroked ringlets of her hair. "You have to trust me, Callie. No matter what has happened before, I would never hurt you."

Her hands came up, timidly touching his face, brushing through his hair and then slipping down to his neck.

The simple touch was at once so delicate and sensual that his back arched in pleasure. He bit down on his lip. Sliding his hand between her thighs and nudging them apart, he stroked her soft skin, placing light but lingering kisses from her neck to her waist. The raw sexual predator in him wanted to ravage, hard and fast and rough, but this strange new feeling was intriguing. And ruling. Something he'd never felt before, both frightening and exhilarating. This new instinct, driven by emotion and need he'd never known, was making him slow down, stoking the primal lust with something deeply spiritual. Deeply hungry. Deeply vulnerable.

He took her hands, guiding them slowly to touch him. On contact, her small warm hands were trembling and tentative, but the soft touch electrified him and he stifled a groan. When he released her hands, they went to his chest, first in a kind of restraining gesture and then, as she gingerly moved them across the taut muscles, in a more receptive way. Meeting his intense gaze, seeing the broad smile on his handsome face, she reached up and stroked his hair again.

He drew her legs up around him, felt the moist warmth in between. Reaching down, he slid a finger across and into the wetness, pausing at the peak with a light caress that caused her to shudder. When he pushed firmly into her, she gasped and tensed again. "Relax, sweetheart," he soothed, "relax. Take a deep breath." She did, and he immediately felt her muscles slacken. "Slow, deep breath," he repeated, and eased himself further inside.

"Jake," she whispered, quivering inside and out.

"Am I hurting you, love?"

"No, but I'm scared," she rasped, holding onto him as if she feared falling off the world.

And he knew why. He could feel her body beginning to respond as he moved inside her, the rhythm slow and deliberate but gradually increasing in pace. "It's okay, Callie. I need you to let go of the fear. Will you do that for me, angel? Open up your beautiful self and let me all the way inside. Come on, angel, open up to me." And as she did, he plunged deeper, moaning with the building pleasure. He was thrusting harder, driving to an ecstasy so intense it felt supernatural. It went beyond the physical sexual connection; he felt as though he was plugged into her heart, and with every beat he was making love to that sacred inner core. At the same time, he felt the core of his aching emptiness filling with her, finding secret places within himself he never knew existed. All at once he felt bigger, harder, unconquerable—but the emotional vulnerability exposed also made him feel weak, made him yearn to keep taking her, as much as he could get, as much as he could have.

As he had entered her, roughly at first, then more gently as he met resistance, she felt the pulsating power of him inside her and her mind went into a chaotic frenzy. She had never known this, these intense sensations and emotions, and at first she was desperately afraid. But she was being drawn closer and closer to him, being pulled toward a precipice she was terrified to scale.

Despite the fear, she was losing herself to him now. "No, Jake," she said weakly, a muffled cry coming from the back of her throat.

"Come on, sweetheart, don't be afraid, don't fight it," he urged, and felt the hot, wet center of her embrace him in a torrential rush, tightening, tightening, tightening. "Oh God..."

He groaned as the pleasure became almost unbearable, waves of bliss crashing over and over and over. Every cavity of his heart, mind, and body filled with her as she took him and held him.

At the height, her hands squeezed his waist and shoulders and she was half-sobbing, half-panting, pleading his name.

The release, for them both, was like plunging down a thundering waterfall and then floating over rapids. Feeling the rush continue as the roar and speed ebbed away. And then the stillness that dropped like midnight's final blanket quieted everything but the rhythmic beating of their hearts.

He rolled onto his side, kissing her, pulling her close. Still lost in the scent and feel and essence of her, his spirit still gliding somewhere high above himself.

Somewhere high, so high in the light. Life and light in the darkness

...and something more.

Outside, the moon pined for its lover lost.

18

JAKE WAS IN A strange place as he stood in the cockpit of the cruiser, watching dawn take her first sultry yawn over the cobalt water, sliding diamond-covered fingers through its ripples. As if electrified by the caress, the sky blushed and filled her face with a fervid flush of mango that lightened by layers until the morning's blue seeped through. Sunrises, he thought, were like a blood infusion of the soul, a time of spiritual solitude for rewiring the mind and nurturing the spirit.

It could also be a time to delve haunting questions. As he did now.

He was not sure what had happened last night, to him or to her. And instead of basking in the euphoria that his physical and emotional self still felt, he was troubled. Because what had happened between them had altered him—deeply. He knew it had altered her. The question was, how? And could he embrace it? Most worrisome of all to him was the fragility of the life that now hung somewhere within the balance of their new intimacy. Because in the dead reckoning of hard truths exposed at dawn, he was realizing that he might have to let go.

He was also realizing that he might not be able to.

He felt the air shift ever so delicately, a tingle under his skin, and turned to see her standing by the companionway. Wearing the slip dress, curls tousled around a sleep-softened face, she glowed like a vision from a dream.

His mind was reluctant but his eyes and his heart were riveted. She looked like a fawn caught in an open thicket, not sure whether to flee or step forward.

She took the step, and he extended his hand.

The morning opened up around them and spread day across the ocean.

JAKE TOOK THE BOAT out around the southern tip of Cabo Matapalo and they spent most of the day sailing in the tropical splendor of the Costa Rican Pacific. A small pod of bottlenose dolphins joined them for a swim, and watching Callie's enchantment filled him with a joy he could not recall ever feeling. She exclaimed in surprise and glee as the dolphins nudged and brushed against her. She pet their smooth, warm bodies and, at Jake's urging, took hold of their dorsal fins and let them guide her through the water. Hearing the music of her laughter, the excitement in her voice, feeling her in his arms enveloped by the warm cocoon of water, transported him back to where he'd been last night.

Midday, they lunched on snapper Jake caught after releasing a luminous silver-and-blue sailfish the size of a surfboard that almost pulled him off the boat. Afterward, they sunned themselves atop the cabin trunk roof, dozing intermittently, hands intertwined.

At one point, Jake said, "Callie, how do you feel about last night?" He felt her hand stiffen in his, then quiver, heard a shaky intake of breath.

She took so long to respond, he was about to ask again when she said, "I never imagined it was like that." She rolled toward him, gingerly placing her hand on his chest. His skin was comfortingly warm from the sun, but the hardness of the muscles beneath started a new tremor in her fingertips. Timidly exploring the smooth, hard landscape there, she crossed thin ripples and ruts of scars and a divot of something deeper, more intrusive. She pulled back, grazing the gold ring that pierced one of his nipples. Her voice seemed to float from somewhere else as she asked, "Didn't that hurt?"

"Uh, yeah, " he said with a low chuckle. "Being really drunk at the time made it bearable. But you're changing the subject, missy. You never imagined it was like what?"

"It was like...what I think skydiving must feel like."

He grinned, gave her hand a squeeze. "Well now, maybe you should let me take you skydiving next so you can find out."

"Are you trying to kill me?"

He laughed. "No, love, just open you up to the world."

And me, an inner voice added. She had been clearly traumatized by what had happened with the guy who'd obsessed on her. He suspected there might be something more from the past that had scarred her, left her fearful of feeling and tentative of living. The two of them were as different as two people could be. He had himself been scarred, deeper than he'd like to admit, but the experiences had toughened him. Maybe too much. As a result, or perhaps not, he lived like he expected to die tomorrow, surviving by constantly moving—like a shark. Fast and furious with raw appetites he fed on flyby. And then she came along and…and the rest of that thought tumbled over the edge of his mind like rocks skittering off the side of a cliff. He had no idea, no idea at all, what came next.

Aloud, he said, "You really never had sex before that guy?"

She shook her head.

"And with him, it was…?"

She shook her head again, looked away. Finally she said, "I just never imagined…"

"No, I guess not," he said, and in his mind he heard the thought that had eluded him. *And everything changes.*

AFTER RETURNING TO THE beach house, Jake responded to the multiple voice messages from Falcone and Niles. They were eager to get started and wanted to have a dinner meeting. Watching Callie sway on the porch swing, her dangling bare feet casting thin shadows that floated over the wooden floor planks, he sighed. *And everything changes.*

Bringing Callie with him, Jake joined Falcone and Niles back at the Río Mar restaurant. The duo was charmed by Callie and spent the time waiting on their food discussing her book. When they began to get more inquisitive, making her squirm uncomfortably, Jake deflected talk back to them.

"So," he said, draping an arm over the back of Callie's chair, fingers lightly massaging her neck, "how did you two get into this project?"

"Bit of a funny story, actually," Niles replied, casting Falcone a bemused look. "I was working for a tour coordinator in London—I've been in the music business ever since I started working—and last year during that big concert for disaster relief, headlined by Springsteen and U2, I ran into this bloke." He crooked a thumb in Falcone's direction. "Eddie was working for the trucking company that was moving Springsteen's equipment. I'm a huge fan of Springsteen's and had never met him, so I was running 'round, bugging everybody I could find, wanting to meet him. Word got back to Eddie that there was this annoying bloke going around pissing everybody off, so he finds me and says he'll take me to Springsteen's dressing room. Needless to say, I was thrilled. He takes me down this dingy hall, past all the activity and commotion, to this unmarked door. He opens it and lets me go in first, but then I hear it slam behind me. Turns out, it's some kind of electrical closet and it locks from the outside. After banging on the door and screaming my bloody lungs out for a while, I notice a fire alarm."

He giggled boyishly. "When the arena had to be evacuated, Eddie had no choice but to come back and let me out. You know, just in case there was a real fire." Niles laughed more boisterously. "Eventually, the promoter found out what happened since they were able to trace the alarm back to the source and I had left my tour jacket in the closet. I was pretty pissed off at the time, so I spilled. We both got fired.

"So we're having at each other when this guy comes up and says he's looking for a couple of mates to work on a television show. Seems he found the whole fiasco rather entertaining. Liked our moxie. Or something like that."

"Yeah, something like that," Falcone mumbled, but he was grinning, too.

Appetizing platters of seafood and beef with accompanying vegetables and sauces kept them engaged for a while, the conversation shifting to the television project.

"Here's what I propose, gents," Jake said in between bites. "First, I'll take you around Costa Rica for activity ideas, introduce you to some of my associates who will be working with you over the course of this assignment. Then, as you requested, we'll head for the Amazon to scout locations. Have you given any thought to security, medical services, translators, and the like?"

Falcone and Niles exchanged vacuous glances. Falcone said, "You do all that, I take it?"

"I do. I can put a team together and be ready within twenty-four hours, quicker if necessary. One thing I strongly recommend is that my team goes in first so the locations can be swept."

"Swept?" Falcone asked.

"For existing or potential threats, elements of danger."

"Elements of danger," Niles repeated, sounding like the narrator of some B-grade slasher flick. "Ooh, I'm bloody liking this!"

Jake was not amused. "I'm serious here. I cannot emphasize enough that the area you have chosen is not the most stable. I will steer you to locations with the lowest risk, but the whole area is still dangerous. You do *not* want to be ill prepared for this environment. You will need to know basic survival skills, be physically and medically protected, and have solid contingency plans in place in case of emergency."

"You know, you could do every bit of your filming right here in Costa Rica and no one would be the wiser."

"Look," Falcone said, stabbing a piece of steak and stuffing it into his mouth, "if it was up to me, that's exactly what we'd do. But it's not. Which is why we hired you."

"Fair enough," Jake said evenly. "Just wanted you to know what you're getting into."

"There's lots of snakes in the Amazon, aren't there?" Niles queried, taking a big swig of his Pilsen beer.

"Some of the deadliest in the world, in fact. Coral snakes, fer-de-lances, rattlers, bushmasters. Those are nasty buggers you don't want to get nailed by. But there are plenty of equally noxious insects and other reptiles. There are some giant spiders that eat birds. I'm sure you know about piranhas and caimans and anacondas and jaguars and—"

"Holy shit, Curran," Falcone interrupted. "What the hell are we doing?"

"I dunno, mate," Niles said, "sounds kind of cool to me."

"We'll see if you say that after a day or so over there," Jake remarked wryly. "Oh, and Curran? With that fair skin, you better slather on the sunscreen, bro."

"Okay," Falcone said, summoning the waiter for their bill, "when do we get started?"

"O-five-hundred."

"What?"

"Five AM."

"Jesus Christ, you can't be serious!"

"Got a lot of territory to cover," Jake said flatly. "Working with me, get used to it."

"Five o'clock in the freaking morning. Shit."

They left the restaurant with Falcone grumbling and Niles chattering excitedly. Grinning, Jake slipped his arm around Callie and bid the duo goodnight. A Latino man seated at the bar watched them leave. Just as he had watched them arrive. He waited a few minutes, then slapped some money on the counter and walked out. His eyes followed the rear bumper of the old Toyota truck as it disappeared in the darkness. But he knew where it was going.

OVER THE NEXT FEW days Jake took Falcone and Niles to some key locations, in much the same way he had Callie, introducing them to friends and associates who worked with him on SpecOps projects. They covered territory in and around Arenal and Monteverde, also Manuel Antonio—a national park northwest of Dominical—and Bahía Drake, a beautiful and geographically intense locale at the northern tip of the Península de Osa. They concluded with a day at Hacienda Barú, a wildlife preserve in Dominical run by a friend. While Jake and his associates prepared Falcone and Niles for what they could expect of their chosen destination, providing details for activities, instruction for stunts, and survival basics, Callie was encouraged to document their collaborative proposal for the production team. When all was said and done, Falcone and Niles were extremely pleased with what she had written for them and satisfied they were ready to move on with Jake.

On the afternoon of the day before departure for South America, Jake was sorting through a stack of mail when he came to a large manila envelope. In the upper left-hand corner was the stamped insignia of a law firm in San José, the attorneys he and Delaney had retained there.

Palacios, Barquero & Mora. He knew what was in the envelope and felt a lump the size of a clamshell lodge in his throat.

He opened the envelope as if it contained anthrax and slid out a copy of Delaney's *fidecomiso testamentario*—Last Will and Testament. A recent phone conversation with one of the attorneys had prepared him for the contents, but it was still hard to grasp the finality of the decree.

The pages felt thick and starched, the font stark and permanent. They felt heavy, so heavy, in his hands.

Scanning the pages of the document, he read what the attorney had already revealed: he was now sole owner and operator of SpecOps, sole recipient of Delaney's personal possessions and property—property, as in owner of Delaney's beach house and the Beneteau. And over a million dollars in drug money in an offshore account that Palacios, Barquero & Mora knew nothing about. He looked up at the dark wood beams that stretched across the house's high ceiling, eyes misting. Faintly, he felt Callie's tender touch on his shoulder.

"Jake? Is everything okay?"

His inhaled deeply. "Why don't you get some rest, love? I'm just going to go for a run. Okay?"

Her face was clouded with concern, but she said, "Okay," and slowly climbed the stairs. Pausing at the top of the stairwell, she looked down at his hunched shoulders. At his hands on his hips. The waves in his black hair. His tanned neck. Heard a heavy intake of air, and felt her own lungs fill. She wanted to touch him then, but felt the impenetrable depth and distance.

She watched as he lifted his head, squared his shoulders, and strode through the front door.

WHEN JAKE RETURNED FROM his run, he strolled through the house that was now his, feet crossing the cool tile floor, hands aimlessly touching the tops of chairs, tables, lamps. His eyes roved the walls, lighting briefly on the spot near the French doors where damage done by the intruder's bullet had been patched, sanded, and painted. He wandered into the kitchen, eying the brightly glazed ceramic plates neatly stacked on an open cabinet shelf, and wondered when Delaney had last dined on one. He gazed out to the pool, imagined Delaney running and leaping and landing in the middle with a big whoop, imagined him wedged between a pair of bikini-clad beauties sipping from tall glasses of rum-spiked cocktails.

Come on down to Dominical, Bubba...we'll have us a good time.

Just wanted to see him, hear him laugh one more time.

He went back inside, climbed the stairs. It seemed to take an impossibly long time.

He stood outside Delaney's bedroom as if it were the sacrosanct chamber of an Egyptian pyramid. When he finally crossed through the doorway, he felt as if a crowbar was strapped to his chest. His head turned slowly, scanning the walls, the floor, the bed. Everything looked placid, undisturbed. Not like the man who'd slept there. Not like the man who had lived there.

The housekeeper kept the room as tidy as the rest of the house, so the only visible thing of a personal nature was a grouping of framed photos on a teak bureau, pictures that more or less duplicated those on the Beneteau. Now they were snapshots of life in freeze-frame. Freeze-frame forever.

Jake moved to the closet, peeled back the louvered doors, looked inside. The space was mostly empty, just a few pairs of slacks and some Oxford shirts, a couple of sports jackets, and uniforms. Some old marine dress blues, encased in plastic. More recent army greens and blues. He fingered them through the plastic, brushing over the epaulets, the Special Forces tab, the specialty badges and ribbons. On the floor, several pairs of civilian shoes and an equal number of gleaming military dress shoes and combat boots. For some reason he could not fathom, Jake stared at the laces. He knelt down and touched them. *Laces, they're just shoelaces.* And then, thought about his own army uniforms, stashed in a storage facility outside Fort Bragg.

He rose and looked around Delaney's room again, and thought, *This is not my house.* Palacios, Barquero & Mora said it was. But Delaney's boots were in the closet. With his laces.

He backed out of the room and turned toward the one across from it.

Callie was lying on the bed, atop the covers, eyes closed, lips slightly parted. A window was open, the ceiling fan overhead swirled a light breeze across her. He paused in the doorway, peered over and felt the rush of warmth at the sight of her, inhaled stoically and started to retreat. But the pull was too strong, the ache too deep, the need too keen.

Barefooted, he padded to the bed, removing clothes as he approached the side.

Callie's eyelids fluttered open. She saw him and sat up. She was wearing a simple cotton chemise, which he easily lifted up and over her head. Eased her back, slipped his hand inside her panties and slid them off. Her hair was slightly damp from the shower, a clean floral smell blending with her soft, natural scent.

This time, though her anxiety level rose just as quickly, her hesitance began to abate almost immediately. He could feel her heart beating just as fast, like frenzied hummingbird wings, but the fear he'd seen in her eyes the first time had diminished.

And when he entered her this time, after the initial shudder and deep intake of breath, her thighs widened and her arms encircled him, clasping tightly. He plunged up inside her with an urgency that seemed to reverberate through his whole frame, feeling a desperation that intensified his movements. Above the pounding of his own heart, he could hear her whimpering, the pitch of her voice rising with each of his pushes. Her hands clutched him tighter, her legs clenched around him.

In one final driving thrust, she cried and he let out a sound that was a combination wail, grunt, and growl. Heat radiated from his heaving body, the air charged with expended energy and emotion.

He rolled onto his back, breathing heavily, and then drew her into his arms.

They slept.

Sometime later, in the gathering evening shadows, he made love to her again, this time slowly. Touching, tasting, feeling, smelling, savoring every intimate inch.

Just before he drifted off to sleep again, he felt her warm breath in the crook of his neck, her small hand on his stomach, and thought, *Oh God, I think it's really happening.*

Outside the window, the sound of twinkling chimes drifted up from the patio.

* * * * *

IN THE WEE HOURS somewhere between midnight and dawn, Jake leaned over the bed and kissed her in the dark.

There was no moon, the air was still and quiet.

"I have to go, precious," he whispered, and felt the now-familiar ache gust through his gut like a desolate canyon wind.

She blinked up at him groggily, then seeing him standing over her fully dressed, sat up with a start. "Jake?"

"I have to go," he repeated, trying but not succeeding in keeping the heaviness out of his voice.

"You have to go now?"

"Yes, sweetheart." He took her in his arms and held her for several minutes, inhaling her sweet scent, feeling the quiver of her heart, the touch of her fingers at the nape of his neck. Then he kissed her, deeply, and for the first time in his life really didn't want to let go. Her flesh so soft and warm against him, the tingle that sparked with every touch, spread with every move. *Oh God...*

And everything changes.

When he pulled away, he felt as if his chest was gaping open. He held her face in his hand, lightly stroked her cheek with his thumb and said, "You'll be okay, angel. And I will be back."

He was only half right.

19

CARTAGENA FROM THE AIR is an amazing panorama of contrasting images against the vivid Caribbean blues of sky and water. It is an ancient city of narrow, cobblestone streets lined with brightly painted colonial buildings, enclosed by heavy stone walls built in the 16th century as a defense against pirates. Beyond the Murallas, an L-shaped peninsula crooks into the Bahía de Cartagena, sprouting luxury high-rise hotels and casinos. Two worlds, the old and the new, connected yet set apart.

Having decided this was an ideal starting point for their Colombian locational scouting expedition, Jake got them an early morning Copa Airlines flight out of San José and spent most of it in studious solitude, leafing through copies of *TIME* and *Newsweek* he'd purchased at the airport. His clients spent much of their time studying him in rapt fascination, seeing a man who, at this particular moment, reading on a plane, looked like any normal man. Not like a seasoned special operative with top-secret clearance who probably knew more ways to kill than a world-class jeweler knew how to cut diamonds. It appeared to them that he had consciously made himself as nondescript as possible in an effort to protect his identity; even so, the man had a magnetism that drew the interest of males and females—especially females. Both men wanted to talk to him, ask him things about himself and his work, but discretion prevailed and they afforded Jake his privacy, conversing quietly amongst themselves.

After a brief layover in Panama City, the Boeing jet set down at the Rafael Nunez Airport. It was mid-afternoon and typically hot and humid as they hurtled along the busy Avenida Santander in a battered old taxi, the vast Caribbean on their right and the fortressed city on their left. They were navigating toward Bahía de las Animas. Making the first turn, the big yellow dome of San Pedro Claver's Church rose above the sea-weathered walls and distantly behind it, the tall red spire of Torre de la Catedral. The next turn, alongside the Muelle de los Pegasos, a picturesque old port full of fishing, cargo, and tourist boats, took them near the clock tower, Torre del Reloj. It stands, as it has for centuries—la Boca del Puente—massive stone gateway to El Centro. The taxi continued south along Carrera 1 to Bocagrande, depositing them at the Caribe Hotel.

The five-star Caribe is a wing-shaped structure spanning a corner of oceanfront avenue in front and El Laguito in back, a small round inlet within the very tip of Bocagrande. Built in the 1940s on four hundred thousand square feet of greenery dotted with palm trees and tropical plants, its opulence was a bit high-end for Jake, but since it was on the expense account of his clients he was certainly not going to complain. After getting checked in, Falcone and Niles took one look at the hotel's big pool, dripping with attractive women, and went digging for their swim trunks.

Jake got a sandwich from the poolside café and took it to his suite, taking advantage of the time alone to stretch out on the bed and make a few calls. It unsettled him a little to find that his first inclination was to call Callie. Resisting the urge, he began contacting associates instead, letting them know he was back in country. He conversed at length with Alberto Hernandez who was in Bogotá, and Raúl Aguilar who was still operating in and around the Amazon basin. Hernandez, who made frequent Amazon expeditions, discussed some arrangements he had made for Jake and offered suggestions for their itinerary. Aguilar had already allocated some men and a local guide to accompany them, but there was something in his tone that caused Jake to veer off subject.

"Raúl, have you heard anything?"

There was a long pause before Aguilar replied, "Some things, yes. Not for discussion now. I will catch up with you." His voice was low, cautious.

Jake felt his pulse quicken. "When?"

"Soon." Without another word, Aguilar clicked off.

Jake felt a vague stirring of dread in his gut.

THEY HAD DINNER AT the elegant and renowned Club de Pesca, a yacht club with a bustling marina across the bridge from the Old Town, just below Getsemaní on Isla Manga. Earlier that evening, they had taxied to the edge of town and entered through the clock tower, a mustard-and-white painted spire surmounting the weathered stone walls. Inside, they strolled through the city streets and took in the sights, sounds, and smells of a place mired in an era of marauding pirates and Spanish conquistadors. They wandered around plazas and gardens, cafes and churches, monasteries and museums and palaces. Colonial and Middle-Eastern flavored homes were both noble and modest, with varnished wooden gates and painted doors that sheltered lovely, well-tended courtyards. Balconies on every street were lush with ferns and palms, bright flowers spilling over and dangling down from the railing edges. The temperature had dropped to a pleasant level, a light breeze spritzing the air with floral fragrance and the occasional waft of cooking oils and spices from restaurants they passed.

Jake felt a heavy tug at his heart, imagining how much Callie would have enjoyed being here in this place.

Fuerte de San Sebastián del Pastelillo, while not as impressive as many of the other forts around the city, was one of the first defense posts constructed in the 16th century, and it is inside these walls the yacht club resides.

They were seated at a white linen covered table on the terrace overlooking the dock, and while Falcone and Niles chattered about their coming trip to the Amazon, Jake's gaze was fixed on a point well out into the bay—a point where there were no images, only thoughts. Thoughts chasing an emotional helix that continued to narrow and tighten inside him.

"Jake," Niles said for the second time.

Snapping out of his haze, Jake turned his attention back to the table.

Precisely arranged plates of seafood entrées with coconut rice and fried plantains had just been placed before them. Falcone and Niles had already dug in with relish and were making contented noises. They were both drinking Club Colombia beer from chilled glasses.

"Sorry," Jake apologized, cutting into his lobster. It was dressed in a savory béchamel sauce flavored with dry sherry. With a restrained smile, he said, "Your production company sure gave you guys a generous travel allowance."

Niles snickered around a mouthful of crab. "Let's just say we might have a creative interpretation of our expenses."

"Well, enjoy the frills now, gents. Tomorrow's going to be a drastic departure."

"Bring it on, mate," Niles declared.

Falcone was a little less ardent. "When you say drastic departure, what exactly do you mean? It's not like we're going to be trekking through the jungle or anything, right?"

Jake's brows lifted in astonishment. "Just how did you expect to scout locations? By looking at maps?"

"Well, yeah, I guess."

"Why do you think I made sure you had all those shots and sent a very specific packing list? Sure hope you brought everything on it, by the way."

"Uh, yeah," Falcone stammered. "Most of it, yeah."

"And the shots on the list?"

"Nasty, those," Niles said with a repugnant shudder. "One of those buggers made me sick as a bloody dog." He mopped a forkful of crabmeat through Gruyere au gratin sauce and popped it in his mouth. "Mmm-mmm, this is divine."

"Well, you'd be a lot sicker, or worse, without the protection."

For the next hour, they concentrated on their meals, comments limited to the food and the restaurant's scenic location.

Pushing his plate aside, Jake said, "Okay, here's the deal. We'll actually be scouting locations by land, air, and water. If you're going to drop people in the middle of the jungle, you better damn well know exactly where you're putting them and everything that's going on within a hundred miles of them."

"A hundred miles?" Falcone repeated.

"All hell has broken loose from greater distances than that, I can assure you." He wiped his mouth, took a final sip from his glass of Cabernet-Sauvignon, and rose from the table. "Now then, gents. I would show you the nightlife around here, but I'd recommend we retire and get a good night's sleep. You're going to need it, we have an early start in the morning."

"We talkin' crack of dawn again?" Falcone grumbled.

"Five AM."

"You've got to be freaking kidding me." He gaped at Jake, open-mouthed. Saw no change in expression.

"Shit."

JAKE HAD BOOKED A charter flight to Leticia, a King Air 200 that cruised comfortably for a little over two hours. Leaving the coast they flew over steep mountains that swept down into breathtaking gorges, then over nothing but the endless roll of jungle, the vastness of which was nothing short of staggering. Toward the end of the flight the Amazon snaked its muddy tentacles through the green, spreading hundreds of tributaries out into the forested terrain.

Deplaning the air-conditioned turbo prop, the three of them stepped into the equatorial sauna called Amazonas, their minds and bodies taking an instant hit of near 100 percent humidity with a temperature past the centennial mark. Falcone and Niles, who had never experienced it, felt like all the oxygen had been sucked out of their lungs by an industrial-strength vacuum cleaner. Before they had crossed the short distance from plane to terminal—a one-story metallic building that looked and smelled more like chop-shop than airport—every stitch of clothing on their bodies was permeated with sweat and sponged to skin.

"Oh my God," Falcone intoned, wheezing for air.

Niles, for once, was speechless.

"Takes some adjustment," Jake said, handing their passports over to the customs agent. The agent gave Falcone and Niles a quick, bemused look, glanced at their passports and stamped the pages. His eyes lingered suspiciously on Jake.

"*Un momento, Señor.*"

"What the—?" Falcone began before Jake held up a hand to silence him.

"No worries, it happens all the time."

Several minutes later, the agent returned with a military officer who handed Jake's passport back to him. "*Tome usted, Señor Tyler. Gracias.*"

Niles leaned into Falcone and murmured, "Why do I feel like we're traveling with some kind of bloody mutation of James Bond, Rambo, and the Terminator?"

"Because I think we are," Falcone said. "Jesus Christ, they've lost their freaking minds to do this in the Amazon. Why couldn't we do one of those lush tropical islands? Shit, right now Siberia sounds appealing."

"Don't get your knickers in a wad. I think it's brilliant."

"You would. I could really go for a cold brew right now. Wonder if they have any in this godforsaken hellhole."

AS IT TURNED OUT, they did. A little more than an hour later, they were drinking *cerveza* in the air-conditioned comfort of the Hotel Anaconda. Overlooking the Amazon River, the hotel is located by Francisco de Orellana Park, one of a very few that even has air-conditioning. They were assembled around a small table in Jake's room, studying a map of the region.

Falcone and Niles emptied the contents of their first cans of beer in just a few long gulps and snatched two more from the room service tray. Jake was drinking bottled water, and lots of it. Watching them guzzle the beer, he admonished, "Better go easy on that here."

Finishing off his second, Falcone said, "Hey, I'm just starting to feel halfway human again. Is the air-conditioning working in here? Curran, turn it all the way up."

"It *is* all the way up, mate."

Jake rolled his eyes, thinking these two were going to be a handful.

LETICIA IS A TOWN of fewer than twenty thousand people and serves as the Colombian gateway to the Amazon. In the southeast corner of a trapezium bordered on all three sides by Peru and Brazil, it is a busy but laid-back portal crowded with street markets and an unkempt collection of river vessels. A continual stream of long, narrow canoes is the only commonality in watercraft; otherwise, every kind of barge, outboard, dingy, houseboat, raft, outrigger, and steamboat chugs, floats, or skitters along. The Brazilian border town of Tabatinga is a few minutes' walk away; a few days by boat upstream passes Iquitos, Peru, and a good bit farther downstream is Manaus, Brazil.

Shortly after dawn, Jake bundled his groggy charges up and pointed them in the direction of the wharf. Wearing khaki cargo shorts, light t-shirts, and athletic shoes, strapped with backpacks, they trudged down the mud-caked street toward the river. Jake thought they looked like they'd been sold off to slavery and were being herded to work the fields. He stopped at a corner café and got some coffee, hoping that would invigorate them.

On their way they passed elderly native women working fruit stands and young barefooted boys hawking fish slung over their shoulders. The fruit hung in citrusy smelling bunches of orange, yellow, and red; the fish were fat and gray and smelly. A few cars puttered through the streets, but motorbikes outnumbered them. When a red one with a pair of teenagers astride came buzzing around the corner, almost plowing into Falcone and Niles, adrenaline kick-started the caffeine and their heads snapped up in startled unison. Before they caught a glimpse of the water, they smelled it in the stench of diesel fuel simmering up from the congested riverbanks. Already, the heat was thick and heavy. Falcone and Niles were panting.

Halting at the wharf, the duo scanned the rickety looking assortment of boats crammed at the edge in stupefied disbelief. There wasn't a single one, large or small, that looked capable of holding together in a bathtub, much less rolling along the robust currents of what was, arguably, the mightiest navigable river in the world. There were a number of large double-tiered wooden and aluminum boats that resembled the African Queen. A medium one, made of wood, dilapidated and peeling white paint, was being loaded with supplies.

Falcone, still slack-jawed, muttered, "Please, God, tell me that's not the fucking boat."

Niles snorted with glee. "I love it! I absolutely love it! We've got to work this into the show somehow. Got to!"

"You're goddamn kidding me, right?"

"Eddie, it would be great! It's not been done before!"

Behind them, Jake said, "Well, we're doing it now, so load up."

"You're serious," Falcone said incredulously.

"Get a move on, gents."

The no-nonsense tone in his voice sent them tottering up a wooden plank that stretched to the boat, both flailing their arms to maintain balance. Jake stepped deftly across, snatched the plank and dropped it onto the boat's deck. A group of boys rushed forward and laughingly untied the lines and tossed them. The old riverboat's engine coughed, sputtered, then rumbled with half-hearted determination. Falcone and Niles grabbed the sides as every timber on the vessel shook. The boat actually began to move in the water. They were amazed. The riverbank drifted away, the swarm of activity diminished with distance. The big river suddenly yawed and pulled them into its strong, murky currents.

THEY HAD BEEN CHUGGING along for close to two hours, Falcone and Niles taking in the scenery with a combination of dread and fascination. Handmade dugout canoes with native river dwellers streamed by, fishermen were scattered along the banks tossing out lines with hooks or pronged spears, scantily clad children frolicked, farmers herded anemic-looking cattle. And the massive umber-colored river churned on. Jake spent some time conversing with the boat's captain. He was a short, thickset man in his late fifties with skin the color and texture of an old leather belt. Most of his teeth were missing, black, or gold-plated, but his head was full of gleaming black hair. He seemed competent enough, but the fact that he downed cans of Águila like it was Gatorade was a little disturbing.

When Jake rejoined his clients, seated on the splintered remains of a wooden bench crookedly nailed to the deck, Niles commented, "I hope the captain can hold his pints."

"Probably," Jake replied, frowning, "but I told him to slow down. His son will relieve him in a while and he can take a nap."

"That makes me feel much better," Falcone said sarcastically, swatting at a large black insect that looked like a fly on steroids. "But then if I lived down here, I'm sure I'd stay drunk."

"Let's talk about the folks you're going to be dropping off in the jungle," Jake said. "What kind of provisions will they have?"

"As in supplies?" Niles asked.

"Yes."

"Actually, just the clothes on their backs," Falcone said.

"Not in the Amazon. Unless your contestants are survival-trained, they'll be dead before the second episode. You'll have to make sure they have safe drinking water at the very least and a machete. Possibly some food or at least knowledge of indigenous food sources."

"Okay."

"Now," Jake continued, "the reason I'm taking you into the jungle this way is so you can see their logical way out, in reverse. And you definitely don't want to drop them too far in, not more than, say, twenty to thirty miles. You'll find that a mile here is like five or ten anywhere else. So as long as they track like the natives and follow the water, the tributaries, they'll find their way to the Amazon and the way out."

"Hey, that would make a cool title for the show, wouldn't it, mate?" Niles said. "*The Way Out*. I like it!"

"Yeah, it would," Falcone agreed. "Don't think they've decided on a title yet."

The raucous engine sounds had settled into a more monotonous drone as the boat's spasmodic movement modulated, so Falcone and Niles began to settle down themselves.

Jake reached into a cooler and tossed them bottles of water. "All right. For now, drink lots of water, watch your time in direct sun, and enjoy the cruise."

Flinching as a cockroach the size of a bar of soap scuttled across the deck, Falcone caught his bottle and said, "Royal Caribbean it's not."

FURTHER EXPLORATION OF THE boat revealed just how not like the Royal Caribbean it was. For one thing, much to their shock and repulsion, there was no toilet. Instead, tucked in a closet barely big enough to shoulder into, was a hole covered by a square piece of plywood. Neither Falcone nor Niles wanted to know what was in the hole or where the contents wound up. And neither inhaled when they were inside. They did keep an eye on the hand-sized spider meandering around the ceiling of the stall, and wondered how they would know where it was later, in the dark.

Their beds were woven rope hammocks, strung across the covered middle deck, and when Falcone and Niles grew fatigued from clutching the side rails for fear of being slung overboard, they quickly concluded there would not be much, if any, sleep on the boat. Unlike typical hammocks, these hung loosely to form a deep center pocket for the body, and despite Jake's direction for optimal positioning—which was to lie diagonally across in a way that kept the spine aligned—neither man could get comfortable. And even in the shade, the midday heat was stifling. Falcone and Niles tossed and twisted and tangled the afternoon away while Jake snoozed as effortlessly as an infant on cool crib sheets.

Until his satellite phone stirred him, vibrating at his waist.

Jake's eyes blinked open and, instantly alert, he glanced at the incoming number on the display. Raúl Aguilar. He swung out of his hammock, put the phone to his ear, and strode out to a side deck.

THEY DISEMBARKED AT A small village about ten kilometers south of Amacayacu, a national park covering some 1130 square miles of jungle. Jake would have preferred that Falcone and Niles remain behind, but after nearly eight hours on the creaking riverboat they were desperate to set foot on solid land. So after making sure they had slathered on sunscreen and DEET, Jake waited for them to gather their backpacks and helped them into the boat's dugout. He rowed to shore, tethered the canoe, and led them through the mud to a sandy swath cut into the side of a scrub-covered bank. There were long, shallow steps leading to the top, all meticulously rutted and squared in the soil. They looked like Mayan ruins. Small children, two boys and a girl, sat at the top. Behind them, the sky was pale with dollops of cloud, the sun so close it was omnipotent, backlighting the whole canvas in colorless radiance.

When they reached the top of the steps, the children had scampered away. Falcone and Niles bent over, having a hard time catching their breath. Their clothing was soaked with sweat, and carnivorous *jejenes*— no-see-ums—were already hovering over exposed flesh in anticipation of the DEET barrier dissolving in the humidity. For some reason, they didn't seem as interested in Jake. He immediately set off toward a group of huts, his own breathing unchanged. Falcone and Niles exchanged dispirited looks and laboriously jogged to catch up.

The Amazon flood season, typically April and May, August and September, necessitated that housing anywhere within its reach be elevated on stilts, but the huts in this village were among the few high enough to be built on the ground with under spaces and short ladders to their doorways. They were constructed of palm wood, chosen in part because termites would not feed on it, and the roofs were made with dried fronds from the yarina palm, lashed to the rafters with lianas for a watertight seal. Windows were fly-screens. The village road was a dirt path that encircled the settlement, which was foliated with lemon, papaya, and mango trees, banana plants and coconut palms. Large, Day-Glo colored parrots and macaws chattered and squawked from tree branches overhead, roosters and chickens picked and poked lazily on the ground.

Jake strode purposefully down the dirt path, turning into the center of the settlement where a sturdier wooden hut with a front porch was surrounded by villagers and a number of men in olive military fatigues. Aguilar was sitting on the porch, beer in one hand, cigar in the other. The paramilitary commander, who was about the same age as Jake, wore his usual maroon beret and jungle fatigues, longish hair neatly combed, beard trimmed. His boots were propped up on the railing. When he spotted Jake, he swung them down, raised his beer, and shouted, *"Qué mas, mi amigo!"*

Jake gave him a wave and called out, *"Hola!"* He waited for Falcone and Niles to catch up, introduced them to Aguilar, and climbed up the ladder to the porch. When the duo made it to the platform, Jake suggested they go inside the *bodega* to get a beer and cool off, which they did without hesitation. He peered inside, watched until they had collapsed into a pair of chairs, then turned back to Aguilar.

Jake gave his friend a quick embrace and took a seat next to him at the railing. Eyed him expectantly, waiting for him to say what was important enough to bring him from the other side of Amazonas to the river edge. He had to wait a while as Aguilar puffed on his Robusto and seemed to be contemplating something of a grave nature. He flicked ashes to the floorboards, sipped his beer. Wiped his mouth with the back of his hand. Put his beer can on the railing and sighed.

"Jake," he said, and looked him squarely in the eye. "There is a bounty on you."

For a moment Jake said nothing, as if it took his mind that long to process the words. Then, he laughed with a husky guffaw, tossed his head back and grinned at Aguilar. "*That's* what you came all the way out here to tell me?" He studied Aguilar's face. "Seriously?"

"You do not believe it?"

"Oh, yeah, I believe it. But shit, Raúl. I had a bounty on me the second my feet touched Colombian soil."

Quietly, Aguilar said, "Jake, this is different."

"How?"

"This bounty is from a cartel."

Jake's face lost some of its elasticity. "A cartel?"

"Yes."

"Tell me."

"Five hundred thousand."

"*What?*"

When Aguilar did not answer, Jake asked, "Pesos?"

"No. American dollars."

Now Jake was silent. Somewhere out in the trees a monkey jabbered, a branch crackled, and a bird screeched.

Aguilar said, "You should not be here."

"I didn't exactly want to come back right now, but"—he jerked his shoulder toward the inside of the *bodega*—"I have a private contract."

"You should not be here," Aguilar repeated thickly.

"Well, I am. But I should be wrapping this phase in a few days. You have any intel that puts hostiles anywhere in my AO?"

Aguilar shook his head slowly. "No. I think you are secure here, but everything can change in an instant. You know that."

Jake nodded. Yes, yes it could. And did.

"Be careful, my friend. I will have your back as much as I can. My men and your guide will be with you here."

"Thank you, Raúl."

"But be careful."

"Of course."

Aguilar stood, gave Jake a solemn look, and headed for the ladder. Stopped and turned around. "This cartel is the one responsible for Haskell's death, Jake."

Jake felt the porch become very light, his weight very heavy. His lungs labored for air and his skin was on fire. Impossibly, he could hear his watch ticking. It sounded like a cannon.

"Who are they, Raúl?"

"Valentín."

20

THEY STOOD SIDE BY side at the railing in stunned silence, captivated by the Amazonian fireworks. The boat was still, its engine mercifully quiet, the captain, his son, and two crewmates below for the night. All around them, the sky was ablaze in the full throes of sunset, the river surface shimmering orange beneath it. A deep violet was bruising its way into the color palette, with a soundtrack of rumbling thunder coming from a few miles downriver. Soon, veins of heat lightning streaked the sky. The air was still heavy and hot. The thunder alternately faded to almost a mumble and then, without warning, would detonate with an earth-rattling boom. Then fade back again. The sky grew sultrier.

"Wow," Niles remarked finally.

"Amazing," Falcone agreed.

Jake said nothing, just stood watching the sky.

Earlier, joined by captain and crew, they had sat around a table with plates of fish, rice, and plantains. The fish, caught that day by the captain's son, was pirarucú, and surprisingly delicious. Falcone and Niles had not been as impressed with the other greasy mess on their plates. The beer, though a little on the bland side, was tasting better and better. Standing at the railing, watching the sunset, the two of them were finishing off their third.

Jake walked away, strolling to the bow of the boat. He placed his forearms on the railing, and peered over the river. It was calm but for the faintest ripples and, distantly, the stealthy swish of caimans coursing through the shallows. He tilted his head up and gazed at the darkening sky where stars were firing on, millions of them. Several yards away he could hear Falcone and Niles exclaiming as they viewed the same lightshow. Their talk became more muted as they retreated toward the stern.

For hours Jake had been weighing whether to tell his clients about the danger they could possibly be in just by association with him. It went against his personal code and professional standards to put any civilian at unnecessary risk. That was, after all, a big part of why they had hired him. On the other side of the dilemma was the confidentiality factor, along with the nature of the beast in which it truly was a case of the less known being the better. True, they had been fully warned of potential danger in the entire region, had read all the warnings in SpecOps' comprehensive contract, had signed all the waivers and releases. But he also knew that, ultimately, no matter what the legalese stipulated, they were his responsibility, and he did not take that lightly.

He stared at the river. Thought about all his options. And decided to go forward.

He looked up at the stars again, and wondered how they looked tonight in Costa Rica.

SOMETIME BEFORE DAWN THE boat began moving again. The gastric chortle of the engine starting up did not wake any of them; only the captain and crew had slept through the night.

Falcone and Niles tossed uncomfortably in the folds of their hammocks, swatting at the insect-covered mosquito netting draped over them. Flying things with wings the size of birds buzzed and swarmed around the naked light bulbs hanging at the corners of the covered deck. And the mosquito nets, it turned out, fell decidedly short of infallible. Either that or the bloodsuckers were biting through the fibers of the hammocks. Added to that misery was the surprising drop in temperature, and in the hours that followed midnight, they shivered in the cool, damp air. After suffering in the unrelenting heat all day, it would seem an embraceable balm, but here on the river, it was a chill that sunk into the bones like a day-old toothache.

Jake managed to doze intermittently, but his mind was restlessly mired in the information he'd received from Aguilar.

By the time the sun spilled over the river, everyone was prowling the deck of the boat. Strong coffee was brewed and copiously consumed until the heat returned promptly at daybreak and began to climb. The crew served a breakfast of eggs, *arepas*, and bananas, and then channeled their energies into moving the old boat upriver. Quite a few hours later, around noon, they passed Isla El Cacao and pulled up to a sandy shore that was utterly deserted.

The Amazon's umber water rolled over the edge of a beach that looked as if it had gone untouched for decades, smooth and unblemished as an Alpine slope or a Sahara dune. Just a short way in, palms and evergreens towered to the sky and obliterated everything beyond. A great mass of green with no beginning or end.

This time, Jake packed the dugout canoe full of gear and supplies, sending one of the crew to shore with it before returning for them. He had instructed Falcone and Niles to dress in long sleeves and pants in dark greens and browns. Sweat saturated their clothing before they stepped out of the canoe, but they quickly saw the reasons for covering up as the sun's heat scorched their faces and could be felt radiating from the ground even through the soles of their hiking shoes. Protection from the mosquitoes and other biting insects ran a close second. Jake's head was wrapped with his faded cravat, while Falcone and Niles wore ball caps.

When Jake finished discussing estimated time of return with the crewmate, he came striding back to where Falcone and Niles stood by the pile of supplies already looking wilted in the brutal midday sun. It reflected off the light sand in blinding blasts that had them squinting despite the shade of their sunglasses.

Noting the butt of Jake's gun above the waistband of his pants, knife sheathed at his side, Niles whistled and Falcone said, "Plan on needing those?"

"Hope not," Jake replied evenly. "But we will need these." He reached into one of the gear bags and drew out three very big, very sharp, very wicked looking machetes. The Cold Steel blades were eighteen inches long, curved, and thicker at the point end. Jake spent the next ten minutes demonstrating their proper use, but when he handed machetes over, the duo clutched them as if they'd just been used to butcher a family of four.

Turning his machete handle over and over in his hands, Niles said, "God, it's bloody hot out here."

"Drink lots of water as we go, but pace yourself," Jake said. "Ready?"

"I guess so," Falcone said without much enthusiasm.

"Okay, listen up. Stay close to me, watch where you're walking, and avoid touching branches and vines or reaching into the bush."

"No problem."

"All right, then. Let's go."

THE SANDY SHORE STOPPED abruptly about fifty meters inland and jungle took over. They entered at what appeared to be an established path, but which soon closed in around them. In the lead, Jake began thrashing through seemingly impenetrable jungle, swinging his machete in wide arcs to his right and left. The Kukri made a whisking and thwacking sound and did a pretty adequate job of clearing the way. Behind him, Falcone and Niles mimicked his movements with their own blades and eventually got the hang of it. To an extent. Most of the way it was a rich, tropical mix of lianas, palms, and trees that were either stemless, bushy, climbing, or towering to the canopy. Massive buttresses, stilt roots, spiny and gnarled trunks sprouted from ground that was a boggy and often fetid compost of mulch, peat, fallen flowers and fruits. The greenery was a multi-textured array of large, heavy leaves and thin, feathery ones with unexpected color bursts from orchids and bromeliads scattered at different heights. The dark evergreen of forest was occasionally broken by shrub-and-grass savannas, more often than not crossed by streams, which were a welcome relief from the sun that blazed high above the open stretches of woodland.

Less than thirty minutes in, Falcone stopped to take a drink of water, panting, "Where exactly are we going?"

"We're working our way to the linkup point."

"Linkup point?"

"Where our guide will meet us. Aguilar, the man you were introduced to yesterday, is an associate of mine, and he has arranged a native guide. We will also be accompanied by some of his men."

"His men? Who exactly is this Aguilar guy?"

"He is a paramilitary," Jake answered obliquely. "The only way to safely get around and get along in this region is to know the right individuals."

"So he's one of the good guys?" Niles asked.

"Here, sometimes good and bad is a fine line," Jake said, and a flatness filled his dark eyes. When he realized Falcone and Niles were staring at him, he nodded. "Yes. He's one of the good guys."

"And when we get to the linkup point, then what?"

"Then we hike through the jungle to the place where you intend to drop your folks."

"But that will be in the middle of nowhere," Falcone said.

"Don't you think you should see where that is?" Jake asked. "You need to know what they are going to go through. Am I right?"

Falcone's shoulders slumped. "Yeah, guess so."

Brightly, Niles said, "Hey, it'll be like *Survivor*."

"Fuck *Survivor*," Falcone muttered, capped his bottle of water, and trudged on.

EVEN NILES' ENTHUSIASM DISSIPATED after the first hour. The heat was torturing them like a methodical executioner, alternating fingers of fire that reached down through openings in the canopy with liquid heat permeating even the thickest jungle cover. It was like taking a steam bath fully clothed, with occasional beams from a thousand-watt heat lamp. Watching Jake skillfully maneuver through the dense forest undergrowth—effortlessly climbing over fallen trees, ducking under hanging vines, and marching across the swampy layers of decay beneath it all— Falcone and Niles exchanged an array of looks ranging from unconcealed envy to fatigued frustration. At one point, they stumbled backward as a lime green vine snake dropped in front of Jake, coiling and hissing. Almost offhandedly, Jake slipped the end of his machete under the snake, rotating it in a way that caused the reptile to wind around the blade. Then, in one quick, forceful motion, he whacked it against a tree.

The butchered snake fell to the ground in several wriggling pieces. Falcone froze, gaping dumbly, while Niles flinched, feeling his breakfast hitching up in his stomach.

Jake nudged the snake's remains aside with his boot, leaned down to cover it with brush, and continued on.

They followed him in sullen silence, now desperately watching the ground and overhanging branches for snakes. They spotted a couple more, but the flying, leaping, and even crawling insects proved needier of their attention. As did the branches themselves. Not long after the snake encounter, Falcone was peering so intently into the foliage overhead that he walked right into a protruding limb, jabbing him in the eye. He let out a wail of pain and grabbed his face. Jake spun around, and the instant he saw Falcone he knew what had happened.

Falcone did not protest when Jake sat him down to tend to his eye, which was swollen and bloodshot. The branch had also scratched up Falcone's face, and blood- and grime-streaked sweat was dripping into his eyes, stinging like a siege of wasps before rolling down into the lacerations on his cheeks. When Jake had finished irrigating his eye and applying tetracycline ointment, Falcone joined Niles who was splashing water on his own scratched face. Despite sunscreen with high double-digit SPF, it was the color of rare sirloin and, in addition to the scratches, was pocked with welts from mosquitoes and *jejenes*.

"Don't you look a bloody sight," Niles remarked wearily as Falcone sat carefully beside him.

"So do you, pal."

They were on a fallen limb, keeping a nervous eye out for anything moving On a perpendicular cecropia tree, a procession of Azteca ants trundled toward the limb like the world's tiniest battalion. They looked like they meant business. Falcone and Niles scooted farther down, watching the ants, then scooted down some more.

"Jesus Christ, my feet are killing me." Falcone tugged off his hiking shoes, and when he inspected his feet he felt tears misting his eyes, causing renewed stinging in the injured one. "Oh God," he moaned miserably.

Seeing Falcone's blistered and bloodied feet, Niles gingerly removed his own shoes and found the same—torn hunks of tissue oozing pus and sweat-thinned blood. They were both about to dip their feet in a nearby stream when Jake's voice resonated from behind.

"Don't do that. You'll only make it worse." Peering down at their heels and toes, he frowned. "Lovely. You didn't break those shoes in, did you?" Shaking his head, he groaned, then knelt before them and dug into his bag for ointment and gauze. Tending to them, he said, "You want to keep your feet as dry as possible—that's why I told you no socks. But we can't leave these sores open for infection…when it comes to bacteria, the jungle's like one big Petri dish."

Jake stood. "All right, we need to get going again if we're going to reach our rendezvous before dark."

The thought of hiking in the dark with the snakes and hundreds of their reptilian cousins, not to mention all the four-legged predators, motivated them to quickly put shoes back on and resume their course. Catching up to Jake, Falcone said, "I see your point about the provisions. We sure as hell can't ditch them out here without food, water, and supplies. So what do we do?"

"Well, I think you can get by with basics, but they have to know or be taught how to adapt to the environment. Harsh as the Amazon jungle is, it contains everything necessary for survival. As Special Forces, I am comprehensively trained in survival and can tell and show you a lot, but one of the reasons I arranged for a local native is so you can learn things more specific to the region." He reached up and whacked a thick vine hanging overhead, slicing it first at the bottom and then at the top before extended it toward them. "Open your mouths."

Niles gulped. "What?"

Jake rolled his eyes.

Reluctantly, Falcone stepped forward, tilting his head back while Jake held the vine above his mouth. He was amazed when sweet-flavored water trickled onto his tongue and down his throat. Curiously, Niles leaned in and sampled a mouthful.

"Not bad!" he remarked. "What is it?"

"It's known as *Sipo de Agua*, which roughly translates as 'sip of water.' There are, literally, hundreds of natural water sources in the jungle. The natives do drink from the river, but they have built something of an immunity to disease over the years. In the case of your people, bottled water and a water purification kit will be essential."

"What do the natives eat?"

"Fish, obviously, and meat from animals they hunt, but a lot of raw produce from the jungle. The yucca root, which is like potato, palm hearts for a cabbage noodle-like food and manioc, which is used in dozens of ways, including flour. Nuts and seeds provide nourishment, too, but are also used as ingredients and spices to flavor food and sweets. By boiling and fermenting, they can also make some liquid refreshment that will kick ass over the most potent alcoholic beverage you've ever had."

Jake turned thoughtful. "You hear a lot about the poaching, deforestation, and the like that goes on in Africa, but it's becoming a big problem here. And because of the medicinal goldmine found in the thousands of plants exclusive to the rainforest, the outcome could be tragic."

"You mean as in the loss of a potential cure for cancer or HIV?" Niles remarked.

"Precisely. Already, over 70 percent of the plants identified as having anti-cancer characteristics have been found here. Quinine and curare comes from here." Jake glanced around, spotted what he was looking for, and pointed to a vine with large heart-shaped leaves. "See that? That's curare."

"I thought curare was a poison," Falcone said.

"It is. One of the deadliest. The Indians boil it down to make a syrup or paste for their blowguns and arrows. It only works as a poison if it gets into the bloodstream. But from a medical research standpoint, it's highly valued because it's been used for everything from general anesthetics to muscle relaxants to drugs benefiting Multiple Sclerosis and Parkinson's disease."

"Wow," Falcone marveled. "I had no idea. This place is pretty amazing." He removed his hat, a sweat-stained black Yankees ball cap, and wiped his forehead. "But just too goddamn hot."

THEY HAD TREKKED SEVERAL miles when Jake abruptly halted them with an upraised hand. He turned, motioning them to be silent.

Listened intently to a very faint rustling in the trees to their right. Then to their left. He looked up and saw birds and monkeys flittering about the limbs. Something was agitating them from below. The rustling stopped, but the birds flew off and the monkeys scattered with high-pitched screeching.

Jake gestured for Falcone and Niles to retreat, pushing his hands out to indicate that they should move slowly and quietly. They did their best, but thatch crackled beneath their shoes and they were breathing so hard Jake could hear them from a few feet away. In front of them, Jake unsheathed his combat knife and prepared to draw the Glock 17 if necessary. The brush rustled again, closer, and Jake carefully backed down the path they had forged, slightly crouched and swiveling in both directions as his eyes scanned the forest.

Behind him, Falcone and Niles were frozen in position against the base of a towering Brazil nut tree. Breathing hard, sweating profusely, hands clamping the bark. Both were watching Jake with spiking consternation. And saw, in glassy-eyed horror, two men emerge from the forest and lunge for him from either side.

21

BUT JAKE WAS READY—he had seen the preemptive stutter of leaves seconds before the brush whipped apart—and sprang forward of their landing. The two men were clad in woodland BDUs and partially draped in Ghillie, their faces smeared with olive grease paint. Both had knives drawn. Timing his attack with their landing, Jake pounced behind the one on his right, grabbed the knife-wielding wrist and wrenched it around in a way that caused the man's body to spin. He propelled the spin into the second man, and the force and momentum of the first pummeling into him took them both down.

Jake planted his hiking boot on the back of their heap and knelt down, his KA-BAR blade poised over the necks of both. For several moments his face was a mask of lethal intent.

And then, incredibly, he laughed.

His laugh echoed across the jungle canopy, drifting far then intimately close.

Still pressed against the tree, Falcone and Niles looked on in reeling bewilderment, eyes bulging like startled fish.

Jake slipped the KA-BAR in its sheath, removed his foot from the back of the top man, and extended a hand to assist him to his feet. The man, in turn, helped his fellow attacker up from the ground. Jake said, "Well done, gents. Hope I didn't hurt you too bad."

That got a muted chorus of grimaces from the pair.

Falcone and Niles finally moved, cautiously approaching Jake and the two would-be assassins. "What the fuck?" Falcone said. His heart was still slamming his chest like a frame carpenter's hammer nailing two-by-fours.

"Pardon my manners," Jake said amiably. "These are two of my operatives. Tangeman and Petropoulos. Tang and Petrie, Eddie Falcone and Curran Niles."

Tangeman and Petropoulos, solid-looking men camouflaged to look like they had morphed out of the jungle's undergrowth, extended their hands and proffered supplicating smiles.

Niles shakily accepted the handshakes but Falcone was still honed on Jake. "What the fuck?" he repeated.

"At ease, bro, at ease. This was a planned maneuver to give you an idea of what it will be like when your folks are ambushed. Not sure exactly what the show's producers have in mind, but I thought you needed to get a taste." He grinned, obviously enjoying the moment.

Niles laughed, relief ebbing over anxiety in giddy waves. "That was the bomb! Don't you think, Eddie?" When Falcone did not reply, he glanced around. "Eddie?"

Falcone had stalked off past the Brazil nut tree. He was not feeling particularly exhilarated.

DUSK CAME ON LIKE an after-dinner mint, a pastel of powdery sugar that seemed to melt with leisure and then was suddenly gone, leaving a syrupy coating on the tongue. Evening, like the syrup, was cloying and sticky. They made the rendezvous point minutes before the sun had begun its meltdown. Aguilar's appointed guide was waiting at the designated spot and was already starting to set up camp.

The native Yagua Indian whose name was Cano spoke very little English but passable Spanish. Like most of his tribesmen, he was diminutive, reserved, and attentive. He was ill at ease in the rumpled clothing he wore, khaki shorts faded nearly to tan and a tattered cotton shirt unbuttoned all the way. His bony feet slipped in and out of a threadbare pair of Keds without shoestrings. He appeared as fascinated by Jake's group as they were of him. While Falcone and Niles quenched their thirst by downing a bottle of water apiece, warily eying Jake's associates,

Jake conversed with the Indian in Spanish. A minute later, he said, "Cano welcomes us and says he will make dinner while we settle in."

"Settle in? For how long?" Falcone asked, his brow creasing. He had peeled the gauze from his eye and was blinking tearfully.

"For the night, Eddie," Jake said lightly, and stepped close to look at his eye. Falcone flinched as Jake fingered the swollen skin around it, sucking at his lip as Jake's thumb pushed his lid back for further examination. "Put some eye drops in before sleep."

"Okay," Falcone replied, his voice surly. As Jake moved away, he added, "Thanks."

Tangeman and Petropoulos, now looking more human without their Ghillie netting and war paint, set about to gather limbs for the framework of a small shelter. They instructed Falcone and Niles to collect vines and palm leaves. In little over an hour, they had lashed together a basic structure that would shield them from rain, should there be any. Hammocks were slung, mosquito nets draped.

Quincy Tangeman and Steve Petropoulos were both affable and outgoing, regaling Falcone and Niles with stories of their backgrounds and association with Jake. Like Jake, on the military parts, they were intentionally vague. Tangeman had worked counternarcotics with Jake and now served as an advisor to state narcotics task forces and hostage negotiation teams. Petropoulos, a communications specialist, was a decorated vet of the Iraqi wars, serving with Jake most recently in Afghanistan. The pair of operatives made an effort to engage Falcone and Niles by asking about the television show they were working on. Niles was predictably congenial, but Falcone was still fuming over the exploit that had brought them here.

While the others collected wood for the fire Cano had built, Jake pulled Falcone aside. "Listen, Eddie," he said, his voice somehow managing to sound both stern and compassionate, "this is the way it has to be. You knew going into this it wasn't going to be Disney World. And you knew it had to be on my terms. Right?"

Falcone said nothing but nodded slightly, looking away with a scowl.

"I know you're pissed," Jake continued. "But I wouldn't be doing you any favors by going easy on you. It's my job to show you the reality of the place and the concept, not the bullshit that's slicked over for TV.

The reality that you and those producers will have to work with."

"I'm just not sure this is such a good idea anymore. I was never totally sold on it."

"On the contrary. I think it has the makings of a great project—in the right hands. Which is why we're doing this. How they choose to manipulate it is up to them, but I want you and Curran prepared to keep them on the right track. Okay?"

Falcone looked back at him. "Yeah, okay. I'm sorry. It's just...I always thought I was tough. I guess I had no idea—" His voice broke.

Jake put a hand on Falcone's shoulder. "Hey, you are tough, bro. You're here, with me."

A sideways grin wormed its way to Falcone's face.

"So," Jake said, "let's see what Cano is making for dinner."

"God, please tell me he's not cooking bugs and roots and shit."

Jake laughed heartily. "Well, don't get your mouth set on a cheeseburger."

DINNER, MUCH TO FALCONE'S considerable relief, was not bugs. But, as Jake prophesied, it was not a cheeseburger, either. It was, however, not bad. In fact, some of it was pretty good.

They sat cross-legged around the fire with Jake translating as Cano explained Indian hunting, fishing, food procurement, and cooking. For this evening's meal, he had utilized both the bonfire and a more traditional stone pit. Some feet away, it had been dug out and layered with thin branches, large rocks sprinkled with river water, and thicker dry wood. A fire was built and burned down until the rocks became red-hot. Banana leaves were then placed on top, followed by the meat and another layer of leaves. While the meat was seared and smoked, Cano had prepared manioc meal and yucca, which he toasted on the fire. He also grilled a large tucunaré—peacock bass—brushed with cooking oil extracted from palm fruit. Desert was a selection of fruits flavored with purple acaí paste and cane sugar.

They scarfed all of it up hungrily, even going for seconds. Jake and his associates ate with a satisfaction tempered by seasoned bush experience, but Falcone and Niles ate with unrestrained relish. Wiping meat juice from his chin, still chewing, Falcone said, "This is good. Really. What is it?"

Jake exchanged a smirk with Tangeman and Petropoulos. Cano replied in Spanish, but Jake already knew. Jake asked Falcone, "You really want to know?"

"Yeah, it's good. What is it, like wild boar or something?"

"*Marimba.*"

Falcone shoved another piece of meat into his mouth, chewed noisily. "What?"

"It's monkey."

Falcone coughed up his last swallow, scrambled to his feet, and headed into the brush gagging. Jake managed to keep his composure, but Tangeman and Petropoulos fell into each other laughing. When Falcone returned, Tangeman said, "Sorry, man. Sometimes it's better not to know," and handed him a bottle of water.

For the final course, Cano had boiled an aromatic concoction from various vines, seed extracts, and fruit. Falcone and Niles watched warily as Jake and his associates sipped it. When none of the three heaved or spit it out, Falcone and Niles took a tiny taste. At first, it was sweet and went down smoothly, washing away the psychological distaste of the monkey revelation. Several more generous sips produced a pleasant, numbing warmth that spread from tongue to throat to chest. Dimly, Falcone became aware that Jake, Tangeman, and Petropoulos had stopped after just a few swallows. And were watching them with amusement.

"Oh God," Falcone slurred. "Don't tell me this is some kind of...Jesus, just don't tell me. Fuck."

Jake shook his head, grinning. "No, it's fine, Eddie. But if I were you, I wouldn't drink any more. At least you will probably sleep a lot better, and sooner." His grin broadened.

"Shit."

Not long after that, Falcone and Niles had stumbled to their hammocks and collapsed into them. Jake made sure the mosquito netting covered them and returned to the fire, rejoining Tangeman and Petropoulos. Cano was tidying up his food preparation areas.

"Poor bastards," Petropoulos said. "They didn't know what they were in for, did they?"

Jake shook his head. "No, but they're good guys. I like 'em."

"Yeah," Tangeman said, "and funny as shit."

For the next few hours, the three friends caught up. Talked about life and their trials and errors in pursuit of liberty. Talked about war and trying to reconcile their placement in and out of it. Just talked in a way only Special Forces brethren can. Between them, they had over fifty years of military service and shared life experiences that no civilians could begin to understand or relate to. Since Delaney's death, Jake had not realized how much he missed the bond, the camaraderie. It felt good, and he was grateful for the interlude.

It also made him miss Delaney all the more.

"Hey, bros," Jake said when the conversation dwindled to yawns, "thanks for making it on such short notice. You going to be able to stick around?"

"Nah," Petropoulos replied. "Unfortunately, we've both got to head back for another course at Benning. Never ends, does it?"

"No, it doesn't seem to." Jake's expression turned solemn. "Too bad you can't join me for a bit."

Tangeman caught his eye. "Anything wrong?"

Jake hesitated, shook his head. "No, everything's good."

ABOUT A DOZEN YARDS from their campsite, Jake managed to find a small break in the canopy. Standing in the stripe of a thin moonbeam, he took out his satellite phone and hit the speed-dial for Delaney's—his—beach house. And heard nothing. No dial tone, no static. Nothing. His heart thumped and the familiar ache washed through him. He tried again, got the same results. Cursing under his breath, he paced in the darkness, feeling the ache swell inside.

No, no, no, he told himself. He would not—could not—let this happen. *No.*

But minutes later he was trying the number again. And again. He still could not get a signal.

He walked back to the camp, sighed despondently, and told his associates he would take the first watch. It was a long watch; he never woke either of them to relieve him. There was no point.

TANGEMAN AND PETROPOULOS DEPARTED the next morning, and the remaining day was spent hiking with Cano to his village. He told them it was only a kilometer or so. His math was a little off; it took them several hours to get there. During that time, Cano shared his knowledge of jungle life while Jake continued to impart survival techniques and strategies. They reached the village late in the day and were only too happy to find most of its meager population napping in their thatched huts. With respect to their traditions, Falcone and Niles willingly strung up their hammocks and joined them in *siesta*.

Jake, too, was exhausted, particularly after keeping watch for the duration of the previous night, but he simply lay in his hammock and let his thoughts drift. Unsurprisingly, they drifted back to Costa Rica. This time, he didn't fight them.

He had just let his eyelids close when a small hand touched his arm.

A young boy, naked except for a grass skirt, stood beside the hammock. His hair looked like a black bowl, his skin the color of caramel. Jake smiled at him and got a toothy grin in return. Before he could say anything to the boy, he had darted off. Stretching, Jake swung out of the hammock, ran a hand over the light stubble shadowing his face, and went to find Cano.

The Yagua Indians are one of the many indigenous tribes of the Amazon, found mostly in the western basin near and inside Peru and are attributed to the origin of the great river's name, after the Greek myth about Amazon women warriors. On seeing them for the first time, the Spaniards took note of the grass skirts and thought they were an all-female tribe. They continue to dwell in much the same way as they did then, as an extended family that survive by slash-and-burn agriculture, hunting, and fishing. Both men and women are known for their expert craftsmanship and blowgun hunting skills.

The guide, now wearing only his native skirt made of chambira palm fiber, was conversing with the village shaman, an old Indian who looked to be closing in on ninety. Their discussion seemed tense, the shaman shaking his head emphatically as Cano gestured with his hands. When

Jake approached, Cano pointed toward him and the shaman turned. He listened to Cano for a few more moments, then nodded. But clearly, he was not happy.

Speaking in his broken Spanish, Cano said, "One of our hunters attacked by giant caiman. Tekeh, our healer, treat him but he not get better. I tell him you medic. He not trust medicine of White Man."

"I understand," Jake answered, casting a look of reverence toward the old shaman. "Tell him I will be glad to help in any way I can. Does he want me to look at the man's injuries?"

Without waiting for Cano to translate, the shaman nodded with weary resignation.

"Okay, then," Jake said. "Take me to the man and I will get my medical bag."

The "man" turned out to be a boy of fourteen or fifteen. His wife, a bare-breasted girl of thirteen, stood next to him wearing a red cotton skirt with a naked baby propped on her hip. The boy's wounds were extensive, masticated flesh along both legs, and already seriously infected. Mindful of the shaman watching distrustfully over his shoulder, Jake examined the legs with care and thoroughness. Again, Jake asked Cano to make sure the shaman was agreeable to whatever treatment he felt necessary. Grudgingly, the shaman gave his consent, and left the hut. Jake's patient seemed relieved, and for the first time his eyes reflected the pain he felt.

"Okay, big guy, " Jake said, "let's get you fixed up." Cano translated and the boy smiled weakly.

Treating the caiman victim took some time as Jake had to first clean the wounds, then stitch some of the lacerations, and finally apply dressings. He finished with antibiotics and follow-up instructions for care of the puncture wounds, which were left open to drain. Cano translated to the boy's wife, who nodded earnestly. When Jake began to pack up his medical bag, he found that he had a small line forming outside the young hunter's hut.

He spent the next few hours in the role of visiting village doctor, with Falcone and Niles squeamishly assisting. They found it difficult to watch Jake poking and prodding, with fingers and instruments, and sticking needles. They found it equally difficult to avoid staring at the naked-breasted Yagua women and wondered how Jake was able to stay so focused and professional.

When Jake's medical clinic closed shop, the village cooks had prepared them a feast. Only after determining there was no monkey roasting in the pit did Falcone and Niles partake. They didn't bother to ask what else they were eating. It worked better that way.

After strolling through the small village to digest their meal, the three of them were ready to retire for the night. As they flopped into their hammocks, Niles said, "That was amazing."

"The food?" Jake asked.

"No, you. What you did earlier. Bloody amazing."

Jake didn't respond.

Falcone said, "Yes. Yes, it was."

Jake smiled, and closed his eyes.

AFTER CHECKING ON THE young caiman victim the next morning, Jake summoned Falcone and Niles, bid his thanks and farewell to Cano. The young Indian recited a customary tribal blessing of good fortune and gifted the trio with necklaces made from seeds, shells, animal teeth, porcupine quills, fish bones, and pirarucú scales. Jake's included a feather, special recognition for his medical services.

With a final bow to Cano, Jake led them back into the jungle. Startled by an invasion of brown capuchin monkeys scampering across their path, Falcone and Niles picked up the pace, shuddering at the dinner reminder. But their spirits were high; they were returning to the boat. To shorten the trek, Jake had previously arranged for the captain to take the boat farther upriver, so they could circle back.

They were about two hours into their hike, making their way through a spread of primary forest that wasn't nearly as dense, when crackling and crunching noises emanated from one side. Jake paused to listen, but Falcone and Niles kept going. When the noises didn't seem to get any closer, Jake resumed his stride. But he kept an eye and ear out for additional movement and sound. Twenty minutes later, Niles tripped over a thick root and Jake watched as he went down, yelping on impact.

Kneeling beside him, Jake checked the ankle Niles was holding and determined that he had sustained a mild sprain. He was reaching into his medical bag for an ACE bandage when the brush on their right snapped with the strident solidness of a tree coming down. Instinctively, Jake lunged in front of Falcone and Niles, shoving them back. He drew his gun, finger by the trigger guard.

Behind him, Falcone groaned, "Shit, not again."

"Quiet, Eddie," Jake hissed. "And get back, as far as you can."

They did as they were told, scrambling to the cover of trees on the other side. Seconds later, they saw a gang of heavily armed men break through the layer of trees closest to Jake. There were a half-dozen in view, all wearing bandanas over their mouths and noses. The leader moved swiftly toward Jake, who kept his gun near his side. Facing this number of armed men, his gun could inflict plenty of damage but not enough to hold them all off; the better option was to appear non-threatening. Watching the guerrilla approach, he hoped Falcone and Niles were slipping away.

"*Venga para aca!*" the guerrilla barked, but Jake stood his ground. He took another step toward Jake, repeating his order. The men that flanked him raised their weapons, AK47s.

And that was when the trees shattered with a barrage of gunfire that seemed to come from everywhere. But it was coming from one direction—behind Jake. Rounds soared over his head like miniature missiles, thwacking into trees, snapping branches, pulverizing leaves. Pieces of bark sprayed out like shrapnel. Jake dove to the ground and clambered back to where Falcone and Niles were hunkered down petrified by the horror unfolding before their eyes. Grabbing them, Jake yelled over the blasting, "Come on, we've got to get out of here!"

They moved then, running jaggedly through the trees, away from the gunfire. Branches jabbed and snagged their backpacks, lashed at their arms and legs, roots and vines sent them sprawling. Niles yowled in pain with the jarring pressure on his ankle as both he and Falcone fought to breathe through lungs laboring to keep up.

A few minutes later, all was quiet. Jake stopped them and listened. Soon, the sound of footfalls crunched in their direction. One set, coming closer. Jake raised his Glock, stiffened, readied his aim. Felt a bead of sweat stream down the side of his face. A mosquito hummed by his ear.

The footfalls ceased. And a familiar scent wafted through the bush.

"Jake, *aquí.*"

A branch was moved aside, revealing the tip of a cigar. A Robusto.

22

JAKE INSTRUCTED FALCONE AND Niles to stay put, and accompanied Raúl Aguilar back to the site of the ambush. Neither man spoke. When they were standing where the guerrillas had confronted Jake, he noticed a blood trail. It might have been hard to see in the dark decomposed mulch of the jungle floor were it not for the excessive amount. Jake's eyes followed the still-wet trail for several feet, stopping on the body that lay in a matted thatch of brush. It was that of the guerrilla leader. Flies were already sorting out landing patterns. Aguilar reached down and tugged the bandana from the dead man's face, and gazed questioningly at Jake.

"Do you know him?" he asked.

Before he looked down, Jake said, "They were after me?"

"Do you know him?" Aguilar repeated insistently.

Jake looked, tilted his head, leaned closer. Something stirred, but at first he could not grasp the familiarity. He thought hard. Fuzzy images swam in the pool of his memory. And then something came into sharp focus. He remembered. And felt a glacial chill in the sweltering heat.

He had seen this man the day Delaney died.

The image came to him, like a slow-motion flashback in a movie. The small town, the young couple, a wedding celebration...the music, the celebrants eating and drinking along the street. The pair of guerrillas seated alone, detached from the crowds. He remembered thinking then that he recognized one of them.

This one.

Jake studied him more intently. Where had he seen him before that day? He closed his eyes in concentration for several minutes, but he could not make a connection.

Shaking his head in frustration, he said, "Yes, Raúl, I know him…but I don't know how or where. I do know I saw him the day Haskell was killed. In a small village I passed through on the way to the airstrip. This is an awfully long way from there." Jake's eyes jelled with piercing clarity, met Aguilar's. "He was here to kill me, wasn't he? *Sicario*." Assassin.

"Probably," Aguilar answered. "Or possibly to take you alive."

"Does he work for the cartel?"

Aguilar shrugged, glanced around.

"How did you know they would be here?"

Aguilar simply pointed to his eyes and ears. Then he took out another Robusto, rolled it between his thumb and forefinger, held it to his nose, inhaled the aroma. Cut the end off the cigar with a small knife and lit it with a silver lighter. His initial, R, was engraved in fancy calligraphy.

Jake sighed. "Well, thanks for having my back. Again." He gestured toward the vicinity of Falcone and Niles. "I need to get these guys out of here."

"I think you will be fine, for now," Aguilar said. "But yes, that would probably be a good idea. I will be around." Which, Jake knew, meant Aguilar and his men would have a discreet presence until they were safely underway.

Jake embraced Aguilar, thanked him again, and said goodbye. He made his way back to Falcone and Niles, his mind brimming with rampant thoughts and emotions. He quickly corralled them and turned his full attention to the welfare of his two clients.

They stood right where he had left them, rigid and riveted and scared.

Seeing them, Jake felt a protective twinge and maybe a little regret. In a self-assured voice, he called out, "Okay, gents, let's move out!"

WHEN THEY RETURNED TO the boat, the captain's son and his two crewmates were soaking in the river, looking cool and contented. Seeing their passengers, the crew swam back to the boat, scrambling up to the deck. Both Falcone and Niles halted in their tracks and exchanged *do-we-dare* looks. Reading their expressions, Jake said, "Go on, it'll do you some good. You've been flirting with heat exhaustion since noon." *And since we almost got ourselves killed*, he thought gravely. As further endorsement, he added, "It will get your body temperature down."

Falcone and Niles slipped their backpacks off, removed the rest of the gear they were toting, pulled off their hiking shoes, and made a dash for the river. It was warm as bathwater but refreshing nonetheless. They immediately felt the tensions of the day begin to abate. Jake smiled, gathered the gear, and transported it to the dugout canoe on the beach. After he had relayed and stashed everything on the boat, he stripped off his boots and shirt and dropped into the water.

Falcone angled toward him. "You going to tell us what the hell happened out there?" Overhearing the question, Niles shimmied over.

Jake considered his answer carefully before replying. "I told you this is a highly volatile region where anything could happen at any time."

"Yes, you did," Falcone said tightly. "But I get the feeling that was not just a random occurrence. How did your paramilitary guy just happen to show up exactly where we were, just in the nick of time?"

"That wasn't a coincidence. I had already given him our itinerary so he could provide additional security. He had some intel about guerrilla activity and put us under tighter watch."

"So he was around when they came after us?" Falcone asked, still skeptical.

"Yes." Jake paused, weighing the scope of his responsibilities and then, his honor. It was his honor that prevailed. "They might have been after me," he said.

"What?"

"I also told you I had just been working over here, very high-risk stuff. So yes, it's possible."

Falcone and Niles both went quiet for a moment as that sank in, then Falcone looked directly at Jake and said with conciliatory sincerity, "Well, I'm glad we're safe and you're okay."

Niles' eyes suddenly widened and he looked around the water in alarm. "Oh my God. What about piranhas?"

Jake chuckled. "Relax. If there were any right here you'd know it. They'd be nibbling on you. Despite what you hear and see in the movies, they typically aren't man-eaters, unless there's blood in the water. That's what attracts them." He paused. "Now a really nasty little bugger is the candiru."

Their heads swiveled fiercely toward him and Jake could feel them both tense up in the water. "What's that?" Falcone asked, already certain he didn't want to know.

"The toothpick fish. It's a small parasitic catfish, about an inch long, that is known to swim into the urethra, and—"

"Wait," Niles practically shrieked, grabbing himself. "That's your pecker, right?"

"Ah, you get an A for anatomy," Jake said, grinning.

"You're jerking our chain now, right?" Falcone snapped.

Without the slightest hint of jest, Jake continued, "It swims into the urethra, spreads its fins and lodges there. The pain is supposed to be excruciating and it can't be extracted without—"

Niles was out of the water and climbing into the boat, screaming, "Don't tell me! Let's get the bloody hell out of here!"

Falcone was right behind him. "Yeah, what he said."

Jake was not laughing. His gaze shifted to the shoreline, beyond the beach to the jungle edge. "Yes, let's get the hell out of here," he muttered.

JUST BEFORE SUNSET THEY saw one of the true wonders of the Amazon, pink dolphins. The boat was moving at a brisk clip, propelled by the stronger downriver currents, trees along the shoreline sharp in silhouette against the backdrop of another fiery Amazon sky. Falcone and Niles were standing at the railing in somber contemplation, drinking canned beer, when Jake came up beside them and pointed to a vivid pink flash about thirty feet from the boat. He handed a pair of Steiner binoculars to Niles, who put them up to his eyes and directed the lenses to the spot.

"Oh my God, Eddie! Look!" Niles exclaimed, handing Falcone the binoculars so he could see, too.

Soon, the single dolphin was joined by several more, and for a while they watched them at play. The dolphins ranged in color from the blush of cotton candy to the confectionary pink of bubblegum. Botos are the only freshwater dolphins in the world, found in the Amazon and, to a lesser extent, Asia. With long beaks and a hump in the place of a dorsal fin, they have a brain capacity 40 percent larger than that of humans. There are thought to be less than a thousand remaining.

Falcone handed the binoculars back to Niles, who was enchanted. He jogged to the stern, sat on the edge, and continued to watch them frolic in the boat's wake. Standing next to Jake, the dolphin sighting was only a fleeting diversion for Falcone who could not clear the more indelible images of the guerrillas from his mind.

"How do you do it?" he asked.

"How do I do what?" Jake replied, though he knew what Falcone meant. His gaze was on the river but the dolphins had left his radar, too.

"That, today." Falcone studied the side of Jake's face, taking in the dark, stoic profile. They had seen glimpses of his compassion, his levity, certainly his integrity, but the darkness never seemed far below the surface.

Jake shrugged. "It's all I've ever really done. It's what I know, what I'm good at."

"You don't get scared?"

"Well, sure I do. But knowing how to channel fear is what defines a true warrior."

Falcone regarded him inscrutably. "What do you mean by that?"

"Fear is a journey from oneself to oneself. It takes a man deep inside himself if he is brave enough to go. And if he does, then he truly knows who he is and what he needs."

The power of Jake's words stunned Falcone to silence. Finally, he said, "And do you know? What you need?"

Jake didn't answer. He remained at the railing for a few more minutes, then he left Falcone standing there.

JAKE LAY IN HIS hammock listening to the old boat creak, the steady drip of water somewhere in the hull, the buzzing and clicking of insects wheeling aimlessly around the cabin. Occasionally, there would be a snort or a murmur from Falcone or Niles, but after dinner and several more beers they had practically fallen unconscious. Over the course of the evening, nothing else had been said about what had happened in the jungle, but Jake knew it would be hard for them to dismiss. And he was having a hard time dismissing the feeling that he could have been responsible for harm coming to them, possibly something worse. A lot worse.

The face of the dead guerrilla floated up from somewhere in the recesses of his mind. Where had he seen him before the day Delaney died? It continued to teeter on the rim of cognizance, just out of sync. He was certain he had seen him, but he just could not place where. One thing was for sure. Meeting him in the middle of virgin forest, in the Amazon, well over five hundred miles from Bogotá, was no coincidence.

His hand brushed his satellite phone, unclipped it from the waistband of his pants. He stared at it in his hand for a while. Pressed the speed-dial and listened. Waited. Heard it dialing. The connection clicked and he felt his heart lift.

And then sink.

"This is Haskell, I could be here or maybe I'm not. So leave me a message...HOO-rah!"

He pressed *end* after the electronic beep. Banging the Iridium phone against his temple, he realized he had forgotten to disconnect the answering machine at the house or at least change the voicemail, and Callie had not yet acquired a new cell phone. *Damn.* Before he could consciously stave it, despair flooded over him like a wave out of sequence.

Jake tossed restlessly in the hammock, willing his mind to empty. The dripping below seemed louder. Insects smacking against the wood were undaunted. *Whap, whap, whap.*

Like the sound that kid's bike had made, the one down a street from his childhood. He'd put playing cards in the spokes, a hip thing at the time. It was one of those fancy Schwinn Stingrays, royal blue he recalled, with the banana seat and deep handlebars. Jake had wanted one in the worst kind of way, had asked for one over and over again. He never got one, never got a bike of any kind in fact; his parents could not afford it.

And he just wanted to see what it felt like to ride...so one summer day he'd snuck into the kid's backyard and gotten on the bike. He was only going to ride it around the block, but he never made it out of the yard. And the kid made him pay. So had his stepmother.

Drip, drip...whap, whap, whap.

Now, a rusty faucet, droplets leaking to the ground as a gaunt child from another time and place tried to capture just a few in his tiny hands. But they kept slipping between his fingers. More moisture on his face, in the tears streaking through the grime encrusted.

Whap, whap, whap.

The rotors of the helicopter overhead, the child looking up as bullets rained down.

And do you know? What you need?

When Jake's mind finally shut down and let sleep come, it was that thought that followed him.

FROM LETICIA, JAKE TOOK them up for a helicopter tour of the Amazon basin, making suggestions for the best locales. Given what had happened the day before and given that he could not guarantee it would not happen again, he strongly encouraged them to consider the Peruvian or Brazilian regions, which he felt might be safer. Falcone and Niles spent some time talking with Jake about the information they would be presenting to the television show's executive producers and made plans for the next few weeks of developmental meetings and pre-production work in Costa Rica.

Then they flew to Bogotá.

On arrival, Jake took them to an El Corral where Falcone and Niles plowed into massive Corralisima cheeseburger combos like a ravenous pair of cattle rustlers after the last roundup. They'd had enough fish— and jungle grub—to last them for quite a while. When they finished their cheeseburgers and fries, Jake said, "I think you guys have more than earned a night of fun, so next stop is a place called Molotov's."

Sunburned face even ruddier with the gratification of a full stomach, Niles said, "That sounds appealing. I take it Molotov's is a bar or club or something like that?"

Smirking, Jake said, "Yeah, something like that."

They walked the length of Carrera 15 to the entrance of a building that looked like just another of the street's seedier establishments. There was no signage out front, only a pair of men the size and density of Olympic shot-putters. Jake spoke to them in Spanish, got nods, and led the way inside. Then he watched with amusement as Falcone and Niles took in the experience of Molotov's, the Russian House.

Men of all types generate instant attention in places like Molotov's, so three good-looking and indisputably fit men drew females like speed to a Ferrari. As the trio made their way to the long mirrored bar, they were watched with predatory interest. A steady chorus line of women brushed past them, making sure they made some kind of bodily contact in the process, their sensual invitations as subtle as a fire walking ceremony. Jake found himself biting his lip to keep from laughing at Falcone and Niles. Turning around to ask if they wanted a beer or perhaps something stronger, he saw them staring with open-mouthed astonishment at the seemingly endless supply of drop-dead-gorgeous Colombian women parading past them: tall and slender, short and petite, full-bodied and curvy; dark and full-blooded Latino or the many variant mixes of American, European, Caribbean, Spanish, Indian, and African ancestry. All of them dressed to kill and radioactive with sex appeal.

"Hey, guys," Jake said, trying to get their attention. "You should know that things are different here in Colombia."

"No shit," Falcone muttered. "God, look at the women. Are you sure we didn't take a wrong turn somewhere and wind up at the Miss Universe Pageant?"

"In the States, prostitutes are sleazy and disreputable, not to mention unsafe," Jake explained, "but in Colombia, the cat house thing is a totally different deal. It's manly and accepted, and as you can see the women are of an entirely different class."

"These women are *hookers?*" Niles asked, incredulous.

Nodding, Jake said, "Most of them, yes."

"Goddamn," Falcone said, but a lusty smile was plastered to his face.

The club's owner was behind the bar, and Jake exchanged introductions over a complimentary round of Aguardiente, more or less the national liquor of Colombia. It was anise-flavored and strong. A round of Club Colombia beer followed to mellow the bite. "So," Alfonso beamed at his new patrons, "you will make yourselves comfortable in my house, yes?" He gave Jake a conspiratorial wink.

Absently licking his lips as he eyeballed a tall, long-legged, longhaired woman strutting past in a very short and very tight leather skirt, Niles said, "Oh, certainly."

In a more serious tone, Jake said, "Listen, you gents do what you like. Have some fun. I'm meeting a friend of mine. Okay?"

As Jake moved off into the crowd, Niles shook his head in disbelief. "Did he mean what I think he meant?"

Falcone chortled, "He's telling us to get laid. You can stay here at the bar and have a few drinks if you want, but I'm suddenly horny as hell and if I don't do something about it pretty soon I'll—"

"All right, arsehole," Niles retorted, "you don't have to paint a bloody picture." He looked around, eyes gleaming. "God, talk about being a rooster in a hen house."

AS JAKE SLOWLY WORKED his way through Molotov's, scanning the crowd for the face he sought, his eyes also roamed over the many erotic flavors of sex candy. Any other time he would have been stoked and ready to pounce. The abysmal ache was back, gnawing its way through him, but none of the beautiful women held the slightest appeal to him tonight. Several stopped him, inquiring if he wanted to buy them a drink. *I should want to*, he thought dismally, but he didn't. He was surrounded by more female companionship than a healthy male could handle in a lifetime, and yet he was as profoundly lonely as he had ever been.

He was on his way back to the bar to get a drink when he heard someone call his name. The sound of the familiar male voice sent a feeling of comfort coursing through him as he turned to see Alberto Hernandez, seated on one of the couches with a lovely, classy-looking woman. She was dressed in an elegant but low-cut peach-colored suit that defined curves and revealed a lot of leg. They appeared to be sharing an intimate but possibly not amorous conversation.

The two men exchanged fond smiles and embraced. Before they sat down, Hernandez introduced his companion as Carmen Cassalas, from the US Embassy. After engaging in some polite small talk with both men, she tactfully excused herself, parting with a few words and a light kiss from Hernandez.

Jake took a seat opposite his friend and said, "I'm glad you could meet me. I need to talk to you."

"Of course," Hernandez said. He was clad in a white cotton shirt, black slacks, and boots, drinking a beer. "So how was the Amazon?"

"Hot as hell," Jake said, "and almost deadly."

Hernandez said nothing, his expression indicating that he probably already knew what had happened.

Lowering his voice, Jake asked, "Alberto, had you heard about the bounty on me?"

"After you got down there, yes. Raúl told me. But I also picked it up from other intel."

"The ambush wasn't a coincidence. Aguilar's men killed the guerrilla leader. I recognized him. I saw him passing through a small town on the way to the airstrip where Haskell's plane blew up."

Again, Hernandez said nothing.

Jake eyed him uneasily. "You don't seem surprised." He looked deeper into his friend's eyes, leaned closer. "Alberto, what do you know? There's something you're not telling me."

"Jake, it goes much further than the bounty. And yes, I was certainly going to tell you. But I am more than a little worried about what you will do with the information."

The din in the room suddenly ground into white noise, dull and distant. Jake's eyes flashed like flint, his chest constricting. "Tell me."

"The bounty was put out by a cartel. Not a new one exactly, but newly emergent. Restructured."

"Yeah, Raúl told me. Valentín is the name, right?"

"Yes. Two brothers, Adonís and Angel Valentín."

"Raúl said they were the ones responsible for Haskell's death."

"Yes, intelligence confirms this. But there is more to it." He paused again, sighed heavily, clearly loath to continue. Finally, he said, "Jake, the Valentin brothers are the sons of Hector Valentín."

Jake's face was empty of recognition, but he felt a weight of unknown size drop in the pit of his stomach like a rock careening off the sides of a deep hole.

Hernandez said, "Hector Valentín was La Víbora. The kingpin killed on the last mission."

23

LA VÍBORA. THE VIPER.

The name sucked all the oxygen out of the room and Jake felt his head go hollow. When he managed to pull breath through his lungs, he said, "You mean the kingpin *I* had killed on the last mission."

Hernandez lowered his head and raised it, not quite a nod, looking at Jake with deep concern in his eyes. He seemed at a loss for words. Finally, he said, "Why don't we go to my house and talk?"

"Yes," Jake said, and then remembered Falcone and Niles. "I've got to find my clients first. We've got rooms at the Charleston, but I want to make sure they get there later."

Spotting the twosome at the bar with a pair of women draped around them like angora mufflers, Jake headed over. "Hey, you guys mind hanging out here for a while?"

Falcone's eyes focused hazily and he waved a passive hand. "Hell, no."

"Curran?"

Niles spooned him a caviar- and champagne-sated smile. "Do I look like I mind, mate?"

"I'll see that Alfonso gets you to the hotel when you're ready."

The brunette next to Falcone slipped her tongue in his ear, her hand slipping somewhere much farther southward. "No hurry," he said, and ordered another round of drinks.

*   *   *   *   *

HERNANDEZ'S HOUSE WAS A tidy five-room single-story located in one of the more modest residential sections of Cedritos in the north. He spent very little time actually living there, and the scarcity of furnishings and décor reflected it. There was a brown leather couch, a tweed armchair, a coffee table, lamps, a kitchen table and chairs, and a bedroom set; the fifth room was cluttered with global artifacts and a travel debris field large enough to fill a small cargo plane. That, as much as anything, was representative of the life he led—the mercy missions, military operations, jungle expeditions, and emerald excavations. Evidence of the latter was displayed on a wide table partially covered in black velvet. Loose gems, both rough and finished, were scattered in all shapes and sizes; jewelry boxes contained both simple and elaborate sets of necklaces, earrings, bracelets, and pins. Emeralds were not only Hernandez' guilty pleasure and a sideline source of income, they were his romance.

Hernandez dug out a bottle of Warre's Warrior that he kept on hand just for Jake, pouring some of the plum-colored port into two etched crystal brandy snifters he'd bought on a recent jaunt to Spain. He handed one to Jake, who was pacing in the limited real estate of his living room, took the bottle and his own glass to the leather sofa. "Jake," he said quietly, "have a drink."

Jake slumped into the tweed armchair and took several sips of the port, leaned back against the top of the chair and closed his eyes. Minutes passed before he lifted his head, took a few more sips, and said, "God, Alberto, what am I going to do?"

"Well, NAS and the embassy are—"

"Fuck them," Jake muttered. "You know good and well they are not going to do a goddamn thing but dance around this cartel, just like they have all the rest. Do the full-investigation-politically-correct-joint-government-operation shit. In other words, absolutely nothing."

Hernandez sighed. There wasn't much he could say to refute that. He worked with them on a regular basis, attended many of their meetings and briefings, socialized at some of their functions, wined and dined often with several—one in particular—and knew Jake was right.

Jake sprang from his chair and began pacing again.

"I can't wait for them to conduct their investigations, gather their intel, share it with all the government agencies, map out strategies, solicit funds." He sat back down, then stood up again. "And I can't wait for this cartel to fucking kill me."

"I certainly understand how you feel," Hernandez conceded. "But Jake, you cannot go after them."

"What else can I do? Tell me." He ran a hand through his hair, dropped it to his hip.

"Maybe get a contract or some other kind of assignment state-side for a while, let things cool off."

"They came after me in the middle of the Amazon. What makes you think they can't or won't come after me anywhere else? No, I don't think I have any choice. It's eat or be eaten." He sank into the chair, leaned forward with his elbows on his thighs. "I have to do something."

Hernandez poured some more Warre's into Jake's snifter, topping off his own. For several minutes they drank in somber silence.

"I have to do something, Alberto," Jake said again, more emphatically.

"You cannot take on a cartel," Hernandez said, matching his tone.

"As I see it, I have no choice." He looked over at Hernandez, and their eyes locked. "Tell me honestly that I should leave this alone. Brother to brother. Tell me, Alberto."

Hernandez held his gaze for several moments, inhaled deeply, and said, "I guess I cannot tell you that. I guess if it were me, I would feel the same way you are feeling. Because I know you are right. These are ruthless men."

Another chasm of silence hung between them, and then Jake asked, "So how do I get to them?"

Hernandez stroked his mustache, sipped his port, thinking. Before he could come up with anything, Jake said, "I have to turn the table on them. I have to do something that will deflect their attention from me long enough to make them vulnerable."

"Okay, let us look at this from a logistical standpoint," Hernandez suggested. "They are a business, an organization. Intel indicates they are aggressively building their operations, trying to reestablish themselves as the powerhouse cartel in the region. Which means they will be doing what?"

"Seeking heavyweight distributors, major buyers and players."

"Exactly. Intel also has unconfirmed reports that they are sitting on an extremely large cache of product, very high purity. Some rumors have it as big as fifteen to twenty tons, which would be worth over $500 million."

Jake whistled and his eyes widened. In almost a whisper, he said, "Fuck, are you kidding me?"

"No, I have seen the intel."

"*Fifteen to twenty tons?* Holy fucking shit. That would be one of the largest hauls ever. Where do they think this cache is?"

"So far, no one knows."

"Do you think they're keeping it classified at the State Department or DOD or DEA?"

"No, it is really my feeling that no one knows."

Jake felt the nerves in his neck tingle. He cupped the snifter, swirled the port inside the etched crystal. "I wonder if Haskell knew, if he found out."

"That is a distinct possibility," Hernandez said.

"God, he was playing with matches in a dynamite factory." An image of Delaney flashed before him so vividly that Jake felt himself flinch.

Standing on the beach in the Bahamas, a bottle of Kalik in his hand, taunting him. "*Come on, Wildman, just one more wave. The ladies are watching…just one more.*"

Standing in the hatch of the plane.

And then gone, forever gone.

"I need to come up with a plan," Jake said. "Something that will draw them into a trap, corner them." An idea popped like a fluorescent light that has been flickering and then finally beams on in bright illumination. "You said it, Alberto. Buyers, they're looking for buyers."

"Yes," Hernandez said slowly, following the trajectory of his thought, "but you would have to implement others to pull something like that off, obviously. They know you. *You* could not do it."

"That's true. I'll have to see if any of my operators are up for it."

"Jake, this is really—"

"Hardcore. Yes, I know. And yes, I know even if I pull it off, I stand a chance of jeopardizing my military status and everything that goes with it. But fuck it, I can't *not* do something."

"Well, you know I will stand behind you and do anything I can," Hernandez said, and Jake knew he meant it.

"This may not have all started with Haskell," Jake said softly, "but I know his involvement, whatever it was, lit the fuse. And now it's going to burn until it detonates or until it's stopped. Alberto, I want them and I want them bad. They tortured and killed those people in Afortunado. They murdered Haskell. Now I have to get to them before they can get to me."

24

JAKE HAD LOST TRACK of how many calls he'd made. The only thing that mattered was that none of them thus far had yielded the results he needed. Seated in a chair next to the bed, he was flipping through the pages of a compact four-by-six ringed binder—his proverbial Black Book—and ticking off names as he made the calls. One after another, he was striking out. Voicemail, no answer, out of the country, on assignment, under the weather, previous commitments, deployed, under contract.

He dialed another. Heard the click as someone answered. A female voice said, "Hello?"

"Hello. This is Jake Tyler. Is Luke Sampson there?"

A moment later Sampson's robust voice came on. "Jake?"

"Luke, my man," Jake said. "How's life?"

"Good to hear from you, it's been a while. Life is good…great, in fact. I just got married!"

"Well now. Congratulations, bro. That's wonderful."

"To what do I owe the pleasure?" Sampson asked.

Jake hesitated, felt a hitch in his chest. "Oh, I was just updating my address book and when I came to you I decided to call, see how you were."

They talked for a few minutes, during which Jake mostly listened to Sampson's glowing account of his newly married life. Joy inflated every word the man spoke, and Jake felt his heart lighten and then, inexplicably, leaden. Finally, Jake said, "Luke, I am truly happy for you. You deserve it, bro. Take good care, okay?" And clicked off. The hitch in his chest dug in, spread wider, deeper.

He closed the binder and circled the room. Went to the arched floor-to-ceiling windows and looked out. Thought about her.

He padded back to the bed, sat down, and dialed Costa Rica on the hotel phone—specifically Luis Ayala, his friend with the Dominical police. When he heard the familiar youthful voice, Jake said, *"Hola, mi amigo!"*

"Jake! *Qué mas?*"

"Hey Luis, I forgot to change the voicemail at the house. I tried to call Callie to check on her…you've been keeping an eye out, right?"

"Oh, certainly, yes," Ayala assured him. "Every day. She is fine."

"You're sure?"

"Yes." There was a pause and then Ayala said, "She is missing you, I can tell. But she is fine. I am keeping watch."

"Okay. Thanks, my friend. Oh, Luis?"

"Yes?"

"Tell her I called, okay?"

"Certainly. Anything else?"

"Tell her it's okay to answer the phone."

He replaced the receiver and changed into running shorts and t-shirt. And then he left his suite, headed for the hotel gym.

THE GRAND OLD HOTEL'S brick veneer with its simple red awning defied the five-star luxury inside. There, the Charleston is a stylized blend of polished wood, gleaming marble, and shining metal, much of which is arranged in geometrical designs. Around the checkerboard-floored lobby, statuettes and elaborate fresh floral arrangements are distributed among rounded or squared surfaces. The neutral whites, beiges, grays, browns, and black lend it the quality of a modern art museum. With only sixty-four suites, it is considered a small hotel among those in the city's luxury class, but its grandeur rivals any of the larger world-ranked establishments in the city.

Falcone and Niles were taking in the hotel's opulence for the first time really, as they approached the restaurant inside. After an utterly unforgettable night at Molotov's, they had tumbled into the massive beds in their suites sometime in the wee morning hours and slept until late afternoon. Dressed in rumpled slacks and jackets, they strolled into the dining room and found Jake already seated, looking freshly showered and invigorated, having what looked to be a disappointing conversation on his cell phone.

La Biblioteca which, as its name indicates, once actually had the classy look and feel of an upscale library—complete with book-lined shelves—is now more an artisan gallery in a wash of honeyed tones and flat surfaces. In keeping with the hotel's geometric order, tables were angled, leather chairs were simple, and the white china service was square. Cylindrical glass vases held red calla lilies.

A waiter slipped in behind them with the smoothness of a silk scarf and retracted chairs. Glancing up, Jake hastily concluded his phone conversation and clipped the BlackBerry back on his pants. His face had been tense when they came in, but as Falcone and Niles took their seats he managed to produce an engaging smile. "So," he said, eying the haggard duo, "had fun, did you?"

"Except for the bloody hangover from hell," Niles murmured morosely. There were bags under his eyes that needed their own luggage cart. "I haven't had that much sex since…well, ever." He peered down at his lap, lamenting, "I think I may have broken it."

"Ditto," Falcone said, rubbing his temples.

Jake laughed. "Well, get some food in you."

They spent the next several minutes ordering dinner, foregoing alcohol. When the waiter moved away, conversation shifted to the television project. Jake listened briefly as Falcone and Niles launched into a dialogue about plans for the coming days, but found his mind quickly jumping track to the talk of last night with Alberto Hernandez. Plates with salad and bread appeared, forks and knives chinked lightly against the china, piano sonatas floated through the elegant room. Falcone and Niles continued to talk, but Jake registered little of what they were saying. When he heard Niles finish a sentence with his name, he said, "Gents, I'm afraid something has come up that requires my immediate involvement."

They both just looked at him, the grave tone in his voice and somber expression on his face causing them to stop chewing.

"Hopefully I won't be out of the loop for too long. In the meantime I think it's best that you return to Costa Rica and work from that end."

Swallowing a mouthful of bread, Falcone said, "Why? What's going on?"

"I can't discuss it," Jake said tersely.

"Is everything all right?" Niles asked, his forehead creased with worry.

"Do not let it concern you," Jake replied evenly. "Enjoy yourselves here, now, then move on with your pre-production work and I'll reconnect with you as soon as I can."

"How long will that be?" Falcone asked.

Before he could respond, Jake's cell phone vibrated. Reaching for it, he automatically rose from the table and excused himself. Falcone and Niles watched him stride from the dining room, Niles mumbling, "Bloody hell."

"Yeah," Falcone said, "that doesn't sound good. You know what? I think I need to visit the men's restroom." He wiped his mouth, got up, and headed in the direction Jake had gone. Spotting Jake standing off by himself talking on the cell phone, Falcone found a corner nearby and tucked himself into it. He reached into his pants pocket, extracted his wallet, and pretended to look for a particular credit card. And listened. Snippets of conversation began to filter over.

"...really frustrated. I've been making calls all day and so far I'm coming up empty. Everybody I've talked to is otherwise committed. Of all times to run into a shortage of operators...no, I don't think I can take a chance using somebody I don't know...probably two guys, yeah...no, I can't wait...have to act now...yeah, had to tell them I'd be out of service for a while...okay, thanks...and I'll continue to make calls, there's got to be somebody available in the next—"

Sensing the conversation was coming to a close, Falcone hustled back to their table. A minute or two later, Jake rejoined them, his face grim. "My apologies," he said, taking his seat.

As entrees were served, Jake parlayed the dinner conversation to their exploits of the previous night. Plates were set before them yielding tenderloin medallions in béarnaise, sea bass in mushroom, and chicken in tarragon. While they ate, Falcone and Niles recited wantonly colorful stories of their sexual trysts, but as soon as their plates had been cleared from the table, Falcone said, "What is it you need a couple of guys for, Jake?"

Jake's face flushed with unexpected anger. "You listened in on my conversation?"

"I was on my way to the restroom and caught some of it, yeah."

"Like I said, Eddie, it's not any of your concern. Leave it at that, okay?"

"Hey, we hired you and you're having to break away. I think you can at least tell us why."

Jake shook his head, feeling his temper rising. Taking a deep, bracing breath, he said, "I can't. For your own security, I can't."

"What if we want to help?" Niles suggested.

"I appreciate it, guys," Jake said, lightening. "Really, I do. But there's nothing you can do to help."

"Maybe there is," Falcone said. "You said you needed a couple of guys. We're not 'operators,' but maybe you could use us for whatever it is."

"Sorry, no," Jake said bluntly.

"Sounded like you're needing a couple of guys pretty bad," Falcone pressed.

"Eddie, leave it alone," Jake bristled. "Now, that's all I'm going to say on the matter." He dropped his napkin on the table and stood. "I'll give you a call later with your flight arrangements."

JAKE STARED AT HERNANDEZ as if he had grown two heads and begun speaking in Swahili. "Did I hear you right? You can't be serious."

Shortly after retreating to his suite Jake had received a call from Hernandez, suggesting that they meet at the hotel's bar to resume the conversation they'd been having earlier on the phone. Jake told him about Falcone's eavesdropping and what was said afterward. Toward the end of Jake's recount, Hernandez had smiled in a way that hinted he'd come up with something. That was when he had shocked Jake by saying, "Maybe they *can* do it."

Now, sipping from a glass of Grand Old Parr, Hernandez said, "I have been thinking about this, Jake. And maybe they are really the ideal ones to do this."

"What makes you think so?" Jake asked, his face still reflecting skepticism.

"First of all, there is obviously a very small window of opportunity here."

"Granted," Jake said, and took a swallow from his drink. The bar echoed the décor of the restaurant, bathed in honey-hued lighting that glowed off the rich wood trim and two-toned flooring. The effect was subtle and soothing, but it was totally lost on Jake who was growing increasingly agitated.

"By the time you line some operatives up and get them in place," Hernandez continued, "most likely that window will have closed."

Jake gazed bleakly into his whiskey, clinking ice against the sides of the glass.

"Finally, I believe these narcos will smell SpecOps guys a mile away."

"Why do you think that?"

"From what I have heard and what I have picked up from intel, I just believe it. They will be especially wary and vigilant until they feel their position is solid. I would not be at all surprised if they even know the identity of many of your guys from their own intel."

"But Alberto, how could I put a couple of untrained civilians in a situation as dangerous as this would be?"

Hernandez shrugged. "I suppose that is the moral dilemma. But they are grown men and if they are game, I say put it on the table and let them decide for themselves. The DEA uses civilian informants in sting operations all the time."

"That's different. Informants are usually in it for the money and have been around the scene enough to know something of the risks involved. I don't know, Alberto," Jake said doubtfully. "I just can't see it."

"Can't see what?"

Jake and Hernandez swiveled around from their table to see Falcone and Niles, holding bottles of Club Colombia.

"Ah, these must be your clients," Hernandez said, standing and extending his hand to each of them as introductions were made. "Join us, gentlemen."

"Why don't you cut the bullshit and just tell us what's going on," Falcone said, dropping into one of the scant leather chairs. "Curran and I have talked about it and we both want to help, if it's something we can do and if you'll let us."

"Well, truthfully, I don't know if it is something you can do and I don't know that I'm willing to let you," Jake said stubbornly.

"So tell us and we'll decide."

Catching a nod from Hernandez, Jake heaved a sigh of reluctant acquiescence and told them. When he came to the cartel, he gave them a carefully filtered version of their lineage and playbook. He finished by confirming that he was now in their sights.

"As a result of" —he paused judiciously—"my work over here, I have now become a target, and I've come to the conclusion that I need to take them on before they can take me out."

Falcone and Niles had been quietly riveted throughout Jake's discourse, their expressions deepening in intensity as the revelations grew increasingly ominous. "You were working counternarcotics, weren't you?" Falcone speculated.

Jake said nothing.

Falcone and Niles exchanged ponderous looks, mentally deciding something in tandem. The process took all of ten seconds.

Putting his elbows on the small table between them, Falcone leaned in and said, "So what do you need us to do?"

25

JAKE PRESSED HIS LIPS together, tilted his head up toward the lounge's ceiling. Then he looked across the table at Falcone and Niles, two television show coordinators—or whatever their actual titles were—who no more belonged stepping into the roles they were auditioning for than astronauts with vertigo. Looked at the spiky-haired Jersey guy and his ponytailed Brit partner of whom he had grown exceedingly fond, and shook his head.

"No," Jake said decisively. "I can't let you get involved in this. I cannot be responsible for putting the two of you in that kind of extreme risk—and it is extreme. No."

"Jake, c'mon," Niles pleaded.

"No."

Jake unclipped his vibrating cell phone, glancing hopefully at the display. Seeing a familiar name, he flashed a quick grin at Hernandez. "One of my best guys," he said, and left the table to take the call in privacy.

"Evan, hey bro…what? Can hardly hear you. Where are you? Where? Shit. What the fuck…when will you be back? No, it's okay…yeah, me, too. Take care, my brother." Jake stood with his back to the table for several minutes after the call had ended, his shoulders slumped in defeat. Evan Neville had just about been his last candidate. The army had other ideas. Damn. *Maybe it's a sign from the Buddha Man,* he thought. Problem was, he wasn't sure what the sign meant. Abandon his intentions, or take a very risky—probably foolhardy—gamble?

When he took his seat again, he drained the Grand Old Parr from his glass and said, "Okay, I'll tell you what I have in mind and we'll talk about it some more."

Another round of drinks was ordered and Jake outlined his plan-in-the-making.

"Alberto and I talked about this the other night as we were theorizing ways to draw these guys out, make them vulnerable so I can get to them. These narcos are building their organization and reputation, so like any power-hungry cartel they are going to be keen to get their product pipeline flowing. That means they will be actively seeking buyers, major players. So the idea was to have a couple of my operatives pose as buyers and bait them with a buy so big that the head guys—a pair of brothers—become involved directly. If my guys could entice them to set up a meeting in a remote enough location, they could then exfil and we could take the narcos out."

"Exfil?" Falcone queried.

Jake cracked a slight grin. "Sorry, that's military for get the hell out of Dodge."

"Wouldn't you have to show them the money so to speak?" Niles asked.

"If you mean like a briefcase full of cash, no, not necessarily. As long as they can verify funds, they will talk." Mindful of his inflated offshore bank account, Jake added airily, "I have a source for the funds."

"So, you wouldn't actually be making a transaction," Falcone said.

"No, it wouldn't get to that point. All I need to do is get them personally involved and isolated."

"Wouldn't they do a background check of the buyers?"

Hernandez spoke up, replying, "Yes, they certainly would. Very astute, Eddie. We have ways to create identities."

"Well, sounds pretty straight-up to me," Niles said. "I don't see why we couldn't do this. Do you, Eddie?"

"Just role-playing," Falcone agreed.

"It's a lot more than role-playing," Jake countered sternly. "This is teasing sharpshooters while wearing a Kevlar vest. Any exposure and they're going to nail us." He gave each of them a harsh look of reproach. "This is *not* a game, gents. Do you understand?"

"Of course we do," Falcone snipped. "I'm just saying it's something we can handle. We'd be under your supervision, right?"

"Absolutely. But to some extent you'd be working without a net. You'd have to be ready to think on your feet. Without the background and training we have, you'd be very vulnerable if anything went awry. We'd be around, but since this wouldn't be an officially sanctioned operation, it's not like we could come in with the cavalry and guns blazing."

"Just curious," Niles mused, "why wouldn't the narcotics blokes— what are they, DEA?—take this cartel on?"

"Because it's too soon. They'll act quickly and indiscriminately when it comes to wiping out labs and coca fields, but for the kingpins they sit with their thumbs up their asses and conduct investigations, surveillance, all that shit. That's all fine and good, but since *my* ass has a target painted on it, I'm not waiting. I just never intended to involve anyone who—"

"Save it, Jake," Falcone interjected, nudging his beer bottle toward the center of the table. "We know that. We're volunteering, okay?"

"Tell me why you would want to do this."

Without hesitation, Falcone said, "Because it's for you. There doesn't have to be any other reason." Beside him, Niles nodded.

"I'm still not comfortable with this," Jake said grudgingly, "but unless I come up with something else, I guess we'll go forward."

"So what do we do next?" Niles asked, his eyes bright with anticipation.

"I have to find a thread to the cartel, something, or someone, who will take the bait to them." Jakes eyes narrowed as a thread suddenly unspooled in his mind. "I think I know just the person." He shot Hernandez a glance. "Where can we put some feelers out?"

Hernandez gave it some thought. "There is an embassy party Friday night. I believe that might provide you with your answer."

THE AMBASSADOR'S RESIDENCE WAS packed with invitees and their guests, most of who were milling about within grazing range of the long and elaborate banquet table set up in a capacious reception room. Men wore either designer suits or tuxes; the women were clad in cocktail dresses and gowns with enough extravagant bling around their necks and wrists or dangling from their earlobes to rival a red-carpet premiere. A notable grouping of embassy officials and diplomats gathered in conversation below the American and Colombian flags. Nearby, high-ranking military and police officers intermingled. Hovering between the two groups was the US Ambassador, the Chief of the Colombian National Police, the Chief of the Colombian Armed Forces, and various officials from the US State Department, and the DEA. In the next room a band was playing moderately loud, watered-down versions of popular American and Latino songs, to which little more than a dozen couples danced. A rendition of Green Day's *Know Your Enemy* turned a few heads and picked up the pace as guests circulated, the conversations buzzed, and the alcohol more fully infiltrated bloodstreams.

Hernandez had no problem getting an invite for Jake but had to pull some strings to include Falcone and Niles. Dressed in modest eveningwear, the foursome sampled food from the banquet table and procured drinks from the well-stocked bar. They were munching on buffalo wings and *empanadas* and *chorizos* when a tall man in an Armani tuxedo crossed the room and approached them.

For the benefit of Falcone and Niles, Hernandez introduced the man as Vince McCauley, his embassy supervisor. Bearded and looking considerably younger than his mid-fifties, McCauley was cordial but fastidious, dispensing with small talk in favor of what was germane to their work. Addressing Hernandez, McCauley said, "I understand you conducted some new surveillance recently?"

"Yes, during the last mission."

"Can you have a report on my desk by noon tomorrow?" McCauley asked peremptorily.

"I have spoken to Carmen Cassalas about this information," Hernandez said calmly but with a trace of weariness. "I would really like to investigate it further before submitting anything."

McCauley made no attempt to conceal his impatience. "All right, but I want everything you have as quickly as possible so we can formulate our next mission agenda."

A shadow of annoyance passed over Hernandez's typically serene face. "We need to go slowly here, Mac. If we act too quickly we may lose the opportunity for a more comprehensive and successful effort. I do not have enough information yet for us to initiate a major operation. I need to do a thorough assessment, talk to the police and agents in the field, and take a hard look at security."

McCauley turned to Jake. "Are you still looking into Delaney's death?"

"Well, I haven't exactly given up," Jake admitted evasively.

"We definitely believe it was the act of a narcoguerrilla group," McCauley said.

No shit, Jake thought, and looked away to hide his disdain.

But his feelings were not lost on McCauley. "Look, Jake, you certainly have my deepest sympathies and understanding, and I know it's been frustrating for you, but there's only so far these official investigations can go. You know that."

Jake did not respond.

In an effort to lighten the tension that had developed, Falcone spoke up. "I had no idea the Drug War was still such a major problem. Since 9/11 and the Iraq War, you never hear much about it."

McCauley drew himself up with manifest ostentation, appearing even taller than his six-foot-three height, and Jake thought, *Here we go.* "Let me tell you about our Drug War, Mr. Falcone. We call it the 'Dirty Little War,' because it has so many similarities to the Vietnam War. Its successes have been tempered by the vacillating support of both the US and Colombian governments, not to mention the criticisms we've drawn. When the Clinton administration launched the eradication program in the year 2000, it focused primarily on aerial eradication. It was deemed a success with reports bragging that the amount of coca cultivation in Colombia fell from 420,000 acres in 2001 to 280,000 acres in 2003. Those results might seem impressive on the surface, but while the focus was on Colombia, cultivation rose in Peru and Bolivia. And while we shifted our focus to fighting the War on Terrorism, they redoubled their efforts and pretty much made up the ground we gained. The bottom line is that the supply of cocaine flowing into the United States and other markets is as plentiful as ever.

"The new Plan Colombia has added another means of attack, which is training and equipping more Colombian police and military. There have been more captures and surrenders, more successful extraditions."

He continued, "On the other hand, we're constantly criticized by human rights groups and citizens who, admittedly, have some pretty valid arguments. They counter that our eradication drives the farmers farther into the jungle—if we don't take away their livelihood altogether and convert them into homeless migrants working the fields. And if we take away their livelihood, there are not enough economic development assistance programs being offered by the governments. The herbicides and fumigation methods arguably pose some health risks and environmental damage. We're always being blamed for wounding or killing innocent civilians with eradication-related gunfire. The army and police are blamed for raiding their homes. And worst of all, our actions incite counter-actions from the FARC who destroy property—like dynamiting pipelines and hydro-electric plants—and kill villagers they believe are informants or sympathizers."

Falcone shook his head dumbly, rattled by the overload of information.

"After dismantling the Cali and Medellín cartels, there seemed to be a shift to small independents who are younger, more sophisticated, Internet savants, with a shrewd grasp of world finance and new money-laundering sources. They work in conjunction with both right-wing paramilitaries and leftist rebels. They send the coke out by the kilo instead of the ton, making it more difficult to track. They have smaller labs but a greater proliferation. The strategy is to spread the product out to minimize the loss in the event of a bust. They still use small planes and speedboats, but they are relying more and more on couriers they can recruit and turn into mules..."

McCauley was still talking, but Jake did not have the stomach to keep listening. The last sentence had immediately evoked the image of Delaney standing in the doorway of the DC-3—the DC-3 loaded with God only knew how much product or money or both—Delaney standing there talking to him one minute, trying to convince him everything was fine, blown up and dying in his arms the next. He moved away, oblivious to the guests he passed, nodding vaguely to some he knew. A few minutes later, Hernandez caught up with him.

"Are you okay?"

"Yeah," Jake muttered. "That guy just talks to damn much. Eddie and Curran hardly needed to hear all that shit, either."

"Maybe they did, Jake. They need to know a little more about what they are getting themselves involved in."

"Well, preferably not from the fucking bureaucrats," Jake remarked. "Funny how fast they want to move on the narcoguerrillas and their village serfs, yet they won't even—"

"*Qué más, papacitos?*" a feminine voice inquired from behind them.

They both turned to see Carmen Cassalas, elegant in a long black dress slit to mid-thigh. The low-cut front revealed a strand of black pearls. This drew playful and predictable admonition from Hernandez.

"*Qué? Nada de esmeraldas esta noche?*" He gave her an affectionate kiss on the cheek.

Flipping her long hair sinuously off bare shoulders, she said, "If you have any new pieces for me to model, I'd be more than happy to slip these pearls in my bag."

Winking at Cassalas, Hernandez said, "I always have emeralds with me." Reaching into an interior pocket of his gray tweed jacket, he produced a necklace of gems the green of an Irish countryside, emerald-cut and graduated on either side to form a V at the center. When he fastened it around Cassalas's neck, the point of the V rested just above her cleavage. Chuckling, Hernandez commented, "On you, the emeralds might not get too much attention."

Cassalas smiled, feigning embarrassment, but the coquettish play quickly gave way to what could have been either professional formality or intimate invitation. "Alberto, I need to have a word with you." She glanced pointedly at Jake, adding, "In private."

Withdrawing with a slight bow and a tight smile, Jake said, "I need to check in with the guys."

FALCONE AND NILES APPEARED to be holding their own, alternating between the banquet table, the bar, and the attractive women on the dance floor, so Jake decided to take a break from the stuffy rooms and the self-important people unctuously working the circuit within them.

He pushed through a pair of French doors and stood on the verandah in pensive solitude. The cool mountain air felt good on his face as he gazed up at the moon. Tonight it was big and full, the color of a pale flame.

He remained there for a while, unaware of how much time passed, his mind in another place.

At some point Jake felt a hand on his shoulder and turned. It was Hernandez. He said, "I may not have told you that Carmen works with both the DEA and NAS."

"I suspected as much."

"I think I may have found your 'in.' The other day I asked her if she knew or had heard of Elena. She did some checking. She says there is no one by that name working with the DEA."

"No?" Jake asked, but he found himself unsurprised.

"Of course, she may be using an alias, but I described her and Carmen said she checked the databases quite thoroughly."

"That's going to a lot of trouble," Jake observed.

"I suppose so," Hernandez said as if he were dangling a hypothetical theory.

Watching the subtle shift of light in his eyes, Jake caught it. Said nothing.

A few moments later, Hernandez said, "So this is how you want to play it?"

Jake inhaled deeply, caught sight of Falcone and Niles inside dancing animatedly in the company of an attractive pair of Colombian women. Felt a twinge of uncertainty. The moon glowed overhead, illuminating him like a laser sight.

"Yes," he said. Following Hernandez back inside the ambassador's mansion, he whispered, "God help us."

26

THE CALL CAME AT 5:45 PM on Tuesday.

Hernandez listened, his side of the conversation spare, and after ending the call cast Jake a provocative gaze. They were seated at a secluded table in the back of the Red Lion, a British pub in the trendy Parque 93 zone. The air smelled of beer and cooking oil, but it was not an altogether unpleasant odor; it was an olfactory promise of comfortable fellowship over a simple cooked-to-order meal to be washed down with a couple of pints. Several pairs of jacketless businessmen lined the bar, bent over after-work drinks and low-key conversation; a small grouping of young men in jeans stood laughing around one of the big-screen TVs; a scattering of couples munched on burgers and other light dinner fare.

Across from Hernandez, Jake didn't have to ask who the call was from. He reached for his cell phone, inhaled deeply, punched in the numbers. Into the mouthpiece he said, "Okay, you're on."

A FEW BLOCKS DOWN, Falcone and Niles casually sidled into Molotov's and meandered toward the bar. The bodies mingling in the nightclub this evening numbered significantly less than their previous visit, but the place was still fairly crowded. Alfonso drifted over like a passing shadow and set bottles of Club Colombia in front of them, adding shot glasses with Aguardiente.

The Saturday after the embassy party, Alberto Hernandez had

stopped by Molotov's to enlist Alfonso's help. As a former sergeant-major in the Colombian army, the club's proprietor was happy to oblige. Fifteen minutes ago, Alfonso had made the call that brought Falcone and Niles to the bar.

Now, sipping their beer, the duo tried to quell their nerves and hyped adrenaline by mentally reviewing the instructions Jake had given them. They were designer-dressed in a combination of street-chic and business suave—Kenneth Cole, Ermenegildo Zegna, Versace, DKNY, Perry Ellis. Falcone wore fitted stretch slacks, a black silk shirt with gold-tan striping open at the collar and loose beneath a charcoal two-button blazer; Niles was slightly more casual in a suede safari jacket over a cotton Tencel shirt and linen trousers, all in muted shades of buff and gray. Both were cologned, coiffed, and smartly accessorized. The gold watch on Falcone's wrist, on loan from one of Hernandez's jeweler acquaintances, cost more than his last car, something French and so exquisite he was afraid to touch it, let alone look at it. So he watched the women instead. Almost immediately he spotted several he remembered, though names escaped him; what they had done with their lips and tongues and teeth and other parts was, on the other hand, quite memorable.

Niles gave him a swift jab in the side. "Keep your tongue in your mouth and the beast in your pants."

"Hey," Falcone huffed indignantly, color rising in his face, "I know what we're here for." He continued his surveillance of the crowd, one hand tapping a nervous rhythm on his thigh as he honed in on faces, trying to strike a balance between social intercourse and focused study.

Several minutes passed. They drank their beer, felt themselves begin to loosen up. The music throbbed, bodies bobbed, eyes sought and caught and then released. Sex permeated like an electrical field that builds right before a boisterous summer thunderstorm. Hot and close, hovering.

Behind them, Alfonso cleared his throat. Both felt their pulses skip.

They twisted around to see him tip his head slightly toward the opposite end of the bar. Making a point not to look right away, they lifted their shot glasses and downed the Aguardiente, then let their eyes slowly gravitate in the direction Alfonso had gestured.

And saw her.

Elena Torres García was standing perhaps twenty feet away, moving sensually with the beat of the music, hips and shoulders gyrating. She was, at least for that moment, alone. And she was spine-tinglingly gorgeous. Her curves were sheathed in a black spandex dress, the top of which was cut and fit like a bathing suit with white satin piping swirling over her ample breasts and crisscrossing her bare back in spaghetti straps. Her hair was loose, the coppery highlights glinting even in the dim light. While they observed her, several good-looking men approached with carnal invitation. In each case, after briefly indulging in their verbal foreplay and virile posturing, she sent them off with frosty rejection.

Watching her, Falcone made sure he established solid eye contact before he and Niles began their pre-rehearsed role-play. For his part, Alfonso had made some subtle adjustments and enhancements to the lighting around the bar. So when Niles extracted a velvet pouch from an interior pocket of his Zegna jacket and emptied its contents, the sparkle could be seen from a distance; more importantly, from the corner of his eye, Niles saw that the sparkle caught Elena's attention. He removed a white silk handkerchief from another pocket, shook it open and smoothed it flat. Next, he displayed the emeralds that Alberto Hernandez had discriminatingly collected for them, selecting various gems and holding them up to catch a thin stream of the spotlight.

The effect was, as Hernandez had predicted, magnetic. Falcone and Niles had barely launched into their discussion when Elena materialized between them.

"You gentlemen certainly know how to get a lady's attention," she said, her voice low and sultry, oozing enough sex to make Viagra as irrelevant as a Tic-Tac.

"And I thought diamonds were a girl's best friend," Niles quipped.

"Not in this country," she replied, twirling a strand of hair with one of her long, shellacked fingernails. She reached between them and picked up a cushion-shaped emerald the size of a postage stamp, examining it closely. "Are you buying, selling, or coveting?"

"Could be all of the above," Falcone answered cryptically, sipping his beer. He signaled to Alfonso who promptly brought them another round, adding a Stolichnaya on the rocks for Elena.

Swirling the ice in her drink before taking a sip, Elena said, "Now that is an interesting response. If I may be so bold, what is your business here?"

"That is rather bold of you, madam," Niles said, smiling, "but since you asked, we're...investors." Indicating the emerald she was still admiring, twelve carats of startling clarity, he said, "You have excellent taste. That one's from Chivor, worth close to half a mil."

Her eyes widened like a ripple pool in a dark lake, her lips parting to allow a small gasp before she regained her icy composure. "Oh, so the emeralds are an investment." She tilted her head inquisitively, stroking the gem with her fingertip. It was the green of a newly minted dollar bill.

"Not so much," Falcone replied casually. "Just an interest. What we're actually seeking is an investment of another kind...of another color you might say."

"Is that so?" Elena asked, her eyes flashing with new interest. "And what color would that be?"

"A paler color," Niles answered.

"A paler color," she repeated.

"Yes. Emeralds are a very good investment, but they are known to have flaws. We're looking for something of exceptional purity, something with high marketability."

"I see," Elena said, and glanced across the vast room, searching the crowd as if she might be seeking someone in particular. "I am constantly amused at the diversity of people I meet here at Molotov's. Most men come here with one thing foremost on their minds."

"Who said we didn't?" Falcone countered huskily. He waited until he had her full attention again, and offered his hand. "I'm Tony Messina from New York and my partner is Bart Fletcher, obviously from London."

She took his hand, letting her fingertips slide across his as she released the grip. "Very pleased to meet you both. I'm Elena Torres García. It just so happens that I have a direct line to such investment opportunities."

Toying with the other emeralds as he spoke, Niles said, "You have our attention."

"I should tell you," Falcone said, pushing his silk shirtsleeve back to expose the outrageously expensive timepiece, "that we can't waste our time on the local level. We only deal in large-scale investment."

Eyes drawn briefly to the watch, she said, "Then I think I can put you in touch with some businessmen in the line of investment you are seeking." She handed the Chivor gem back to Niles, finished her drink and gave her hair a light toss. "But first one of you better dance with me."

HERNANDEZ PUSHED HIS PLATE aside, popping the last french fry into his mouth. Rubbing his scant stomach, he glanced over at the tall Englishman who had taken Jake's seat and said, "Excellent as always, John."

"I aim to please. So when are you going to do that Amazon trip you keep talking about? I'm right ready to do some fishing."

Hernandez smiled. "I am as well. The quest for the giant catfish continues. Perhaps this October."

"Well, count me in, mate."

"Of course."

The proprietor of the pub rose from the table and took his place back behind the bar, soliciting refills as he popped in and out of conversations among the locals. Hernandez got up and walked to the pub's front entrance where Jake had been pacing for the past twenty minutes.

"Jake, come and sit down. I think it is going to be a long evening."

Frowning, Jake looked at his watch and said, "Yes, I know. Okay."

Following Hernandez back to the table, he dropped into a chair with a heavy sigh. Hernandez said gently, "You told them what to do. They are sharp and seem focused. Now you have to let them stand or fall on their own."

Jake clawed agitatedly at his hair. "I know, I know. But Alberto, I don't have the confidence yet that they know what the hell they're doing."

"Well then, now is the time to find out," Hernandez replied simply. He looked intently at Jake. "Is there something else about this that is bothering you? You had a relationship with her, after all."

Jake did not respond right away, looking off when he said, "It was just an occasional hookup, anyway." Facing Hernandez again, he added,

"And as far as I'm concerned, she's every bit as responsible for killing Haskell as if she'd rigged the fucking plane herself."

"I happen to agree with you," Hernandez said solemnly.

They fell into an uncomfortable silence as Jake reflected on the briefing he had given Falcone and Niles earlier, rehashing and scrutinizing everything he'd told them, hoping he hadn't given them too much information, hoping he'd given them enough, hoping they'd know how to react to whatever unfolded—hoping they wouldn't overreact and expose themselves to what could be perilous consequences. Hoping he hadn't made the wrong decision.

He had given them only a sketchy background on Elena, rationalizing that much more would make them either tentative or too aggressive. The one thing he emphasized was her ruthlessness, his parting comment to them being: "Never forget who she is."

An assassin, he thought, *she's nothing less than a cold-blooded assassin.*

And he had just sent Falcone and Niles to set up play in her parlor.

John had returned with another beer for Hernandez. Regarding Jake ruefully, he said, "I think you could use a drink yourself, mate."

"Yeah," Jake said thickly, "I think I could probably use several."

JAKE STOOD BEFORE HERNANDEZ'S living room window, finally tired of pacing and only faintly aware of the sun beginning to erase the night. And a long night it had been. He'd had a few drinks with Hernandez, even started to relax a little, but his mind maintained a continuous percolation of doubt peppered with worrisome what-ifs. Hours passed with no word, and then hours more. Finally, sometime after two AM, John had summoned a taxi for them, and Hernandez took Jake back to his house. He watched Jake's fretful laps for another hour before giving in to exhaustion and retiring to his bedroom.

As the hours mounted, Jake's emotions vacillated somewhere in the middle of anger and concern, a cavern he'd occupied many times with Delaney. He was concerned that something might have gone wrong and angry that whatever was happening was totally out of his control. It was not a feeling he was used to, certainly not a feeling he liked.

Once during the long wait he had slumped back on the couch and, before he realized it, briefly dozed. His subconscious mind took him to another place, across the ocean, and just before he snapped awake he remembered flying—embodied as a hawk—through a blinding white light, actually shuddering as he was suffused by an otherworldly exhilaration. He awoke in a tingly sweat.

Now, as he stood on the preludial edge of day as it slowly crept toward the window, he glanced at his watch for perhaps the twentieth time. And, also for the countless time, thought distractedly about calling Luis Ayala—or the house. *No*, he told himself resolutely, *got to stay focused, can't go there.* But his self-denial inflated a small hollow place in his chest that lingered until the moment he heard the door thump open.

Falcone and Niles stumbled into the living room, looking drained and bedraggled, and immediately dropped onto the couch. Looking blearily at Jake, Falcone said, "We're in."

Niles muttered, "God, I could use some bloody strong coffee."

"I think we all could," they heard Hernandez say as he emerged from the short hall. He padded into the kitchen and put a pot of coffee on to brew. In minutes the piquant aroma of Colombian coffee filled the room and their sinuses. The rich brew was poured, mugs distributed.

"Okay," Jake said, his eyes as dark and intense as the coffee, "talk to me."

Falcone yawned, stretching back against the couch. With the insouciance of a tomcat back from birding, he said, "Tony Messina and Bart Fletcher have a meeting with the brothers Valentín." Then, unable to stop himself, he grinned with boastful accomplishment.

Despite his expectations of the outcome, Jake was surprised. "When?"

"This Saturday, at noon," Falcone answered around another yawn.

Jake's forehead creased as his eyes narrowed, the veil of suspicion instantly going up. "Where?"

"Don't know," Niles said. "We were told a car would pick us up promptly at eleven."

"I am not sure I like that," Hernandez remarked, stroking his mustache thoughtfully. "That gives them total control. They will be picking you up at the hotel?"

"Yeah. After you made the arrangements, we checked out of the

Charleston and got settled into the Radisson, just as you told us to do."

"Good. I will follow up with a phone call, make sure the Charleston has wiped you from their records."

"How can you be sure they will do that?" Falcone asked.

"They will do it," Hernandez assured them.

Coming from the kitchen after refilling his coffee, Jake stopped by the couch and stood over the haggard pair. "So how did it all go down?"

"Pretty much exactly as you wanted," Falcone replied. "The emeralds worked like magic. Once we started talking investment opportunity we had her interest, but she kinda strung us along for a while. We had some drinks, did the small talk thing, danced...you know."

Niles picked it up there, saying, "Elena invited us back to her suite at the Tequendama to talk business. When we got there, we had a drink while she made a few phone calls. Then she told us that she'd set up a meeting with some business associates, the identity of which she was not at liberty to divulge."

"I told her we would not be interested in any meetings on those terms, that it was our policy to know up front who we were dealing with," Falcone said.

"Good for you," Hernandez asserted.

"She told us she'd have to think about it."

"And then what?" Jake asked.

"And then Curran excused himself," Falcone said, diverting his gaze to the contents of his coffee mug, "and I closed the deal."

Jake said nothing.

Falcone continued, "She gave it some more thought, and before I left, she let me know we'd be meeting with the Valentíns, Adonís and Angel, at one of their estates near Bogotá."

Arms crossed over his chest, Jake inhaled stiffly, looking from Falcone to Niles and finally to Hernandez. "All right then," he said briskly. "We've got a lot to do, guys, so let's get to it."

27

THE MASSIVE TELEPORT BUSINESS Park is across the street from the ABN/AMRO building that towers just beyond the Fundación Santa Fe Medical Center, bordered on the other side by the Santa Ana Mall. Within its complex are hundreds of high-profile businesses, ranging from banks and financial institutions to scientific and technological companies to oil and manufacturing headquarters. It also houses the Radisson Royal, rising fourteen stories in glassy techno-eminence above Avenida 7, which runs nearly the entire length of Bogotá, north and south. A succession of gleaming cars turn onto the sweeping terrazzo drive on any given day, Saturdays possibly being the busiest. This day was no exception, nor was the car.

At precisely eleven o'clock AM, a black Lexus sedan eased up the hotel's drive and idled in routine cortege. It could have contained an ambassador or a rock star or a sheik. Or represent someone equally as powerful, possibly more so.

From his covert vantage point, less than a dozen yards from the Radisson's main entrance, Jake saw it roll up to the curb and recognized it as the same car that had picked Elena and Delaney up from Molotov's. The driver got out of the car, went around to open the passenger-side rear door, and stood beside it. Astride an old Honda Shadow, a motorcycle Hernandez had borrowed from an acquaintance, Jake watched as Falcone and Niles— a.k.a. Tony Messina and Bart Fletcher—emerged from the hotel's grandiose entrance, spotted the car and driver, and strolled over. He had to admit they looked the part. Niles was wearing a Paul Smith tonic suit in gray with Ferragamo loafers. He'd pulled his hair back and had fashionably draped some kind of silk scarf in a funky chartreuse color around his neck. Falcone, sporting a three-day stubble, gelled hair, and dark-tinted oval glasses—all Sonny Crockett retro— wore a black Etro blazer with an untucked jewel-tone striped shirt, seamed pants, and boots. He carried a black attaché. Between them, the cost of their assortment of designer threads and accessories had to be staggering. Jake couldn't help but wonder what their production company CFO would have to say when they turned in their receipts. But it was all part of the charade, and it had to be pitch-perfect. He and Hernandez had spent hours briefing the two of them, trying to prepare them mentally and intellectually for the roles they had assumed, but now as Jake saw them get into the Lexus, he knew it was out of his hands. All he could do was watch and wait, and wonder if he was sending them off to an ambush or to the deal that would take them to the next level. The final one.

He waited until the car had merged into the traffic snarl of Avenida 7, then took off after them. They turned west onto Calle 116. By the time he hit the Autopista Norte, the Lexus was lost in the throng of speeding cars and trucks. But Jake had no trouble picking them back up several minutes later—he knew where they were going.

IT WAS A CRISP, cool day, and the cloudless blue sky defined the edges and emboldened the colors of everything below it. The Suesca estate, viewed in the unfiltered sunlight of midday, was all the more impressive. That such an immense and elegant place could materialize in these isolated hills, its handsome colonial design harshened by the iron-and-stone barricade, seemed abundantly illogical. On the other hand, knowing its true identity and purpose rendered it thoroughly credible. In any case, the name etched in the bronzed plaque at the main gate was entirely appropriate. It read: CASA SOLITARIA.

During the hour-long drive from Bogotá to Suesca, Falcone and Niles had been silently rehearsing lines for their respective roles in this Colombian passion play. But now as the electronic gate slid shut behind the

Lexus, the reality of the business at hand was settling in like the heavier rocks rolling to the bottom of a deep quarry. It was game time.

The chauffeur steered the car around the cobbled drive, pulling up in front of the triple-arched façade. A moment later, he opened the door with a soft whump that sent sunlight spilling in and the quiet vacuum of the car opening out to the innocuous sounds of chirping birds and whisking sprinklers over a freshly cut lawn. Looking back toward the iron-gated entrance they could see a handful of groundskeepers tending to the plush carpet of grass, deep green shrubbery, and bright flowering ornamentals. From somewhere within the house, a pair of vaguely mil-itary-looking men appeared and immediately commenced the predictable security check, which consisted of a quick but thorough frisking, inspec-tion of cellular phones, a look inside Falcone's attaché, and a few waves of a metal detection wand. During the search, they stiffened, perspired heavily in their designer duds, and shared a shaky exhalation when they passed. Falcone and Niles then followed the driver through the stucco arches dripping with fuchsia-colored bougainvillea, across the elevated courtyard and past the fountain, stopping beside the kidney-shaped pool. There, a female servant intercepted them, inquiring in Spanish if they cared for a drink while they waited. When she realized neither under-stood her, she gestured to a chrome-and-glass drink cart containing everything from bottled water and various juices to beer, Aguardiente, and assorted liquor with the mixers.

For a brief moment, they were alone in the picturesque terraced courtyard—a courtyard that might have belonged to any legitimately affluent Colombian businessman or woman, but which instead be-longed to the head *narcotraficantes* of a newly emergent mega-cartel—and exchanged a sobering look. Their heads turned in unison toward the arched doorway of the house and saw Elena emerge with a man they assumed was one-half of the brother partnership.

They weren't sure what a drug lord was actually supposed to look like, movie characterizations aside, but this brother was tall and trim, tanned with longish dark hair worn loose. He was casually dressed in a navy-and-red striped workout suit and a navy crewneck shirt. His wrist sported a jeweled Rolex, his hand a diamond-and-onyx ring, on his feet were spotless Nike Air high tops. His cologne was a sea-salted blend of mandarin, musk, and bergamot.

Beside him Elena smiled hazily. She watched Valentín from the corner of her eye and the second he shifted his sight from Falcone and Niles, she gave Falcone a sly wink. A silk double-breasted suit covered very little of her, clinging in all the usual places. Beneath it, she wore no blouse or stockings, and her feet were stacked into stiletto heels that matched the mint-green suit. She was wearing an emerald necklace and earrings she'd acquired from Falcone and Niles several evenings ago. Worth quite a few thousand dollars, the set had been the equivalent of a buy-in for this meeting—a meeting worth quite a lot more. Now, as her eyes played on Falcone, she fingered the teardrop-shaped gem dangling between her lapels and lifted it to her mouth, flicking it with her tongue. Abruptly letting it fall back in place, she put one hand on Valentín's arm, while extending the other toward their guests. "Angel, this is Tony Messina and Bart Fletcher. Gentlemen, meet Angel Valentín."

Angel Valentín stepped forward offering a guarded smile as he stiffly shook their hands with the grip of a Sumo wrestler. He vacillated inquisitively from one to the other, but his primary focus seemed to settle on Falcone.

As the target of Valentín's scrutiny, Falcone willed himself to project the confident elusiveness of a savvy financier. He could feel his underarms growing warm and damp below his fine silk shirt.

Angel Valentín grinned expansively and swept his arm toward the drink cart and cluster of elegant chrome-accented patio furniture, brightly cushioned chairs arranged around a beveled glass table set for lunch. In articulate, Latin-accented English, he said, "Gentlemen, let us sit. I apologize for my casual appearance. I assure you this is not my normal business attire. I was working out and let the time get away from me. You understand." Again, the wide ingratiating grin, displaying fastidious dental hygiene.

Falcone and Niles shared a knowing look as they took a seat. This man was in impeccable shape and therefore no stranger to the gym—there was probably a good-sized one right on the premises—so if he'd just been working out he would hardly be so freshly groomed. No, this was the image he wanted to project, a carefree image designed to put them at ease. Jake had informed them about such strategy, warning them not to buy into it.

Angel Valentín snapped his fingers and the female servant who had greeted them earlier swiftly reappeared, her demeanor being one of someone fearing a government overthrow at any minute instead of merely overcooking the rice. Addressing Falcone and Niles, Valentín asked, "What do you like to drink? How about rum? I have some excellent twenty-three-year-old Guatemalan." When his guests nodded, he turned back to the woman and said, "Alma, *Cuba libre, por favor.*"

Alma hastened to the beverage cart and began to pour from a bottle of Zacapa Cententario, adding Coca-Cola and slices of lime.

After their drinks had been served, Niles spoke up, commenting, "What a lovely and impressive place this is."

Valentín shrugged, examined fingernails buffed smooth as butter. "Is nice for entertaining...and some business...but me, I prefer the city."

"Will your brother be joining us?" Falcone asked, and looked pointedly at Elena, whose gaze had shifted to the pool.

"Adonís usually does not make the initial meeting," Valentín remarked glibly, taking a sip from his drink and then clasping his hands neatly over crossed legs. "Why don't we discuss what type of business opportunity you are seeking. First of all, do you represent an organization?"

"Does that matter?" Falcone asked, following Hernandez's advice to keep his tone light, with a minimum of inflection.

"That depends on the type of business we wind up doing with you," Valentín replied. "If you have affiliations and are looking for a certain amount of product, then yes, it could matter. But if you are independents and—"

Falcone leaned forward and looked Valentín directly in the eye, a move on par with unlatching a tiger's cage and stepping inside. "I can save us a lot of time, *Señor* Valentín. We are not affiliated with anyone, but we have a multitude of connections in our own circles. We have a shitload of money burning a hole in our pockets, and a lot more sitting in offshore bank accounts. What else do you really need to know?"

Valentín's close-set eyes narrowed and his lips pursed as he digested that. Then he said, "At this level, yes, that is all *I* need to know. Which is why we have others in the organization"—he tipped his head to

Elena—"to seek, investigate, and evaluate potential clients."

Conversation was momentarily interrupted by the return of Alma, accompanied by a young male servant who looked like he might be her son. He shared her anxious demeanor. They had brought out generous platters of food, which were now being arranged around the table. A marinated vegetable selection included artichokes, asparagus, mushrooms, and hot peppers; a pineapple-centered fruit tray displayed guayaba, mangos, maracuyá, and papayas; the main course was *arroz con mariscos*—rice with shrimp and lobster.

After they had all begun eating, talk resumed with Valentín inquiring about their business background. He watched them intently as he stuffed forkfuls of the rice-and-seafood entrée into his mouth. Occasionally, he'd cast a sidelong glance at Elena to gauge her reaction. If she was conveying anything to him, it was imperceptible.

Adding a few more vegetables to his plate as he worked on the main course, Niles said, "Mr. Messina and I have been involved in several lucrative investments. He is well connected in shipping and distribution, while my expertise is in marketing. Our primary contacts are in the international music and film business."

"Interesting," Valentín remarked keenly. "We may want to discuss some opportunities within our own organization with you."

Falcone took a turn building their hand. In preparation for this meeting, Hernandez had briefed them on the most recent narcotics trafficking, providing them with key names and information. Now, as Falcone mentioned some previous deals consummated by Messina and Fletcher, he spiced the dialogue with just enough to up the ante.

Valentín was showing a moderate amount of interest as the pieces of their profile began to fit neatly into place, and when Falcone stopped talking, he said, "I think you will find that we run a tight organization. My brother and I believe in a hands-on approach. We are both operations and operators. We go out in the field, inspect the product and the producers. We coordinate the security and those who provide it. We are there when it ships out. Unqualified success demands total control of the whole process. This is our philosophy and it has served us well." He licked his lips, his dark eyes gleaming as he added, "Is the only way."

Abruptly, Valentín wiped his mouth with a linen napkin and pushed his plate away. "So," he said curiously, "what kind of volume are we speaking of?"

"A couple hundred keys to start," Falcone replied, "and if we like what we see, we'll move up to the thousand range."

Valentín absorbed that, automatically running the figures through the calculator in his head, and then rose from the table. "Gentlemen," he announced, draining the last rum-and-coke from his glass, "if you will excuse me for a few minutes, I must make a call."

When Valentín had gone inside the house, Elena smiled and said, "It is going to be a pleasure doing business with you." Beneath the table, Falcone felt her bare foot navigating up the side of his leg. The touch made his skin grow hot again, his clothes moist and snug. It also clicked the mental and physical hyperlinks to his first encounter with Elena, part of which included, regrettably, some of the most incredible sex he'd ever had. And then he thought of Jake's friend Delaney, and shivered as if a cold wind had blown through. Glancing at Niles, he noticed the color had drained from his partner's face. Maybe it wasn't the wind, he thought grimly—maybe they were being warned by the ghostly touch of one who had been this way before.

WEDGED IN THE WIDE branches of a tree well outside the security wall surrounding the estate, Jake had a perfect view of the courtyard. Camouflaged by woodland BDUs and obscured by thick leaves, he was able to monitor the meeting with the aid of a pair of Swarovski's. Ironically, the binoculars had belonged to Delaney, a gift from a Russian Spetsnaz soldier they had worked with for a brief time and who had sought their help in successfully landing post-military employment in the States.

Peering through the high-powered lenses, Jake felt an uncomfortable sense of disengagement, something to which he was not accustomed. He was an elite operator, a specialist with the skills and intelligence and fortitude not only to plan missions but carry them out. He knew he was a good leader and trainer, had in fact trained a significant number of military colleagues and subordinates, but he did not like the role of observer. And there had simply not been sufficient time to thoroughly prepare and properly train Falcone and Niles. They did not understand the ideology of the narcoguerrillas, much less know their tactics. These were not imbecilic thugs they were dealing with; high-level narcos were intelligent, militant businessmen whose organization was more intricately wired than the Mafia and had refined the best tricks of the world's most formidable terrorists. And here were two regular Joe's having lunch with possibly the most powerful *narcotraficantes* in South America. No weapons, no monitoring devices, and for all intents and purposes no way out if anything went awry. Even though Jake was maintaining visual support, from a tactical standpoint there would be very little he could do if things suddenly went sour. He was in radio contact with Hernandez, who had quick and direct access to the police and military should the need arise, but they all knew that if the need arose it would most likely be too late. Fortunately, watching them now as they ate lunch, all appeared to be going smoothly.

When Jake had seen Elena appear in the courtyard, accompanied by one of the Valentín brothers, he'd found himself coolly detached. But as he continued to watch them and observe her in the true role and environment to which she belonged, he could feel the heat of his animosity roil inside like lava. His thoughts cycled back to the night Elena had brought Delaney here, drugged and sexed up, to excavate whatever it was the organization wanted from him. Remembering the sight of Delaney stretched naked across the bed, in a drugged and drunken stupor steamed by her seduction, sent a sour rush of air into his lungs. Once again, as he had so many times since, he wondered if he could have saved Delaney's life if he'd stormed into the mansion and confronted them then instead of later. And once again, he concluded that it probably would not have made any difference. In the end, Delaney would have been just as dead, but he might have been as well.

Jake's attention was drawn back to the courtyard below as the meal was finished. He watched as Valentín went into the house where he remained for approximately fifteen minutes, watched as Elena laughed and flirted, watched as Valentín emerged again. This time he was accompanied by another man, a man who could have been his twin. Almost, but not quite.

*   *   *   *   *

ANGEL VALENTÍN HAD STEPPED back into the courtyard, but he was not alone. When the other man came clearly into view, Elena's face underwent a subtle but discernible transformation, a carnivorous sheen in her eyes, a sensual swell in her lips.

Realizing someone new had joined them in the courtyard, Falcone and Niles rose and turned to be introduced. The man, as tall and trim and tanned as his brother, wore his dark hair tautly pulled into a short ponytail. He was wearing a white cotton shirt with long cuffs and slightly flared sleeves, tight black slacks neatly tucked into leather boots, looking a little bit like he belonged on the deck of a seventeenth-century Caribbean schooner. He strode over to the table and stopped just short, obviously accustomed to sibling deference and social obeisance.

From beside him, Angel Valentín said, "Gentlemen, my brother... Adonís Valentín." His tone was predictably reverential.

"Tony Messina"—Falcone waved his hand toward Niles—"and Bart Fletcher. Very pleased to meet you." He extended his hand but quickly let it drop to his side when no reciprocal gesture was made.

"Likewise," the second Valentín said, coolly regarding them as he strolled to the drink cart and poured himself a shot of Aguardiente. He tossed it back in one swallow, poured and drained another, then dug into an iced bucket of bottled beer. Indicating they should take their seats, he said, "Please, gentlemen, as you were." Straddling a chair next to his brother, Adonís Valentín said, "Angel tells me you are interested in doing business with our organization."

"Possibly, yes," Falcone remarked, trying to match Valentín's aloofness. He was finding it difficult. The elder Valentín brother had a daunting hardness about him that reminded Falcone of Jake, disconcerting given who he was.

"And what, may I ask, are your expectations if such an alliance may be accomplished?" Valentín inquired as he extracted a leather cigarette case from one of his pockets, flipped it open, and selected from the contents. Putting a cigarette to his lips, he lit it with an engraved gold lighter, inhaled briefly, and passed it over to Elena. As their hands touched in the interchange, there was a palpable sexual chemistry that Elena played off by cutting her eyes at Falcone. Valentín offered the case to Falcone and Niles, saying, "The finest Colombian tobacco, a custom blend."

"No, thanks," Falcone said crisply. "To answer your question, our expectations are simple."

"Meaning what?" Valentín inquired. "For example, will you use your own distribution network or will you require point-to-point delivery, which we can of course provide."

Mindful of Jake's friend Delaney, Falcone thought, *Sure you can provide it, you son of a bitch. Fly the friendly skies of Air Colombia, one-way tickets available at a special rate.* "We can go either way, depending on the price and terms," was Falcone's succinct response. "And we have a variety of payment options," he added, positioning his hand to afford Valentín a good view of the exquisite emerald ring Hernandez had loaned him. It was one of Hernandez's most prized pieces, a multi-carat, perfectly cut and set gem from the Coscuez mines. It was both very rare and very valuable and, as intended, both Valentín brothers honed in on it as Falcone rolled it around his ring finger.

Niles spoke up, saying, "Bottom line is—as we have already told your brother—if you have the product, we have the capital and we're ready to deal. Simple as that."

Acknowledging Niles with a nod, Adonís Valentín said, "Well, Mr. Fletcher, I admire your directness. So I will be direct with you also. We are interested in your business, but find it very strange that the two of you do not seem to exist." Valentín's gaze snapped back and forth between the two of them.

There was a weighty moment that dropped like an unfettered anchor, but Falcone recovered with aplomb. "Does it *look* like we don't exist?"

Valentín finished his beer and cigarette, unstraddling the chair. Walking slowly around the table, he said, "What it looks like and what it is could be two different things, yes?" Looking off in the distance over the quilt of green hills beyond the estate, he continued, "But this business is full of unknown variables. That is the challenge, and I embrace it." Abruptly, he turned back to face them, now with a caustic smile. He made eye contact with his brother, then strolled away without another word.

When he had disappeared into the house, Angel Valentín stood and said, "Gentlemen, it has been a pleasure. We will be in touch."

Determined to have the last word, Falcone said, "Fine. We'll give it a week. After that, we'll have to move on to other business. You understand."

"Perfectly," Valentín replied, and extended his hand as they rose from the table.

Falcone accepted Valentín's farewell handshake and moved off toward the archway from which they had entered. Just before exiting, Falcone turned to offer Elena a polite goodbye, but she was already out of range. He could see the back of her mint-green suit moving snugly around the curvy ass beneath, high heels clicking below long tanned legs as she disappeared into the house with one final swish of coppery brown hair. Inside, her lover and business partner awaited with the sex, and the decision.

28

THE FLYING WEATHER AND visibility was, at least from the outset, favorable as Jake and Hernandez flew south along the Río Putumayo toward the Amazon basin. While Falcone and Niles were holed up at the Radisson waiting for the anticipated phone call, Jake had decided to go along on what was, for Hernandez, an official field op for counter-narcotics. For Jake, it was a perfect opportunity to obtain more intelligence. They were cruising in one of the Colombian military's Cessna Caravans, roughly ten thousand feet over the winding river and jungle canopy that so effectively concealed narcoguerrilla activity. For the past couple of hours in flight, Hernandez had been absorbed in collecting more aerial photographs, shooting video, and adding to his already copious notes. Jake was also scanning the terrain but immersed in the vortex of his own deep thoughts.

Earlier, the two of them had contacted Raúl Aguilar by radio to obtain field recon information on the latest guerrilla movements; they tended to trust the veracity of his information more than that from official briefings. But today when Aguilar related that things were generally quiet for the time being, both Jake and Hernandez were inexplicably troubled. It had been their experience in narcotics trafficking, just as in terrorism, that when chatter and activity dwindled it could mean something more ominous was brewing. Now, peering through his window at the deceptively serene sky, Jake remembered the way it had looked just before Delaney was blown up. And how fast, how mind-numbingly fast, the blue serenity had shattered and turned into a raging black inferno.

He looked down, surveying the vast mottled green terrain that was believed to be part of Valentín territory, and wondered if Falcone and Niles had the *narcotraficantes* on the hook. If they did, the big question was how to take them out. He was weighing possible scenarios and various counter strategies when he realized Hernandez was speaking to him.

"What?"

"I was asking what you were thinking," Hernandez said, his hands busy working the controls of a new CAT repeater he was testing for viability of extending handheld radio coverage.

Wrinkling his brow, Jake replied, "Well, I just want to cover every possible angle in the event we're put on the spot with little or no warning."

"Of course. You know, Jake, I have to tell you, I think the guys are conducting themselves surprisingly well."

"They are," Jake conceded, quickly adding, "but I didn't like that 'you don't exist' stuff."

"Valentín was just testing them, and from how they described their response, I think they passed."

"I hope so, but I wish there was a way to get them out of the picture now. There are a hundred different ways a meeting or transaction could go down and a hundred different ways it could go totally to shit. I could be sending them off to be killed."

Hernandez nodded his head somberly. "I cannot say that I disagree with you on that. You knew this was going to be extremely risky and dangerous."

"Which is why it should be me going in instead of them, and it frustrates the hell out of me that I can't because of Elena."

"More than that," Hernandez said. "You can be sure the Valentíns know a lot about you, including what you look like."

"That's true. I also impressed upon the guys that they would be watched from here on out, that they will have to take great care in every move they make."

"As will you, my friend," Hernandez warned.

Jake said nothing, his thoughts splintering as he felt a strange twinge in his chest. It was an unfamiliar feeling, coming from an unknown place, and it burrowed deep within him.

Hernandez had returned to his spot in the front of the plane and Jake to his mental strategy session, when the Cessna was violently tossed out of its smooth flight path by the updraft of an enormous explosion below, a muted ka-boom that shook the earth and the plane flying above it. The Cessna rotated right then left, lurching up and then dropping down as the pilot fought to regain control and altitude. Hernandez's equipment—camera apparatus, pages of notes, maps, rucksacks, duffels, plastic water bottles—cartwheeled in all directions. While pilot and co-pilot worked to stabilize the plane, Jake and Hernandez, who had not been belted in their seats, were struggling to stay planted.

"The FARC must have hit another pipeline," Jake said.

Trying to keep his balance and look through the window at the same time, Hernandez replied, "I think so. We were flying over some petroleum rigs just now."

Below, rolling black smoke and orange flames swept across the ground and billowed into the air. Dozens of miniature figures could be seen scurrying to escape the swiftly expanding firestorm. Jake and Hernandez watched in morose silence as the inferno consumed everything in their view, including the petroleum workers who could not outrun it.

Once the Cessna was above and beyond the turbulence generated from the explosion, Hernandez instructed the pilot to land at a nearby military base in Araracuara. Undergoing some renovations, it was not by choice but by necessity as the plane was running low on fuel. And, as if taking a cue from the thick black smoke of the explosion, the sky's pallor had begun to change from its unblemished blue to a smoky gray. When they were less than fifty miles from the base, rain began to splatter against the windows and spasms of wind were causing the plane to heave and shudder. The sky's ceiling continued to drop, the clouds massing in dense patches and turning from ash to tarnished pewter. Rain splatters soon became torrents that noisily pummeled the glass, virtually obliterating visibility.

Belting himself in next to Jake, Hernandez said tensely, "The pilot and co-pilot are having a tough time."

"No shit," Jake gulped, gripping the armrests of his seat a little tighter.

"The GPS coordinates are off and they are searching for landmarks to guide us in."

"Can't they get assistance from air-traffic control?"

Hernandez shook his head dismally. "They just told me the FARC killed one controller last month and the other was given political amnesty to another country."

"Fuck, are they going to be able to land this thing?"

Hernandez didn't answer right away, trying to pick up something from the intense dialogue in the cockpit. Jake listened, too, and heard the pilot say he was following a road that paralleled the military base. Hernandez and Jake watched and listened silently as the pilot and copilot took the plane lower, dropping several thousand feet, then several thousand more. They were below four thousand feet and beginning descent for what they could now see was a half-obscured landing strip, when the pilot suddenly increased power and airspeed, and pulled steeply up.

"What the hell?" Jake exclaimed, but he quickly saw the reason for the abrupt change in plan. As the Cessna regained altitude and the airstrip shrunk below it, a break in the stratum of clouds exposed the military base where they had been about to land. It was crawling with FARC troops.

Bad act, bad weather, bad blood. Just bad. Grimly, Jake found himself wondering if this was all a bad omen of something worse to come.

SPRAWLED ON THE BROWN leather couch in Hernandez's living room, Jake was hearing but only half-listening to the day's events being delivered with forced joviality by the nightly news anchors on RCN News. It was a dire replica of the previous day and would be repeated with few minor alterations on the following evening's broadcast. Political protests, car bombs, brutal murders and kidnappings, drug seizures and terror strikes. Pipelines being blown up. Surreally, this dreadful fare was followed by a buxom female anchor launching into the *Farandula* segment, cattily commenting on the latest J-Lo movie and a dress worn by Beyoncé at a music industry awards show. "That little number probably caused more jaws to drop than the outcome of Santa Fe and Nacional," she pronounced. Smile wider than a broad jump by Jesse Owens, teeth as white and straight as piano keys.

On that cheery note, the sports anchor relayed the story behind the soccer match.

A plate with a ham sandwich sat untouched on the coffee table. In the chair across from Jake, Hernandez was finishing the last of his. When he stopped chewing, he said, "Not hungry?"

Rubbing his eyes, Jake sat up and gave the sandwich an apathetic look. "Not really," he said. "It's okay, I'll eat it in a little while."

But food was the last thing on his mind. It had been hours since the pipeline explosion, but the image remained soldered in his mind. As it replayed, he began to see Delaney superimposed, the plane exploding instead of the rigs. Delaney smiling and then Delaney blowing up.

After the Cessna's pilot had aborted landing, they had flown a few miles west and made an emergency put-down in low brush just outside the small town of Angosturas. Hernandez had radioed the military base commander at Tres Equinas, and in a few hours a refueling plane had located them, filled the Cessna's tank, and escorted them back to the base. From there, Jake and Hernandez had caught a flight back to Bogotá. Hernandez had just gotten off the phone, checking in with the embassy and NAS, and was now jotting some notes on a legal pad for his written report.

Just as the news went off, there was a knock on the door.

It was Falcone and Niles, both wearing dark hooded jackets. Hernandez herded them inside, glancing furtively up and down his street. Reasonably satisfied they had not been followed, he withdrew to his living room.

"Don't worry, mate," Niles remarked blithely, removing the hood of his jacket and freeing his lean arms from the sleeves. "We're being very careful."

"Let's hope so," Jake commented, not happy to see them knowing the chance they took in coming to Hernandez's house.

"We are," Falcone countered with a scowl. "We took a taxi, split up, walked a block, took separate taxis, then walked here from separate points, all after dark. It was like something straight out of *The Bourne*

Identity."

"Good, very good," Hernandez said evenly. "You have news?"

"They called," Falcone announced triumphantly. "We have another meeting, this one to make the first transaction. And you're never gonna believe where." He paused for dramatic effect, which to his disappointment was totally wasted on Jake. "On their yacht."

"Where and when?" Jake asked tersely.

"It's docked in Cartagena, but they didn't say where we'd be going."

"Going?" Jake repeated.

"Well, you know, just cruising out and back."

"Cruising out and back, that's what they said?"

"No," Falcone snipped impatiently, "that's not what they said, Jake, but I wasn't going to ask for the itinerary. That would have made them suspicious."

"Yes, it probably would have," Hernandez offered. "So when is the meeting?"

"Not quite a week. This Sunday."

The room became heavy with silence as the reality dropped with the delicacy of a coin in an empty hallway, then with the slow, dead weight of a sinking ship. And then, as if in resumed-play mode, the air electrified.

"Okay," Jake said tightly, "why don't you gents get something to drink and chill. I need to think about this."

But in actuality, he didn't need to think about it much at all. He already knew exactly what they were going to do—and what *he* was going to do. After all the mental debate and indecision earlier, as soon as he heard about the meeting, it had started to come to him.

When Falcone and Niles were seated in the living room, each with a beer, Jake said, "There's only going to be one transaction, and it's going to be cut short. You guys better grow some gills."

29

SHE SAT IN THE porch swing, reveling in the soft breeze, listening to the chimes jangle with its tickle. The sun was in that hovering place, deep and dark and disappearing behind the approaching night. Ocean sounds were so close she could almost touch the waves that made them. Another beautiful idyllic day that would be followed by another soothing tropical night.

But she was despondent.

By day she sat at her laptop computer and tapped out words and sentences and chapters. The story was developing. Characters were shaping, the plot was forming, the pace was picking up. It felt good, it felt solid, it felt liberating. But she was missing Jake. His solid presence, his penetrating gaze, his tender and torrid touch, the intimate connection of mind and body and spirit. Him.

She inhaled deeply, filling her lungs with the salty air, tasting it in her mouth. But her lips hungered for the taste of him, the feel of him, the dominance of him. Just him. Soon, the lick of the ocean's tears bit into her eyes and she cried.

Until she heard the sound of the pickup truck coming down the road, gravel crunching, the engine abruptly silenced with the shift of a gear and stroke of a key. The thump of shoes scrunched, then squished into the fragments of shells that lined the drive. As he had each and every evening since Jake's departure, Pablo Luis Ayala was checking on her. Other officers from the local police rode by, often stopping to say hello and inquire about her wellbeing, but Ayala made a daily visit whether he was on duty or not. There had been no further incidents with the intruder Jake confronted, but neither had the man been located or apprehended. She knew Jake had requested the police patrol in his absence, but the regularity of their presence and solicitous inquiries were as genuinely nice as they were reassuring.

She smiled as Ayala stepped up to the porch.

"Hi, Luis."

"Hola, Señorita. How are you this evening?"

"Fine. I'm fine." She sniffled, wiping her eyes.

Ayala saw the slight gesture but did not comment.

Callie regarded him with a sudden bloom of hope. "Did you hear from Jake?" she asked. "Did he call?"

"No, I am sorry to say. Not since the other day. But I am sure he will. Remember he said, is okay for you to answer the phone here."

Her head drooped and she inhaled with a shuddery sigh as the hope withered. "Yes, you said. But I feel funny answering the phone in someone else's house."

"I understand." Ayala shifted into more protective conduct, hand on his gun belt as his eyes panned the lush foliage spread about the property. "Everything has been quiet?" he queried. "No strangers?"

"Everything has been quiet," she replied, managing a small smile.

"Okay," Ayala said, "I will check for you tomorrow." He backed down from the porch, paused, and turned. "Callie, he will be back soon."

She watched as Luis Ayala trod back to his truck, started the engine, and pulled out of the drive. Steered onto the access road and drove toward the Costanera Sur, off into the advancing dusk. With another forlorn sigh, Callie rose and stepped inside, heading straight to the kitchen bar. Her eyes went immediately to the answering machine by the wall phone, as they always did now each time she entered the house. The little green light was not blinking. Her heart deflated, but in an instant it was throbbing giddily as she punched the Play button and listened to the message Jake had left day before yesterday. She'd listened to it countless times, over and over again, feeling the same rush, the same warmth, the same giddy quiver each time— followed by the hollow emptiness.

His deep masculine voice resonated from the speaker. *Hello, love, it's me. If you're there, pick up the phone…it won't bite.* Throaty chuckle. *Okay, so I just wanted to call and let you know that all's well. I trust everything's good with you…hope Luis and Camilla are looking after you. Not sure when I can call again, but I will try later. In the meantime, you take care, get some writing done, get out a little, and I'll see you soon. Bye, sweetie.*

Her heart jittered, the room, the house, the world, everything was drowned out by her beating heart and the sound of his voice.

She strolled back onto the front porch and rocked in the swing for a while, listening to the calming whisper of the ocean. It was still light enough to see the waves through the dunes, rushing then rolling then smoothing, then starting all over again. The sound, the sight, the smell, was as primal and hypnotic as a lullaby. She got up from the swing, cast a yearning look, hesitated. It would be dark soon, but she hadn't been on the beach today. The sand's soft caress pushing through her toes, the warm weave of waves. Feeling so small at the edge of something so immense and all encompassing.

And yet, feeling so safe.

She glanced around, saw no one in the distance. It was dinnertime. People were tucked inside bungalows or lounging on patios having cocktails, mingling poolside, sucking down oysters and steamed shrimp, tossing salads. Freshly showered and perfumed for night, beach towels draped over railings, sand sprinkled across their thresholds. Flip-flops tossed aside for loafers and stacked sandals.

The ocean whispered, so soft, so soothing. She walked across the drive. Behind her, fading as she slipped down through the dunes, a ringing.

WHEN SHE RETURNED TO the house, perhaps an hour later, deep plum had washed over the sky and the faint stirrings of nocturnal insects were warming up for their evening's concert. A lone bird issued a shrill last-call for the departing day. As she mounted the porch, a swift breeze broke from around the corner, thrusting palm fronds into her face and clanging the chimes in a riotous tangle overhead. She looked back and saw the dark rim approaching from the west. The salt in the air tingled, the gusts picking up force.

Inside the house, she secured the front door and padded over to check the French doors. And stopped several feet short.

They were swinging open, rattling in the windy passes, occasionally banging against the sides of the house.

She knew the doors had been closed when she'd left the house earlier. She *knew* they had, she remembered checking. But had she locked them? She could not recall.

Her mouth went dry with panic and for several moments she could not move. Her eyes darted around, looking for signs of any disturbance, but nothing appeared to be displaced. Everything in the living room was neatly arranged in exactly the same order as it had been after Camilla's routine cleaning. In the foyer, the big Bulova clock ticked quietly. Loudly. Every tick sounded like a drumbeat.

Tick, tick, tick.

Cautiously, Callie rounded the bar and peeked in the kitchen. The wine rack sat in the corner, bottles stacked in each of the slots. Near the spotless stove, the coffeemaker was clean and ready for service. Next to the sink, the glazed clay pitcher with its tiny chink near the top of the handle. Above it, the neatly shelved plates and dishes. She turned, surveyed the dinette. Colorful woven mats with matching napkins rolled and tucked in bamboo rings squared each place. Untouched.

Her breathing eased, her heart rate slowed.

Just the wind, she told herself. The wind had loosened the doors' latch and yanked them open. With a sigh of relief, she paced over to close the French doors still being knocked about by the gusts, making sure she pulled them tight and slipped the lock firmly in place.

She took a deep breath, felt the relief flow through her with the warmth of a whirlpool jet.

Tick, tick, tick.

She was about to go upstairs when the familiar tug caused her to reach for the Play button on the answering machine, now desperately wanting to hear the assurance in his voice. She pressed the button and closed her eyes, waiting for the first husky notes of his voice. *Hello, love, it's me...*

Instead, she heard nothing but hissing. Her eyes blinked open and she stared at the machine, depressed the button, then pressed it again. More hissing. She felt her throat close up as a new surge of panic welled inside.

Jake's message was gone.

CALLIE LAY AWAKE IN bed, cringing with every creak and groan of the house as the wind blew. Huddled and shivering beneath the covers, her eyes nervously flicked around the room, watching as shadows crawled and crossed the walls and ceiling. Increasingly, their shapes became indiscernible as the last light faded into night. In between the gusts and gales and groans, the only sound was the gentle paddle of the fan moving air overhead.

And then, a murmur of thunder. The wind died as abruptly as the steam stream of a tea kettle removed from the stove, stopped and held its exhale. An eerie quiet floated through the house, and all she could hear was the swish of the fan's blades.

Or did she—could she—hear the latch on the French doors downstairs?

She sprang up in the bed, heart jolting to full-throttle again. Listened. Heard nothing. The latch? Filled with dread, she got up and tiptoed gingerly to the bedroom door. To the landing. Waited, heart hammering. The clock downstairs beating. Looked down, squinting into the darkness. She didn't dare turn on the lights, waiting for her eyes to adjust. Stared down at the French doors.

Tick, tick, tick.

She could not see them.

After several moments of fearful immobility, she bit her lip and crept slowly down the stairs, stopping at the bottom. Listened. No banging, no whistling wind. Just the clock. *Tick, tick, tick.* She tiptoed toward the doors, guiding herself through the dark by grasping the tops of the barstools and feeling for the edge of the counter, then the wall.

She looked, caught her breath, and found the doors intact.

At that instant, the house illuminated like the bath of a camera flash, throwing everything in a glare of white light, and thunder cracked like the sky had ripped open.

A hoarse scream rasped from her throat and she tore up the stairs, stumbling on the risers. She scrambled into bed and pulled the covers over her as rain drummed a timpani on the roof. Her heart kept up the beat for a long time after that.

Sometime close to midnight when the rain had settled into a steady, soporific rhythm, the exhaustion of surging adrenaline overcame anxiety, and she fell asleep.

But not before she wondered again what had happened to Jake's message.

30

JAKE LISTENED TO THE repetitive ringing on the other end of the telephone connection, six rings until Delaney's machine picked up and played his old message, now grating like the chant of a carnival barker. Jake dropped the receiver back in its cradle. He stood staring at it listlessly for another full minute, and was caught thoroughly off guard by the degree to which his spirits plummeted.

Sitting on the side of his hotel bed, he glanced at his watch and frowned. Only an hour's difference in time between Bogotá and Costa Rica, which would make it five-thirty there. It would be getting dark. He felt a knot of worry, but quickly released it.

For the next hour, he busied himself with email and phone calls, still trying to connect with some of his associates. Still not having much luck. As he logged off his BlackBerry email and connected his phones to their chargers, he checked his watch again. Almost seven-thirty; six-thirty in Dominical. He dialed the number again, waited for the connection to go through, heard the ringing start. And continue until the machine clicked on again. This time, he left a brief message.

"Love, I'll try to call again in the morning."

He hung up, gazed harshly at the phone, and then let out a remorseful sigh. His message had been coarse. He should have said something else, should have lightened his voice. But damn, what was she doing out of the house after dark? And then something occurred to him and he felt a strange upheaval of emotion. Maybe she had met someone. He let that thought have some breadth and decided that wouldn't be the worst thing to happen. Maybe he was right after all about her not being his type—or maybe it was more him not being her type. In any case, she should have someone stable and settled. A regular guy with a regular job who would take her out on dates and bed her in a more traditional fashion.

Not a warrior with a $500,000 bounty on his head.

Not someone so dark.

That new thought should have made his heart lighter, should have afforded him some relief for the emotional quandary he had been grappling with.

But it didn't.

JAKE WOKE SWEATING IN the chilled air of his suite at the Charleston. He sat up in bed, breathing heavily. She had been in his dreams, and not in a good way. He reached for the phone without even looking at the clock on the nightstand, letting the receiver slip back in place with the realization that it wasn't even light outside. Wooden Roman shades were rolled down over the suite's windows, enough space between them to see that dawn had not yet nudged night out of the way.

He got up, went to the bathroom to relieve himself, then lay awake in bed until palings of light began to filter in through the miniscule spaces in the shades. Room service brought a coffee tray, and he drank several cups while he waited for it to be six o'clock in Dominical.

Unable to wait any longer, Jake placed another call at 5:55 AM, and this time was taken aback when it was answered on the second ring. In a breathless voice that snagged at his heart, he heard Callie say, "Jake?"

"Mornin', sweetie," he said, his voice infused with warmth. "Sorry to call at this hour, did I wake you?"

"I...I couldn't"—her voice sounded weak and strained—"there was a bad storm last night."

"Is everything all right?"

There was a slight pause before she replied, "Yes...just didn't sleep very much."

"I hope you'll excuse the message I left last night. I was just, I don't know, tired and tense."

"Oh?" she asked, and he thought she sounded bewildered.

"It would have been getting dark there, so I figured you'd be in for the night," he said lightly, without consciously conceding that he really wanted to know.

"I took a walk on the beach kind of late."

"Not such a good idea after dark, love," he admonished gently.

"I know. I won't do that again. Jake?"

"Hmm?"

"Will you be back soon?"

"Hope so, but don't know for sure." He turned at the sharp rap on his door. "Callie, I have to go. Take care for me, okay?"

Her last words, *Okay, Jake,* replayed in his head over and over throughout the day.

THE BOAT WAS SOME hundred meters or so off a deserted stretch of beach near an obscure inlet south of Tierrabomba, tucked along northern Barú, hove-to in the turquoise waters of the Caribbean. With the proliferation of coral reefs in the area, Jake opted not to drop anchor to keep from damaging them and also to prevent getting stuck. The waves were fairly calm, lapping languidly against the boat's hull, and a hot pre-summer sun presided in a sky of shocking blue brilliance. Postcard paradise in another time, another circumstance, but not now.

Wearing only a pair of navy swim trunks, Jake was sifting through diving gear he had rented with the boat. Spread around him on the deck was an assortment of underwater apparel and apparatus: suiting, gloves, booties, fins, masks, snorkels, belts, gauges, weights, lighting, tools, buoyancy control vests, scuba tanks and a rebreather. He was checking the equipment as he monitored the progress of Falcone and Niles. Hearing them splashing close to the boat, he glanced at his watch to note their time.

Both were sputtering and heaving as they climbed up onto the swim platform. Jake handed them each a bottle of water, letting them drink and drip for a few minutes before he said, "That was pretty decent. You're progressing nicely, but you're gonna have to do better, gents."

They stared at him open-mouthed, their breathing too labored to speak.

After a few minutes, Jake asked, "Okay, ready to go back in?"

"Son of a bitch," Falcone panted, and guzzled the last of his water. "You've got to be kidding."

"No," Jake said evenly, meeting his hostile gaze with unnerving equanimity. "I am not kidding. This time, I want you to do the swim above water to the beach and underwater coming back. Try to pick up your pace with longer strokes and by kicking more vigorously."

"Shit, Jake," Falcone muttered irritably. "How many freaking times have we got to do this?" He and Niles had already swum to the beach and back to the boat a half-dozen times. There were more stitches in his sides than a moth-eaten teddy bear with its stuffing falling out.

"As many times as I think you need to," Jake replied dryly, his jaw set. He clapped his hands together briskly. "So okay, let's go."

But Falcone stood gaping at him, feet firmly planted, his expression incredulous. "You're serious! Are you trying to kill us?"

"I'm trying to ensure you stay alive," Jake said. "You don't get it, do you? These guys are not playing with you. This is not a game where whoever loses simply cashes in and then goes home."

"We know that and we get it," Falcone retorted defensively. "I just don't understand why we can't make this first deal and then—"

"Because you might not get past the first deal," Jake interrupted. "Now, you need to get back out there."

"And you need to—"

"Eddie!" Curran grabbed his partner by the arm and tugged him toward the bow. "Jesus Christ," he blubbered in Falcone's ear, "don't piss him off! We'll be out here all bloody day!"

"We will anyway," Falcone grumbled sourly, glancing over his shoulder at Jake who stood glaring at him, hands on his hips.

Watching them dive into the water and start back for the beach, Jake felt his frustration mounting. How could he possibly get these guys ready in just a few days? They were both in better-than-average shape, particularly having survived the arduous jungle course. And from snatches of conversation, he'd gleamed that Falcone was into the typical all-American sports play—baseball, basketball, football—and worked out some. Niles was more of a wildcard, but his enthusiasm and energy helped to compensate for what he lacked in physical stamina. Even so, and not for the first time, Jake was having serious doubts about letting them be involved in—no, letting them *execute*—something that skilled and seasoned SpecOps guys should be doing.

Going on the premise that the Valentíns' yacht was berthed somewhere in or around Cartagena, Jake had taken special care in selecting a secluded place where he could get Falcone and Niles into shape. Earlier this morning they had taken separate flights from Bogotá—the duo flying commercial and Jake on military craft—and once they'd arrived, he had wasted no time getting them started on a training regimen. He began with general physical training, after which they'd run the equivalent of two miles. Just prior to the swimming, he'd had them stretched out on the boat's deck for a session of flutter-kicking, a strenuous exercise that simulated finning and strengthened the abdominal muscles. In the beginning, he had worked out along with them—the PT, the running, the swimming—but when he realized that his own superior fitness was demoralizing them, he gave it up. He knew his expectations were high, but there was precious little time and they would have to be ready.

When Falcone and Niles made it back to the boat, Jake told them they were done for the day. He had repacked the diving gear and was adjusting the headsail.

"Well, mate, did we make the grade?" Niles asked hopefully, still out of breath from the exertion.

"You guys had a great first day," Jake said, giving him an encouraging smile.

"I'm *so* glad," Falcone said sarcastically as he brushed past Jake.

Sighing, Jake said, "Look, Eddie, I know this is not fun, but if you want to pull this off—and it's your choice, you don't have to do it—I've got to get you physically ready." Falcone had stopped and swung around to face him. Looking Falcone directly in the eye, Jake asked, "Do you want to do this?"

"Yes," Falcone snapped, "I said we did and we meant it. But I don't see why—"

"*Do* you want to do this?" Jake repeated emphatically.

"I said yes," Falcone exclaimed in exasperation, fists clenched at his sides. "But I—"

"Then you've got to do what I say, Eddie, whether you like it or not, and you've got to trust me. And that's all I've got to say about that." Jake's face and voice reflected a steely calm that was somehow more intimidating than temper.

Falcone held his stare for several seconds before he was forced to look away. "Got it," he muttered, and stomped below to shower off.

"What are we doing now?" Niles asked Jake, giving him a hand with the sails.

"We're returning to the marina. I need to go ashore, pick up some supplies and do some scouting." He gave Niles a scant grin. "You better get some rest, bro, you're gonna need it. You think today was rough, wait until you see what I have in store tomorrow."

Groaning as he headed below deck, Niles murmured, "Bloody bollocks."

WHILE FALCONE AND NILES spent the late afternoon napping aboard the boat, a forty-five-foot Jeanneau, Jake rented a Jeep Cherokee and drove through town. On the seat beside him was a printout from Google Earth encompassing the Bay of Cartagena with several areas circled or highlighted. Now, as he navigated Avenida Miramar along the bay, he realized that unless he could locate the Valentíns' boat, his plan was useless. From Santa Cruz Marina, where he'd left the sailboat with his exhausted recruits, Jake's first stop was Club Nautico. One of the two most upscale marinas in the area, it teemed with sailboats and cruisers of all sizes, bearing flags from a mélange of origins. None particularly caught his eye, and chatting with dockhands revealed nothing of interest. Next, he hit a knot of traffic at the San Sebastion entrance for Club de Pesca and had to turn back toward the city to bypass the congestion, making a mental note to hit it on return. He crossed the Roman Bridge and nosed into the increasingly thick traffic on Calle Larga, headed to Todomar Marina. There, he spent another hour or so canvassing dockhands and boats. The only thing he had to go by was a general idea of type and size. So far, he'd only seen a handful that came close to fitting the criteria, and he conceded it was entirely possible that the information

Falcone and Niles had been given was intentionally vague or misleading. After all, 'docked in Cartagena' could mean *near* Cartagena, and if that was the case, odds of finding it were practically nil. Standing at the end of the Todomar dock, looking back across the bay, he could see the crowded slips of Club de Pesca and, much to his astonishment, a yacht that out-sized and –classed all.

Hiding in plain sight. *If* it was the one.

Leaving Todomar, Jake reversed his course on Avenida Blas de Lezo, past the convention center back to Calle Larga, across the bridge and into Manga. A sharp right turn and he now had a cleared path to Club de Pesca, the very place he'd taken Falcone and Niles for dinner on the eve of their Amazon expedition. At the dock, he made a casual circuit before striking up conversation with a marina employee. It seemed the sleek tri-deck superyacht parked at the very end of the right-side pier was registered to an Ecuadorian flower exporting company, Flora EquaExquisitas.

Strolling toward the vessel, Jake made out a name in elaborate gold script. *Javiera.* Just like the company, the identity meant nothing to him. But as he knelt down to take a closer look, something else did. Below the name was an emblem, painted in blue and purple, yellow and black—an orchid, with feral eyes in the background.

Elena's tattoo.

His hand reached out to touch the white fiberglass hull and his eyes narrowed.

You and me, baby…soon, just you and me.

SEATED AROUND THE COCKPIT of the Jeanneau, sipping beer under the stars, Falcone and Niles were silently suffering the aftereffects of the day's abuse. After showering, they had collapsed on beds in the cabin and slept until Jake returned about an hour ago. He'd come on board with a bag of groceries from a nearby Carulla market, the contents of which produced an enthusiastically received steak-and-pasta dinner, protein and carbs. He also had a box of materials he'd acquired from a warehouse rendezvous; these, he stored in a secure place.

Jake had remained below to clean up and check his email. Before logging off, he googled Flora EquaExquisitas and found the company referenced but very little substantiative information. On a whim, he typed *Javiera* in the search bar and surfed his way to a Spanish names site. Scrolling through the J's, he found it and clicked on the meaning. *Owner of a new house.* He mulled that for a moment. Owner of a new house. Or, he thought, perhaps a new cartel. Rejoining Falcone and Niles topside, Jake leaned back against the cockpit and gazed thoughtfully up at the stars speckling the night sky. In his mind, he saw the *Javiera*. In his heart he felt Delaney…Delaney and something else.

"Well, gents," he said eventually, looking solemnly from one to the other, "I'm going to ask you one last time."

With a dismissive shake of his head, Falcone said, "No need. Right now I hate your frigging guts, but I haven't even come close to changing my mind." He glanced at Niles. "Have you?"

Niles concurred but did not seem to match Falcone's degree of conviction.

Tilting his head, Jake asked, "Curran, are you sure? I wouldn't think any less of you if you want out."

"No," Niles said quietly. "I don't want out. I'm all the way in." A tired, crooked grin slid over his sunburned face. "I just feel like raw hamburger after it's been chewed up in a grinder and then pulverized with a bloody meat-cleaver."

Jake nodded sympathetically. "Yeah, I can imagine."

"No," Falcone sneered, "I doubt if you can. I think you're fucking bionic."

"Eddie," Niles chided, rolling his eyes.

"That's okay, Curran, I understand how he feels. I'm not bionic, just in condition. And I'm sorry this is so hard, Eddie, really. But it's necessary."

"Well, do you think you might at least tell us *why* the hell you're putting us through all this shit?" He shifted, wincing as a spasm rippled through first one leg and then the other.

Kneeling in front of him with concern, Jake asked, "Are you having cramps?"

Gritting his teeth, Falcone groaned, "Son of a bitch, yes. But just leave me the fuck alone."

Calmly, Jake said, "Hey, relax, okay? I want to make sure you haven't strained any muscles or torn any ligaments. Curran, there's some ibuprofen in my bag. You should both take some." Despite Falcone's fractious objections, Jake continued to examine his legs, checking the hamstrings, quadriceps, and calves. When he was satisfied there were no strains or tears, he massaged the muscles for several minutes until the cramping had subsided. Then he dug into his bag, which Niles had retrieved from below, and got the ibuprofen and some hydrocortisone cream.

"Thanks," Falcone said glumly.

"Okay," Jake said. "And you guys better switch from beer to mineral water for a while, for several obvious reasons, but it will also help ward off the cramps." When Falcone and Niles were finished applying the cream to their sore limbs, Jake put everything back in his bag and went below to get them some water.

When he returned, Falcone said, "You never answered my question."

"Until this afternoon," Jake began, "I wasn't sure if we would be able to execute the plan I had in mind, but since I located their boat we can proceed."

Niles almost choked on the water he was swallowing, coughing and blowing it through his nose. "You found their boat? How?"

"Just pure luck," Jake replied.

"Unbelievable," Niles marveled. Mulling it over, his forehead furrowed in puzzlement. "Of what significance is finding their boat? Before the meeting, I mean?"

With a cryptic smile, Jake said, "Everything."

"Okay," Falcone said, all animosities quickly dispelled, "tell us what we're going to do."

UNDER JAKE'S INTENSIVE AND indefatigable command, Falcone and Niles began to turn the critical corner by week's end. Having spent more time in the water than out of it, they were finally gaining a reasonable level of comfort and proficiency, and their endurance had greatly improved. Still, Jake knew that the success of his planned operation depended less on water skills and survival techniques than it did confidence and precision in the execution. In his military career he had undertaken many riskier tasks with a much greater danger factor, but he could recall few with so many variables and unknowns. He had two inexperienced civilians that would now be totally dependent on the thoroughness of his training, a limited selection of technical equipment, and a highly volatile window of time within which to operate—not to mention the need of military personnel and equipment to complete the mission. But he was determined to make it work. In the final analysis, that was the most important aspect of any mission, the determination that drove it. He had that covered.

Several times during the week, while Falcone and Niles took respite from their workouts, Jake drove back to Club de Pesca. Each time, he rented a different vehicle, and varied the times of day and night. The purpose for his surveillance was, first and foremost, to make sure the location was not changed and second, to monitor any activity. The boat remained in its berth, and activity on and around it seemed normal. As the weekend approached, food and supplies were loaded. Everything was progressing perfectly.

On Saturday morning, they reviewed every aspect of the plan one last time. Seated around the dining table in the galley, they discussed the operation while Jake checked and packed their gear.

"Hey!" Niles said suddenly, startling Falcone into nearly spilling his coffee. "What about sharks?"

"What about them?" Jake asked lightly, putting encrypted SIM cards in the pair of refurbished, throw-away satellite phones they would be carrying.

"What do you mean, what about them?" Falcone retorted. "Curran's got a good point. We never talked about sharks and I sure as hell don't want to be shark scum."

"That's chum," Jake laughed. "Yeah, after living through this, that would be a hell of a way to go. Tell you what, we'll go out today and I'll teach you shark-punching."

Falcone and Niles stared at Jake speechlessly until a smirk broke the surface of his staid demeanor.

"Asshole," Falcone muttered, but relief was audible in his voice.

"Don't worry, bro," Jake said, "I've got you covered in that department." He reached into one of the gear bags and extracted a pair of black devices the size of transistor radios with cables attached. "This is the latest anti-shark technology, SEAL buddy of mine put me onto it. It's called Shark Shield and basically, the way it works is by generating an electronic field around you. The electronics make the sharks uncomfortable as it kind of scrambles their sonar, so they stay away"—he grinned—"usually." He handed them one of the devices, demonstrating its operation.

"My luck, I'll get the one it doesn't bother," Niles remarked.

"Do you Rambo types really punch sharks?" Falcone asked sarcastically.

Jake chuckled. "Believe it or not, yes. I've got a good friend who teaches that stuff in our water survival camp, but personally I'd prefer this little gadget any day. Less likely to donate an arm to Mr. Shark."

"Jesus Christ," Falcone groaned.

"Okay, you two," Jake said at last. "I've checked everything out and you're ready to go. I've synchronized our watches and made sure everything else works."

"Techno-gadgets and synchronized watches," Niles quipped with a nervous giggle. "I feel like Jack bloody Bauer."

"Call me after they've contacted you and then I'll call you after you've been on board the boat a little while. Unless something starts to go wrong, in which case don't wait for me to contact you. Whatever you do, don't take for granted that things are going smoothly. At the same time, try to manifest the attitude that you are there to strike a mutually lucrative deal. And yes, there's always the possibility that they already know this is a setup, but hopefully you'll be out of there before they act on it. They wouldn't be where they are if they were not highly intelligent and well-connected, but you are, too."

Just before Falcone and Niles disembarked from the boat, Falcone stood before Jake with a look of soulful sincerity. "I know I've given you hell all week and you were only doing what you had to do. I just want to say I'm sorry."

"No sweat." He gave Falcone an understanding smile.

"Are you sure you don't want us to help you tonight? That's gonna be dicey."

"Negative," Jake remarked with a sly little smirk, "I've done it all before. No, you guys need to be at the hotel. So get going."

Stepping off the boat, Niles said, "Be careful, Jake."

"Always," Jake replied, handing over the last of their gear. He felt an emotional charge pass through him as he leveled his gaze on them for a few moments. "You two watch out for each other. I'll be fine."

"So will we," Falcone said with conviction, and they were off, trudging up the dock toward the marina office to summon a taxi.

Watching them, Jake felt a knot lodge and tighten in his gut, praying that it was only apprehension and not intuition. And then, as he prepared to set sail, he realized two things. One, if the plan failed, he might not see Falcone and Niles again. And two, if the plan succeeded, it would all be over. Once and for all over, with no looking back.

JAKE SPENT MOST OF the afternoon and part of the evening preparing his diving gear and the materials he would be carrying.

The call from Falcone and Niles came about 6 PM. The sailing excursion had been confirmed, with departure set for 8 AM Sunday morning. The *Javiera* would be sailing down around the Islas del Rosario with the return planned for sometime later that night.

At midnight, Jake slipped into a black Wrangler and headed down Avenida Miramar toward Club de Pesca. About a hundred meters from the fortress bastion that fronted the marina, he slowed and pulled off the road, nosing the Wrangler into a section of brush. From there, it was a few yards to the water. Previous surveillance here had revealed some walkers and joggers along the promenade, but after dark he'd encountered only an occasional vagrant. Tonight, he saw no one.

Clad in his wetsuit, he strapped on a BC and bulky rebreather, and adjusted the rest of his gear. Then he checked the package in the pouch strapped around his waist a final time to make sure he had everything he needed, padded to the walkway edge, and dropped into the warm Caribbean.

He felt more tense than usual, something he attributed to the fact that other, more vulnerable lives were at stake. But as he swam the half-mile to the marina, he began to relax and his confidence elevated. Along the way, he saw very little in the murky waters except what was in the cone of his LED beacon, passing through more fields of debris than fish. He knew he was closing in on the dock by the haze of diesel and thicker silt shifting around him. When the hulls of boats came into shadow above him, he surfaced briefly to get his bearings. In the sodium glow of overhead lighting along the dock, the *Javiera* gleamed like a Titan rocket on silent countdown.

Jake slid back beneath the surface and closed the gap with a few quick kicks. When he was directly underneath the boat, he spent a few minutes familiarizing himself with its external structure. It was designed with a tunneled hull, the chambers of which were located directly below the engine room. Maneuvering in front of the tunnels, he extracted a brick-sized metal box from his pouch. Locating the sea chest inlets, a pair of one-foot-square steel holes that took water to the engine, Jake thrust the box into the recess until the strong magnet inside jerked it to a wall of the intake, hard and solid.

When he was done, he gave the hull a pat. *Not long now, big girl...not long now.*

He resurfaced to take a last look at the boat, and movement aboard caught his eye. He drifted to a concealed spot beneath the pier, removed his dive mask, and reached for the waterproof Yukon scope looped around his neck. Two people came into focus, standing along the yacht's port-side railing—a man and a woman. In the green Jell-O world of night vision, they morphed together, arms intertwining. The man hefted the woman up, her bare legs encircling his torso. Their bodies jerked, their heads bobbed.

Adjusting the zoom on his scope, Jake brought the couple's faces into greater detail. But even before doing so, he knew who he was watching.

I could do it right now, he thought.

They would never see it coming. He could take them one at a time or both together, and in two quick motions slit their throats. Nice and neat, then over the side and into the water, their dark eyes staring back at him in unsuspecting wonder, mouths agape as their lungs filled with seawater and their blood bloomed out. Yes, he could do it right now. But he was content to wait, let his plan play out. It was, he knew, the better way, leaving no loose ends.

Jake dove deep below to the clearer depths and swam back to the promenade, feeling nothing. Nothing but the warm, watery world. Tranquil and whole. For tonight.

31

THE SLEEK MOTORYACHT WAS boring into the deeper waters eight to ten kilometers from the coast, its powerful 5400-hp twin engines maintaining a comfortable cruising speed of 45 knots. On departure from Cartagena, the boat had navigated through the Bocachica strait, passing between two historic Spanish forts, the Batería de San José and the Fuerte de San Fernando, at the tip of Isla de Tierrabomba. Against the vast blues of sea and sky, she sped forth like an ivory missile armed and aimed at some distant target.

Not more than two hours ago, Falcone and Niles had been chauffeured from the Hotel Caribe to the marina. Pre-boarding had been initially tense, the security checks of person and possessions considerably more comprehensive than those conducted at Casa Solitaria. They were both sportily dressed in Tommy Bahama and Ralph Lauren ensembles, pale lightweight slacks, striped and tropical print silk shirts, and deck shoes. When Angel Valentín had called with confirmation of the meeting, he'd instructed them to bring bathing suits and one change of clothing, and so they had. They each carried a medium-sized duffel and attaché, packed into which were the phones and assorted businesslike documents and paraphernalia. Nothing was really brought into question until one of the security men came across the Shark Shield packs.

"*Qué es esto?*" he queried, suspiciously turning the black neoprene pouch over in his hands. It looked both sinister and innocuous, an accessory of unknown function with a short textured coil and a flexible cuff.

Niles had told him precisely what it was, and the tension lightened as his explanation brought a robust volley of laughter from the trio of security men.

"*Vaya! Buen viaje!*" one of the men said finally, and waved them toward the boat. The security team was still snickering as Falcone and Niles had stepped aboard the *Javiera*.

Fine, Falcone had thought, let the sharks eat *them*. But then sharks would be the last of their worries. He'd exchanged a relieved smile with Niles, feeling a small surge of confidence with the passage of their first test.

Now, little more than thirty minutes later, they stood on the flybridge with the Valentíns, being boastfully regaled with specifications and statistics about the *Javiera*. This, as a wrap-up to the introductory tour that had taken them through automatic aft deck sliding glass doors into a marble foyer resplendent with curio tables displaying Erte figurines and Versace crystal, to the frosted-glass and 18-carat gold-leaf etched bar dominating the skylounge, to the svelte and sophisticated pilothouse with an array of controls, monitors, and screens befitting a spaceship. Looking out over the glistening Caribbean, Falcone and Niles were struck by the utter inconceivability of finding themselves here, on this megayacht, after slugging along the murky waters of the Amazon on a threadbare barge that was one splinter away from becoming river flotsam. Custom built by Millennium, the multi-million-dollar high-performance yacht with its combined diesel and gas-powered turbine engines produced 20,000 horsepower and could, according to the Valentíns, do top speeds approaching 70 knots—just over eighty miles per hour. As if to prove it, Angel whistled sharply to the captain, yelling, "*Más rápidame!*"

Immediately, the twin diesels spooled up, the whine of the turbine increasing to a feverish pitch. With barely a rumble, the ride of the 140-foot yacht was as smooth as a Cuisinart in puree. At top speed the motoryacht's movement became only slightly choppier as it churned up waves that left a trail of spume thick as meringue. Falcone and Niles shared a few nervous minutes, thinking about the seismic vibrations being generated by the heavy horsepower, but Jake had assured them it would have no effect.

"Yeeee-haaa!" Angel hooted, displaying an absurdly lunatic grin contorted by the wind's pressure against his face.

Managing to suppress his own cocky exhilaration, Adonís ordered the captain to resume cruising speed, and led them to the rear of the main deck for al fresco dining. In contrast to the mixed Mediterranean and Oriental décor that luxuriated the rest of the yacht's interior, this space was light and summery, particularly with everything opened up and the tropical sea breeze blowing through. Calypso music with an aberrant hip-hop flavor played in the background, and the piquant smell of freshly grilled, highly seasoned fish wafted out from a barbecue somewhere within. As they took their seats around the linen-covered table, Elena emerged from the staircase and crossed the flybridge, sliding onto the circular settee. Her perfume swirled a trail behind her, a heady blend of jasmine, licorice, and some indeterminate musk. Soon afterward, a uniformed servant began to set ice-cold shrimp cocktails before them, followed by green salads speckled with crabmeat. The main course was blackened tuna, complimented by Chilean chardonnay which Falcone and Niles sipped sparingly, filling up instead on the mineral water.

The Valentíns were dressed in similar fashion to Falcone and Niles, whites predominating. Adonís wore a thin, long-sleeved cotton shirt with the cuffs rolled up and the front half-buttoned. Elena's eyes traveled frequently to his tanned chest, across which ran the faint groove of a scar that stretched diagonally from beneath his right nipple to the waist of his form-fitting white slacks. Elena, by contrast, wore a sleeveless black dress, breasts swelling against the smocked top, long legs visible through a thigh-high slit. Silver bracelets chinked up and down her lower arms as she raised her fork to her mouth, a simple motion with which the men seemed inordinately fascinated.

Table conversation centered on the boat and its gadgetry, fast and pricey cars, food and drink, and entertainment. It was tacitly understood that business would not be broached until later in the afternoon or early evening; the day was for informal talk and leisure. After lunch, they all changed into swimwear, Elena suited in an infinitesimal zebra-striped bikini with angles sharp enough to cut a solitaire diamond. They lounged in the upper-deck Jacuzzi for a while, allowing the substantial lunch to digest and then, as the sun peaked overhead, began to hanker for the sea's cool refreshment.

The yacht had slowed on entering the protected waters of Corales del Rosario and was now gliding through more shallow channels near Isla Grande. The captain dropped anchor, and the five of them spent the next few hours in and out of the Caribbean. Had it not been for the omnipresent foreboding in knowing that the passing hours were bringing them closer and closer to the scheduled time, Falcone and Niles might have actually enjoyed it.

FOLLOWING AN EVEN MORE gastronomical dinner of stuffed lobster and filet mignon, business talk began over coffee and tiramisu. They moved from the formal dining room, separated by a columned sideboard housing Baccarat crystal and Lamose china, into the main saloon. Its dark burl wood was offset by light marble floors overlaid with muted-color Oriental carpeting and dramatic fiber optic lighting; a fawn-colored sofa curved around a gold-edged oval coffee table, accenting easy chairs with end tables on the opposite side. The large Serdinelli- and Miele-outfitted country-style galley was just beyond on the port side, while the luxurious owners' cabin consumed nearly half of the main deck. Inside the suite, a king-sized pedestal bed with etched headboard was surrounded by mirrors and art panels. The twin his-and-hers heads joined in the middle with a freestanding shower and giant black onyx Jacuzzi. The audio-visual toys would have sent a media maven into a delectable overdose of sight and sound, the components of which were blended seamlessly into cabinets. Even the giant-screened TVs were concealed in pop-up credenzas and dropped down by mechanical lifts.

Standing beside the granite bar, Adonís Valentín waited while a male servant set two snifters out, pouring Courvoisier in one and Grand Marnier in the other. Vintage, high-dollar stuff, Remy Martin Louis XIII and Cuvée Spéciale Cent Cinquantenaire. As he sipped the cognac and handed the Grand Marnier to Elena, he asked Falcone and Niles, "What will you have?"

While neither wanted anything else to drink—there had been more wine with dinner—they both knew how important it was to stay within expected behavioral boundaries and keep scrutiny to a minimum.

Glancing purposefully at Niles, Falcone said, "I don't know about you, Fletch, but I think some more of that excellent coffee would be good, maybe with a little brandy."

"Ah, just the spot," Niles chimed. "Need to keep my wits about me when we talk numbers."

"Yes, numbers," Adonís purred, swirling the caramel-colored cognac in his snifter, inhaling its distinctive aroma with his eyes closed in pleasure. But only for a moment, and then his expression distilled to one of veiled emotion. "So you know, we have verification of your funds."

Falcone and Niles said nothing, felt the air in the saloon grow thick and heavy.

Adonís eyed one and then the other. Casually sipped the Courvoisier. And said, "Gentlemen, I am pleased to tell you that we are prepared to offer you our highest level product at a very attractive price." Tipping his head toward Angel, who began scribbling some figures on a notepad, he continued, "If you will take a moment to consider this, we can—"

The soft chirring sound coming from Falcone's attaché gave him a start until he remembered what it was. Jake had already called him once, checking in just after lunch, and had told Falcone he'd call again at about this time. Glimpsing at his watch and feigning a look of annoyance, he said, "Christ, I forgot about the New York deal." Looking at Adonís, he said, "I need to take this call, do you mind?"

Smiling politely, Valentín said, "Not at all."

Excusing himself, Falcone took the satellite phone outside. "Yeah, it's me," he said, lowering his voice.

"Hey," Jake said on the other end of the static-laden connection. "Everything all right?"

Pushing the phone closer to his ear, Falcone said, "Shit, Jake, I can hardly hear you. Yeah, so far, so good."

"Okay, look"—fading out—"time...soon...get ready."

Falcone heard just enough to know what he was saying. "I know and we're as ready as we'll ever be."

"Watch the time, Eddie," Jake urged, "one hour." And the connection was lost.

Returning to the main saloon, Falcone said, "Sorry for the interruption."

"I understand," Adonís Valentín replied dryly. He strolled back to the bar for another Courvoisier, watching Falcone intently as he returned to his seat next to Niles.

Peering at the notepad Angel Valentín had passed to Niles, Falcone studied the mind-warping figures as if he crunched such numbers every day, penning a few minor adjustments. He leaned close to Niles, whispered in his ear. Niles nodded vaguely and handed the notepad back to Angel.

Reviewing the changes, Angel contemplated a counter-offer, then decided the price was acceptable. Adonís strode over, gave the notes a quick glimpse, then faced Falcone and Niles. Raising his snifter, he said, "Mr. Messina, Mr. Fletcher, we have a deal. Here is to a long and prosperous business relationship. *Buena suerte para nosotros.*"

Falcone and Niles raised their glasses in response, acknowledging first Adonís, then Angel and Elena. As Falcone's gaze met Elena's, she winked. Things could not be going better, Falcone thought with growing confidence as he finished his brandy and coffee and leaned back into the couch's cushions.

Across from them, Elena's cell phone played a muted musical ringtone from her purse. They watched distractedly as she reached down beside her chair, dug the phone out of her bag, flipped it open and held it to her ear. She said nothing, merely listened. A moment later, she snapped it shut and dropped it back into her bag without so much as a change in expression. Fleetingly, Falcone wondered how she could possibly get cell service where they were.

"One of our associates will be joining us momentarily," Adonís was saying airily, finishing the last of his drink and setting the crystal snifter down on the bar with a decisive clunk. "This worked out well. He has been spending some recreational time here in the islands, so we stopped to pick him up. If you will excuse me now, I have a little business of my own to tend while I retrieve him."

Watching Adonís Valentín leave the main saloon, headed for the foyer, Falcone's mind unleashed a chaotic mess of reactive signals and thoughts. Cell service range. Another person coming on board...and they were docked at one of the islands? For how long? he wondered. He felt his pulse throbbing in his temple. Not good, this was not good at all.

Ordering himself to stay calm, he addressed Angel and Elena, saying, "That was some dinner." He stood up, flexing his arms and legs, and glanced candidly at Niles. "I think I'll take a short stroll, walk some of it off. I need to call New York again anyway."

Walking back through the galley to the outside, he frantically punched in the stored number for Jake. It was answered almost immediately. "Thank God," he mouthed into the receiver.

"What's wrong?" Jake asked tightly, this time through a clearer connection.

"You've got to hold off."

"You know that's impossible, Eddie. What's going on?"

"We're docked at some island. They're picking someone up." Falcone felt his composure lifting like weak glue from paper.

There was a pause, voices in the background, and then Jake said, "Okay, I see…the GPS tracker has you just off Rosario. No sweat, they'll probably head back out as soon as the person boards. Did they say who it is?"

"No, just 'some associate'."

Calmly, Jake said, "Just stay focused, Eddie."

Falcone felt his bowels twitch and twist. "Yeah, okay."

Before disconnecting, they compared time to verify that their watches were still in sync. It was 19:21:32 PM. Less than forty minutes to the target time, and counting.

Falcone stepped from the galley and almost walked into Elena returning, apparently, from the adjacent powder room. Before he could speak, she pushed her body against his and sucked him into a very hard and very long kiss. When it was over, he opened his mouth to say something only to have it filled with her tongue. Wrestling himself free, he panted, "God Almighty, Elena! Adonís—"

"Adonís has gone ashore," she said throatily, slipping her arms around his torso. "He will be a while. Come, we will entertain ourselves until he returns."

Again, Falcone's mind shifted into overdrive. *Oh God*, he lamented, *get me out of this*. And, absently, *What would you do now, Jake?* How long was *a while*? What was Niles doing? Was he with Angel? Something felt dreadfully wrong. As Elena tugged him into the owners' suite, Falcone snuck a peak at his watch. 19:26:11. Not quite thirty minutes. *God oh God oh God.*

Inside the suite, Falcone's instincts rallied like a running back racing the clock in overtime. There was, quite simply, no time to resist her, so he made a conciliatory decision. He would get it over fast.

He grabbed Elena, kissing her voraciously. She moaned pleasurably and worked at his pants until she had ripped the front open. He lifted her up, lunged onto the bed, and was on her and in her before she could take command, but his aggression only served to light the fuse of her determination to dominate. She bucked, rolling him on his side, and they slammed roughly into each other for several minutes. At one point, she lifted up and looked down at him with hooded eyes, long hair hanging around his face, planted her hands firmly on his shoulders. Falcone knew she was trying to take over, slow him down, so he pulled her to him, centered his energy in one final thrust. His gratification came with the release of tension and simultaneous wash of stimulation, but hers was about to culminate in an entirely different way.

Reaching for his neck, drawing his face close to hers, she said, "I know who you are, Tony Messina." The voice soft as silk, and as hard and hot as a driven rivet.

He blinked, did not know what to say. His breathing raged like a brush fire, filling his lungs and pumping his heart.

"Seems you have stayed at the lovely Caribe once before. With someone else. Someone I knew. Intimately." Her breath on his neck felt like it was boiling his skin, from the inside out.

The ocean beyond the portholes seemed to roar in his ears.

"I know a lot of things." She ran her tongue across his lips. "*Adios, Eduardo.*"

She rose from the bed, straightened her dress, gave him a final scorching look, and left the suite.

Heart galloping, he hopped off the bed and adjusted his pants, coaching his breathing to regulate. Fastening his fly, he checked his watch. 19:43:51. *Sixteen fucking minutes, sweet Jesus.* A lot could happen in sixteen minutes. *Calm down,* he told himself, *nothing's going to happen until we're clear.*

Adios, Eduardo.

Oh God.

He opened the door to the cabin and was stopped dead in his tracks by the approach of Angel Valentín. Right behind him was, apparently, the just-boarded associate.

Who looked vaguely familiar.

Like a wayward Frisbee, it hit him. The boat captain's son, from the Amazon excursion. Falcone's mind reeled. Playback of the jungle ambush flashed through his brain. *Son of a bitch.*

He pulled back inside and tapped the speed-dial for Niles' phone, praying he would get service as Elena had earlier, agonizing as it finally began to ring once, twice, three times.

His watch screamed 19:47:09. *Answer the goddamn phone, Curran!*

Four rings, then five.

"Hello?"

"Holy shit, Curran," he blathered, words coming out in breathy gusts. "Elena cornered me...she knows who we are. The boat captain's son is here. We've got to get the fuck out!"

"What?" Niles gasped.

"Is anyone around you?"

"No, but—oh, bloody hell I think they're coming this way!"

"Well, get a move on!" Falcone barked into the phone. "You need to discreetly get yourself out of there. You know where I'll be." If nothing—or nobody—intercepted him.

Numbly, Falcone realized the connection had ended.

19:50:39. Less than ten minutes. And he didn't even know if they had left the island dock. While crossing the cabin, just before he'd stepped into the companionway and seen Angel Valentín, he thought he sensed movement but could not be sure. Now, as he slipped through the door and made his way past the spiral staircase, he could definitely feel movement, could hear the soft rumble of the big boat's engines. He edged out onto the side deck. Glanced quickly down, squinting into the evening shadows, saw no one. Checked his watch.

God Jesus Mary God it was 19:53:59. Six minutes left. Where was Niles? *Okay, okay,* he told himself, if Niles was detained he would just wait, simple as that. And then it hit him like a flying block of concrete—what if Niles couldn't get away? What if he had walked into Elena, too? Or, worse, Angel with the boat captain's son? If Elena knew who they were, did the Valentíns know? And, if not, how long before she would tell them? Incredibly, he realized that Jake's timing was dead on—and they had passed the point of no return.

Frantically, he tried to think of how he could extricate Niles if he got caught, but God, oh God, there was just no time. His mind was about to launch into a full-blown panic when he spotted Niles shuffling around the corner, sprinting toward him along the outer deck.

"Let's get the bloody hell out of here!" Niles called to him.

Falcone kept an eye on Niles approaching as he swung his legs over the railing.

With less than five feet between them, a figure seemed to morph right out of the fiberglass, snagging Niles before he could join Falcone on the overhang. Twisting around, Niles fought to extricate himself from the crew member who was speaking in heated Spanish. From his precarious perch, Falcone watched as Niles wrestled free and climbed over the railing. He was sidling toward Falcone as the yacht's smooth ride took a minute lurch. From anywhere else aboard it would pass largely, if not totally, unnoticed, but standing on the outer deck lip it was like a riptide. Falcone's feet slid out from under him, and the sudden shift of momentum broke his grip on the railing. As Falcone's body went sprawling over the edge, he saw Niles being yanked back onto the deck by the crew member—one muscular arm around Niles' neck, the other brandishing a gun.

In the deafening vacuum of wind and space and speed, Falcone screamed, *Nooooooooooooooooooooo!* And was swallowed in a vortex of churning water that felt like a pit of gravel. Dimly, through the numbing rush of submersion, he felt his briefcase bumping around his body, felt some distant and disconnected thought bumping around with it.

Pumping his way to the water's surface, he thrashed around desperately looking for Niles. Spitting water, tasting the salt in his mouth and throat, his body still tingling from the shock of impact with the water, Falcone screamed for Niles. He struggled against the undertow created by the boat's big props. It was dark, only a deep orange glow clinging to the western horizon as a remnant of the day, the moon not yet bright enough to illuminate the sea. He was dazed and disoriented, uncertain of his position in relation to the boat. Scissoring his legs to stay afloat, he clutched the briefcase to his chest, his fingers on the top, pinching the clasps. On the clasps…*oh God, the clasps, the—*

The Caribbean exploded, shaking the reefs and rumbling the sandy bottom, unfurling a shock wave across and below the water's surface and flame-throwing fire out above and high into the new night sky. The *Javiera*, every board and beam of her being—and all those toasting the social hour within her—had been blown away.

32

"CURRAN!" FALCONE SCREAMED. "CURRAN where are you?"

He thought he heard a gasp and splashing, but debris from the yacht was raining from the heavens, a missile shower of flaming chunks of metal, wood, fiberglass. Falcone took a huge breath and dove under the water, thought he caught a glimpse of Niles nearby doing the same. Swam underwater as far as he could go, slowed by the food, the drink, and the sex, going until his lungs ached to the point of bursting. He broke the surface, sucked deeply at the air and immediately began choking on the acrid smoke.

Coughing, he called again for Niles. Heard nothing, saw nothing. His pounding heart tripped. Niles had to be here, somewhere, he thought desperately. He had seen him. Hadn't he?

"Curran!"

Nothing, nothing at all. Just the fire raging as it consumed the thousands of gallons of fuel, the sea current still violently lurching.

Falcone dove underwater, trying to see through the murkiness created by debris, pieces of reef, and sand. Just as his eyes began to adjust and his breath was about to give out, he saw Niles' legs and torso. He swam the seven or eight meters and looped an arm around his partner.

"Curran? Hey!" He smacked lightly at Niles' cheeks and was rewarded with a murmur. "Hey, come on pal, no time for slackin' now. God, you scared the shit out of me."

"Jake," Niles slurred foggily, his head drooping and his eyes fluttering, "can't do it, just can't." Blood was oozing from his nose and the corner of his mouth.

Shifting his weight and adjusting his hold, Falcone also noticed that one of Niles' arms was bleeding profusely. "Oh God," Falcone said softly. "Curran, it's me, Eddie. Can you hear me?"

"Jake...can't," Niles said, his voice draining to barely a whisper.

"Yes, Curran," Falcone said insistently. "Yes, you *can*. You have. We have. We did it, it's over. But you've got to hang with me, bud. Okay? Curran, do you hear me? Look at me!"

Niles' eyelids blinked fully open for a few seconds and his gray eyes seemed to regard Falcone with wonder. Then, his lashes were fluttering again, and he whispered, "No...can't Eddie...can't."

"Yes, you can! Come on, Curran," Falcone pleaded, pinching Niles' jaws, tapping the sides of his face. But this time, there was no response. Niles' head lolled to the side and his body was limp. Falcone felt for a pulse—something he wasn't even sure he knew how to do, but he had watched Jake enough—and found a weak one. Okay, he told himself, time to move onto the next part of the plan. Evac. He held onto Niles and scoured the singed sky, seeing nothing but the spreading umbrella of black smoke.

JAKE SAW THE EXPLOSION from his position near the door of the Blackhawk UH-60. At their distance it was a sudden spot of red-orange that appeared in the evening sky like a Fourth-of-July Maroon with a solid boom and dazzling flash—only the flash didn't fizzle away, it plumed and billowed and brightened. As they flew closer, it loomed larger and higher, sprawling out across the water.

During the hours he had been tracking them by GPS, interspersed with the few phone conversations, he had mentally constructed every sequence of events, pondered every conceivable complication, envisioned every outcome. But in the end, it all came down to fate and faith. His life had been filled with moments like this, and he was still not sure which tipped the balance. He wanted to believe it was faith, but it was always a very fine line. And despite the fact that he had planned the op with as much care for failed contingency as for a successful outcome, what was happening below him now was largely out of his control with the lives of two guys he'd come to care a great deal about now hanging in that balance. Falcone and Niles had jettisoned from the yacht at the designated time, the detonator had triggered as the briefcases' clasps made contact with the salt water and the signal had alerted him to the ninety-second countdown.

With the explosion, the wait was over. He could now resume control, call the shots, run the operation. He was back in his customary role, his brain issuing commands based on both intellect and instinct.

He scanned the darkness, searching, seeing nothing. He donned NVGs and looked again. Saw the forks of flame, just the fire writhing across the water. Nothing more. He strained through the goggles into the green-tinted night, watching for something, anything, to indicate they had made it.

Despite the fact that it was over, he could not feel the release, could not feel the relief, because it might have cost him something he was not prepared to lose. They were just a pair of regular guys with ordinary lives, who had taken a job that took them into something that should have been only a little edgy. Something they could go back and recount in dramatic fashion to their friends and families, not something that took them so far over the edge that they never stood a chance of returning to their regular lives. Or returning at all.

The helicopter closed in on the field of fire spread over the water and Jake leaned against the open door, looking and hoping that faith would have the upper hand this time.

WHETHER IT HAD SEPARATED from him on impact or been left behind, Niles' was without his briefcase. Falcone's had hit the water with him and its clasp-trigger had started the countdown and detonated the bomb—a bomb that would have blown up Niles, too, had he not managed to free himself in the last couple of seconds. For that, Falcone was immeasurably grateful, but being without the second case and all its rescue paraphernalia—not the least of which was the personal floatation device—was going to be a real challenge, hopefully not an insurmountable one.

Falcone paddled his legs to stay afloat, now thankful for Jake's insufferable workouts, unlatching his case and fishing for the signaling ChemLight. Finding it, he looped the cord around his neck. From the briefcase he extracted the floatation device they had passed off to the security men as part of the much-ridiculed anti-shark paraphernalia. Thinking about the sharks spurred him to work a little faster. Slipping the PFD around Niles, Falcone popped the CO_2 cartridge to inflate it and then ducked underwater to attach the Shark Shield. Since there was now only one of everything, he didn't hesitate for an instant in activating the Shark Shield on Niles. Hopefully it would protect them both, but if not...well, it would just have to.

Next, he checked the Motorola phone. The briefcase was supposedly waterproof—and it was actually floating on the water—but Falcone had his doubts, especially since everything inside seemed moist. Niles stirred slightly, moaned faintly. Suddenly remembering his friend's bleeding arm, he cursed out loud, replaced the phone, closed the attaché case, and wrestled out of his shirt. Lifting Niles' limp arm, still bleeding from a long and what looked to be fairly deep gash, Falcone tied his shirt tightly around it.

Opening the case again, he clutched the phone and punched in Jake's number. *God, please let it work*, he prayed. But there was no dial tone, no sound at all, nothing. Shaking it, Falcone muttered, "Son of a bitch!" He tried again. This time, he got a dial tone. And this time, Jake answered.

"Jake!" Falcone said with a relief so profound he felt tears spring to his eyes.

"It's about time, my man," he heard Jake say as a muted cheer went up in the background. "You guys okay?"

"No," Falcone replied shakily, looking over at Niles bobbing listlessly next to him. "Curran's unconscious. He must have gotten hit by some of the debris. He's bleeding pretty bad."

"Okay," Jake said, his voice as reassuringly steady as ever, "listen to me, Eddie. I'll get back to you on Curran's condition in a minute. We saw the explosion, so you must be in range. You have the ChemLight?"

"What? Oh, the light, yeah," Falcone stuttered, his teeth chattering with nervousness. He gripped the light around his neck.

"Light it up."

Falcone bent the plastic tube and shook it as he'd been instructed, but saw nothing. "It's not working! I don't see anything!"

"Calm down, Eddie. Remember what I told you about it—it's the infrared kind, so you can't see it and we won't see it until we're closer. Now, about Curran. I want you to feel for a pulse."

"I did. He's got one," Falcone blurted glibly. He couldn't feel his feet.

"Good, but I want you to do more than that. When I say start, I want you to count the beats until I say stop. Okay?"

Falcone did, and then Jake said, "Have you got the penlight?"

"Oh shit," Falcone muttered, "I didn't see—oh, wait, it's in my pocket...I think." After fighting with the wet material of his pants, he came up with the waterproof pen. "Okay, got it."

"Shine the light into his face and pull back his eyelids. Tell me if the pupils react to the light."

Frustrated, Falcone jabbered, "I don't know what you're talking about Jake."

Patiently, Jake said, "Eddie, just do as I say."

Rolling one of Niles' eyelids back, Falcone shined the strobe into the iris and squinted, not exactly sure what he was supposed to see. "I don't know, Jake. I can't tell."

"Flash it away and then back again. You should see the pupils contract. Get smaller," Jake said.

Falcone tried again, but to no avail. "I still can't," he said with a distressed sigh.

"That's all right, Eddie," Jake told him. "Tell me where he's bleeding and how much." Falcone did, adding that he had tied his shirt around Niles' arm. "That was exactly the right thing to do," Jake praised. "But we need to make sure it's not too tight or it'll cut off the circulation. You should be able to slip two fingers under it. Can you do that?"

Falcone checked, found that he could, and reported affirmatively to Jake.

"You did good," Jake said.

But instead of feeling glad, Falcone could only think about the minutes that had passed and the blood that had flowed while he'd been fumbling with other things that might have waited.

"Jake?"

"Right here, bro."

"Is he going to make it?"

"Don't know, Eddie," was Jake's blunt response, catching Falcone totally off guard. He wasn't sure what he had expected to hear, but Jake could handle everything so Jake could handle this. Jake was saying something, but Falcone's mind had shifted to a numb place. Paddling in the water, holding onto Niles and scanning the wide black sky, Falcone heard nothing. Somewhere in the water below him, he felt something nudge him. *It's a goddamned shark*, he thought distractedly.

The blood in the water. Niles' blood in the water.

And then he snapped back, hearing Jake's voice.

"Eddie, just hold tight. We're coming. We're close."

Falcone thought, *I'm not going anywhere...unless the shark eats me.* And then his mind drifted back to the eerily numb place. Where he felt calm and safe and almost dead.

GAZING UP AT THE inky Caribbean sky, Falcone was wearily aware of the tightness in his paddling legs, the heaviness in his chest, the throbbing fuzziness in his head, Niles' chin on his aching shoulder. Moments ago, or maybe hours ago for all he knew, he had seen the hazy outline of some dark, angular mass sliding around them. He was all but certain it was a shark, but before panic had a chance to really take hold, the outline dissolved into the water. The Shark Shield must be working, he thought gratefully.

Blood, there's blood in the water.

There was still fire on the water, but it had begun to die down, and it seemed much more distant from them now. It was over, Falcone told himself, it was really all over. And Jake was coming for them; he'd told Falcone he thought it would only take a few minutes to reach them. It had seemed a lot longer than a few minutes to Falcone. In fact, it had seemed lifetimes. His mind kept returning to what was beginning to feel like a dead zone and he found it hard to stay alert, to concentrate. His thoughts scattered, floated into nothingness, and then came back in a mindless jumble.

Filtered images of his childhood swam through his frenzied mind. He saw his brother, Milo, who he loved shamelessly…his mother who he missed terribly…his father who never understood him and from who he was estranged…a baseball field in Jersey on a summer day so spectacular he knew he would always remember it, as he did now…a Coney Island hotdog and an Atlantic City spree with a feisty gal named Lenore…his old '65 Mustang convertible, tape player cranking out a marathon of Springsteen…

He caught himself drifting and snapped back.

Checking Niles' pulse, Falcone felt his heart flutter with a mixture of anxiety and relief. His friend was still alive. Niles had faded in and out for a while at first before finally succumbing to unconsciousness. Falcone could not tell if his bandaging efforts had stopped the bleeding from Niles' arm. He did know that the shirt he had tied around the wound was saturated.

Blood…blood in the water…it's there, couldn't stop it…couldn't stop it, couldn't stop it.

Brushing Niles' cheek, Falcone said, "You're going to be okay, my man. Jake will be here any minute, and he'll take care of you. We've made it this far, so you've got to hang in there. Okay? You remember what Jake drilled into us, don't you? Never quit! You're not gonna bail on me now, I won't let you." And, in a prayerful whisper, "God help me, I won't let you."

Falcone's legs were cramping severely, paddling slower and slower as he tired, but as long as he kept his arm around Niles he knew he would keep going. Distractedly, he thought of all those stories about incredible rescues at sea where the survivors had managed to stay afloat for not just hours but *days*, escaping dehydration, hypothermia, drowning, and sharks. They became hot commodities on the talk-show circuit, explaining how they had found an inner strength and will to live. Of course, he could easily imagine Jake surviving such and then some, but he could not see himself lasting that long. He felt the undertow of distress pulling him down, prompting him to reach for the Motorola phone. As he did, the unmistakable nudge below of something enormous paralyzed him with fear.

Falcone grasped the phone tightly in his hand, unable to move, breath wheezing from his chest. He saw the arrow-shaped dorsal fin rise out of the water directly in front of him and felt his insides turn to liquid, pain radiating from the base of his testicles. The fear rose up and expanded like a bubble, elastic and floating, ready to pop any second. Something outside himself, an extension of himself that he could not even feel, reached over to the Shark Shield attached to Niles' bobbing body and switched it off. The dorsal fin moved several yards away, turned in slow motion, and then came gliding swiftly back.

Blood in the water, blood in the water.

Falcone switched the unit back on, his heart hammering as he squeezed the phone in his hand. There was a sudden thrashing in the water as the large mass sharply reversed and swam, fast and erratically, in the opposite direction. Falcone heaved a sigh and fought the urge to throw up, bile burning in the back of his throat. A few moments later, shaking violently, he lost the fight, much of the evening's surf-and-turf slopping into the sea.

He dipped his face in the water, to cleanse and soothe, but when he came up for air he was still shaky and nauseated. Somewhere above, distantly, he heard the rotors of a helicopter. There was a momentary rush of ecstasy he would later admit exceeded any sexual one he'd ever experienced. He waved the ChemLight frantically back and forth over his head, and this time saw a bright, strobing red flash in the sky. The chopping sound grew closer, more distinct, and soon the air began to move around him.

Shaking Niles gently, Falcone tried one last time to rouse him, but even the noise of the helicopter had no effect. Almost immediately something dropped on his head, something light and loose, something like...*a rope.*

Falcone tilted his head backwards, blinking in the swath of light now flooding over him, feeling the downdraft generated by the blades whirring above, all thoughts deafened by the roar of the Blackhawk hovering directly overhead. Struggling to hold onto Niles in the sudden upheaval of waves, he grappled for the end of the rope. Finally grasping it, he found the harness Jake had described during their mock-drills. He managed to get it over Niles without too much difficulty, his energy surging with the adrenaline rush. He hooked the D-ring and waved to signal the SPIE rig operator to take Niles up.

Watching Niles' lifeless body dangling in the air as the operator drew him up to the Blackhawk's open door, Falcone felt his emotions lifting and flowing all around him, as if his own life's essence had drained. But it was not the ebb of weakness, it was the release of contained strength.

The harness was dropped for him, and minutes later he was inside the helicopter somberly watching Jake and Alberto Hernandez work on Niles. He shrugged off the concerned inquiries of the pair of Comandos Anfibios—Colombian SEALs—who comprised the crew, accepting only a bottle of water and a blanket draped over his shoulders. Finding a spot where he could observe without getting in Jake's way, he saw for the first time how pale Niles' face was, the blood on his head and the nasty gash on his arm.

Jake and Hernandez worked quickly and aggressively, continuously checking Niles' vitals while they examined and repaired the lacerations. The arm wound had begun to bleed again, and Jake was preparing to suture it. He'd already had IVs in and oxygen running by the time Falcone made it on board.

Glancing briefly over his shoulder as he started stitching Niles' arm, Jake addressed Falcone for the first time since he had made it aboard the helicopter. "You okay?"

Grimacing with each suture, Falcone said, "Yeah, but is Curran gonna be okay?" It looked like an awful lot of sutures.

"We'll need to get him to a hospital for a more thorough evaluation," Jake replied evasively. "He's lost a good bit of blood and he's got a concussion."

"But he should be okay?" Falcone pressed feebly.

Jake gave his arm a squeeze but said nothing, returning his focus to Niles.

Falcone leaned back against the shell of the helicopter and helplessly watched as Jake and Hernandez continued to take care of Niles. The Blackhawk banked slightly, and through the window Falcone could see the tiniest flecks of orange as the wreckage of the opulent yacht they had wined and dined on, some indeterminate time ago, burned off into the Caribbean Sea. Taking the charred remains of the Valentín cartel kingpins down to the sharks.

PART THREE

JUNGLE SHADOWS FALL

33

THE COLNAV BLACKHAWK LANDED, by prior arrangement, at the Cartagena Naval Base in Bocagrande. Falcone and Niles were immediately loaded into a military ambulance that was waiting at the helipad, and the pair of Colombian Navy SEAL equivalents piled into an escort vehicle leading the way to the base hospital. Jake and Hernandez rode in the ambulance, with Jake remaining at Niles' side. He was still unconscious.

The Grupo de Comandos Anfibios is a Colombian Special Forces unit whose primary focus is counternarcotics, and it had been through working that pipeline and calling in a few favors that Hernandez had been able to requisition the chopper and SEAL team. He thanked them vigorously for their assistance and gave them a salute as they returned to their command. Rejoining Jake in the trauma room, he found Falcone sitting forlornly in a corner segregated from the exam area.

Sitting in the chair next to him, Hernandez studied him closely. "You have been evaluated by a doctor here?"

Falcone nodded sluggishly. "Yeah, I'm fine." He tipped his head toward the partition that closed off the exam area. "Curran's not."

"Do you know that?" Hernandez asked calmly.

"If you mean did anyone tell me that, no, but...well, you saw him."

"This is one of the best medical facilities in Colombia. I am sure they will take good care of him. He will be all right, Eddie."

They sat in somber silence for what seemed, to Falcone, an

impossibly long time. In reality it was only twenty minutes before Jake emerged from behind the partition.

"He's going to be okay," Jake said, and pulled a chair over to sit with them.

"Are you sure?" Falcone asked, mining Jake's expression for any sign of placatory deception.

Patting his knee, Jake said, "You can relax now, Eddie. The docs are good here and they're taking care of him, or I wouldn't be sitting with you now. Would I?"

Falcone didn't respond, but Jake's words eased his anxiety.

"How about you?" Jake asked, tilting his head inquisitively.

Falcone shrugged, eyes cast downward.

"Hey, you guys pulled off an incredible operation."

Meeting Jake's gaze, Falcone said, "Yeah, we did, didn't we?" He smiled wanly. "Guess you trained us well."

"Anybody can be trained," Jake asserted, "but it takes individuals with a special aptitude, ability, and drive to apply and execute that training in the way you guys did. I'm very proud of you both."

"As am I," Hernandez seconded.

"Now," Jake said, "I know you are focused on Curran, but I need you to tell me everything that happened while it's still fresh in your mind."

Falcone heaved a haggard sigh and recounted the events leading up to the yacht's detonation, pausing to answer questions from Jake or Hernandez. When he got to the part where Adonís Valentín had made the announcement about an associate joining them, Jake asked, "And did the 'associate' come aboard?"

"Yes. Jake, it was the boat captain's son."

"What?" Hernandez's normally placid face displayed the astonishment of a man who had been smacked over the head with a phonebook. "The captain's son?" he repeated, incredulous. "Raúl and I know the man, have known him for years. He is a retired police captain. Are you sure?"

"Yes, it was his son."

Jake glanced at Hernandez. "That explains the Amazon ambush."

Hernandez was shaking his head, clearly rattled. "I cannot believe this."

"Jake, that's not all," Falcone said grimly. "Elena...uh...Elena cornered me right before we made it off the boat. She told me she knew who we were. She knew we had stayed with you at the Caribe."

"Fuck," Jake muttered, and felt something vaguely troubling slink around a dark corner in his mind.

"Well, none of that really matters now, does it? It's done and over, they're all dead and gone."

Jake reached over and clasped his shoulder. "You're right, Eddie. And *you*," he said emphatically, "need to get some rest."

"I'm not going anywhere and I'm definitely not resting until I know Curran's okay."

Jake saw the determination in Falcone's face and said, "I'll get some coffee."

NILES REGAINED CONSCIOUSNESS SOMETIME after midnight. The doctor in charge of his care allowed them a few minutes, so they quietly filed in around his bedside. Niles' gaunt face had the cast of a raw oyster, his eyes sunken and veiled. He was connected to IVs and monitors, which blipped with reassuring steadiness. His head and wounded arm were bandaged and an oxygen cannula snaked from his nose.

Seeing the grave look on Falcone's face, Niles croaked, "Oh my God, am I dying?"

Jake chuckled. "No, Curran. I told him you were okay, but he had to see for himself. How are you feeling?"

"Like I've gone three cycles in a bloody washing machine and I'm still on spin," he rasped. "I've got all my parts?"

"Unless I cut something I shouldn't have when I was stitching you up," Jake retorted with a grin.

Niles smiled weakly and coughed, throat sore from the intubation that had just been removed. His eyes rolled back in his head.

"Okay, that's it," Jake said, giving Niles' hand a squeeze. "We're outta here so you can rest."

"I'm staying," Falcone announced stubbornly, crossing his arms.

"No," Curran wheezed. "I'm all right, mate. Go, and have a drink on me."

Which is what they did.

34

IN THIRTY-SIX HOURS, Niles had recovered sufficiently enough to trade his hospital bed for the much more comfortable one at the Radisson, and after another twenty-four he was able to fly. While Hernandez returned to Bogotá, Jake and the duo boarded a plane for Costa Rica. They were all more than ready to leave Colombia.

Their Copa flight left Cartagena shortly before 5:00 PM and touched down in San José around 7:30 after the short layover in Panama City.

Standing beside an idling taxi curbside of the Juan Santamaria International Airport, Falcone looked at Jake and said, "Guess you're ready to have us out of your hair for a while."

Jake offered a light smile. "On the contrary, bro. But we all need some downtime, that's for sure." His gaze shifted to Niles. "You doing okay?"

"Just tired. I'll be all right, mate."

"We'll be at the Marriott," Falcone said.

"By the pool with an ice-cold—"

"Hey, *you* stay out of the sun for a while," Jake ordered.

"Okay, doc," Niles scoffed.

"I'm serious, Curran."

Niles sighed. "You usually are, mate. Don't worry, I'll be good." He winked. "Mostly."

"Okay, then," Jake said briskly. "I will give you guys a call in a few days, just to check on you, then we'll link up again maybe in a week or so."

"Sounds good to me," Falcone said.

They stood regarding each other solemnly for several moments and then Jake embraced them. Keenly feeling the newly trenched depths of their friendship, a ripple of emotion passed through him as he said, "Take care of yourselves, gents. Get some good rest before you go back to work."

"Don't worry, we will," Falcone assured him. "You do the same."

"Believe me, I intend to," Jake replied. Smiled. Gave them one last look, watched them get into the taxi, and headed for airport parking to pick up Delaney's old Toyota truck.

JAKE MADE THE FOUR-hour drive from San José to Dominical in just over three, but it seemed interminable. By the time he navigated beyond the city environs and approached the southern central valley, it was fully dark with the mist of a late afternoon rain hanging in the air. He rode with the windows down, the breeze blowing through pleasantly cool and spiced with the musk of dampened earth and moist night-blooming flowers. At this hour, traffic on the winding highway was light to non-existent, so his mind was free to roam as he sped up and down the rolling hills that skirted the Cordillera de Talamanca.

Now that he could finally close the grisly chapter on Colombia, he found himself riding an erratic merry-go-round of feelings. With the obliteration of the Valentín brothers, concerns over a cartel hit on him had diminished to a negligible level, but he knew better than to let his guard totally down. Even so, he felt that leaving Colombia would most likely drop him off the *narcotraficantes'* radar. That Elena had died by association left him void of emotion; he didn't feel anger or regret or bitterness or dismay. He just felt nothing.

For Delaney, a sad sense of finality had settled within him, along with a readiness to move on. It was time, and with the closure afforded by avenging his death, Jake had no desire to continue waging the Colombian drug war. He'd done his time and then some. There were plenty of other challenges and missions for him to take on. Once he finished his work with Falcone and Niles, maybe he would take a short break, travel a little, then get the word out that he was looking for a new gig.

Callie, who had been turning over and over in his heart and mind on a kind of subliminal loop, came to fore with a suddenness of presence and emotion that made his chest ache.

And everything changes.

But did it, he wondered. Did things ever really change? Maybe not for him. Over the years, he had come to feel that was very much the case…which meant he had a difficult decision to make.

He drove on through the night-shrouded valleys, moving his thoughts and feelings around like wooden pegs in search of the right hole. But the closer he got to the turnoff for Dominical, the more wayward and unmanageable they became. When he crossed the Barú River bridge, he felt giddiness fluttering like a trapped bird in his ribcage. With the helplessness of a climber whose rope is slipping away, his mind began to fill with intoxicating thoughts of her soft feminine scent, the touch of her skin, the warm feel of her body surrounded by his. Images floated like a sensual kaleidoscope, images of her golden hair silvered by the moonlight, of the delicate sweep of long lashes over the upper ridge of her cheekbones, of pale petal lips.

By the sheerest will of discipline, he corralled his emotions and forced himself back toward the threshold of decision. Agonizingly, he couldn't seem to find it.

And then he steered off the Costanera Sur, turned down the gravel access road, pulled the Toyota up to the beach house, and a wave of exhilaration washed over everything. As his shoes crunched across the driveway of pea-gravel and ground shells, all he could hear in his head was the pounding of his errant heart.

THE BREEZE HAD DIED to the faintest stirring, barely tinking the porch chimes, the surf beyond the dunes hushed and docile. Even the night birds were strangely silent. The shuffle of his feet across the porch seemed immoderately loud.

Jake took a deep breath and entered the villa. Dropped his bags. Listened.

It was pitch dark and utterly still. He felt for the wall switch to the foyer lantern, flicking it on. Subdued light swept an amber arc into the living room. The space, the furnishings, the décor, everything was exactly the same as it had been when he'd left nearly a month ago. A month that seemed like a lifetime. He stood in the foyer, absorbing the feel of the house, hearing only the ticking Bulova. His eyes gravitated to the clock's finely etched face, saw that its small hand was on the eleven.

It was late; she was undoubtedly in bed, asleep. An ethereal vision of her pretty face in slumber drifted through his mind, causing his heart to jitter.

Dousing the foyer light, once again immersing the house in darkness, he reached for the staircase railing and padded quietly up the steps. His fingertips tingled on the iron, launching an internal sensory countdown to the touch he craved. The phantom taste of tender flesh, his lips and tongue on her nipples, taunted his mouth.

The ache to be inside her was suddenly all encompassing, and with every step his body pulsed with the need to fill her, hold her, the need to take and feel surrender. Raw desire dizzied his senses, but emotion had a stranglehold on his heart.

And everything changes.

He sprang over the last two risers and turned the corner. Stepped to the open door of the bedroom. Tiptoed lightly to the bed and leaned over.

"Love, I'm back," he whispered softly, his eyes still adjusting to the darkness.

No stirring, no sound, no overhead draft from the ceiling fan.

He reached into space, and felt nothing. His hand dropped to the surface, and felt only the quilted top of coverlet over sheets and mattress. Air, stitched quilting, too smooth. Vague outlines began to take shape in his vision. Seconds passed and textures materialized. He could now see the bed.

It was empty.

He felt a spire of alarm as he flipped on the bedroom light switch, revealing the empty bed in full-color detail. The comforter was perfectly tucked below the pillows, the edges evenly aligned along the sides of the frame. Of the unslept-in bed.

He strode across the hall to Delaney's old room and switched on the light. The room was empty and undisturbed. He checked the bathroom. It was expectedly unoccupied, smelling of some citrusy disinfectant, towels neatly stacked and draped. Checked the master bedroom, finding it exactly the way he'd left it. He returned to Callie's bedroom and stepped into the bath.

And was inundated with the soft floral scent of her.

His head reeled and his ears buzzed with a deep inner noise. A single crumpled towel lay on the vanity top. He picked it up, held it to his face, inhaled. Smelled her essence. It was still slightly wet.

Bewildered, he dropped the towel and strode from the bedroom.

Standing at the top of the stairs, he called, "Callie? Are you here?" His deep voice resonated through the empty house like a radio turned up a notch too loud. It echoed off the walls with hollow authority. He thumped back down the stairs, calling her name. Hearing no answer.

"Callie? Callie, are you here?" The command in his voice cracked with a rising note of concern.

His mind was starting to wind in furious little circles, when he heard himself say out loud, "Okay, she's gone somewhere." *At eleven o'clock?* She could have met someone, he reminded himself. But where that idea had seemed feasible—even, he thought idiotically, favorable—a week or so ago, he couldn't sell it to himself now. His mood shifted like a storm front, his emotions rolling like dark, tempestuous clouds.

He turned a lamp on and stood in the middle of the living room, raked a hand roughly through his hair, looked around fretfully. For the first time, he noticed something amiss, something so subtle and yet utterly arresting in its subtlety. Because it was something affectionately connected to Callie—a foyer rug. A small accent three-by-four trimmed with palm trees and monkeys, it was the first or last thing your feet touched on entrance to, or exit from, the villa. And it was forever crumpling or skewing sideways on contact. Jake had found himself sidestepping it, because Callie always smoothed it back in place with her toe—an unconscious gesture on her part, an endearing observation on his. Looking at it now, he saw that a corner of the rug was bunched up and noticeably askew.

He bounded upstairs, back into her bedroom. This time, he opened drawers and scanned the contents of the nightstand and dresser, not sure what he was looking for but finding only garments. Shorts and t-shirts, frilly panties and bras. They felt disconcertingly tiny in his hands. He drew apart the louvered closet doors and peered inside. Saw the lavender slip dress, and his heart flipped.

But what he saw next sent an icy sliver of dread up his spine.

Hanging from a peg just inside the closet was her purse.

Knowing she could have another, he opened it and, biting his lip, stuck his hand inside the small straw bag. He felt papers, some kind of brochure, a compact, sunglasses. When his fingers touched her wallet, alarm flared again. Okay, he reasoned, she could still be out with someone. Maybe taking a walk on the beach?

The rug, the crooked rug. An involuntary shudder racked through him.

Maybe he should call Luis, ask if he had seen her earlier. Maybe he knew if she had gone out. He descended the stairs again, started for the phone at the kitchen bar, and stopped.

The French doors were ajar.

A finger of light from the patio striped the tile floor. His eyes followed the thin streak of light and caught the edge of something out there, something near the pool. He felt his hairline bristle, his breath grow shallow and ragged.

He slipped through the French doors and looked toward the pool.

A few feet from the edge was a body, face-down.

He knelt on a shaky knee, saw a bloody hole the size of a cherry, pulped with brain matter, hair, and seared flesh, and carefully turned the body over. And stared into what was left of the ruined face of Pablo Luis Ayala. Eyeballs protruded from their sockets, above which a gory crater gaped. For a frozen instant, Jake stared down at his dead friend and could not draw a breath, could not assimilate a thought. Just hard, dead air that asphyxiated him. And then the world tilted off its axis as oxygen hit his brain and fire lit his heart.

"Oh God. Callie...oh God."

35

WITH A STEADYING BREATH, he forced himself to look back down at Luis Ayala. But his thoughts were no longer focused on Ayala. Jake grabbed the back of his neck, rocked back on his knee, and squeezed his eyes shut.

"Oh God," he murmured again. He rocked, he gazed blankly at Ayala, then rose quickly, electrified with adrenaline. He panned the perimeter of the pool, pushing his gaze beyond the shadows, probing the darkness. Seeing nothing, hearing nothing.

Sprinting back through the French doors, he plundered through drawers and cabinets until he found a flashlight. He snatched one of his duffel bags from the foyer and extracted the Glock 17, racking a magazine into the chamber. Semi-automatic in his right hand, Maglite in his left, he returned to the patio and began an intensive patrol.

Almost immediately his anxiety ratcheted to another level, because as he covered the pool area and then moved on to the rest of the grounds surrounding the house, it was becoming increasingly clear that something very sinister had happened here—sinister not because of a mass of grisly evidence, but instead a lack of it. He expected to find footprints, tire tracks, disturbed landscaping. Something. Questions attacked his brain like a swarm of angry hornets, buzzing in an incoherent cacophony.

Where was Ayala's vehicle? His department motorcycle or his personal truck? Had he been here on routine patrol, checking on Callie, or had something brought him here? How long had he been dead? Jake supposed once a time of death could be determined, he would know approximately when Callie went missing. Missing or—

No, he implored silently, *God no*.

He knew he needed to call the police and tell them about Ayala, knew he had to bring his rampant emotions under control and slip into the armor of dispassionate and disciplined respondent. But for all his staunch military conditioning and iron-willed command he was having a hard time bringing himself to that point. His head was diligently going through all the mental mechanizations, but his heart was still upstairs in the bathroom where the precious essence of Callie still lingered. He was desperately clinging to the notion that Callie couldn't have been gone long because the towel was still wet. But then the air was humid, so how much would that extend drying time? An hour? Longer?

As he depressed numbers on his cell phone, he sprinted up the stairs once more and headed into Callie's bedroom. Stepping inside the bathroom, he reached for the towel again, handled it and felt its texture. It somehow seemed less wet, merely damp. He lifted it to his nose and breathed deeply. Her scent was already fading. He buried his nose and mouth in the towel. Clenched it just like that for a long time.

A DISTRICT COMMANDER OF the Fuerza Pública pulled up to the house in a blue Toyota pickup that looked a lot like Delaney's. Riding with him was the highest-ranking officer from the Dominical force, a sergeant, and behind the pickup another pair of cops rumbled into the drive on motorcycles. Even with the report that one of their own had been killed, it had taken them nearly an hour to respond. Jake found that incomprehensible and infuriating. He was pacing back and forth between the house and the patio when the group of police filed through the back gate.

Jake glanced sharply at his watch. "What the hell took you so long?"

The sergeant, who was not much older than Ayala, said, "I am sorry, *Señor* Tyler. The Organismo de Investigación Judicial had to be notified, as did our *jefe* the lieutenant." He indicated the older heavyset man who was leaning over the body, nudging and thumping arms and torso as if to convince himself Ayala was really dead despite the bloody crater in his head.

After spending some time picking through Ayala's pockets and examining the contents, the lieutenant straightened up and turned his attention to Jake. Behind him, the other cops wandered uselessly around the patio. "I am Lieutenant Arturo Vega," he said, studying Jake guardedly. "This is your residence?"

"Well, it is now," Jake replied, offering no further explanation.

Indicating the Glock protruding from the waistband of Jake's pants, the lieutenant said, "Your weapon, I presume?" When Jake nodded, he extended his hand. Jake slipped it out of his jeans and offered it to Vega.

Watching the officer examine it, checking the chambers for missing rounds, Jake said, "It's a 9mm. It looks to me like Ayala was shot with a .357."

"Are there any other guns in the house?"

Jake wasn't sure if any of Delaney's weapons were in the house, but he simply replied, "I also have another Glock in my bag. A 26."

"You have permits for these?"

"Yes," Jake said, and retrieved both the Glock and his weapon permits. Handing them to Vega, he added, "The Dominical police know me."

The lieutenant cast a sidelong glance to the sergeant who nodded in affirmation and said, "*Él es militar. Fuerzas Especiales.*"

Vega did not seem impressed. "And what time did you arrive?" he asked dryly.

Jake exhaled impatiently but recounted how he'd come to discover Ayala's body. The lieutenant had produced a small pad and was jotting notes. Aware that a timeline was being constructed, Jake said, "I just returned from Colombia and drove here straight from the San José airport. I've got my passport and parking receipt with the time stamps, also my airline ticket." He continued, "But I think there's something else connected to Luis's death. He was here because I had asked him to keep an eye on"—he paused awkwardly—"on my lady friend, while I was out of the country."

"And where is your lady friend?" Vega inquired.

"That's just it. She's not here. She's gone."

The lieutenant did not respond, his face as expressionless as a goldfish.

"All of her things are here, but she's gone," Jake reiterated, becoming increasingly frustrated. He wanted to grab the police officer by the collar and scream into his face, *Stop fucking around and go find her!* Ayala was dead, he wasn't going anywhere. But for Callie, he could feel each escaping minute as if it were one less breath left in an allotment of air, and his chest was getting tighter by the second.

"Are you saying you think the killer or killers did something to your lady friend?" Vega asked, but his tone was skeptical.

"I don't know," Jake said, feeling his adrenaline punching back like a boxer off the ropes. "I just know Luis was looking after her, he's dead, and she's gone."

"You could be right," Vega said. "Well, we will talk about this some more. But first I must wait on the Judicial Police and the judge."

Jake stalked back inside the house. He didn't want to talk about this some more. He wanted to search for Callie.

WHILE A MIX OF personnel from Dominical and Puerto Cortes wandered about the house and grounds, a contingent of investigators from the OIJ arrived to process the scene. Unlike the lieutenant, the senior investigator, a captain, was quite interested in hearing what Jake had to say. Growing increasingly agitated, Jake again went through his return to the house and the events that followed, producing his travel documents, even allowing his hands to be examined for gunpowder residue or burns.

"Look," Jake implored, as one of the officers swabbed his palm, "I know you have to conduct a thorough investigation, and I'm trying to cooperate fully. But I know whatever happened here *just* happened. Critical time is getting away. I need to look for her. I need to—"

"*Señor,*" a voice intoned from behind him.

Jake turned to see a man in his late fifties, short and squat with a thick head of silver hair. A paunch contained in a white cotton shirt swelled over his jeans. He wore scuffed boots and wheezed softly when he walked. One of the OIJ addressed him as *Juez*. The judge.

In Costa Rica, local police are under the jurisdiction of the Organismo de Investigación Judicial, the national investigative equivalent of the FBI. When a crime of any serious nature occurs—particularly a murder—a judge is called to the scene to evaluate the preliminary evidence and, if a suspect or suspects are in police custody, determine whether they should be detained for further questioning or arrested. In the case of a body, the OIJ arranges for removal and transport to a crime lab, usually in San José.

Jake extended his hand, which the judge clasped briefly. "Jake Tyler," he said wearily.

"Juez Guillermo Obregón," the judge pronounced. Dismissing Jake, he addressed the captain and asked, "What is your evidence?"

The captain proceeded to tick off the facts, his voice trailing as the sum of the parts barely bumped the scales. As he spoke, the judge studied Jake's documents. When the captain had concluded his recap, Judge Obregón moved aside and made a few calls on his cellular phone. One was to airport security at Juan Santamaria International, to verify Jake's flight and arrival time. Another was to the US Embassy. Jake heard the judge read his name and other information off his military ID. Several minutes passed and his phone chirped. He flipped it open, listened, then snapped it shut.

He turned to Jake and said, "Señor Tyler, you are free to go. Please make sure the Policía Judicial have a way to contact you." He gave a vague nod to the captain and lieutenant next to him, and left the scene.

Jake was not far behind him.

WITH HIS WEAPONS CLEARED, Jake slipped the Glock 17 back inside the front of his jeans and took off into the brush behind the house. For the next several hours, he worked his way through densely wooded stands of trees and palms and fruit orchards, thickets of ferns and flowering plants. He moved in ever-widening sweeps, covering every direction. At one point, he thrashed into a bed of philodendrons with leaves the size of elephant ears, and spotted a mass. He pulled in a tight breath and peered closer, shining the beam of his Maglite into the thatch. A moment later air eased through his teeth as he realized the mass was the ravaged carcass of some kind of animal, probably dinner for one of the big cats that prowled the hills. Most likely an ocelot.

He continued his search through the night, crossing the Costanera Sur and plunging into the thicker forest beyond. Crossed back and re-canvassed the area closer to the house. Tired and dehydrated, he thrashed his way past guacimo and cenizaro trees interspersed with royal and coconut palms surrounded by brightly colored heliconias. Another hundred meters, he stumbled onto the beach as the first pale shadows of dawn were spreading over the silvery water. Dropping onto the sand, Jake grasped his head in his hands and listened to the soft wash of waves. At some point, he heard the dull thump of feet, distant then coming closer. Then stopping. He looked up and saw the face of someone familiar, an American named Jerry Hadley, head lifeguard for the patrolled section of beach much farther north.

"Jake? You all right, pal?"

Jake peered blearily up at the six-foot-four athlete. With his blond crew cut, blue eyes, and dark tan he looked like a buff Malibu Ken. He was wearing jogging shorts, a Thrusters tank top, and running shoes. Jake did not reply but thirstily eyed the bottle of water tucked into Hadley's waist-pack.

Following Jake's gaze, Hadley handed the bottle of Cristal to him and hunkered down on the sand. "What's up?" he asked.

Taking a long guzzle of water, he wiped his mouth and said, "I just got back from Colombia and found Luis Ayala dead at the house."

"Jesus Christ," Hadley muttered.

"And Callie's gone."

"What?" Hadley's jaw dropped. "Are you sure? I just saw her yesterday evening."

Jake's eyes speared Hadley's, flaring with hope. "You did?"

"Yeah. Even spoke to her. I always do." He smiled. "She's a sweetheart."

"When was this? What time?"

Hadley thought about it, referencing what he had been doing at the time. He recalled jogging closer to the trees because the tide was coming in, so that had to be around—

"—Six-thirty, maybe closer to seven," Hadley said.

"How did she seem?" Jake asked, voracious for any morsel of information that might give him some thread, however slim, to pursue.

"She seemed all right. Pretty much the usual for her. I see her nearly every day on my morning and evening jogs. She keeps to this secluded section of beach near Delaney's"—he caught himself—"near the villa. She walks along the beach—doesn't go in, just gets her feet wet—then sits and looks at the ocean, sometimes she writes in a notebook."

"Have you seen her with anyone else?"

Hadley thought only briefly before replying, "No, not a soul."

"Do you recall seeing anybody hanging around her, watching her...anything like that?"

Considering a little longer this time, Hadley said, "Don't believe so."

"But she was all right? She's been all right?"

"Yeah. Well..."

Jake waited.

"I can say that she seemed lonely."

Hadley's words hit Jake in the back of the throat like a rock and then sank into the pit of his stomach. Sat there like a boulder. When Hadley responded to Jake's next question, his words were thick and heavy.

"Yesterday...did you see her leave?" Jake asked.

"Yes, I did. She said, 'see you tomorrow.'"

The boulder in Jake's gut cracked open and sent big chunks flying everywhere.

WHEN JAKE RETURNED TO the house, a dawn sun the color of pink grapefruit had led morning across the rainforest and onto the patio. The police were gone, and they had apparently taken the body of Luis Ayala with them. They had left his blood. It had dried on the stone, a dark maroon stain the size of a watermelon.

Absently, Jake stumbled into the kitchen and made a pot of coffee. Poured some into a mug and wandered through the house with it. The utterly empty house. He found his eyes drawn time and again to the skewed foyer rug.

He climbed the stairs and padded into her bedroom. Sat on the bed, ran his hand over the top of the comforter. The comforter that had not been drawn back for a freshly showered Callie to slip beneath. Somewhere between the damp towel that had snugged her soft, soaped skin and absorbed the sweet essence of her, and the bed not slept in…something had happened.

His mind bucked the thought with bullish defiance. There could very well be an explanation that had nothing to do with Ayala's death, at least not directly. Maybe Ayala had surprised a prowler—Jake's mind instantly conjured an image of the intruder who'd called himself Duster— and maybe, he rationalized, maybe Callie had heard the commotion downstairs and gone to see what it was. Maybe she'd found Luis and been frightened, panicked, run away. There had to be a less ominous reason for her vanishing. There just had to be.

His satellite phone vibrated. He snatched it, moved toward the window, and answered.

And all hope of reason died.

36

JAKE STOOD BY THE bed, a stone statue of himself, clutching the satellite phone to his ear. Clutching it so hard his palm burned and his fingers were numb. Staring into a place in the space of the room that now pulsed with ions of volcanic rage and fury, he listened to the dead hum that echoed through his aural canal and buzzed into his brain with the brutality of an industrial chainsaw.

But mere seconds ago, he had heard a sound that broke him more completely than any blade could have cut. He had heard a sob, nothing more than a single sob so faint a hummingbird's wings would have drowned it out—but he knew it was Callie.

Before he could even speak the connection went dead, and the hum of empty air replaced the signal that had bounced among sixty-six satellites cross-linked 450 feet above the earth to a multi-prismed gateway on the ground, where it would have been routed through a wireless switch and transmitted to his phone.

Her voice in his phone.

The fact that she was alive failed to really register as his heart hijacked all brain activity for the next few moments. The rage and fury he'd somehow managed to reign in, detonated, and sent his emotions into a hurtling freefall that pulled all rational thought with it.

A single sob, a severed connection. A source of hope. A promise of despair.

With a guttural growl of anguish and futility, he slammed the Iridium onto the bed. It rebounded harmlessly off the mattress and lay silently on the comforter. Except for the signal-strength bars and menu symbols, its holographic display glowed vacuously green. Jake swirled from the bed and lashed out with his fist, catching a table lamp, sending it to the floor in a pile of bamboo splinters, glass shards, and seashell fragments. And then he snatched the phone and bolted from the room, tearing down the stairs.

His momentum took him wheeling into the middle of the living room where he stopped, breathing heavily and looking from wall to wall. For the first time he could ever recall, he had absolutely no idea what to do next. He tugged at the collar of his t-shirt as if it was suffocating him, clawed at his disheveled hair, and paced like a caged animal. Stood in the middle of the room and stared at the walls, glared at the satellite phone's display. Daylight was filling the villa, mocking the darkness in his soul.

He paced, he stood, he paced some more.

The Iridium vibrated in his hand and he froze, blinking at it as if he'd been stung.

He glanced at the display to see the incoming number, but it read *Caller ID blocked*. Pushing the OK button, he put the phone to his ear and panted, "Callie?"

He listened so intently he could feel every beat of his pulse against the phone. But for endless seconds all he could hear was the distinctive sound of a live connection, a hum filled with the static fluff of air charged with a transmitting signal.

"Callie?" he repeated, more emphatically, pressing the phone harder against his ear. "Callie, where are you? Talk to me!"

Now he heard a faint stirring and what sounded like a muffled whimper. Then a crackling. And then, one word.

"Jake…"

And once again, the connection was broken.

CALLIE'S HOARSE AND TERRIFIED little voice reached inside and pulled his guts up through his throat. But it was what finally succeeded in shifting his brain into gear and his body into action. He sailed savagely around the house, gathering clothing and other items, repacking his bags. Nearly an hour passed before his satellite phone transmitted another call. This time he had the ringer switched on, and the sudden chirring was shrill in a quiet as thick and malleable as candle wax.

"Callie," he rumbled into the phone, every nerve trilling.

But the voice he heard this time was not Callie's. It was snide and confident and noxious. The male caller taunted, *"Venga por su muñequita,"* and spit, *"hijo de puta."*

Come and get her, motherfucker.

Jake was still glaring at the sat phone when his BlackBerry buzzed on his hip. He plucked it from the holder, held it to his ear, and barked, "Tyler."

He heard an astonished intake of air at the other end, followed by, "Whoa, what the hell did I interrupt?"

Recognizing Eddie Falcone, Jake exhaled and said, "Sorry. Not a good time. I can't talk to you right now."

"Sure, okay," Falcone said. "I just wanted to call and let you know—"

"Wait," Jake snapped, a sudden thought splitting the middle of his head like the bullet that had split Ayala's. With an impact every bit as deadly.

On the other end of the call, Falcone waited as Jake's thought pinged for lucidity. He said, "Right before you and Curran got off the boat, did you see the Valentíns?"

"Well, yeah. Just as I was making my getaway I nearly ran smack into Angel. Remember? That's when I saw the boat captain's son and—"

"Did you ever see *Adonís* back on board after they picked the guy up?"

"Yeah, I'm sure he was there. I mean, I guess he was...I never thought about it."

"Well think about it now. Think hard, Eddie. It's important."

There was a long silence and then, in a voice drained of all inflection, Falcone said, "No, Jake. No, I didn't see him. Oh God, what's going on?"

But Jake had ended the call.

The volcanic rage building inside erupted. As did something even more dangerous. His fear.

Adonís Valentín was alive and he had Callie.

37

JAKE BOOKED THE EARLIEST flight he felt he could make from the nearest airport, tossed his bags in the Toyota 4x4, secured the house, and headed up the Costanera Sur. He slowed as he approached the turnoff to town, briefly considered stopping by the police station to let them know his plans, then decided he'd be better off informing them once he was out of their jurisdiction; he wasn't about to take a chance on being detained. He drove on, crossing the bridge over the Barú River, and pulled into the nature reserve on the other side.

Hacienda Barú is 815 acres of pristine and protected Pacific coast wetland and highland ridge rainforest. Jake frequently included it in SpecOps tour packages and knew the owner and staff quite well. As he got out of the pickup, a wave of despair rolled over him so intense it took his breath away. The last time he'd been here was with Falcone and Niles, but just before that he had brought Callie. On a perfect summer day with a sky as blue and sunny as the Pacific could ever create, he had watched a myriad of enchanted expressions play over her pretty face as they strolled through the beautiful orchid and butterfly gardens. Entering the Hacienda's office, a familiar voice pulled him back to present.

In response, Jake said, *"Hola, buena mañana, Señoritas."* The two receptionists, Shirley and Stephanie, smiled coquettishly and jockeyed around each other to see who would get to assist him. Before either could take the initiative, a bearded man appeared at the teakwood counter and extended his hand.

Greeting the owner, Jake said, "Hey, Jack. I appreciate you helping me out."

"Anytime." He reached for the sheet of paper Jake was handing him and passed it off to Shirley who was hovering at his elbow. She slipped the sheet into a fax machine behind the counter and waited for the transmission to go through.

"Can I get you some coffee, Jake?" Shirley asked hopefully.

"Thank you, no time. Got to get to the airport. That's why I had to stop so I could get a credit card authorization faxed over to Lynch Travel."

"There you go," Stephanie said, handing the transmittal confirmation to him.

Nodding to all three, Jake said, "Thanks again."

Briefly catching his eye, Jack said, "Hope everything is all right."

Jake left the office and returned to the 4x4. Back on the coastal road, he started calling Alberto Hernandez and Raúl Aguilar.

Hernandez told Jake he would notify the US Embassy and DOS and work his intel sources. Aguilar's response was characteristically more assertive; he assured Jake that his troops would be mobilized in key locations doing reconnaissance by nightfall. Speeding north along forty-five kilometers of road that felt as if it had been jackhammered and left in avalanche-size pieces, Jake was working the directory of stored numbers in the Iridium when his cell phone rang.

"Tyler," Jake answered gruffly.

It was Eddie Falcone. "Jake? Jesus freaking Christ, what's going on?"

Pushing speeds ranging between seventy-five and eighty-five, which sent the Toyota pickup catapulting over every bump, Jake checked his watch. His flight was scheduled to depart a little before eleven o'clock and it was already after nine. The drive usually took an hour or more—usually, at moderate speeds. He was flying.

"Sorry for being abrupt when you called, Eddie," Jake said, his voice elevated over the rush of air blowing through the open windows. "But I've got a situation. I'm going to be gone, not sure how long."

"Jake, what's going on?" Falcone asked again.

Jake did not respond, focusing instead on steering around the severed limb of a Guanacaste tree straddling the road. The pickup went airborne as it angled off the slope of a hill, then slammed jarringly back on its tires, bouncing Jake off the seat. He clung to the wheel, righted his course, and clenched the cell phone between his jaw and shoulder.

"Jake, please tell me what's going on. You think Valentín is alive? Has he done something?"

"Eddie, I'll call you when I can. I've got to go."

"Is he targeting you?"

Jake felt his throat close up.

"Is he?"

"Eddie," Jake said sternly, "I'll call you when I get back."

"Let Curran and me help. Please."

"No. You've helped. You have. But this is something I have to handle."

"Jake."

"No. Not this time. But thanks. Really. I'll call you when I get back."

He pushed END and concentrated on his driving.

THE AIRPORT IN QUEPOS, a small town trying for tourism but lurking in the shadow of its renowned neighbor Manuel Antonio, is little more than a Quonset hut with an airstrip. It serves a handful of small planes—Cessnas, Pipers, Navajos, Twin Otters—traveling in-country to places like Arenal, Liberia, Tamarindo, and San José.

Jake skidded off the dirt road and came to a rolling stop on pavement that started right at the airport. Grabbed his bags, locked the pickup, and sprinted through the cloud of dust he'd stirred. He went straight to the small line of passengers at the check-in desk, located in the corner of the terminal's restaurant. When he reached the clerk, he asked if they'd received his ticket. They had. Minutes later he was climbing aboard a Sansa Cessna Caravan. It took off on time at 10:50 AM, headed for San José.

Less than thirty minutes later he was standing in the immigration line at Juan Santamaria International. Noting a police officer standing beside the airport employee conducting check-in, Jake felt a stab of anxiety. What if the OIJ had issued a travel restriction on him, blocking him from leaving the country? *God*, he pleaded silently, *they have to let me go.*

When he got to the desk and gave his name, he kept his eyes on the clerk, watching tensely as the young man tapped keys on his computer, consulted his screen, and studied Jake's passport and driver's license. He inhaled slowly, steadying his nerves. The clerk gestured to the police officer, who approached.

Jake's pulse skipped as the policeman peered over the clerk's shoulder, flipping through the pages of Jake's passport. The stamps read like a dossier of DOS travel warnings, which had apparently aroused their interest. Hopefully not their suspicion. They were both eying Jake with avid curiosity.

The police officer commented, "You do a lot of traveling, *Señor*."

Jake shrugged and tried to manifest bored indifference. "Military," he replied. "US army."

The airport employee and police officer exchanged enlightened glances, smiled, and nodded. "That would explain it," the young man at the desk remarked. Adding a stamp for San José, he handed the dog-eared passport back to Jake along with his ticket and boarding pass. "Have a good flight, *Señor* Tyler."

FOUR AND A HALF hours later, Jake was seated across from Alberto Hernandez in his NAS office at the US Embassy in Bogotá. He'd had a huge stroke of luck with his flight out of Juan Santamaria International. Originally booked on a Copa Airlines flight that connected in Panama and would have arrived at 9 PM that evening, Jake had made his way onto a delayed Lacsa flight. Scheduled to depart before his 11:20 arrival time in San José, the non-stop was pushed back to 11:55 AM. Racing to the gate, he made it with only minutes to spare, but it shaved six hours off his travel time.

Hernandez had pulled his chair around to the side of a desk stacked with reports, briefings, proposals, and other documents. Behind him, tactical maps were pinned on a corkboard. Facing Jake, his expression gaunt, he said, "I am afraid I have some very distressing news." He stroked his mustache and amended, "a little bit of good news, but more bad news."

"What's the bad news?" Jake asked bluntly.

"Well, let me give you the good first. I was just on the phone with Raúl before you arrived. He has confirmed that Adonís Valentín is indeed alive and has been seen in Bogotá, and points much farther south, as recently as yesterday."

Jake said nothing but felt a resounding thump in his chest.

Hernandez cleared his throat and steeled himself for the next. "The bad news," he said carefully, "is with our previous intel and the new reports from Raúl, we know where most of his major encampments are."

Jake's forehead furrowed in confusion. "I don't understand. That sounds like pretty good news to me."

Hernandez continued, "Since counternarcotics has been working this intel for some time, they are ready to move on it."

"Move on it," Jake repeated blandly, still uncomprehending.

"Counternarcotics has a massive interdiction operation launching the first of next week."

Jake stared at Hernandez as if he'd just revealed a nuclear code. For a long time he was speechless, and then he said, "Oh, fuck no. Alberto, you can't be serious."

"I am afraid I am," Hernandez said quietly.

"Do they know about Callie?"

"Yes, I informed my superiors as soon as you told me."

"Then don't they realize that she is most likely being held in the very territory they will be targeting?" Jake asked incredulously.

Hernandez nodded somberly. "They do."

"Wouldn't they be treating this like a K&R?"

"But it is not. You and I both know this is a personal score. As such it is highly unlikely that Valentín will set a ransom. He certainly does not need money with the cache that he is sitting on," Hernandez remarked.

"Goddamn," Jake muttered. "Son of a fucking bitch." He began to pace the cramped office. "I've got to talk to them, Alberto. They can't do this now!"

"Jake, I spoke with them at great length," Hernandez assured him. "Since we have no information to confirm or even suggest that she is being held in any of the encampments, they will not consider stopping it."

"What about a delay then?" Jake asked. "Surely they could hold off until we have a chance to at least get more intel."

Dismally shaking his head, Hernandez said, "Mac says they are moving on schedule."

Jake swung around. "Where's McCauley's office? I want to talk to him myself. Who else do I need to talk to?"

"You can talk to them all you want, but you will just be wasting precious time. When money and politics are involved, they will not yield. I have been fighting a losing battle with this ever since they all got the intel. Personally, I think they are moving prematurely, and I told them so. Nothing I have said has made any difference. They are moving forward with it."

Jake looked at Hernandez, said nothing.

Hernandez finally stood and put his hand on Jake's shoulder. "Come on, I will take you to his office."

The Bogotá Narcotic Affairs Section is the largest and most complex NAS agency in the Department of State, controlling a budget of nearly 500 million dollars. As Hernandez steered Jake down the corridor, they passed a myriad of offices staffed with various managers, advisors, contract personnel, and administrative staff, finally arriving at a much larger suite toward the end of another hall. An attractive secretary looked up from her computer keyboard, smiling fondly at the sight of Hernandez. When her eyes flicked to Jake, the smile drooped to a flirtatious semi-pout.

"*Buenas tardes*, Lucia," Hernandez greeted. "Is he in?"

"Yes. I think he is available." She buzzed her boss on the phone, spoke briefly, then rose from her desk to escort them to McCauley's inner office. "Gentlemen," she said, brushing Jake as she opened the door. He forced a smile and she returned to her desk with a flush in her olive-skinned cheeks.

McCauley stood in perfunctory greeting, his tall frame precisely chiseled in a charcoal Hugo Boss pinstriped suit. The dour look on his face affirmed that he knew what this meeting was about and had probably been expecting it. He glanced pointedly at Hernandez, then directed his attention to Jake, waiting. His right hand absently fingered a glass paperweight etched with the embassy seal.

Jake said, "I understand you have a major interdiction planned next week."

"Monday, yes," McCauley replied crisply.

"I'm here to ask that you postpone it."

McCauley leaned back in his chair, folding his arms, again casting Hernandez a quick look. Jake couldn't tell if the looks were meant to be inquisitory or admonitory, but he suspected McCauley would have further discussion with Hernandez about this meeting and it would not be pleasant. With what sounded like carefully coiffed regret, McCauley said, "Jake, Alberto informed me of the woman who has been allegedly taken by the cartel. I'm very sorry to hear about it, but we can't put our plans on hold based on the possibility of—"

"This is not an *allegedly* or *possibly* anything," Jake interrupted, making an effort to keep his tone calm and rational. "It's happened. You have got to give me some time."

"I'm sorry, Jake. To cease our operations based on an abduction would be akin to conceding to terrorists—which is what they are—and you know our policy on that. I hate to sound callous, but at any given time there are many others being held out there. Knowing that they may be harmed or killed by our operations is an unfortunate risk, as is any collateral damage to innocent civilians."

"I'm not asking that you cease operations, just hold off for a few days."

"Listen, Jake. You know we are concerned with the prospect of putting a civilian life at risk. As a military operative you know that we cannot simply stop or even postpone a meticulously planned operation on the basis of a suspicion, not with all the police and government and military personnel in place." McCauley paused, interlocked his fingers. "We take the big scores when and where we can get them. The happenstance"—he cast Jake a perspicacious look—"*hits* on the Valentín cartel will no doubt be viewed as prodigious. But even with that and what we've accomplished most recently, our operations are constantly being criticized. This could be a huge score. Everything is in place and expectancy is high. We have to pull this off. Failure is not an option."

He let that hang for a moment, then changed his tone as if someone else had been speaking. "Now if you can bring me substantial proof, or if you receive a ransom demand or—"

"If this was your woman," Jake said, leaning on the edge of McCauley's meticulously arranged desk, his eyes boring into those of the NAS director, "your wife, your lover…your daughter…would a *big score* matter? Would you be able to stop it?"

McCauley fidgeted with the paperweight, licked his lips, did not reply. Jake glared, pivoted, and exited.

Hernandez lagged behind, and in a few minutes rejoined Jake in front of his own office. He was accompanied by a pair of uniformed men, Major Jorge Saldaña of the Colombian counternarcotics police and General Stefano Silva Paez, the CNP Chief.

Addressing Jake, Major Saldaña said, "Without your information we could not be executing an operation of this scope. I do understand your concern." He handed Jake a business card with some handwriting on the back. "I give you my private contact numbers—radio, cell phone, pager—and if you find the civilian, call me. I will personally see to it the operation is ceased immediately."

Jake said nothing, but he stuffed the card in his pocket. Hernandez exchanged a few words with Saldaña and Paez as they parted, then turned back to Jake. "I am sorry," he said morosely. "That is the best I could do."

"I know," Jake said dryly. "Thanks." But the Colombians' offer provided no appeasement; he knew they were lying.

THAT EVENING, JAKE AND Hernandez sat at the kitchen table in Hernandez's house, a large Jenno's pizza box between them, weighing various options. About an hour into the session, there was a robust knock on the front door. Hernandez opened it with caution, grinning when he saw the two men standing on his stoop. Embracing them, he spread his arm and stepped back. "Come in, gentlemen, come in," he invited, his voice exuding warmth.

Jake looked up from his untouched slice of pizza and managed a wan smile. "My brothers," he said, with a noticeable inflection of relief in his tired voice, and stood to embrace Quincy Tangeman and Steve Petropoulos. Earlier, he'd put out another call to his network, but this time he was unequivocal about the sense of urgency. And this time there was no shortage of volunteers, but after prudent consideration Jake decided two operators would be sufficient.

Tangeman and Petropoulos set down their bags, Hernandez opened his liquor cabinet, and talk began to flow. They polished off the pizza, had a few drinks, and turned in early. Three of the four slept.

IT HAD BEEN DECIDED that the first recon op would be a drive to the Valentíns' Suesca estate, Casa Solitaria. Jake seriously doubted he would find it occupied now that Valentín knew he had been set up there, but he could not afford to leave any stone unturned.

Piled into Hernandez's navy Bronco, Jake, Tangeman, and Petropoulos set off for Suesca after coffee and a light breakfast the next morning. Conversation was spare as they made the hour-long drive. Jake continually scanned the road and surrounding areas for signs of guerrilla activity, but he was still struggling to keep his overall focus unencumbered. Emotion was something he rarely, if ever, had trouble shutting out when he was operating; now, it streamed inside him like a blood-infusion.

Observing him as they drew closer to their destination, Petropoulos queried, "You okay, bro?"

Stonily, Jake said, "Sure."

A few minutes later, as Jake maneuvered the Bronco into a brush-covered area within fifty feet of the estate's front gate, he said, "We're here. Let's see if anyone else is."

As they patrolled the perimeter of the stonewalled estate, it appeared to be unoccupied and unguarded. Jake led them around to the tree he'd first used to vault onto the grounds. This time he had brought some of his basic climbing gear: ropes, throw weights, carabiners, gloves. Jake knotted and hooked the ropes, then tossed the throw weight into the leafy treetop. He went first and cleared the wall with ease, landing on the grounds practically flat-footed. Tangeman and Petropoulos followed suit without incident.

They continued across the lawn to the house, passing under the arches at the entrance and stepping into the courtyard where not so long ago Falcone and Niles, as Tony Messina and Bart Fletcher, had negotiated their way into the Valentíns' organization. Knowing now that the sting had ultimately targeted Callie, Jake felt his chest inflate with grief. *Stay in the here and now*, he admonished himself.

Jake was deliberating over the various methods of breaking and entering when Tangeman surprised him by discovering an unlocked back door. "Well, look here," he was saying, about to step inside when Jake grabbed his arm and pulled him aside.

"Hold on there, my man," Jake warned, and drew his Glock. Motioning for Tangeman and Petropoulos to follow behind him, he kept his finger over the trigger guard and slowly advanced into the house, making angular sweeps.

All was as quiet and still as a closed museum, the impeccably clean interior having the same sterile feel to it. Seeing one of the wall-mounted alarm boxes, Jake determined that it was deactivated. He found that odd, but considering the fastidious order of the house—every surface dust- and lint-free, every wood grain polished to a lemon-scented sheen, every rug grooved with overlapping vacuum swaths, glass shining and streak-free—he concluded it was a glaring oversight on the part of the maid service. Even so, instinctive wariness warned of the possibility of a setup. He went from room to room, finding the same spotless conditions in each. When they reached the master bedroom suite, Jake experienced the disquieting sense of another presence, and immediately felt his guard go on alert. He signaled for Tangeman and Petropoulos to be still, and crept soundlessly around the room. When he was confident no one was overtly present, he began a methodic search of closets. Finally convinced they were alone, he studied the interior more closely. The premonitory feelings, he decided, most likely stemmed from the emotion-charged memories of the night he had watched Delaney and Elena through the window. Watched the sex and the deception, the beginning of Delaney's demise and an incendiary element in Elena's. Now, seeing the big ornamental wrought iron bed in its earth-toned décor, set amidst the mirrors and salmon-colored walls, the Spanish artwork and candle clusters, he felt a sudden rush of sorrow. In the light of day, long afternoon shadows roaming the powdery walls, it took on a wholly different dimension. But the nocturnal images and the musky scent of the sex were indelibly embedded in his brain. Gone was the anger, permanently replaced with the forever absence and the abiding sadness.

"Jake?" Petropoulos, stirring quietly beside him.

"Just want to take another look around and then we're out of here."

"Okay." Petropoulos lingered at his side a moment longer, then backed off, leaving Jake alone in the room.

After a few minutes Jake thought he had seen enough, and brushed past a series of mirrored panels on his way out. But something caught the corner of his eye, causing him to turn back around. A dime-sized smudge at the edge of one of the mirrors, something the cleaning crew missed, something smeared, something red, something like…

Blood.

His heartbeat quickened as he gave the room another, more meticulous search. This time, he found a few more specks and smudges of blood, mostly on dark surfaces, like wood, and more of it on the black wrought iron bed frame. He yanked the bedcovers back, examined the freshly laundered sheets, found nothing. And then, seeing what appeared to be another blood speck on the Aztec-patterned rug below the bed, he leaned down, and saw something that stopped his heart like a train slamming into a mountainside. The world shifted out of focus, sound blared and muted. The center of his gravity floated far away from him and then came spiraling down.

What he saw were tiny fragments of crushed seashells missed by the vacuum and, just under the bottom edge of the bed's dust ruffle, a small piece of opal—the heart-shaped opal from the necklace he had given Callie the night he'd first made love to her. The blood, he now knew, was hers. The presence he'd sensed was hers. Callie had been here, and Callie had bled here.

UPON LEAVING CASA SOLITARIA, Jake somberly revealed his findings to Tangeman and Petropoulos, and the three of them rode the first dozen or so miles back toward Bogotá in bleak silence.

Jake's dark thoughts skittered back and forth across the tenuous threshold bridging despair and delirium. He had touched the blood of that soft, sweet, benevolent spirit—blood on his fingertips as he'd tended her wounds the evening he had come to her aid in San José.

Oh God, why the blood?

On his hip, the Iridium chirped urgently. He snatched it up and put it to his ear, talking and listening as he drove. In the backseat behind him, Tangeman and Petropoulos leaned forward, trying to hear the conversation. All they could get from it were Jake's laconic replies, mostly the word *Okay*. Finally, they heard, *We'll see you there.*

"That was Raúl," Jake told them. "His men have been canvassing Valentíns' territory, and he's got a few possible locations. We're going to fly into Leguízamo and meet up with him tomorrow. A starting point."

As they completed the drive back, layers of day were peeling away the last light of dusk, casting an amber glow over the undulating hills that spread up to the nearby mountains and further out to the distant jungleland. There, somewhere, Jake knew Callie was still alive. And he would find her. He had to find her. Before counternarcotics launched Armageddon, Colombia-style.

38

IT HAD BEEN ANOTHER beautiful day.

Up until the terrifying moment the men had taken her.

She'd gone for her usual morning and evening walks on the beach, spent the rest of her day writing. The book was really progressing, due largely to the increasing level of comfort she felt in Dominical. When she had first come here, she wasn't at all sure what was going to happen—not with her life, certainly not with Jake. Then he had taken her out on the boat...and everything changed. Now, with some income from pre-production work for Falcone and Niles, she was beginning to feel that she could stay here, that she could belong here. It was such an idyllic place, one in which she felt secure and safe. She loved the villa, loved the little town nearby, loved the beach.

But she missed Jake. She missed Jake so much it hurt. She had never felt this way before and it scared her. Because the need was all-enveloping. But it was also the most rapturous feeling she had ever known. But missing him dug new depths of loneliness. She wondered when he would return.

That evening she had stayed a little longer on the beach, watching the sun set over the ocean. It was a sight she never grew tired of. The sun's fire intensifying as it lowered to the sea, growing redder as the sky and water darkened, finally sated and doused by the moon's first flame. It was a mating dance she could watch over and over again.

She had retreated to the house, climbed the stairs still feeling the sun's heat on her skin. Slipped out of her sheer white cotton dress and stepped into a lukewarm shower. Not cool, not hot, just cascading warm water and steam. Soaped herself with lather and shampoo that smelled like hyacinth. Rinsed and felt the foam slide down her body, swirl into the drain. Reached for the big thick towel, drew it around herself and snuggled into it. Thought about the big, comfortable bed with the ceiling fan above, swirling the cool night breeze misted with ocean salt. Thought about him.

She had stepped out of the shower, water dripping from her hair into her eyes, clutching the towel close, when rough hands grabbed her.

She saw the two men in a dark, confusing blur—big and muscular and menacing in black—felt something stick her in the neck, felt the sting of pain, quick and excruciating. And then felt nothing more.

Now, some indeterminable time later, as Callie came groggily awake in increments, all she knew for sure was that she was no longer in Jake's house, she was sick, and she was hurting. She was lying on a small, uncomfortable bed in a plain room with one window set too high to see through. A pale sliver of sun crept across a dusty stucco floor, the light failing to either warm or brighten. A pitcher of water and a glass sat on a wooden stand by the bed, below which was a frayed hemp mat. Overhead, a ceiling fan creaked as she huddled under a threadbare wool blanket, shivering. She felt nauseated and could not quite bring the room into focus. Her head throbbed dully and continuously. As she lay with her knees drawn up and arms tightly cradled to her chest, cold and shivering in the sheer white cotton dress that her abductors had apparently redressed her in, consciousness started to congeal and she did remember one thing.

Jake on the telephone.

But the setting had been different. A large house, elegantly furnished and artfully decorated. And an intimidating man, well-dressed and groomed, laden with overly sweet cologne and an abundance of gold jewelry, dark-haired, swarthy, with an accent. But it was the other man with him, younger and ponytailed, who was clearly in charge and even more frightening. It had been after a heated conversation between the two, conducted in Spanish, that the heavyset man with the cloying cologne had snatched Callie up from the couch she'd been slumped across and carried her into a large bedroom. He had slung her onto the bed, and what happened next was an indistinct blur. She remembered being hurt by the rough handling as she struggled to do what he was telling her, to stay awake, remembered a telephone being shoved against her ear—and remembered, vividly remembered, hearing Jake's commanding voice. For that briefest of instants, she was enveloped by a euphoric wave of relief, but before she could let it take her, the phone was jerked away. She recalled nothing more.

And now, as she lay on the hard bed in the bare, gloomy room, hurting and scared and thinking about Jake, she began to cry. At some point, the reeling blackness came again, and she fell gratefully into it.

SHE WAS VIOLENTLY SHAKEN from the darkness, forcefully drawn into the light. Her eyelids fluttered open, the room spun dizzyingly in and out of focus, and the throbbing in her head distorted coherent thought. But fear was automatic and severe, instantly jolting her heart and setting off violent tremors.

The ponytailed man was shaking her, gripping her roughly by the arms, muttering something in Spanish. When he saw that she was coming to, a lewd grin spread across his dark face. "Ah, good...you are awake, *muñequita*. We have a call to make, you and I."

Pulling her up on the bed, he continued to hold her with one arm while he pushed buttons on a cell phone clutched in his other hand. He waited for the connection, then pressed the phone against Callie's ear, hissing, "Speak to Jake."

But Callie could not manage words. Her chest was heaving and frightened sobs were choking back her voice. Nausea and dizziness rolled over each strained breath. Still holding her in a vice-grip, the man gave her a bone-crushing squeeze about the ribs, and she emitted a weak wail of pain. Tears were streaming from her eyes and she was gasping for air, so he put the phone up to his own ear and spoke into it.

"A little shy with the words, your *muñequita*," he said smoothly. "No matter. Pay very close attention." He placed the cell phone sideways on the wooden stand.

He released Callie and stood. As she crumpled back on the bed, the sobs and gasps becoming weaker and more shallow, he unhitched his belt and unzipped his jeans.

Watching him, her eyes went wide with terror and a faint whine gurgled from deep in her throat. Her eyes were riveted to his hands as they clamped the top of his jeans, and yanked them past his hips.

She could hear a horror-stricken voice inside her pleading, *No, no, no, no,* but her throat, her mouth, her tongue were paralyzed with fear.

He climbed onto the bed, and loomed over her.

The voice in her head called desperately to Jake, knowing he was a few feet away on the phone but probably very far away in reality. The man was over her—*Jake stop him please please please Jake oh no no no...no...*

Grasping her legs behind the knees, he shoved them up and apart, wedging himself in between, and gave her a violent thrust. She cried out as he cleaved into her, the pain searing and excruciating—burning, tearing, pulverizing—but her cries quickly died, overpowered by his heavy, guttural sounds as he pummeled harder and faster. The brutal force of his thrusting sent the bed's wooden headboard slamming into the wall, crumbling plaster as the weak springs below the wafer-thin mattress twanged and screeched. He finished with a long groan, picked up the cell phone, and purred into it, "Mmm...a very fine little *concha*. Welcome back to the jungle, Jake Tyler."

He punched the phone off and rose from the bed. Looking down at Callie, he saw that she had passed out. Plucking at strands of her long curly hair, he mused, "Too bad you could not stay awake to enjoy that, *muñequita*. Maybe next time." He paused, eying her speculatively. "But, not too long for you, *querida*...not too long now."

Hitching up his jeans, he noticed the blood on them, smirked, and left the room.

39

JAKE STOOD GRIPPING HIS cell phone for minutes after the connection went dead, breathing like his lungs had been deprived of air to the point of bursting. His dark eyes were boiling with the fire consuming him, his heart wild with anguish. Hernandez watched him with a mix of empathy and concern, said nothing. In all the years he'd known Jake, he had never seen him like this, and it was more than a little harrowing.

When Jake finally spoke, after a long, agonized silence, his voice was as flat and fathomless as a cave pool. He simply said, "I'll be back."

HE RETURNED TO HERNANDEZ'S house a few hours later, opened the front door, and dropped a small duffel bag on the floor. When he looked up, his blood pressure slammed into his temple like the snap of a thick rubber band. "Fuck, no," he muttered angrily, turning away and pressing a hand against his forehead. He took a centering breath and turned back to face the new occupants in the room. "What the hell are you doing here?"

"Well, that's a bloody enthusiastic welcome," quipped Niles.

Beside him, Falcone said, "Be pissed if you want, Jake, but we came to help." He nodded his head toward Hernandez. "And from what we've just heard, I think you can use it."

Jake fired a look at Hernandez that was a mixture of anger,

frustration, and disbelief.

"Jake, they are here," he said calmly, adding with a touch more poignancy, "and obviously care. We all do." Behind him, seated on the couch, Tangeman and Petropoulos nodded.

Eddie Falcone and Curran Niles stood looking like a pair of somber sentries dressed entirely in camo-green, duffels and rucksacks stacked in the chair behind them.

Jake ran a hand through his hair, stared at the floor, paced in a small but furious circle. Finally let out a noisy breath that was a cross between a sigh and a groan. "Shit." He leveled a grim look of resolution on each of them. Heaved a deeper sigh. "Okay, then, gents. Let's go."

IT WAS MID-AFTERNOON when Jake, Tangeman, Petropoulos, Falcone, and Niles stepped from the Cessna Caravan onto a desolate landing strip somewhere south and east of Puerto Leguízamo, near the Rio Putumayo. A small metal building that served as a fuel depot was the only structure in sight, and there were no vehicles or other aircraft, nor had there seemed to be any recent traffic.

Until a mud-splattered, bullet-pocked Land Rover rolled up in a haze of dust, Raúl Aguilar at the wheel. He greeted them all with merely a nod of his head, singling Jake out with a look of grave import.

They quickly loaded their gear into the vehicle—a boxy old Destroyer model—climbed inside, and Aguilar steered off to the south. As they sped down what was not so much a road as a trail widened by the passage of a previous vehicle, Aguilar shared the latest information.

"Valentín has been on the move, as recently as an hour ago," he said, his voice vibrating like an electric razor as the Land Rover bounced over the trail. "Unfortunately, he keeps moving. He has not remained for any length of time in one particular place. We have not been given any indication from villagers near the encampments that a *gringa* has been seen. If she is being held in one of the known encampments, they have been successful in keeping it a secret."

"Where was Valentín when he was on the move an hour ago?" Jake asked, having to raise his voice to be heard over the engine noise.

"We are headed that way now," Aguilar said. "My information

indicates that Valentín works these guerrilla camps. Angel worked the ones in the north, in Guaviare. Adonís worked the ones in the south, Putumayo and the Amazon."

"Which is where we were last working."

"Yes."

A heavy silence dropped like a dungeon door and no one talked for a while as the Destroyer fought its way over treacherous terrain being consumed by the encroaching reach of jungle. Thick, woody vines and overhanging branches thwacked against the sides of the vehicle, scraped and thudded across the top. The trail continued to narrow, the brush and trees thickened even more.

Tangeman spoke up from the rear. "Jake, don't take this the wrong way, but since you know the son of a bitch is luring you with her, how—"

"I don't know yet," Jake snapped before he could finish. Moment by moment he was struggling to keep his thoughts focused solely on objective—he knew he had to stay in that lock-down mode to be able to function at his highest level—but emotions kept rising and threatening to riot over the wall. Her voice, her cries, her pain, just would not leave him.

Get control, he warned himself sternly. *Now.*

The remainder of the long ride was passed in the unnerving silence broken only by brief exchanges between Jake and Aguilar over map coordinates. They stopped just as dusk was beginning to drain heat and color from the afternoon. It was still hot enough to melt the presidents off coins. Clambering out of the Land Rover, Falcone and Niles felt like they'd been slammed in the gut with a bowling ball and fought to catch their breath. Tangeman and Petropoulos wheezed slightly; Jake merely blew out some air.

Raúl Aguilar and a few of his men had set up a campsite within an area they'd cleared with machetes and axes, just enough to allow their egress but not so much as to show evidence of their temporary occupation. Beyond that, secondary forest built into heavy jungle that closed in to obliterate the sky. Aguilar took them to a makeshift communications center where antennas had been mounted in treetops with various radio apparatus set up below on a stand constructed from tree limbs. One of the logs served as a bench, and the man seated there moved aside to make room for Jake. Aguilar said, "I think we have a fix on Valentín's last location."

"His last?" Jake questioned. "Does this mean he's moved again?"

"No, I am not sure of that. This is the location we scouted about two hours ago." He looked intently at Jake, something significant brimming in his eyes. "Jake, this location is the camp where you were held before."

As he processed that piece of information, there was a subtle change in Jake's expression, just the slightest flicker in his dark eyes. Thinking back to the day when he had been forcibly taken to Castillo's camp to treat FARC wounded, his mind framed a flashback of the exchange he'd witnessed between the *commandante* and Delaney, an exchange his friend died denying. And something else flashed into his mind then—the image of the dead guerrilla in the Amazon jungle, the *sicario* who had spearheaded the ambush—and Jake remembered where he'd seen him before. He was one of the guerrillas who had dismissed him from Castillo's compound. *Estas de buenas, Gringo Doc.* Luck, Jake now knew, had nothing, nothing whatsoever, to do with it.

"So this Castillo is one of Valentín's narcoguerrillas?" Petropoulos asked.

"Yes," Aguilar replied. Consulting a map, he pointed out the FARC compound in relation to their present location. The two points were fairly close together, a matter of miles.

"Do you think Callie's there?" Niles asked hopefully, the heat drawing large apples of rouge on his cheeks.

"No," Aguilar replied, adding, "but we really do not have another place to start. We may get an indication that will take us further." He caught Jake's eye, asking softly, "When did you get the last call?"

Jake swallowed, felt his chest grow tight. "This morning." God, he thought, it seemed like *days* ago. And, for the first time, he wondered just how Valentín had gotten his phone numbers; both his cell and sat phones had elaborate state-of-the-art encryption. In a sickening flash of lucidity, he realized that the procurement, in one way or another, had probably been via Delaney.

"Did he set a ransom?" Falcone inquired.

"No," Jake said, his tongue thick. "He's not interested in ransom."

"So are we going there?" Niles asked.

Aguilar consulted Jake for an answer and, after a brief mental deliberation, Jake replied, "Yes. I want to try to raise Alberto on the radio, see if there are any new developments from his front." Addressing Falcone and Niles, he said, "Get some chow, drink lots of water, rest a bit. After you're through eating, we're going to give you a crash course on weapon handling and a few other things you'll need."

They reached into their packs, scowling suspiciously at the tan MRE meal bags.

Behind them, Tangeman said, "Bon appétit, boys."

AFTER FINISHING OFF THE contents of their ready-to-eat meals, which turned out to be pretty decent beef stew with assorted accoutrements, Falcone and Niles were outfitted and familiarized with gear. In addition to the standard jungle necessities, they were issued semi-automatic handguns and tactical headsets. While Tangeman and Petropoulos helped them become oriented with the sets' earbud, push-to-talk, and tiny boom mic, Jake joined Aguilar at the communications station. When they were finally able to make contact with Hernandez, it was confirmed that preliminary staging for the interdiction was already underway. Hernandez also gave Jake a rundown of the objectives and targets of the operation, as well as the points of infiltration and exfiltration. By the time they signed off with Hernandez, it was full dark and Aguilar's men had a robust fire going.

Rubbing his hands together, Jake said, "Okay, guys, listen up. We don't have much time and you need to get some rack, so—"

"Some what?" Falcone asked.

"That's sleep," Petropoulos chuckled, but catching a harsh look from Jake stifled any further levity.

"As I was saying," Jake said tightly, "we don't have much time and I need to be sure you know how to use what you've got." He took a few minutes to review what Tangeman and Petropoulos had gone over, then launched into basic weapon handling, recon, and camp protocol. He covered everything from working with semi-automatic handguns and submachine pistols, to the most effective placement of insect repellent (boot-tops, belts, and sleeve cuffs) and how to urinate (into holes or crevices as opposed to on rocks or leaves). He repeatedly and emphatically cautioned them against talking out loud as well as getting ahead or falling behind the pace. He spent a considerable amount of time spinning hypothetical scenarios, most of which he fervently hoped would never happen. Especially when he saw their glassy expressions of alarm, stark in the firelight.

After giving each of them individual time to ask questions and voice concerns, Jake checked the dressings on Niles' head and arm. He was pleased to see that the stitched lacerations appeared to be healing nicely. Applying some more antibiotic cream and fresh bandaging, he ordered the two of them to sleep. With Aguilar's men on guard duty, they strung hammocks, mosquito nets, and tarps, and tried to comply. It was, by and large, a futile effort.

LONG BEFORE DAYBREAK, A pair of Zodiac RIBs were unpacked and expertly assembled by Tangeman and Petropoulos. It took them less than thirty minutes to inflate and piece together transoms, floorboards, accessories, and outboard motors. Guided by the navigation of Garmin and the lowered beams of Surefire, they sluiced stealthily and swiftly down a tributary of the Putumayo, killing the 150-hp twin engines just before the arrival of dawn and destination. The rising sun pushed river and jungle into coarse definition, its suffocating heat vaporizing and closing in around them like a fishing net. The Zodiacs were banked and concealed in launch points that were first cut out and then recovered with brush.

It took them about an hour to hike within telephoto range of the FARC compound and, for the next few hours, surveillance was conducted with high-powered rangefinders and binoculars. They spotted Castillo several times during their circuitous path around the perimeter, but saw nothing out of the ordinary. Security did not seem particularly high. Guerrilla soldiers armed with automatic rifles roved the grounds in a lackadaisical manner, chattering and laughing, smoking and chugging Cokes. Some tossed back whiskey chasers from a bottle they passed around. As time lapsed and morning matured to late afternoon, Jake's gut told him Callie was not here. But, he surmised, she might have been at one time, and he needed to know if this was the case. With that in mind, he decided the next move would be divining information from locals.

To Aguilar, Jake said, "Let's send a couple of your guys out by the river. We'll cover them, of course, but I think they can go and come back without much attention. The atmosphere seems to be pretty relaxed. There's some *campesinos* gathered, and if she's been here I'm willing to bet they'll know."

Nodding, Aguilar said, "Pretty blond *gringa*...yes, they will know. Whether they say is another thing."

Surveilling the riverbank where the small group of villagers was getting in and out of dugout canoes and small boats, Jake noticed a handful of children playing. "Tell your men to talk to the kids. If they're not too shy, they'll tell." Reaching into a pocket of his rucksack, he pulled out a fistful of wrapped candy. Handing an assortment of Tootsie Rolls, Bazooka Bubblegum, and Jolly Ranchers to Aguilar, he said, "This ought to do the trick."

Jake's assumption panned out. The pair of men Aguilar sent returned with a thumbs-up. The spokesman for the pair said, "The children smile big for *los dulces*. They say, '*Oye mamacita*'."

"But is she still here?" Jake asked desperately, already knowing the answer.

They both shook their heads, smiles disappearing. "No. They just say she go with *el hombre*."

"Valentín?" Jake asked, feeling the air go out of his lungs and a knot form in his throat.

The two men shrugged.

"And they don't know where?"

"*Lo siento*, no."

Voice heavy, Jake said, "Okay, gents, let's head back. I guess we'll have to call it a day."

JAKE LAY AWAKE, LISTENING to the jungle's nocturnal sonata, the collective chirr of insects, nasal grunts and croaks of frogs, and the wide diversity of bird sounds. But as the night wore on it grew quiet and still under the damp cloak that fell heavily over the trees like a wide black wing. On either side of him, he was aware of Falcone and Niles' fitful fight with slumber; Falcone tossed and moaned while Niles gritted his teeth and shivered. To Jake, the cool night air was invigorating after the relentless heat and humidity of the day, and he allowed it to ease his body's tension as he probed his mind for answers, his soul its entreaty for spiritual guidance. As the pale fingers of morning mist reached down through the gaps in the tree canopy, he thought he might have something.

Aguilar's men were already up and stirring, drinking coffee they had brewed over the fire. Jake poured two cups from the pot and jabbed Falcone and Niles, drawing groans of protest and cranky mumbles. "Wake up, guys," he said firmly, and handed the coffee to them.

They drank it slowly, wincing at the bitterness, begrudgingly coming awake. Both drained and disheveled, their eyes were sunken in puffy pockets of skin.

Jake, by contrast, on practically no sleep, was alert and focused. He had consumed only a small amount of coffee, but he was as wired as if riding the caffeine buzz of a dozen cups. When Aguilar, Tangeman, and Petropoulos joined them, he shared the revelation he'd had in the wee hours. Spreading one of the maps on the ground between them, he squatted down and pointed to an asterisk he'd penciled in about forty miles south of their location. "This," he stated decisively, "is where I believe we'll find Valentín and Callie."

Puffing on one of his Cohiba Robusto cigars, Aguilar scratched his head and asked, "How did you come to this conclusion, *mi amigo?*"

"Well, I was thinking back on our ops down here and how jumpy Haskell was during the last phase. I realized later, of course, that he was jumpy because he knew we were treading just a little too close to some of Valentín's territory. I have also come to realize that Haskell was killed, at least in part, because he knew too much about their operations to be allowed to get out. The contents of a safety deposit box at our bank in the Bahamas contained two things, a letter and a USB drive. In the letter he said that he wanted to get out of it, but he seemed to know he wouldn't succeed."

He paused, his voice dropping off. In the distance, a bird's forlorn cry echoed across the treetops. A monkey screeched irritably in reply.

Continuing, he said, "The drive had a file with a spreadsheet containing a series of numbers that, at the time, made no sense to me. Since it apparently meant something to Haskell, enough for him to put it in the safety deposit box, I eventually printed the spreadsheet and kept it with me."

He reached into the pocket of his woodland-camo pants and pulled out a folded piece of paper. Opening it up to show them, he said, "Last night, I was looking at it again and it occurred to me what's here. The numbers are map coordinates." He placed the spreadsheet next to the map and pointed. "See, here are the coordinates for Castillo's encampment. These other numbers are probably more narcoguerrilla strongholds—they're all located within what we know to be Valentín's territory." Now he indicated a set of numbers marked with an asterisk and moved his finger over to a spot on the map. "I believe this is Valentín's main command center, maybe even his primary residence."

He looked up to gauge their reactions and was met with stunned silence.

Finally, Aguilar said, "I must admit, Jake, that your theory is entirely plausible. Unfortunately, I have absolutely no information to verify it, and surely you must know that we are running out of time. If we go with this and then find out we were wrong, it will probably be too late."

Gravely, Jake said, "I realize that. It's just a gut feeling, but I always trust my instincts."

"That's good enough for me," Tangeman said without hesitation.

"Me, too," Petropoulos chimed in.

Falcone and Niles nodded their support.

"Okay, *jefe*," Aguilar said soberly. "This is where we will go then. *Con Dios.*" He turned and began issuing directives to his men, and in a matter of minutes the camp was being disassembled and packed up.

While his guys were collecting their gear, Jake made radio contact with Hernandez for a situation report. When he relayed their new itinerary, Hernandez was not encouraging. The interdiction, named Operation Dark Sun, was proceeding on schedule, with the heaviest and most aggressive bombardment set to begin sometime in the next few days. The location Jake had disclosed was within counternarcotics' targeted area.

"Jake, I pray that your instincts are right—they usually are—and I urge you to get in and get out as quickly as possible. Keep me apprised of your position and status at all times and I will certainly do what I can to keep these guys from going in there until you are safely out." He paused, and Jake could feel his despair. Hernandez went on, saying, "But you know I cannot make any promises."

"Yes, Alberto, I know."

THEY SPENT THE FIRST part of the day motoring farther downriver by way of several narrow tributaries. Around noon they nosed the Zodiacs into a channel that took them directly to the Putumayo in a big, noisy rush of current. Running some one thousand miles from the Colombian Andes, the big river snakes past the borders of Ecuador and Peru before plunging south to the Amazon. They continued on into Amazonas, eventually slipping down another branch of the river before pulling off into a small cove cobwebbed with overhanging trees. Once again, the Zodiacs were meticulously tucked into excavated pockets of brush near the bank.

As they hauled gear into the forest, Jake said, "We're still a few klicks from the spot, but we have to take it on foot from this point on. Going by river would be quicker and much more direct as this stretch runs past our target, but this is the only way to go in without being noticed. We'll be going through the nastiest bit of jungle imaginable, but because of that we shouldn't run into any guerrillas—at least not until we get a lot closer. We'll set up camp here first."

Feeling his heart jittering nervously, Falcone asked, "But what's the plan?"

"We won't really know until we get there and do some recon," Jake replied truthfully. "Simply put, we'll have to assess the location, get a general idea of the number of men, their arms and ammunition, communications capabilities, and most of all determine if Valentín is holding Callie there."

"What if we can't find out if she's there?" Niles asked worriedly.

"We'll find a way," Jake said firmly.

The next hour was spent setting up camp about thirty meters from the river's edge. Gear and supplies were organized, as were arms and ammunition. Radio frequencies were tested, rucksacks checked. And then it was time to go.

Aguilar's men were organized into one team, spaced twenty-five meters apart from Jake's. Designated point and trail men were armed with M16A2 rifles and 40mm grenade-launchers while the rest carried Gilils, Garands, MAC-10s, Uzis, and one or two higher-tech MP5 sniper rifles. While Aguilar's men maintained about ten meters between each other, Jake let Falcone and Niles creep closer behind him, peering over his shoulder periodically to make sure they were all right. Despite having Tangeman and Petropoulos covering Falcone and Niles from the rear, Jake could see by the shine in their eyes that they were scared.

FORTY MINUTES LATER THEY were standing where the asterisk had marked the spot.

Or was supposed to.

But there was no guerrilla encampment here, only the abiding immensity of jungle. Overhead, very infrequently pocking the deep green canopy of trees, bright holes of stark blue were a glaring reminder that the day's light was peaking and would soon be diminishing. For a stiflingly still moment, the forest's cadence swelled numbingly around them just as the thick-veined leaves crowded in, beaded with ants and jungle sweat and bouncing as a springboard for insect-seeking birds. Organically disembodied sights and sounds, all larger and louder than tangible thought.

Jake's face remained set, expressionless, but for the first time a sliver of anxiety manifest itself in the form of a very slight quiver in his bottom lip. "Goddammit!" he swore, comparing his handheld GPS with the readings from a compass. "It's supposed to be here! Where the hell is it?" He shot another azimuth with the compass and reset the GPS, but his findings were the same as before.

"Let us just go a little farther, closer to the river," Aguilar suggested patiently. "Who knows? The coordinates might have been off."

"Yeah," Jake replied grimly, "maybe so. They also could have been here and moved."

As they continued along the river route, Jake made another radio contact with Hernandez, who confirmed that Operation Dark Sun was underway, with ground troops and counternarcotics operatives beginning to move into position. Jake talked until the signal faded and then signed off. He knew the probability of running into the counternarcotics forces out here was high, and he didn't even want to think about what would happen if they found Valentín's encampment before he did.

He *had* to find Valentín first, and soon.

The guerrilla camp was so well-hidden by jungle that Aguilar's men very nearly missed it or, if they'd been moving in the adjacent direction, would have quite literally stumbled on top of it. A path almost obscured by brush led from a termite-bored river dock into the jungle. But just beyond the edge of forest, below a vastly unbroken tree canopy, the undergrowth gradually thinned to reveal thatched huts and shacks. Armed men were present and roving about, but unlike Castillo's men, these guerrilla soldiers appeared to take their sentry duty seriously. Jake knew the surveillance was going to be as dangerous as it was vital to a successful infiltration. Before they could even try to find out if Callie was being held here, they had to know what they were up against. He also knew they were running out of time, but the intelligence had to be acquired and processed first. So after a quick strategy session, they grouped off and slowly encircled the guerrilla camp for recon.

Jake, paired with Falcone and Niles, had pretty fair vantage points, and while they did gather some useful information—a rough estimate of the number of guerrillas present, possible stockpiles of ammunition, and the location of the radio hutch—they saw no conclusive evidence of Valentín's presence. After over an hour of observation, steeped in withering heat and plagued by unrelenting mosquito sorties, they made their way back to the rendezvous point near the river.

Halfway there, a pair of guerrillas crossed in front of them, slogging through brush not more than ten meters away.

Putting his finger to his lips, Jake gestured fiercely to Falcone and Niles, pointing to the MAC-10s they had been absently carrying up until now. Then he pointed to his eyes and patted his chest with his hand, whispering, "Cover me," into the throat mic of his headset.

In that hot-flash second, Falcone looked shakily at Niles, whose face had gone cheesy pale, but before doubt could cloud his judgment, before thoughts of his inadequacies had a chance to rally, the heat of the moment harnessed his resolve. Gripping the submachine pistol, Falcone took his stance. As Jake had shown them only yesterday, Niles did the same, slightly parting his legs, planting his feet, extending his arms. Sweat poured from their faces, soaked through their clothing. Once again, the jungle cadence vibrated deafeningly in their ears, and their pulses pounded with the primal rhythm.

Jake advanced slowly, treading soundlessly behind the two narco-guerrillas. They were conversing in Spanish, momentarily oblivious to his presence. The vocalise and movements of birds and other small animals created a jungle surround-sound that Jake had learned to plug into. The caws, warbling, and chattering played an eclectic scale against the backdrop of rustling leaves, crackling and snapping branches and, with the right balance and timing, provided a perfect filter for his footfalls. Crouched behind the guerrillas, Jake waited patiently for the right moment and then sprang, swinging both arms wide to encircle their necks in a suffocating lock.

Falcone and Niles rushed forward, guns aimed and ready to fire, but they could already see that was not going to be necessary. The pressure and position of Jake's grip around each of the guerrilla's necks—*murasame*, the pressure points on each side of the neck behind the collarbone—had rendered them motionless, let alone defenseless. The automatic weapons they carried slipped from their grasp and dropped to the ground. While Niles kept his gun unsteadily trained on them, Falcone scurried over to collect the weapons. He got an approving nod from Jake and went back to stand beside Niles.

Slowly releasing the two guerrillas, who immediately began gasping and coughing, Jake addressed them in Spanish, his voice so harsh Falcone and Niles flinched. First, he confiscated the guerrillas' handheld radios and stripped them of artillery bandoleers worn across their chests, tossing them over to Falcone. Then he ordered them to kneel on the ground in a crossed-leg position with their hands behind them, which he quickly secured with plastic tie restraints.

"Donde está Adonís Valentín? Está por aca?" he asked, prompting them to exchange a wary look. They were both young, clad in military olive

with bandanas tied loosely around their necks. When neither appeared to be ready to volunteer any information, Jake reached down to the guerrilla on his left and pressed his thumb into the pressure point behind his ear. He generated just enough pain to be effective without causing loss of consciousness or death. The move brought quick results; although the first guerrilla had to spend some time regaining mental clarity, the second became outwardly more cooperative.

"*Sí, Señor,*" the second guerrilla replied quickly, but then shrugged noncommittally.

Still speaking Spanish, Jake asked, "Is he on the premises or not?"

The two guerrillas now seemed genuinely uncertain, consulting each other and then shrugging again. But when they looked back at Jake, found his penetrating eyes boring into their faces, they both nodded eagerly. The first guerrilla cringed and leaned away from Jake. The color in his face was just beginning to return.

"*La gringa está aca?*" Jake demanded, watching for the slightest telltale betrayal in their expressions.

But it was obvious they knew where the interrogation was going now and looked straight ahead, avoiding each other's eyes. Even so, Jake thought he detected a sneering twitch from the second guerrilla, and that was enough. Taking a few steps back and lowering his voice, he summoned Tangeman and Petropoulos on the radio. The other half of his team appeared in a matter of minutes, taking the two guerrillas into custody.

Striding over to Falcone and Niles, Jake gave them a slim smile. "Good job, gents," he praised, eliciting relieved looks from both. When Aguilar joined them, Jake said, "She's around here, somewhere. I feel it. So is Valentín. He may not be in the camp presently, but I think he's definitely in the area. That's what I read off those guys. So we've got to get in there. It's the only shot we have."

"Okay," Falcone said, wiping furiously at his eyes as he fought a losing battle with the sweat rolling into them, "so how are we going to get in?"

"Well," Jake said slowly, "we could sneak in, but the risk of capture would be great, and we can't afford that. We could force our way in, but that risks casualty and loss of life. The best way is to look for an opportunity, and we don't have time for that. So we'll create one."

Falcone and Niles swapped curious looks and even Aguilar's eyebrows hitched up quizzically.

Jake dug into his pack and took out a stack of paper currency. Colombian pesos in $50,000 denominations. "I think this will work nicely," he said.

"Bloody Christ!" Niles exclaimed. "You've been carrying that around?"

"How much *is* that?" Falcone asked incredulously, quickly adding, "I thought you said Valentín wasn't interested in ransom."

"He's not," Jake replied evenly.

A shrewd grin spread over Aguilar's face. "No," he concurred, enlightenment filling in his eyes. "But his narcos will be."

At that moment, the jungle shuddered around them as rain drummed over the top of the canopy.

40

THE REST OF THE day had come and gone in a haze of pain and paralyzed panic, suspended in a cocoon of fear so tight the room floated around her in white-hot blotches. Except for a couple of painful trips to the tiny bathroom, Callie barely moved from her huddled position on the bed, knees drawn up, arms crossed over her aching abdomen, head tucked to her chest, back turned from the door. She was only dimly aware of light seeping in through the lone window and then draining with the wane of day. There were intervals of clarity that ripped her open, causing her to gasp and heave in a reprisal of torment that left her writhing and sobbing until the ripped rawness turned to numbness. Everything would go black for a while, then disorienting opaque, and finally the blackness bled into night.

She lay huddled on the bed, eyes wide in the darkness, frantically aware of her nakedness beneath the torn white sundress. Her hands trembled against the radiating pain in her belly and the ache that drilled through her pelvic bones. Tears pooled and flowed again. Again, she sobbed brokenly.

The night moved on. Torturously.

THE LYRICALLY SWEET SMELL of roses hung in the air like a fine-linen sachet. Their pinks and reds and yellows blushed color in a tumble of blossoms that bordered the drive and sprawled into the rear yard. On a spring day enthralled with sunshine after an afternoon spritz of rain, their essence was heady and hypnotic. Old garden and English roses, their flowers full and rich in color, their fragrance robust and pure. Her fingertips brushed velvet petals as she passed, felt the dewy blend of pollen and raindrops. The ambrosia of their mix trailed after her as she let herself into the little house, even as she strolled down the hall. Entered the bedroom. Where their scent followed still, but the air grew suddenly thick and hard to breathe. Where the sweet fragrance turned as noxious as rotting flesh.

Her four-poster bed with its pretty comforter covered with a potpourri of cabbage roses was draped with a mound of white organza. A wedding dress. Ripped and shredded and sprinkled with crimson petals, petals and something else...blood. She spun around with a scream caught in her throat and saw the lipstick on her mirror, the big craggy letters smeared in waxy fury.

She retreated in horror, staggering back down the hall to her kitchen where the window over the sink was raised halfway. Where the first whiff of scorched sugar floated in on a shimmering hot breeze. Where the sound of soft crackling turned into a cavernous yawn and then a groan, and then the heat was suddenly a wall of flame. She watched in lame fear as fire lunged and leaped toward her.

She ran through her living room, coughing and stumbling and scrambling for the door, yanking at the knob, coughing and yanking and not opening the door...and then finally twisting and turning the knob and spilling out onto the pavement. Black smoke spilling out over her, heat and flames gorging on the rush of air. Clambering to her feet, she ran to the street...and slammed into the side of his truck, a black Chevy Tahoe. Saw his face and the curl of his lip, just before the SUV peeled off in a shriek of rubber that sent her sprawling to the curb.

Behind her, the house and all the beautiful roses were burning up.

SHE WAS SHIVERING AGAIN. The wool blanket was gone, but light was stealing back through the high window. There was a stale and hollow feel to it, like skim milk in transition. Day was returning, and with it, a drumming dread of the man. The thought, the vision, the anticipation, violently wrenched her stomach and sent a lurch of bile up her throat and into her mouth. Gagging, she pressed a shaky hand to her face and sat up so quickly that the room spun in nauseating vertigo. She vomited over the side of the bed and began to cry, quivering. Seeing the glass and pitcher of water on the wooden bedside stand, she reached weakly for it. But her hands shook so badly she couldn't raise the pitcher to pour into the glass. Whimpering, she set it down with a soft thunk, and wiped her mouth. Slowly, she eased herself back down on the bed and desperately hoped the nausea and dizziness would subside. Desperately hoped the man would not open the door and come back into the room.

Desperately thought about Jake.

CALLIE OPENED HER EYES in a blind frenzy, realizing she must have drifted off again. Thankfully, the nightmare from her past—recent and yet now seeming so long ago—had not repeated. Disoriented, she blinked in the dimness and instinctively flinched in fear, the violation replaying in frightful force and volume like the shocking blast of a subwoofer from an open car door. Slowly, the room came into bleary focus, and she noticed a tray on the wooden stand by the bed. There appeared to be a plate of food on it. Squinting, she saw beans and rice and something she could not make out. The glass and pitcher of water had been replaced by a plastic bottle of Agua Cristal. Her throat was hot and parched, but her queasy stomach rolled at the thought of food or water. Still, she was so thirsty. Gingerly, she reached for the bottle, the movement sparking new tenderness and cramping in her abdomen. Her hand closed around the bottle and brought it gently to her lips. The feel of the water on her tongue and sliding down her throat was surprisingly unrefreshing. Instead, she felt a searing sensation that was quickly followed by a sickening recoil of her stomach which, seconds later, brought it back up, making a wet blotch on her dress. Below, toward the hem, dried blood spots.

She didn't give the food a second look.

Slowly and carefully, she lay back down on the hard bed, her eyes honed anxiously on the door. During one laborious trip to the bathroom earlier she had tried the knob, found it locked. She wondered who had brought the food in, and instantly felt her chest seize with palpitations at the thought of the man back in the room. But she doubted he cared whether she was hungry or thirsty, so maybe it had been someone else.

The room was growing steadily darker, and a glance upward to the window showed a square of inky blue. Night was coming again. So how many did that make, she wondered. Two nights? Three? No, counting the first place she'd been taken, it had to be more than that. And where was she? Since she did not remember anything after being grabbed, she had no idea if she was close to the beach house or not. Which took her thoughts back to Jake. Tears came again, stinging eyes already sore from crying. Her chest hitched with weak sobs. The man knew him and was taunting him—did that mean Jake would come to get her? A sweep of hope gusted through her but just as quickly died with a downdraft of dread. What would happen if he did come? The man was the most terrifying being imaginable, and she had no doubt he intended to kill Jake.

A sharp cry of despair rose from her throat and the tears came harder. The cramping intensified and she felt another wave of nausea riding up with the sobs.

And then a sound outside the door choked the tears off like a wrenched faucet, the pain and discomfort turning to icy spears of foreboding. A desperate voice inside pleaded, *No, no, no, no, no, no...please no...* Terror reared up like a wild breaker.

There was a scratching sound on the wood, a faint metallic jangle.

A key in the lock.

Her stomach lurched and her heart twitched in a paroxysm of fear, then slammed against her ribs.

The tumblers clicked. *No, no, no, no, no...*

The knob turned. The door edged open. Paused. Then creaked another inch. Another pause, longer. A shadow moved into the narrow gap. Callie's breath caught in her throat. The shadow solidified as the figure wedged between door and frame.

It was not the man.

Callie exhaled, but her heart continued to thud.

A short woman, middle-aged and rounded, cleared the door and eased it shut as if it might shatter on impact. On the inside now, she crossed herself in the darkness and tiptoed toward Callie. Seeing Callie's alarm, she quickly put a finger to her lips and whispered, *"Shhh! Silencio, Señorita."*

She stood by the bed, hugging a small bundle to her breast. Slipping a hand into what appeared to be a satchel, she extracted a light-colored cloth and laid it on the bed beside Callie, gesturing for her to pick it up.

Reaching for the article, Callie discovered a pair of cotton panties that had been cut down to size and stitched up on both sides. Incredulously, Callie realized the woman had altered her own underwear. Flushing, Callie started to thank her but was urgently silenced again. The woman averted her eyes, watching the door as Callie struggled to get the underwear on. Pulling the oversized underwear over her narrow hips prompted a twinge of deep discomfort. She inhaled sharply and waited for the sensation to pass.

Next, the Latina woman reached down and tugged off her sandals and knelt down, slipping them on Callie's bare feet. After a nervous glance behind her, she straightened up and placed the long strap of the hand-woven bag she'd been clutching, a *mochila*, around Callie's neck. With the woman's face a few inches from her own, Callie could see the consternation in her eyes, sweat beading her jet-black hairline.

"*Vamos doña, camine,*" the Latina whispered urgently, motioning with her hands for Callie to move.

Wincing, Callie eased off the bed and walked on wobbly legs, following behind the woman. Incredibly, they were going to the door. Callie's heart hammered as the woman nudged the door open and peered first one way, then the other.

Distantly, down the darkened hall, a sonorous rumble. Snoring.

Terrified, Callie pulled back, withdrawing into the room. The foul blast of evil, the brutality of the assault, hit her full-force again, and she moaned plaintively.

Tightly clasping Callie's hand, the woman tugged her in the opposite direction, the sandals making a soft *whap-whap* sound on the ceramic floor. As they entered another room, Callie ran into something solid that hit her in the stomach and made a scuffling noise. She bit her lip to keep from crying out. In front of her, the woman tensed and muttered, "*Dios mio.*"

A chair, a table. Something tall nearby. A refrigerator. They were in a kitchen. From down the hall, the raucous outburst of a louder snore froze them both. Seconds later, all was quiet. The woman's urgency redoubled and she gave Callie's hand a firm yank, murmuring, *"Apurele, vayase ya, rapido."* Pulled her to another door.

Opened it.

On the other side of this one was night.

41

NIGHT HAD NEVER LOOKED so dark and so vast, and for all she knew or could see, it might have stretched out over an endless expanse of ocean or the wide open nothingness beyond the edge of a cliff.

It turned out to be neither and, in many ways, both.

Callie heard the door close with a light click behind her and, for the briefest of instants, felt an absurd pang of separation anxiety. Her hand reached for the knob, almost touching it, then dropped to her side. A muted crunching sound seemed to be gravitating toward her, a crunching sound that grew more distinct by scant degrees. She sucked in a breath, held herself rigid, eyes probing the darkness for a direction to go in. She heard a crisp snap, saw a wisp of flame, and then two tiny dots glowing orange in the night, moving erratically like a pair of drunken fireflies. Cigarettes. Voices drifted as the lit cigarettes jostled, moving up and then down, out and then back. And then they began to float toward her, the crunching of feet on brush coming closer.

A single voice, insidiously intimate, only a few feet away. *"Qué?"*

Callie bolted away from the door, away from the house, stumbling headlong into the night and she knew not what else. Frantically, she thought she heard footfalls behind her and moved faster, but the pain in her abdomen was screaming and her weak legs were already giving out. *No, no*, she exclaimed in her head, *run, run! Can't stop, can't stop!* But she was stopping, her legs folding like a collapsing lawn chair. The last thing she felt as she fell was fire engulfing her belly and the staggering blow of her head hitting the ground.

WHEN CALLIE OPENED HER eyes, all was still and black. Her head had a heavy but empty feel, as if a balloon had been inflated inside and then popped. She became aware of the ground beneath her, felt its firmness, smelled its sphagnous musk. A pale gold hook of moon hung in the sky, stars scattered like chips broken from its orb. It took her several moments to remember where she was, what had happened, and when she did a burst of panic got her clawing and pushing to sit up. Her efforts brought on a powerful wave of dizziness and nausea that almost caused her to drop back to the ground. But fear of being caught proved to be a stronger impetus and she was finally able to stand. Taking several deep breaths, she slowly felt the dizziness lessening and the nausea remaining in check. She peered around in the darkness and, seeing the house behind her, started moving as quickly as she could manage.

She had gone perhaps thirty or forty feet when the sliver of moon vanished altogether, the last nightlight going out. Beneath her feet the ground seemed to be changing, becoming more uneven, brush scratching and climbing up her ankles. She ambled a few feet in each direction and found it all the same, and yet something was different. An overwhelming feeling of despair descended on her as dark as the night—how could she keep going when she couldn't see anything? Again, she turned in every direction in the hope of being able to make out something, anything, and then she felt the *mochila* bob against her side. Felt the weight of its contents. She reached inside and immediately felt the despair flip over to euphoria as her hand closed around a slim cylinder.

A flashlight.

Tears of gratefulness sprang to her eyes.

Aiming it toward the ground, she flicked it on and slowly swept it around her. Cautiously raised the beam. She gasped at what she saw in the powdery light. She was surrounded by trees—tall, thick trees that had crowded out the night and pulled her into an even darker netherworld with no beginning and no end. How had that happened? She had only taken a few steps. Panicked, she turned toward what she thought was the way she'd come, and pointed the flashlight. Nothing but trees. She swung the beam around again, full circle. Trees, a density of mammoth trees. With mounting alarm, she paced several yards in every discernible direction. And found the same thing each way she headed.

She was in the forest.

Stunned, Callie looked for a place to sit and spotted a log. She tried to tuck as much of her dress underneath her as possible, utterly grateful now for the underwear the Latino woman had given her. With the *mochila* cradled in her lap, she held the flashlight over the opening and studied the contents. The first things she noticed, with a surge of relief, were two bottles of water and something that looked like dried fruit. *Plantains*, she speculated. A plastic bag contained a couple of doughy rounds, bread of some kind.

But right now she was not hungry and thirst seemed a distant need. It was night, it was pitch dark, she was alone in the forest…and she was scared to death.

CALLIE SAT ON THE log, blinking fitfully in the pale mist of illumination drifting up from the flashlight. Her first instinct on breaking free of the house had been to flee, but now she was afraid to go anywhere for fear of getting lost. And then a thought of such deep desolation struck her that a sob gurgled involuntarily from her throat. *Who or what would she be lost from?* Where was she? Was this jungle near the beach house? Was it near Dominical at all? Was it even in Costa Rica? She could not imagine that Jake had any idea where she was. But wasn't being lost better than being found by the inconceivably evil man back at the house? Of that, there was no doubt. And what if he had discovered that she was gone? What if he and his men were out looking for her right now?

She rose unsteadily from the log, vaguely aimed the flashlight in front of her, and began walking as quickly as she could. Her pelvis still ached, everything within its cradle tender and hurting, but she had been freed and now had the chance to get away. She had no idea where to go in the maze of trees, but she had to try. Though the trunks were close and the undergrowth thick, there was enough room to maneuver between them. So far. Nudging vines aside and ducking low hanging limbs, she gradually fell into a quiet rhythm.

At first, the only sound she heard was that of the sandals pushing down on the forest floor, alternately soft and spongy and coarse and unyielding. But as she navigated further, the jungle's nocturnal dimension came unnervingly to life in a fusion of noises as large predatory birds thrashed through the canopy on the hunt for bats and monkeys against a chaotic chorus of rumbles, grunts, groans, clicks, barks, whistles, and trilling from frogs and insects. She became fearfully aware of indistinct undulations above and around her, obscured by density and darkness. Something flapped just above her head, so close she could feel the stir of air in her hair. She flinched and tottered, and the flashlight was jarred from her grip. It thumped to the ground and rolled away from her feet, the light clicking off as the switch hit a tree root.

"No, no, no," she whispered in horror as the dark bas-relief of jungle solidified to total black once more. Carefully, she knelt down to feel for the flashlight, sucking in a sharp breath as cramps seized her abdomen. A sudden swishing nearby sent a peal of fear through her like the twang of a tuning fork, the sensation tingling from her jaw to her kneecaps. A scared whimper mewed from her throat as she thrust her hand forward and side to side. Touched something smooth and warm and pulsing. She jerked her hand back and heard a sound that was like air being let out of a tire. *Hissing.* Terrified, she could not move as hissing filled her ears, almost ringing with intensity.

Close, persistent hissing. The air shuddered. Went still. Her heart beat unbearably loud in the stillness.

Seconds passed, then minutes. A faint rustling...inches, just inches...and...receding. Steam swirled around her, bathing her face and neck in moist, sticky heat. The ground smelled of burnt coffee and charcoal and earthy decomposition.

She exhaled and felt her heart gradually slow. But it took a long time for her to find the courage to move again. When she finally did, her shaking hand closed around the flashlight. She went weak with relief as a flick of the switch brought a little light back into the jungle. But the loss of light had made her wonder how much time remained on the flashlight's batteries. Hours? A nighttime's worth? *Please*, she prayed desperately, *please don't let me lose the light*. The thought of that happening made her start shaking again, so much her teeth chattered.

Around her, the jungle thrummed.

Suddenly lightheaded in the humidity and utterly overwhelmed, she sought a place to rest and found a buttress at the base of a wide tree. Slipping her hand inside the *mochila*, she felt a square of fabric wedged in the bottom of the bag and pulled it out. Unfolding the light woven material, she found that it covered enough ground for her to sit and stretch her legs. Just barely. When her calves touched brush, she quickly drew her knees up and tucked her feet. Covered by only the few yards of now-tattered white linen sundress, a crudely altered pair of too-big panties, and sandals that were no more than soles and a couple of straps, out here Callie felt as vulnerable as if she were naked. A ghastly image of the vile man over her, of being exposed and violated, flashed like sky-splitting lightning. She squirmed uncomfortably on the fabric throw, tucking and retucking the short hem of the dress. Sighing, she uncapped one of the water bottles and took a few sips. When she didn't become nauseated and the water stayed down, she took a few more. For the first time, she was really thirsty, and had another worried thought: *How long would the two bottles of water last?* She took one more mouthful of water, twisted the top back on the bottle, and put it inside the *mochila*. Coated with sweat, she leaned back against the tree. Seconds later her neck was on fire, then her arms and legs. Squealing, she jumped up and pawed frantically at her skin, instantly stinging her hands and fingers, the pain as hot and intense as electric shocks. Grabbing the flashlight, she flailed it around and was horrified to find herself crawling with ants, dozens and dozens of them. Disappearing inside her dress, running down her bare arms, climbing up her neck to her face. Over her eyelids, around her earlobes, across her lips. Shaking and slapping them off, she wailed in misery as their bites swelled and circulated heat through her flesh. Soon, her heart was jittering with adrenaline as their venom disseminated. The pain radiated and she found herself gasping for breath. Her throat tightened and she struggled to swallow. A surge of panic pulled her under like a riptide.

She dropped limply to the square of fabric and tried to stay calm, tried to breathe slowly, tried not to cry. She took a few more swigs from the water bottle, splashing a little on the welts rising around her neck. The tightness eventually lessened, her breathing eased, her panic diminished. But the fire spread, and intensified.

And then the mosquitoes came.

THEY FEASTED WITHOUT MERCY, and as Callie tried helplessly to ward them off, flesh itching and burning relentlessly, she was sure she was going to die. Arms hugging her midriff, she imagined it was Jake holding her, and wept.

At some point she heard a faint chirping in the tree directly above her, perhaps fifteen feet up. The chirping had an unsettling urgency to it, increasing in volume and frequency. Next, from the same spot, *wick-a-wick-a-wick-a-wick,* followed by barks and more insistent chirping. *Wick-a-wick-a-wick-a-wick,* and then a shrill scream that sent Callie scrambling. Heart tripping, she pointed the flashlight up into the high branches of the tree, the beam catching a pair of glowing red eyes. Almost dropping the flashlight again, she snatched the square of fabric from the ground below the tree and skittered away.

She had only gone about five yards when she heard something else.

Growling. Deep, serious growling somewhere behind her.

Now her heart was hammering, her mind frenzied with fear. The growling continued, low and menacing. Was it close? Yards away? Feet away? As she tried to ascertain where the growls were coming from, a raucous roar erupted, enfolding and filling the space with the richness of Bose surround-sound. She jumped, cried out in terror, her exclamation all but eclipsed by the shrieks of the creature in the tree. Her heart was beating so strenuously she thought it might explode. She pushed her clenched hands up against the middle of her chest, as if to contain it.

More growling. It sounded closer. *Was* it closer? *Oh God, was it?* Oddly, the creature in the tree had grown calmer, resuming its *wick-a-wick-a-wick-a-wick* chant interspersed with a few chirps. But the growling, where was the growling?

Callie listened. Had it stopped? Was it gone? Distant, crackling noises, a long, low rumble. Then nothing.

She found a cluster of leafy ferns at the base of another tree, dropped the fabric square across them, and sunk onto it. Numbly, she reached into the *mochila*, uncapped a water bottle with a quivering hand, and drank. Not even a minute later, she threw all of it up.

THE JUNGLE BY MORNING was, at least on first impression, a less scary place. With only about five percent of direct sunlight reaching the ground, there is not much daylight in a rainforest. But as the black shroud lifted from the trees, revealing a deep emerald cavern, Callie could see what had surrounded her during the night. And it seemed infinitely less threatening. For a little while.

She flicked off the flashlight, the beam already fading to a dim glow, and reached for the *mochila*. When she looked inside, her jaw dropped in heartbreaking incredulity. The plastic bags that had contained the *arepas* and *plantains* were empty. When she plucked them out, she could see holes gnawed through the plastic and only minuscule crumbs. Something had crawled inside the *mochila* during the night, mere inches from her, and eaten the food. The thought of whatever it was crawling over *her* during the night made her stomach flip. Even so, she was actually hungry, and thirsty. Dismally, she took out a water bottle—and found it, too, empty. When had she drunk all the water? She eyed the second full bottle and suddenly felt a jab of panic. How long could she make it with only one bottle of water left? And nothing to eat?

Think about what Jake would tell you, a small inner voice urged. What would Jake say? And just that simple, solitary thought, brought a new torrent of tears as she heard his deep, authoritative voice in her head. Imagined him talking to her. She loved to hear him talk, could listen to him endlessly. She desperately wanted to hear his voice now, even just one word. Would she ever hear it again?

"*Jake...*" She wept inconsolably, aching to the core of her being.

The insect bites itched maddeningly, the agony magnifying as the temperature rose. Examining her arms and legs, she was horrified to see dozens upon dozens of angry red blotches, badly swollen, some bleeding. There were just as many cuts and scratches from the brush. Biting flies hovered, darting in to taste the blood and add to her misery. She stood, brushed herself off, and glanced around. Surprised that she had enough fluid in her to urinate, she found a spot with relatively thin vegetation and relieved herself. Then, uncertainly, she began walking.

Still thinking about Jake, she remembered their time exploring the Costa Rican countryside—Monteverde, Arenal, Rincón de la Vieja, Río Pacuare—remembered their overnight camping. Before all that, she had never even been in a tent, much less in the woods. But she had been with him and knew he wouldn't let anything happen to her. She bit down on her lip, blistered from ant bites, and tried to throttle the emotion. Okay, so what *would* Jake say? She searched her memory, also thinking back over the time she had accompanied him as he worked with the two television production guys.

A sudden thought broke through the fog like a blinding ray of sunshine. *A river*—Jake had told the production team that finding a river was often a good way to find a settlement of people, Indians most likely. And they would have food, water, shelter! Heartened, she picked up her pace and peered a little more intently through the foliage, looking for any sign of water. Along the way, she also searched for something to eat. The trees, she discovered, were full of produce—seeds, nuts, fruit—but what was safe to consume? Seeing a tree with clusters of golf ball size fruit ranging in color from white to pale yellow, she plucked one from a thick-leafed branch and bit tentatively into it. The sourness puckered her mouth and stung the sores on her lips, but she was so hungry she forced a few more bites, washing the tart pulp down with several mouthfuls of water. But it was for naught when, a few minutes later, her stomach retched and rejected the contents in a slimy mess that left her throat burning. Quivering, she looked around again, bewildered, and noticed another tree. This one was much fuller, sprouting a slightly different-looking fruit, reddish in color. And this one was full of birds—a bevy of small ones and a large pair of toucans—even some monkeys, all pecking away at the fruit. She picked several pieces from the ground and put them in the *mochila* for later. She was too nauseous to eat them now.

Callie continued her hike through the jungle, fervently hoping to find a river. As hours passed, the temperature climbed steadily, and she was drenched in sweat. Her belly wasn't the only part of her cramping anymore; her legs were beginning to spasm and seize with increasing frequency. Exhausted, she stopped to rest, finding a semi-cleared spot that appeared to be free of ants. As she sat, panting in the horrendous heat and rubbing her crimped leg muscles, she watched the creatures that had meandered around her in the night, and wondered if maybe it was a good thing after all that it had been too dark to see them. Several feet away, a massive ceiba tree was crawling with a colony of ants— thousands of them—that had disassembled some kind of reptile and were carrying the pieces back to their bunker. Feet, tail, torso, head. The sight of them made her shudder in revulsion and remembrance, the profusion of festering bites itching with new fire. Her eyes traveled to the base of the tree, where a fallen branch sprouted a cluster of brightly colored bromeliads, a burst of red and purple in an otherwise monochrome of evergreen. A scorpion was stalking their circumference on the prowl of a salamander, while a horned beetle the size of a hand grenade trundled over the branch itself. A thick tangle of lianas twisted around the tree trunk and climbed into a gnarled network toward the top. Vines seemed to stitch every seam of the canopy and rope every narrow gap of decaying mulch. And every one of them she crossed looked like a snake.

And, some of them were.

She had resumed her trek and was concentrating on separating a stand of palm stalks when a movement on the ground caught her eye. Perspiration boiled from her skin, rolling into her eyes. Momentarily blinded, she stepped back and wiped at the sweat, blinking at the caustic sting. Something moved by her foot. And then nudged and bounced off. She heard a throaty burp and released a breath. Probably a frog. She was about to step forward again when a vine as green as the rind of a lime, thick as a fire hose, swung down in front of her. It was variegated with a crosshatched white stripe, coiled, and wriggling. Dizzy and dehydrated, Callie stared at the vine, almost reached for it to steady herself, and then gasped as the end of the vine suddenly shot an arrow-shaped head toward her. A tongue zipped out, amber eyes firing.

Stumbling, she fell backwards over a downed tree limb and rolled several yards before coming to a stop. Dazed, she pulled herself up and started wiping mud from her arms and legs, but only succeeded in smearing it. In doing so, she realized two fortuitous things; the mud seemed to act as a balm for her insect bites, and the mud indicated wetter ground. Hope bloomed as she speculated that a river might be close.

Sweating profusely, her throat ached for refreshment, so with great care she extracted the last bottle of water and gently removed the cap. She'd only had a few sips and was rationing the remaining ounces to make it last as long as she could. But now, having gone hours without any, she was ragingly thirsty. Tipping the bottle to her mouth, she took a tiny drink and tilted her head to let the water slide down her throat. A wave of dizziness sent her reeling and she watched in stunned doom and disbelief as the bottle popped from her hand and went careening to the ground. The rest of her precious water seeped into a compost of rotting leaves.

SHE'D BEEN FOLLOWING THE whimsical flight of a royal-blue butterfly, her thoughts floating airily in a strangely tranquil place, when a robust rumble from high above shook her out of the reverie. For the past few hours, as the day wound imperceptibly toward late afternoon, Callie's mind had been drifting. Heat, hunger, and dehydration were taking a toll and, added to the sleep-deprivation over several nights, hallucinations were not far off. So the percussive rumble overhead sounded, to her, like the beastly growl of the previous night, and she grappled frantically through the limbs to get away from it. Trouble was, it was everywhere, and it was getting louder, closer, heavier. Soon, there was a drumming above, muted at first and then building to a steady staccato.

She stopped trying to escape and listened. Incredibly, it sounded like *rain*. Only there was no rain. Yet the air was permeated with moisture. Her dress was soaked and clung to her skin, her hair hung in damp tendrils. She held out her hands, palms up, but saw or felt no raindrops. Several moments passed as she puzzled over the phenomenon. And then she heard dripping.

Dripping. Water. Dripping, dripping.

Desperately, she looked around and saw, with slack-jawed wonder and raving gratitude, the source. The rain was rolling over the top of the canopy like droplets over a giant umbrella, tumbling over whatever edges it could find, sliding down through the multitude of layers and finally, dripping from trees. Transfixed, Callie watched as a prehistoric-looking creature clambered along a tree branch, jade green scales iridescent in the mist, and stuck out its tongue to lap up a dollop of water captured on an elliptical leaf. Spines bristled from his head to the tip of his tail, his chartreuse eyes fixed and hooded. He was as scary as everything else she had seen in the jungle, but the fact that he was drinking water infused her with mindless joy.

For the next thirty minutes or so, she launched a water-divining mission, sipping a mouthful of liquid wherever she could find it. Her efforts didn't yield much until she discovered that a broad leaf rolled into a funnel cone could collect an inch or two of water. Except for being soaked, she began to feel better, more lucid.

So when she almost slipped off a muddy embankment, it took her only a few dazed moments to realize with weary triumph that she had, in fact, found a river.

SHE FOLLOWED THE RIVERBANK until the trees became too tightly enmeshed for her to pass between. In a few places the canopy ceiling parted at the water's edge and she had been able to see daylight, but now both night and jungle had blended the gaps and blackened the green.

The fading beam of the flashlight bobbed ahead of her as Callie staggered through the trees. Weak with hunger and thirst, profoundly exhausted, she lacked the energy to even swat at the mosquitoes that descended after the rain ceased. Sounds of the night tuned up for another production, a jam session of monkey chatter as they retreated for rest, twilight bird sonatas, and the maraca vibrato of crickets. In the midst of this, she heard the distinctive sound of a splash. She crept slowly in the direction of the river. Could the splash have come from a boat? Perhaps Indians in a dugout canoe? She moved a little faster, pushing through the brush, trying to ignore the branches threshing her skin, raking across her legs, ankles, and tops of her feet. Another splash, this one louder. She pointed the flashlight toward the sound.

And caught the familiar red glow of a pair of animal eyes. Something large and sinewy rose from the dark water and lumbered onto the bank with a grunt. Then a throaty roar that made her flesh vibrate as it resonated in her bones. Vines and brush thrashed in a heavy whisk.

Callie turned and ran jaggedly through the forest, limbs smacking her from the front and back, stumbling and slipping on the marshy ground. Falling, struggling to get back up, running until she could run no more.

Panting, pain piercing her sides and throbbing in her belly, she collapsed against a tree and slid to the roots below and labored to catch her breath. The flashlight rolled from her hand, and flickered out. For several moments she could not move, lost in the throes of another excruciating fit of leg cramps. Shivering from the pain, she slowly recovered enough mobility to reach for the flashlight. Luckily, it had not rolled far. She was drawing it back to her lap when her side was stuck with what felt like a hundred needles dipped in fire. Wailing, she flicked the flashlight on and aimed it over her waist. A branch covered in spikes had penetrated the thin linen material of her dress and was embedded in the tender flesh beneath. As new pain seared, she looked around frantically for some way to get it off. Finally, she tapped the branch with the flashlight and felt it pull free, but not without leaving some of its barbs buried in her side. Heaving in agony, she plucked at them. They felt as big as nails, and it seemed the more she tried to pull them out, the deeper they burrowed. She wasn't able to get them all out, and even the ones she removed left as much pain as if they were still there. Exhausted from her efforts, she laid the flashlight in her lap. And watched despairingly as its beacon dwindled to a faint yellow coin.

Minutes later, it waned to a dot and died out.

Thunder stuttered and boomed and rain soaked through the forest a second time. Callie cried, softly and mournfully, trembling in the darkness where there would be no light to chase away the terrors. She closed her eyes and thought of Jake. Thought of his fingers in her hair, his breath in her ear, saying her name. Just holding her.

ANOTHER DAY AND NIGHT passed, punishingly. The jungle's steam bath of humidity steeped, and it was as if she could feel the wet heat boiling below her skin. But dehydration had advanced to the point that she was not perspiring—her skin felt hot and dry, baked. She staggered on through the trees, vines, and dense vegetation, images dancing dizzily in front of her, coming in and out of focus. At one point, a swarm of ants the size and density of an oil slick undulated right in front of her, sending other insects and reptiles scurrying ahead of them. She backpedaled to avoid stepping amidst the moving mass, careening into a tree and dropping to the ground. For several moments the adrenaline of resurgent fear held her vigilant as the *ronda* passed. She sat there for a while afterward—minutes or hours, she didn't know.

And then, she pulled herself up and shakily continued walking. In circles, it seemed. Impossible to tell because it all streamed together in one vertiginous blur. Sometime later in the day, she stopped, reached to a tree branch to sturdy herself, and fainted.

MORNING SHIMMERED THROUGH, BRINGING the jungle back to darken the sun. Dimly, Callie stirred and heard a rustling. Too weak to stand, she watched apprehensively as movement rippled through the bush, pulling at vines and swaying stalks—watched, knowing she could not move, could not escape from whatever was coming. The flash of a blade ripped open a wall of green with a metallic zing.

Callie looked up to see a man emerge from the slashed brush.

The man was not Jake.

42

BY THE TIME THEY made it back to camp, despite never seeing or feeling the first raindrop, they were all muddy and soaked. Aguilar's camp sentries had a low but vigorous fire going, which quickly drew them in for drying off and scarfing down some chow. After the brief respite, Tangeman and Petropoulos supervised Falcone and Niles in readying and assembling the field gear, weapons, and ammo they would be taking in the morning.

Jake wandered off by himself, mired in thoughts he was fighting to keep unfettered with emotion and locked down behind warrior mode. Never in his life, not in any military op he could recall, had he found it as difficult as he did now.

It was Callie.

He paced, flexed his muscles to release the tension, and shook his head as if by shaking it the emotions would shift to a lower shelf. He checked his cell and sat phones to make sure he had not missed any calls, wondering why he hadn't heard anything further from Valentín. He had expected it, which troubled him considerably. Frowning, he extracted the spreadsheet from his pocket, taking care as he peeled it open. Damp, sweat-stained, and fading, the print was becoming almost impossible to read. He was squinting at it when Raúl Aguilar came up beside him.

Robusto dangling from his lips, he said, *"Qué mas?"*

Jake continued to study the damp, badly wrinkled paper without answering.

"*Qué, mi amigo?*"

Jake shook his head. "I don't know, Raúl. Just reviewing the coordinates, making sure I haven't missed something. One thing that does bother me is no contact from Valentín today."

Aguilar puffed thoughtfully on his cigar, tapping ashes as he scratched at his beard. "Yes. Very strange. Then again, perhaps not. He may have been on the move."

Jake met Aguilar's gaze with inscrutability. "Why the hell would he be moving now? He wants me to find him, to come to him, so why would he make it more difficult?"

Aguilar shrugged. "That is the only reason that comes to my mind. Perhaps there are other things going on."

Jake considered this for a moment, his mind turning over every possible variant, but nothing really clicked. He consulted the spreadsheet again, shook his head, stuffed it back in the pocket of his camo pants. Smacking a mosquito from his cheek, something struck him. "Raúl, will you get a couple of men and come with me?"

"Certainly. Where are we going?"

"To make sure there are no nasty surprises on the back side."

TREKKING THROUGH THE JUNGLE to the north and east of camp, Jake led Aguilar and a pair of his men on a trajectory that would take them behind the guerrilla compound. A set of PVS-7 NVGs was strapped to his head, illuminating the darkness in an alien green glow that exposed everything with surprising clarity. Aguilar and his men used older but functional Soviet Baigish scopes. Before leaving camp, Jake had briefed Tangeman and Petropoulos with a full-range of contingency plans in case they encountered any bad guys or in the event he did not return. Bottom line, it would be *Charlie Mike*—continue mission.

The diagonal route that swung out beyond the compound took them just under two hours. Along the way they encountered nothing more than jungle and its usual nighttime denizens, none of which fazed any of the four. While taking a water break, Jake consulted his GPS and radioed their location to Tangeman and Petropoulos. Relaying coordinates, something snagged in his mind. He took the spreadsheet out of his pocket, adjusting the IR illuminator on the NVGs so he could see it. There was one series of numbers and letters that he'd not been able to pinpoint on the map; the numbers could have been coordinates, but next to them had been the letters *ABCS*. What the hell was *ABCS*? It obviously stood for something, but he never came up with anything that made sense. If the numbers were coordinates, they were close to the grid.

Gesturing to Aguilar that he wanted to continue, Jake led them in the direction of the cross point. They passed the back side of the compound and hiked through a section of forest that seemed to be gradually thinning. A little over thirty minutes later they were standing at the bank of a narrow river, which Jake guessed was another tributary of the Putumayo. Through his NVGs he could see some kind of structure on the other side, at the top of a slight rise. Pointing his rangefinder across, checking the GPS and making the calculations, he felt his pulse quicken—the structure appeared to be right on the mark of the coordinates he'd been tracking. *ABCS*, he mulled again, what could *ABCS* possibly stand for?

Scanning the riverbanks, Jake searched for a way to cross and spotted a dugout canoe tethered on the far side. Removing his gear, he instructed Aguilar and his men to wait while he swam across to retrieve the boat. He dropped into the water and paddled slightly upstream, past the structure, then let the current bring him silently back. He snared the canoe and pulled it across the water. Aguilar tossed Jake's gear into the dugout and the three of them got in while Jake helped to steer it across as he swam back over.

Seeing movement and hearing voices, they emerged from the river in crouched positions and dropped to the ground on their stomachs. Watched and listened. Jake whispered directions and seconds later Aguilar's two men split apart, one going left and the other, right. There were two guerrillas stationed at the front of the structure, but their attention was not on the river below them. They were laughing about a compatriot's snoring inside the structure, referring to him as *un cerdo*. A pig. Machine guns hung heedlessly at their sides, cigarettes smoking from their hands.

Aguilar's men took them out quickly and quietly, rushing in from opposite sides. They were stripped of weapons, ammo, and radios. A hand signal gave Jake and Aguilar clearance to advance.

Clambering up the incline, they stood in front of the structure.

Jake studied it through his NVGs. It was a simple clapboard building with a frayed Colombian flag protruding from the corrugated metal roofline. Peering inside, they saw the butt of the sentries' jokes lying on the floor, mouth open in stertorous emission; another guerrilla was less vocally asleep next to him.

Jake and Aguilar stepped into the building and slipped stealthily around the pair, which lay on their sides. Simultaneously, Jake and Aguilar clamped a hand over their victims' noses and mouths. The pair of dozing guerrillas came quickly and alarmingly awake, but the knives at their throats instantly checked any struggle they might have launched. Jake gave Aguilar a shake of his head, conveying a silent directive that Aguilar understood implicitly. Then, as the second guerrilla watched, Jake jammed his knife into the throat of the first—under the chin and straight through to the base of the skull. Paralysis was instant, death very nearly. The second guerrilla was visibly shaken, eyes bulging as Jake jerked the knife from the other guerrilla's throat, prompting a thick spout of arterial blood for the few seconds that remained of the man's life.

Stepping around to kneel beside Aguilar, Jake addressed the second man. In Spanish, he said: "You will say nothing until I ask you a question. When I do, I want a straight answer. Understand?" With Aguilar's hand still tightly clamped over his nose and mouth, the guerrilla nodded. Jake glanced to Aguilar, who slowly lifted his hand from the guerrilla's face. He kept the knife at his throat.

Immediately, the man wheezed for air, but almost as quickly he spat a string of profane threats. Jake grabbed a fistful of the guerrilla's hair, wrenching his head back. Calmly, but through gritted teeth, Jake said, "I told you to say nothing until I asked you a question." He waited until the guerrilla stopped muttering and looked at him. Jake flipped back his NVGs, leaned closer, looked directly into the man's eyes. "Where is Valentín holding the woman?"

For an instant the guerrilla's eyes held Jake's without a change in expression. Then they narrowed, and a sneer played over his lips as he realized he had one final move on his predator. Grinning with sadistic pleasure, he snarled, *"Su mujer esta muerta."*

Your woman is dead.

Before Jake could react, the guerrilla yanked his head to the side, away from Aguilar's knife, and swung an arm up behind Jake's head. Aguilar caught it in midair, twisted it into an impossible angle, and stabbed the guerrilla in the chest. Jake released the man's hair and grabbed his face in both hands. "Where is Valentín holding her?" he repeated, as if he had not heard the guerrilla's edict.

The guerrilla's snarl grew slack, his eyes glazed, his face collapsed. His last words seemed to now register in Jake's head, like flickering neon letters on an electrically challenged marquee. Angrily releasing the guerrilla, he stood and growled, "No! Goddammit, Raúl!"

"Jake," Aguilar said quietly, "do you really think he was going to tell you?"

Jake stalked off, stared furiously at the ground. Felt the room close around him so tightly he could not catch his breath. But he refused to let himself be swept into the emotions that were storming the gate. He slowed his breathing, slowed his pulse, let his mind flatline. He raised his head and surveyed the building interior.

The room smelled of mold and decay, with cobwebs as thick as window sheers draping every corner. Small tables and chairs, splintered and rotting, were scattered in no particular order across the muddy floorboards. Sections of the walls had papers tacked in groupings, the edges curling. Stepping over to examine some of the papers, Jake was surprised to see crude drawings—childlike drawings—and it suddenly dawned on him where they were. In a schoolhouse. The thought tumbled as randomly as a sneaker in a dryer, and then it thumped against a door in his mind. *A schoolhouse.*

Not ABCS...*abc's.* Delaney's shorthand for school.

The fact that this obviously long-abandoned schoolhouse was being guarded by guerrillas could only mean one thing— contraband. Or, possibly, something else. A hostage. Not a body, a hostage. Judging from Aguilar's heightened interest, he had come to the same conclusion. Despite Jake's steely resolve to stay on operational track, a trapdoor in his heart creaked open. Contraband or *hostage*…but where the hell could a hostage be stowed?

Your woman is dead.

God, he prayed, let there be some magic door, some secret opening, some hidden panel. *Let me find her here.*

He did a cautious circuit of the room, looking first for the obvious, any additional entrances. There were none. Neither were there any closets, pantries, or cabinets, and the few boxes and crates contained little more than mildewed paper products and books. His eyes roved over the tin ceiling then dropped to the floor, but he saw no sign of irregularity. No seams, no gaps, no loose edges. As he walked around the schoolhouse, Jake tested the wooden planks in various places with the toes and heels of his boots. Stopping near the center of the room, hands on his hips, he was stumped. Staring at a pair of tables that seemed sturdier than the rest, chairs tucked a little too neatly, he noticed a woven hemp rug beneath.

Shoving the tables and chairs aside, he rolled back the rug. And found a pair of padlocked doors. His adrenaline kicked. From his rucksack, he dug out a lock pick set and went to work on the keyhole. In seconds, he jogged the tumblers and rattled the shackle loose. Drawing his Glock, he leaned over and yanked the doors open. What he saw made his eyes go wide and his mouth go slack. And his heart plunge. Through the lenses of his PVS-7s he saw a green dungeon of cocaine—a cellar stockpiled side to side to side with cellophane-wrapped bundles, thousands and thousands of them. Judging the height and depth of the stacks, Jake did a rough calculation in his head and whistled. "Holy shit," he murmured, stupefied.

They had found the mythical cache.

And that was not all. In another area there were, literally, hundreds of stacked crates. Jake knew what they contained before he looked. Using his knife to wedge one of the tops open, he found weapons of every conceivable make and model—mostly of the heavy variety and all of them high grade. Everything from AK47s to rocket-launchers and RPGs, mortars and ammunition. They were well-packed for long-range shipment. Jake took it all in, exhaled heavily.

No hostage. Your woman is dead.

Jake straightened up, took a step back, and felt something hard press into the base of his skull. He knew immediately what it was.

"*Lo siento, mi amigo*," Aguilar said softly from behind him.

"Raúl, what the fuck?"

"Listen very carefully," Aguilar continued, still pressing the barrel of his Uzi against Jake's neck. "I do not want to shoot you."

"Raúl—" Jake began, his voice breathy, a slithery feeling in his stomach. His hand gripped the Glock tighter, finger brushing the trigger guard.

"Listen to me," Aguilar said sharply. "In a minute, I am going to let you turn around. It is up to you what will happen next."

"What the hell are you talking about?" Jake demanded.

"Turn around, Jake."

Jake heard the shuffle of Aguilar's feet on the dusty wood floor, felt the barrel of the submachine gun removed from his neck. Slowly, he turned, the Glock nose-down but his trigger finger ready. He caught movement by the doorway and saw one of Aguilar's men start to enter. His gun arm stiffened.

"*Fuera!*" Aguilar called out, waving him back. Bewildered, the man retreated. To Jake, Aguilar said, "I can shoot you, you can shoot me."

In a voice calmer than he felt, Jake said, "Raúl, we are friends. Neither of us is going to shoot the other. Talk to me. Tell me what this is about." His mind was ablaze with thoughts, all of them too volatile to touch.

Aguilar was holding the Uzi at his side, could swing it up and fire in milliseconds. The paramilitary did not respond for several moments, looking at Jake through solemn, hooded eyes.

"What's going on, Raúl?" Jake pressed gently, his face hot in the close, musty air. He could hear his heart thudding in the stillness. His fingertips tingled.

"Walk away now," Aguilar responded, matching his tone. His voice was as soft as a puppy's fur, but there was a hint of the dog in his diction.

"I'm not going anywhere until you tell me what's going on." Jake crossed his arms, but he kept his finger by the trigger of the Glock. When Aguilar was not forthcoming, he asked, "Did you know this was here?"

"I did not. This is the truth. But I thought you might find it along the way of the mission. And so you have."

"I don't understand," Jake said, his expression becoming more incredulous as he was realizing the seriousness of Aguilar's intent. "You've been with me all along, supporting me in every way—even as Haskell turned on me—and now you're turning on me, too?"

"No, no," Aguilar said emphatically. "That is not the case. Jake, surely you know how I feel...I will forever be in your debt for coming to my aid when my wife and children were murdered. I have been with you and remain so but"—he shook his head sadly—"I must leave you for now."

Jake took a step toward him, causing Aguilar to raise the Uzi.

"God, Raúl, this is crazy-ass shit," Jake sputtered, perspiration beading at his temple as his muscles went rigid.

"*Vaya, mi amigo.*"

Jake swung his arm up, bringing the Glock 9mm within inches of Aguilar's face. "I can't let this be," he said, adding, "whatever it is you have in mind. You know I can't."

"This is as I expected," Aguilar said evenly. "And most regrettable."

There was a long pause, both men aiming their weapons, both gazing steadily at the other, both unyielding. The air was hot and heavy with traces of gun oil simmering like steam off asphalt.

Finally, Aguilar said, "Go, Jake. Get your lady."

"Is she dead, Raúl?"

Aguilar said nothing.

"Is she dead?" Jake asked again, a hairline crack in his voice.

And again, Aguilar said nothing. Whether it was because he didn't know—or because he did—Jake couldn't tell.

JAKE WAS PISSED AND, at the same time, feeling an effervescence of grief. He stormed through the jungle at a brisk clip, anger beginning to gnaw through his daze of disbelief over what had just happened; the grief continued to fizzle through his head, bubbling into cavities, exploding, and then resonating like charged air. He had taken the dugout back across the river, glancing once over his shoulder to see Aguilar watching him from the top of the incline. Jake felt like he had tripped and fallen down the Amazonian rabbit hole. This was not the kind of nasty surprise he had expected on the back side, but Colombia seemed to be full of them.

Speaking to Tangeman and Petropoulos on his headset, in a rigidly controlled voice he said, "Talk to no one. Get Eddie and Curran, get as much gear as you can carry, take a Zodiac with fuel if you can manage it, and get the hell out of that camp." He issued the coordinates for a linkup and hiked toward the point. It struck him then the irony of Falcone and Niles showing up at Hernandez's doorstep—without them now, he would never be able to pull off the operation he had planned.

Checking his watch, he saw that dawn was less than an hour away.

43

THE MAN WHO EMERGED from the bush looked nothing like a man at all. Wielding his machete, he stared at Callie with hostile intensity. A strip of red cloth the size of a tube sock was draped around his loins, covering his genitals but only just barely. The rest of his skin was the color of cognac, painted in streaks of an even darker brown. A headdress strung with seeds reined in a whisk of coarse black hair; his neck, arms, and ankles were banded with adornments made of animal teeth. Incredibly, his feet were bare.

Callie's heart stuttered, her pulse pricked, and then she slumped back against the tree. The world swam in a layered sea of green. Dimly, she was aware of wetness on her lips, followed by liquid warmth in her mouth that slid down her parched throat. She felt a calloused hand behind her neck, inhaled an earthy but somewhat fleshy smell, heard vague grunting. Her focus began to slowly clear, the spinning reduced to a sense of imbalance.

She was being pulled to her feet, but her knees kept buckling. When the brown man could not get her to remain standing, he hefted her over his shoulder. The jog of his stride as her head bobbed upside-down brought the liquid rushing back to her throat and mouth, filling her sinuses. The green sea pitched and swallowed her.

* * * * *

A FAINT, FUZZY SENSATION traveled lazily along her arm, but Callie could not find the surface. She was hot and weak, her mind floating in a delirium of simmering quicksand. The fuzzy feeling brushed her neck, then her chin, and her eyelids sluggishly opened. A black leggy thing meandered delicately up her cheek, stopping directly in front of her eye. Somewhere inside her, a scream fought to get out, but the sound was turned off. A brown hand scooped the fuzzy thing off her face, a soft laugh tittering down. The penny-colored head that went with the hand leaned over and showed a mouthful of teeth that looked like the pickets of a very old fence. The face was contrarily young. An Indian, Callie realized, still coveting the fuzzy thing—a spider that looked like a black velvet glove.

His other hand materialized over her head, suspended for several seconds, fingers curled in a cupping gesture. It lowered gingerly, touching her hair with the delicacy and reverence of one touching something rare and exquisite. His eyes were bright with a curiosity that was either whimsical or erotic, his lips pursed in concentration.

Then, as if snapping out of a trance, the young Indian scampered off, leaving Callie to her slow reveal. She was no longer surrounded by trees, but she sensed them nearby and could still hear the sounds of chattering monkeys and squawking birds. As her sight and senses worked to become lucid, she recognized thatched surfaces and, when she tried to rise, grasped the fact that she was lying in a hammock. Keenly feeling the perforations and embedded spikes in her side, she sank back down, gazed up at the thatch ceiling, and succumbed again to the soporific vacuum of quicksand.

Somewhere below that grainy surface she heard voices, peppered with static.

Another Indian face appeared above her and as she focused, he began to babble. None of the words made any sense, but when he held up a two-way radio and gestured, her heart sprang in her chest. Seeing the flicker in her eyes, the Indian nodded, saying something else she did not understand. But the last thing he uttered sent her pulse skipping: *"He come."*

Could they have found Jake? Hope kindled a desperate rally.

And then, like a screened door had slammed in her face, she was suddenly thrust into the forest again.

The young Indian watched as the pretty blond woman was taken away, his expression pensive. He looked back to his elder, who was still clutching the two-way. After a minute, the older Indian set the radio on the ground, gave it a disdainful look, and walked away.

TREES WERE COMING AT her from high and low. Branches snapping, vines pulling, bark scraping. Bare skin being torn, new fire breaking out like embers landing up and down her arms and legs as the flies and mosquitoes fed in flight. Heat pulled oxygen from the air in vast sweeps. She was being roughly jostled through the harsh corridor of ever gloom green ushers, then some interminable time later, tilted and dropped.

The bed, in stale darkness, was familiar.

For a fleeting instant, shamefully, she felt relief to be out of the jungle. And then, imploding terror as she saw the shadow that loomed over her in the dark.

44

SOMEWHERE BEYOND THE DENSE canopy, the sun had begun to lighten the sky, but beneath the many layers of jungle the only sign of impending dawn was the stirring of its wild underbelly. Infinitesimal sights and sounds of the night-dwellers and those of the day passing them on the way out. Crawling, climbing, ambling, slithering, flying, hopping. Hiking.

On reuniting with his team, Jake had led them to a new location for staging, slightly closer to the guerrilla compound. Still stunned over Aguilar's defection, he had managed to check his anger but would not talk about what had transpired with the others, channeling his thoughts instead to the critical operation they would be launching very shortly— an operation severely compromised by the absence of Aguilar and his men. Now, as Jake's foursome sat in a square finishing off breakfast MREs, he eyed each in turn, his expression grave.

"Okay, gents, when you're done with chow, let's gear up and head out. It's time to go hot."

What remained of scrambled eggs and hash browns was quickly washed down with final swallows of strong coffee. Stifling groans of muscle-sore misery, Falcone and Niles stood and stretched. Tangeman and Petropoulos, knowing Jake's expectation of expediency, immediately turned their attention to the gear. Wisely, Falcone and Niles followed suit. When everything was ready, they assembled for rollout.

Loaded down with packs, supplies, weapons, and ammo, Falcone and Niles were already sweating heavily. Jake's experienced operators cast them mildly sympathetic looks.

Jake lifted a duffel bag and tossed it to Niles, whose arms came up to catch it only by reflex, almost dropping it. Grasping it clumsily, he looked at Jake in bewilderment. And then, a second later, he realized what he had.

Days ago, after the last phone call from Valentín—in which he had listened in tortured anguish as Callie was brutalized—Jake had gone to the Banco de Bogotá and opened an account by having money transferred from the Bahamian branch. The office manager had been most accommodating when the amount requested was a little over 800 million pesos, but not as happy when Jake withdrew most of it. Now, packed in stacks and rolls, the pesos bulged against the sides of the canvas bag. All 350,000 dollars' worth.

Niles gulped, hugged the duffel tighter to his chest.

Jake had decided to bait the narcoguerrillas with the $350,000 based on several factors, one being the estimated wealth of the cartel—despite its recent personal losses—and another being the average K&R payouts. Less might have been a temptation but possibly not enough to get the anticipated results; more would have likely invited a quick and homicidal reversal of fortune. This amount would be presented as a down payment with a balance-on-delivery condition. It was an inconsequential detail anyway, as Jake did not really expect the money to change hands, at least not for Callie's release. It was merely a point of his strategy to get to her.

If she's still alive, a demonic internal voice tormented. Ignoring the voice and abolishing the thought, he reviewed the mission objectives one final time, making sure each man knew exactly what he was doing and when. Precision timing for all tasks would be critical.

Addressing Niles and Tangeman who were paired up, Jake said, "Remember, the purpose of this is to compromise their security, get as many of their key guys together as you can. Diversion and distraction, that's the game. Secondly, you want to play on their greed to find out whatever you can about Callie's location. That's it, nothing more. And move it along quickly, we have to get in and get out. Be alert and listen for us so you can be ready." Jake looked pointedly at Niles. "Okay?"

"You got it," Niles responded crisply, trying to sound more confident than he felt. Deep down, he was as scared as he'd ever been during their entire time in Colombia. His heart was pounding a conga against his rib cage and his stomach was churning like a whirlpool. He took a bracing breath, and shifted the bulk of the rucksack strapped to his back. The weight of the duffel seemed implausibly heavier. He got nods all around and said, "Let's do it."

THE HIKE TO THE guerrilla compound and the reconnaissance that followed took them into the hottest part of the day. The sun, though darkened by the crown of trees, bore down without mercy. They took an hour to rest and rehydrate, then fell into their appointed roles. For the first phase, Jake and Petropoulos circled the compound, stealing up to the edge in between guerrilla patrols. They jockeyed swiftly and silently, in flawless synchronization, their handiwork masterfully undetectable.

The next phase belonged to Niles and Tangeman.

Through his Swarovski's, Jake watched as the pair strode up to the entrance of the compound, where they were met by a handful of guerrillas. Jake tensed as dialogue was exchanged, a pair of guerrillas withdrew in conference, then Niles and Tangeman were escorted inside. What happened next was largely out of his hands and a gigantic leap of faith. Or maybe utter stupidity. He prayed to the Great Abiding Spirit, the Buddha Man, God, or Whoever was listening, that it was not the latter.

NILES AND TANGEMAN WERE led straight to the command center. It was one of the larger and more sturdily built huts, located toward the core of the compound. The elements of construction suggested that it had been an Indian village not so long ago; unsurprisingly, there were no signs of any natives. Navigating a wooden plank walkway, they passed numerous barracks, smaller shacks, and other huts along the way, taking note of the personnel and armament as they went. Once inside the structure, also considered the safe house, Niles and Tangeman were presented to a guerrilla chieftain who was introduced as *Teniente* Lizarazo. At the entrance to the camp, Tangeman had authoritatively informed the sentries that he and Niles were expected. Niles had opened the duffel, giving them a fleeting glimpse of the cash, and they were subsequently ushered inside with little hesitation. Now, just as Jake had predicted, word of the money was spreading like wildfire throughout the compound, and in a matter of minutes several more ranking guerrillas materialized. Perhaps even more importantly, the hut was occupied and surrounded by armed security personnel.

In Spanish, *Teniente* Lizarazo curtly inquired about the nature of their business. He stood before Niles and Tangeman, beefy arms crossed over his olive uniform with an inimical expression on face. An armed man was planted at each elbow.

Tangeman, whose level of Spanish was competent, did the talking. Keeping his tone cool and concise, he explained that they were here to make a down payment on the ransom for the American woman.

This was met with raised eyebrows and a conspiratorial interplay between Lizarazo and another high-ranking comrade standing nearby. Their eyes locked, looks passed, and Lizarazo said, "I was not aware we had made such a demand."

"We were contacted initially by *Commandante* Máximo Castillo, and then by Adonís Valentín himself," Tangeman replied.

"*Señor* Valentín contacted you?" Lizarazo inquired, brows raised. The fingers of his hand drummed across the top of a cellular phone clipped to his belt. "When was this?"

"Today," Tangeman answered. "Just a few hours ago. Call him yourself if you wish. He said you were given full authority to make the deal."

Lizarazo plucked the cell phone from his belt, palmed it, paused, flipped it open. Punched a few buttons. Watched them as he lifted the phone to his ear. Then abruptly snapped it shut. "Let me see this money," he said stiffly, casting a skeptical eye toward the duffel Niles carried.

In response, Niles lifted the bag, braced it on one arm, and drew the zipper back. Tugging the opening aside, he tilted it enough to show the greens, browns, blues, and purples of large-denomination peso notes.

Sweat glistened over Lizarazo's thick brows and there was an oiliness in his eyes as he stepped over to finger the money, doing some kind of mental calculation as he poked through it. There was a collective murmur among the other men assembled.

Abruptly, Niles zipped it shut and let it swing casually to his side.

Before Lizarazo could say anything, Tangeman said, "Now, you understand this is just the down payment. The other half will be paid at the time of release."

"The other half," Lizarazo repeated, wetting his lips as he did the math and visualized the abundant possibilities of $700,000. "I see." Drawing himself up with a snide grin before slipping back into his callous demeanor, he said, "Yes, I have the authority to negotiate this deal."

"Before we proceed any further," Tangeman said tightly, "we must see the woman to make sure we are not paying for the release of a dead body. *Prueba de vida.*" Beside him, Niles' arm twitched. Tangeman nudged him discreetly to conceal the movement.

Yet another ranking guerrilla had emerged, this one referred to only as Rocha. Eying the duffel with salacious longing, his response to Tangeman was acerbic. "Certainly the woman is alive, but she is not on these premises."

"There is no deal without proof of life," Tangeman said dauntlessly, repeating the standard K&R term known to every Colombian abductor and hostage negotiator.

"Well, if you require—"

His words were lost in a series of explosions, ear-numbingly near and rumbling the ground beneath them. This sent everyone but Lizarazo and Rocha scrambling. They were both staring at Niles and Tangeman in livid surprise when a close, powerful series of shots blew a large hole in the side of the hut.

WHILE NILES AND TANGEMAN had been discussing ransom with the guerrilla chieftains, Jake was taking advantage of the scattering personnel and security weakened by their diminishing numbers. Quite a few of them had gravitated to the vicinity of the command center to see what was going to transpire with the civilians that had unexpectedly shown up. With Falcone nervously covering him, Jake slipped up behind the sole guard remaining at the entrance, clapped one hand over his mouth and thrust a knife up his rectum with the other.

Falcone watched in raw, mouth-gaping horror as Jake jerked the knife out, wiped it on his pants, and released the man who was already paralyzed. Blood vessels rupturing massively, the guerrilla sentry was dead when he hit the ground.

"Je-suus!" Falcone hissed, his eyes popping like hot embers.

Wordlessly, Jake grabbed Falcone's arm and pulled him on, heading for the radio shack. On the way, he took out several more men, some with his hands, others with his knife; there could be no noise until they got closer. Crouched in some brush near a group of guerrillas, Jake and Falcone waited for the next phase of the operation.

They did not have to wait long, only a matter of minutes.

Jake checked his watch just as things began to blow up.

First, vehicles parked near the camp's entrance went up in rapid succession, big booms producing huge, shooting fireballs and rolling black smoke. Next, random targets around the perimeter of the compound exploded, mostly barracks and huts. These splintered apart, collapsing like matchsticks, and then burned. Finally, munitions storage shacks began to go up in spectacular, incendiary displays that generated their own series of explosions. Guerrilla soldiers were running haphazardly from one detonation to the next, shouting chaotically back and forth across the compound.

Where there had been several guerrillas stationed at the radio hooch, only two remained when the fireworks started. Now, the pair was working feverishly to establish radio contact, something that Jake promptly made impossible by slicing the support wires to the antenna rig. When he and Falcone emerged from behind the hooch, the two guerrillas rushed them.

Falcone, whose only fighting instincts involved fists, never went for his weapon, but instead began to block and counter-strike his assailant. The guerrilla, outsizing him by several inches in height and a good many more pounds in weight, swiftly gained the advantage and landed solid shots to Falcone's upper body.

Keeping an eye on Falcone, Jake brought a quick end to his own skirmish with a direct strike to his attacker's throat, followed by a powerful throw that fractured the guerrilla's skull on impact with the ground. Now coming to Falcone's defense, Jake grabbed the second guerrilla and spun him around, but before the guerrilla could engage him in combat, Jake jabbed his knife into the man's collarbone. The guerrilla's aorta burst, pulsing thick red streams of blood as he dropped to the ground.

Running toward the command center, Jake yelled back to Falcone, "Come on! And use your fucking gun! That's what it's for!"

Panting, Falcone shouted, "Okay, okay!" and checked his MAC-10 to make sure it was ready to fire.

They slowed about eight meters from the command center, crouched low, and scurried around the side. Jake peered through the entrance as they passed, catching a glimpse of Niles and Tangeman, noting their position inside. Then, waiting for another explosion, he leveled his Galil rifle, aiming it behind Niles and Tangeman, and blasted a hole in the wall of the hut. The edges crumbled, widening its aperture. He extracted the automatic pistol tucked into his waistband and tossed it in to Tangeman. As Tangeman shielded Niles and ducked away, rushing from the command center, Jake tossed a frag grenade in their wake. It skittered inside and went off with a concussive boom, blasting the building apart. Bodies and pieces of bodies flew out in all directions.

Catching up to Niles and Tangeman, Jake shouted, "Where are they holding her?"

"Don't know," Niles yelled back, "but not here!"

Jake stared at Niles in quivering intensity. "Did you get *anything* from them?" he demanded.

"They said she's still alive," Tangeman offered, adding soberly, "if we can believe they weren't just playing for the money."

"Fuck," Jake barked.

He put his hands on his hips and deflected his stare to the ground. Corralled his frustration and growing desperation, then raised his head. Another check of his watch told him that the charges he and Petropoulos had rigged earlier were done. Jake was about to try to raise Alberto Hernandez on his radio when a familiar sound from above stopped him. And hit his gut like an iron wrecking ball.

Rotors. Lots of them. Growing louder, closer.

"Oh God," he murmured as he looked up, wiping grimy sweat and blood streaks from his face. A pair of green UH-60 Huey helicopters roared overhead, followed by a fleet of Blackhawks. They were flying at treetop level, door gunners with M60 machine guns and M79 grenade launchers clearly visible. Doing final recon and security for the imminent interdiction. "Counternarcotics are moving in," Jake told them. "You guys have got to get out of here."

"What do you mean *we've* got get out of here?" Falcone demanded.

"Just what I said," Jake replied emphatically. "I've got to find Callie, but you guys are outta here—now."

"No fucking way!" Falcone blustered, stepping up to Jake. Then, rethinking his aggression, took one step back.

"We don't have time to argue about this," Jake muttered hastily. "Let's just see what's on the far side of this compound."

As they zigzagged their way to the rear of the encampment, dodging burning remnants and passing a few dazed-looking guerrillas who were too busy tending the fires to launch any initiatives, Jake tried to make radio contact with Hernandez. He was unsuccessful.

They plunged into the jungle beyond the camp, finding a path that cut through a stretch extending about a hundred meters. On emerging from the forest edge about an hour later, the first thing they became aware of, dramatically, was a fiery tangerine sunset, the light of day all but gone. The next thing was the electrifying image of a dark silhouette against the deep orange of dying sun—a hacienda at the top of a short rise. Fenced cattle grazed lazily around it, as did pastured horses. A satellite dish and HF radio antenna sprouted from the roof of the ranch house.

"Piss damned, what do you know," Jake marveled. "I think we found the son of a bitch."

45

"SO LET'S GO GET the bloody bastard!" Niles exhorted.

"Okay," Jake cautioned, "just because we practically wiped out his narco camp does not mean we're home free. Far from it."

Petropoulos nodded his head in accord. "Jake's right. We must be very, very careful."

Jake instructed Tangeman to keep trying to make radio contact with Hernandez. He really needed a situation report from Hernandez so they could minimize their risk by exiting at the infil points, but he realized the chance of this was growing slimmer by the minute.

As they advanced cautiously up the hill, Petropoulos relayed GPS and compass readings while Tangeman again attempted to make contact with Hernandez. They closed in on the ranch house, which was surrounded by metal fencing topped with concertina. Petropoulos went to work with tensile wire cutters and opened a section large enough for them to fit through. Tersely instructing Falcone and Niles to stay back with Tangeman, Jake and Petropoulos crept low along the lengthening shadows.

They spotted four men, paired off at the corners of the house. The guerrillas were clad in dark fatigues tucked into rubber boots, draped with bandoleers of ammunition for the M16s they carried. They appeared to be taking their guard duty seriously enough, periodically surveying the surrounding landscape through the scopes of their rifles.

But boredom prompted some distraction in the form of picking off small animals that scampered across the gap between fence and forest. Their silenced M16s made thumping sounds as shells hit the ground or something like a thwack with a high-pitched screech when hitting a target. Jake and Petropoulos waited until the second pair tired of the game and ambled around to the back of the house, and then tossed a rock to divert the shooters' attention. When the pair headed over to investigate the noise, Jake and Petropoulos rushed in and struck them from behind, knifing both simultaneously in the base of their skulls. They dragged the bodies a short distance from the house, just out of viewing range, and returned for the others. When the second pair of guards came back around the front of the ranch, Jake and Petropoulos were waiting at the corner, and took them out the same way as the first.

Standing in the open garage bay where a freshly washed and waxed Lexus GX 4x4 was parked, Jake turned to Petropoulos and said, "Okay, my brother. I need you to go back and take care of my guys."

"No, Jake. Tang is with them. I need to cover you. You don't know what you're going to find in there."

Jake shook his head resolutely. "No, Petrie, I can handle him. Watch the guys. Please. And keep trying to get Alberto on the radio for a sitrep."

"Okay," Petropoulos sighed, frowning in disapproval. "Be careful."

"And Petrie, if counternarcotics start striking anywhere close, don't wait for me. Get the hell out and take the guys with you." When Petropoulos did not answer, Jake said, "I mean it."

Petropoulos nodded without another word. As he retreated into the afterburn of sunset, he glanced over his shoulder and saw Jake disappear through the interior garage door.

IT WAS EERILY QUIET, but Jake sensed Valentín's presence as soon as he entered the house. It was a primal feeling.

He detected the faintest musky scent as he crossed the foyer to the hall. It was a scent vaguely sexual, steeped in masculine sweat, and one instantly repulsive to Jake. He gave the living room and adjacent areas a cursory scan. Twilight shadows were swiftly overtaking the interior, drifting across from heavy window panels that lined the back wall. The décor was almost identical to that of the Suesca estate, Spanish-Mediterranean with dark furnishings and artsy accents. A pervasively greasy smell emanated from the kitchen, cooking odors from a recently cooked dinner, some kind of beef. He padded down the long, dim hallway, careful to minimize the sound of his boots on the ceramic floor, listening intently with each step. Heard nothing. Just the eerie quiet.

With his Glock in front of him, he peered cautiously in an open doorway on his left. And felt his heart clutch. The room was spare, with one high window, a wooden stand below it, and a bed with a worn wool blanket. Jake felt the bony fingers of foreboding drum up his spine, felt the wraith of helpless desperation that hovered in the room's dank air. As did a trace of the repulsive musk, musk and something else. He smelled fear. *She had been here.* But how long ago? Was she still here, elsewhere in the house?

He quickly checked the small bathroom, then slipped back into the hall and resumed his search, passing servants' quarters on both sides. Neither was occupied though they appeared to have recently been so. When he reached the end of the hallway, he tensed, halting several feet from what appeared to be a larger bedroom.

Listening, still hearing nothing, Jake swung into the door opening, leaned in.

The room was empty. *Goddammit, it was empty!* But not, he saw immediately, undisturbed. Not at all. Even from the doorway, the disarray of bed linens was dramatic, with spread hanging over the footboard, pillows on the floor, and sheets half pulled out. His gut wrenched. She wasn't here.

No, no, no! He fought the urge to scream, felt his lungs fill and burn.

Now he looked frantically around the room, even though he knew there was nothing else to see. And he'd seen more than enough.

Where had the son of a bitch taken her? *Valentin had to still be here. Had to.*

Pivoting on heel, he left the room and sprinted back through the house, this time looking for another way in or out. He spotted a door off the kitchen and headed for it. Found it unlocked. Stepping outside, his boots touched gravel and then dirt and then grass. The horses and cattle he'd spied from below the rise were corralled to his left, with the rest of the rear yard encircled by a tall wooden fence. Like the metal one in front, it was strung with barbed wire and embellished with concertina. He strode to the gate centered at the back and found it latched and locked.

"Fuck!" he exclaimed, uselessly jerking the heavy steel padlock. But, as it was locked from the inside, obviously no one had left through this gate. In the rapidly dwindling dusk, he surveyed the right side. Paced over, sweeping the Glock in an arc around him. Stopped at another gate.

This one was ajar, presenting him with two directions to take. To the right was a dirt airstrip and a hangar large enough to house two small planes; only one, a Cessna Citation, was berthed. To the left was a tree-lined pathway leading into progressively thickening woods. Distantly, but coming closer, he could hear the sound of jet aircraft and artillery. He knew it wouldn't be long now. "God, no," he implored to the sky he could no longer see. "She's got to be here. She's just got to be here somewhere."

He pushed through the gate, pulled his NVGs over his eyes, and started down the path.

JAKE HAD HIKED THE length of the trail, some two hundred meters, when he heard the sound of muted clanking. A strange sound in the jungle. He edged past the tree line and stepped into the clearing on the other side.

And halted dead in his tracks.

Another hundred meters from where he stood was a second ranch house, but his eyes were riveted on what was pastured in the yard that led to it. A block of large cages ensnared a collection of jungle cats, a half-dozen of which were pacing just behind the metal bars. From the muffled rumblings in the background, a good many more were concealed by the brush-covered enclosures spread within the housing. There were solid-coated, striped, and spotted ones, healthy specimens all, but their hunger was unmistakable as they drew to the sides of their cages and honed in on him with voracious eyes. Moving slowly, Jake reached into his ammo pouch and extracted the Glock's silencer, palming another seventeen-round magazine for good measure. Screwed the suppressor onto the muzzle. Slowly advanced, keeping his eye on the pacing cats. Their eyes followed him as well.

He had cleared the cages and was within fifty yards of the house when a deep growl—much too loud, much too close—rolled behind him, curdling his testicles and resonating in the base of his spine. He turned slowly around and found himself gazing into the face of a spotted beast, uncaged, eyes reflecting white through the PVS-7s' filter. Its teeth were white, too, showing from behind twitching lips. A vice of perfect sabers. It was the distance of a parking space.

The cat hunkered down, tensed, its eyes riveted on Jake, tail swishing—attack posturing. Watching, deciding. His legs moved, slightly. His eyes never did.

Jake inhaled sharply, held his breath for a few beats, then let it ease back out. In a low, measured tone, he said, "Easy, big guy…easy now. Let's do this real easy." The cat eyed him warily, still hesitating. Jake stood perfectly still, held his ground. But the cat began to advance, creeping almost imperceptibly. Jake fought the impulse to back away— something he knew never to do with an animal, especially a wild one— and remained still. He held the Glock with both hands but did not point it.

The cat was on him in one powerful leap, roar ripping from his chest as he thrust his body into the air. He hit Jake just as the Glock came up, knocking the gun out of his grip. The cat's bulk felt like a car had dropped on top of him, and he sucked at the air to catch the breath crushed out of his lungs. Jake angled his elbow up beneath the cat's chin and jabbed hard, which bought him a few precious seconds during which he was able to draw his knife. Swinging his arm wide of the cat's torso, he targeted the collarbone but missed and struck somewhere near the shoulder blade. The animal screamed in furious agony and bore down, jaws gaping wide with teeth splayed, and Jake felt its claws digging through his sleeves and into his flesh. In seconds, the teeth would be tearing into him, serrating muscle and pulverizing bone. Channeling all of his energy in one concentrated move, knowing if he failed it would probably be his last, Jake pummeled his knee up into the cat's groin. Hit his spot, in the big male's genitals, and rolled away from the yowling beast. Grappled on the ground for the Glock.

But just as Jake thought his aggression would deter the cat, as was the typical response, it launched another attack, catapulting through the air. Jake shot him twice in the chest and dodged to the side. Pivoted and squeezed off several more rounds. The big cat screamed and writhed and finally dropped to the ground with a resounding thud, inches from Jake's feet. Blood flowered from the gunshots, spreading over the ringed rosettes that dotted the luxurious pelt. The massive male jaguar flailed for a few more moments and then stopped moving, eyes glassy and nostrils still.

With a deep but shaky breath, Jake tucked the Glock back in his pants, turned and moved on toward the house.

THE DOORS WERE SECURELY locked, constructed of heavily reinforced material, the windows high and shuttered. This, Jake deduced, was a safe house. As such, by intent and design, it would be virtually impenetrable. But was it Valentín's? Was he here? Was she?

Your woman is dead.

Once again, he felt the tide of desperation washing in, further onto the rapidly receding shore of hope. He had to find a way into this house. Completing a circuit from front to back, he found no obvious breaches. Looking up, he wondered about the roof, speculating that maybe there would be a vent he could pull out or, if not, some loose roofing material that could be peeled back to expose underlayment that could be punched through. The roof was constructed of clay tiles over a wood frame, but with the satellite dishes and other communications antennas, there was a good possibility of a gap or weak spot. He shimmied up a corner, using a window frame for leverage, and hoisted himself onto the top of the house. And instantly saw his way in.

Centered over what was probably the living room, was a rectangular glass panel. A skylight. Clambering over to it, he removed the NVGs and looked down inside. As he had guessed, the space below was a living room, and even from here he could see that it was distinctly more elegant than that of the other house. The furnishings were designer, expensive, and pristine. Accents were selective and provocative. Art was abundant and dramatic. But who did it belong to? More importantly, was anybody home?

Poised over the skylight, Jake suddenly heard the clatter of helicopters above, the distant hum of planes, sporadic bursts of firepower. Counternarcotics were here. *God, dear God, they were here.* He wondered if Tangeman or Petropoulos had made radio contact with Hernandez. And, if they had, he wondered if it would make any difference. The interdiction, it seemed, was well underway.

He had to get into the house.

Before he had a chance to examine the skylight closer, a deafening clamor gnashed above and, simultaneously, a powerful downdraft swept across the roof, knocking him flat. A helicopter passing directly overhead. The gust sent him sliding to the edge of the house, boots scudding across the tiles, hands grasping but not taking hold. He felt the whistle of night about to eject him. Just as he was about to go hurtling off the side, his hand latched onto an elevated tile. Holding on, he twisted onto his stomach, got his knees under him, and regained his footing.

Zero time left, he admonished himself. Zero time.

He scuttled hastily back to the skylight and began working on the frame. His fingers poked and prodded but found no give. He peered through the glass, saw what was directly below. Made his decision. Straightening up, he jumped into the center of the panel and punched through the glass, bending his knees as soon as he cleared. And landed, bouncing off a wide overstuffed chair that matched the indigo sofa.

Uncertain of how much commotion he'd made in the crash and landing, he took cover behind the chair and crouched there for a minute, listening for any stirring within the house. While he waited, he checked himself for injury and was relieved to find only one substantial laceration along one arm. It wasn't bleeding too badly but while he did not want to waste precious time tending it, he knew better than to risk exposure to jungle infection, so he quickly ripped a strip of fabric from his camo fatigues and wrapped it. When there appeared to be no response to his forceful break-in, Jake stood and took in the surroundings.

As he had observed from the rooftop, the house's interior had *Architectural Digest* quality elegance. The indigo living room group was offset by lighter Satinwood tables, the tile and wood floors partially covered with intricately patterned rugs. There were several big lamps distributed through the room—a couple on surfaces, one hanging from an ornate chain in a corner, and one standing in another corner—but none of them were illuminated. The house was filling with darkness and deadly quiet.

God, she had to be here—*had to be*—where else could she be? An image of the half-empty airplane hangar flashed into his mind. *No!* No, no, no.

He proceeded cautiously toward the hallway, passing a formal dining room on the left and a kitchen twice its size on the right. Still, he heard nothing. But this hallway was much lengthier than that of the other house and, he was betting, the soundproofing substantial. He continued his advance, but a large room near a bend in the hall stopped him. What he saw both mesmerized and horrified him. The room was set up as a command and control center, outfitted with the latest communications and computer technology. But that wasn't what arrested his attention—it was the corkboard above an electronic console. Next to a collection of mapped locations, places he knew most intimately, were high-resolution enlargements of photographs. Of himself in Colombia, framed in the door of a Huey and standing in a jungle clearing, with Delaney…and of Callie, on the beach in Dominical. The picture of her, so utterly vulnerable in the sights of the photographer, nearly brought him to his knees. The telephoto shot was so graphic he could see her eyelashes, fine as an artist's paintbrush. Jake's heart felt like a cannon in his chest. Valentín had not called today.

He pulled out of the room in a blind frenzy and turned the hall corner. Here, thick carpeting started and extended the remaining distance to what was, undoubtedly, the master bedroom. He held back, flattened himself against the darkest wall, and listened.

For the first time, he began to hear sounds.

The same guttural animal noises he'd heard on Valentín's call grunted into the silence—and the effect was like the brutal force and shrieking sound and crushing weight of a train wreck in his brain. His pulse throbbed, his heart pounded, his muscles tensed, all of his senses heightened. Adrenaline pumped through his body like rocket fuel. The breath passing through his lungs felt like shattered glass. Fighting the overpowering urge to race the rest of the way down the hall and into the bedroom, he maintained his slow, cautious pace. Tilting his head, he listened closely, needing to hear more—not wanting to, but needing to. And he did. When he was halfway to the bedroom door, he heard Callie.

Hot and cold waves in his universe collided, crashing against the hard rocks of his inner turmoil.

She was alive, and Valentín was hurting her again.

He could hear Valentín, muttering irritably, slamming something hard onto a wooden surface, shattering something. Seconds later, Jake stiffened. The cell phone on his belt was vibrating. He turned it off without looking at it; he knew who had called him.

That's okay, you fucking son of a bitch...I'll be answering you soon enough.

He continued silently down the hall and was just outside the bedroom door when he heard the metallic creak of the bed as Valentín vaulted onto it. Then he heard a pained cry from Callie, shrill but weak, followed by the violent heaving of the bed. It was Callie's cry more than Valentín's grunts that impaled his heart and set off the rage he'd been suppressing. It burned savagely inside him, exploded deafeningly all around him, like an apocalyptic war of galaxies. But the instant he burst into the room, a cold iron fist reached from somewhere deep within and closed around the inferno of wild emotion.

Valentín was so caught up in the fervor of his assault that he failed to hear Jake behind him.

In one fluid motion, Jake slipped his open hand beneath Valentín's face and, using it like a knife, sliced upward to his nose. The move peeled Valentín off Callie with effortless force—Jake did not want him dying in her or on her—and finished with his body slamming into the wall with bone-cracking impact. Momentarily stunned, Valentín stared at him, wheezing for his breath. Then, unbelievably, his mouth snarled into a smile of triumph. "So...I got you here, after all," he murmured, and took a step toward Jake.

Jake said nothing, did not move. But his peripheral vision had swept over Valentín's groin, where blood was beaded stickily in the thatch of pubic hair protruding from his open jeans; he was still rigid, grotesquely tumescent. Jake felt fury of indescribable depth burst like a mortar in his head, but he pulled all of that fury into the very center of himself and waited.

Valentín took another step. "The first time I saw your pretty *muñequita*, I knew how to make you come." He laughed crudely as if he had made some lurid joke. "So, let us do it. Show me what you are really made of. No weapons"—he gritted his teeth—"no fucking explosions...just you and me." He extended his hands, wriggled his fingers in a *come-on* gesture. One more step put him less than an arm's length away. Tongue swirling around his lips, he oozed, "She is a very fine little bitch and I had her begging for my—"

Jake's hands came up and snapped his neck with a quick angled twist to the right.

He released his grip and let Valentín's body drop to the floor. Hell could have him now. His focus shifted to Callie.

She was cowering on the bed in a fetal position, wearing the same bloodied white dress, trembling fearfully and sobbing convulsively. When he reached for her, she recoiled in terror, quaking even more severely, her chest heaving. At the sight of her lacerated and insect-bitten skin, blistered and infected, his throat knotted.

Still not seeing him, Callie whined, "No, no, no"—then, in a pitiful voice that broke his heart—*"Jake?"*

"Yes, angel," he soothed. "I'm here. It's all right. Take it easy, love," he said, gently stroking her forehead. It was as hot as toast.

Her eyes opened wide at the sound of his voice, and for a moment she desperately held the gaze.

"It's all right," he repeated reassuringly. "Let me just take a quick look and then I'm gonna get you outta here." He checked her pulse and, slipping his hand between her legs noted the considerable bleeding. The sheets were spattered and smeared with more of her blood. Distantly, he heard the rumble of artillery and knew there was no time to do anything for her now. He ripped a strip from the bed sheet, wove it between and around her thighs. Tied it gently. "Okay," he said, "let's go," and carefully scooped her up in his arms.

As he cradled her quivering frame against him and began to retreat down the hall, he felt the tension drain from her body, the quivers subside, and knew she'd lost consciousness. She was in bad shape and urgently needed medical attention. Carrying her out of the ranch house, he kissed her cheek, whispering, "Stay with me, precious…stay with me. We're gonna get out of here."

He hoped no more cats were on the loose.

46

THE NIGHT VIBRATED WITH the invasion of helicopters, the whisk of blades swirling artificial coolness through the oppressive humidity. At first the sounds had been distant, along with the steady drone of jets. But within the last ten minutes or so, ever since Petropoulos emerged from the ranch house without Jake, the sounds had gradually amplified, and now they were deafening. The helicopters and planes were almost on top of them, counternarcotics closing in. Dusk had given way to evening, and below in the narcoguerrilla compound the fires were finally dying out. Darkness was descending swiftly.

Following Jake's instructions, Tangeman continued to call Hernandez on the radio, but the efforts had so far proven futile. Now, listening to the approaching aircraft—squadrons of Fantasma gunships trailed by Kfir jets and OV-10 Broncos—Petropoulos and Tangeman were grappling with an agonizing dilemma.

"Jake said when they got close, he wanted us outta here," Petropoulos said, more to Tangeman than to Falcone and Niles, who had been huddled in fretful abeyance.

This got a vehement reaction from Falcone. "Not without Jake!"

"We've got to, Eddie," Petropoulos insisted. "He made me promise. I'm betting he'll be right behind us. But we go...*now*."

"No!" Falcone screamed over the engine noise thundering above.

"Sorry, Eddie," Tangeman said, "but I'm with Petrie. We always do what he tells us. Jake will make it. If we don't get out of here now, we may not."

"I'm not fucking leaving! I'm going after him, he may need some help!" He started up the hill toward the ranch.

"Eddie, listen to them!" Niles pleaded.

The commanding voice Falcone had come to dread and respect boomed from just beyond them. "Let's get the hell out of here! You should already be gone!" They all turned to see Jake coming over the rise, Callie in his arms. "The cavalry's here in case you hadn't noticed, but they won't know the good guys from the bad."

"Is she—?" Falcone began.

Jake did not respond, brushing past them. They followed him down the hill, away from the house. When they reached the bottom, Armageddon hit ground zero.

Bombardment seemed to come from every level and direction, underscored by the constant rattle of gunfire. Nearby, they could hear frantic rustling in the jungle, guerrillas or counternarcotics or both. Shouting to Tangeman, Jake asked, "Did you get Alberto?"

When Tangeman shook his head, Jake yelled, "Keep trying!"

Petropoulos fell in stride beside Jake. "So how are we going to get out of here?" he asked. "You think there's any way we can exfil by river?"

"Since we had to leave the Zodiac, I don't see how. But I don't think we're going to make it in time on foot. There's a Citation parked in a hangar back at the house, but since none of us are pilots I don't think that's an option."

"A Citation, no shit?" Petropoulos whistled. "Wow. Maybe between us we could manage?"

"Possibly. But there are two problems with that...one, we don't have any idea if it's fueled and no time to take the chance and two, with all the firepower in the air we'd be the biggest fucking target outside of the ground structures. No, we've got to get as far away from here as quickly as we can. I say, let's just head to the river and we'll figure something out."

They jogged through the outlying jungle, the artillery practically on top of them. Just ahead, through the green filter of the PVS-7s, Jake saw the river. And, incredibly, after hiking a short distance along the edge, he saw something he least expected—a boat. It was a small aluminum fishing dinghy, with oars and an outboard motor. A tight fit for all of them, but with the interdiction operation closing in, they would have to make it work.

When the others had climbed into the boat, steadying it by pairing off at opposite ends, Jake handed a lifeless Callie down and stepped in at the center. As Petropoulos pushed off, the boat caught the current and began pulling downriver. Tangeman and Falcone worked feverishly on what turned out to be a frustratingly dysfunctional motor, only getting it to work for brief intervals, but it was enough to get the boat's momentum going upriver. While Falcone and Tangeman fought the outboard, Petropoulos divided his time between rowing and trying to raise Hernandez on the radio. He continued to get nothing more than static. They also tried to connect by sat and cell phones, to no avail.

Drawing Callie across his lap, Jake leaned down and was relieved to hear very faint breath sounds. Next to him, Niles asked tentatively, "Is she going to be all right?"

"Things are not good right now," Jake said grimly. "I'm going to need you to get some stuff from my bag." With that, he immersed himself in Callie's care, and as his hands moved over her in the darkness, he could feel her blood on his fingertips. Always stoic on the line and in the heat, Jake could feel his armor breaking down with this fragile life in his lap.

As the boat sputtered up the dark river, penetrating the even darker night, they became suddenly aware of another presence. Jake signaled for them to kill the gurgling motor. Petropoulos also suspended his paddling as they listened and heard the approach of other boats. In minutes they would pass within meters of each other. Indians or narcos, and probably the latter, escaping the counternarcotics raid.

"Everybody down!" Jake urged in a whisper, covering Callie with his body. Reaching beside him, he pushed Niles down just as gunfire whizzed over their heads.

Tangeman and Petropoulos were paddling furiously to get past as bullets splashed all around them in the water, some pinging off the aluminum sides of the boat. Jake kept his body over Callie's but rose up enough to fire his Glock. Tangeman joined in and dug out additional magazines for their weapons, tossing some to Niles for Jake's. They reloaded and continued firing. Through his NVGs, Jake saw guerrillas in speedboats, racing past them. Many fell over like metal shooting gallery targets, others kept firing.

There was a splash near the rear of the boat, followed by a muted boom and a violent roiling that sent the stern into the air and then slammed it back down. The boat pitched sharply sideways and water sprayed up and over the sides as Tangeman and Petropoulos fought to keep it from flipping.

"Somebody try to get that goddamn motor going!" Jake yelled. Just as Falcone succeeded, eliciting an anemic cough from the engine that stuttered into a choppy buzz, Jake heard him yelp.

With the boat now sluicing upriver and apparently out of shooting range, Jake shouted, "Did you get hit?"

"I think so!" Eddie shouted back. "I feel like my face is on fire!"

"Okay, shut the motor off now," Jake instructed. "Tang, can you check him?"

In a minute, Tangeman called out, "It's okay, just a graze."

"It sure as hell doesn't feel like just a graze," Falcone grimaced.

"Get some gauze from my bag and put pressure on it."

Jake's attention returned to Callie. Shining a penlight over her, he saw that she was still unconscious and very pale. "Stay with me, precious," he pleaded. "Stay with me, we're almost there."

But as they rounded a bend in the river, they plowed into a wall of mud that had slathered down the increasingly steep embankments. The nose of the boat hit the mud damn with a solid thud, water cascading down on top of them. Looking ahead, Jake could see there was no way to proceed further by river. At least not without hiking some distance with the boat in tow. The other four climbed out and then helped him with Callie. Jake knelt on the ground and held her against his knee, pausing to check on her. She stirred with a moan, her eyelids fluttering open, and immediately began shaking. Holding her face, he could feel her jaw trembling in his hand.

"Hurts," she sobbed, hands weakly clutching her abdomen.

"I know, baby, I know," Jake said, pained, noting that she was going into shock. Gesturing to Niles for his medical bag, he dug out an ampoule of morphine. Filling a hypodermic, he injected her thigh. She flinched against him, crying, but several seconds later her shaking eased. She was still bleeding. "God, I've got to give her more medical attention," Jake said, his voice strained with anguish. "But we've got to get the hell out of here. Still can't get Alberto?"

Tangeman shook his head in frustration. "But I'm still trying."

Jake stood, lifting her up in his arms again, and said, "Let's just hike a ways and see if we can find a semi-cleared area. Maybe then there might even be enough reception for cell or sat. Hell, there was back at that bastard's ranch."

They began to maneuver along a series of switchbacks winding toward a steep ridge, following the river as the basin dropped farther and farther down. Aside from jungle sounds, it had been mostly quiet for the past thirty minutes or so, with only an occasional fusillade of fire in the distance. On one hand, that was good, meaning they were moving away from the interdiction; on the other hand, it meant they were also moving further out of exfil range. And then, all at once, the wind of fate— and the battlefield—shifted again. Thunderous artillery rolled in from just beyond the embankment they skirted, and from the rumbles beneath their feet and the increasing volume, it seemed they were about to find themselves right in the crosshairs.

"Jesus Christ, what are they doing?" Petropoulos screamed.

"Shit, I don't know," Jake ranted, beginning to feel the weight of desperation. "Must be some labs over here somewhere. No river navigation, no bird, no radio contact, we are fucked." He looked around, peering through the NVGs, and saw some kind of platform about five or six meters in front of them.

When they got to it, halting right at the edge of the embankment, there was a collective gasp.

"Holy shit," Falcone exclaimed.

The platform, which consisted of a few dozen crudely cut boards that had been anchored into the ground with heavy metal spikes, overlooked the abyss of a cavernous gorge. Strung across the river basin was a steel cable.

"Tang, Petrie, one of you scope out the other side," Jake directed. "I want to know why there's a cable here. There's got to be a reason."

Petropoulos raised a night vision scope and scanned the far

embankment. "Well, for one thing, there's a big clearing. Might even be an LZ."

"What?" Falcone asked, feeling ignorant for the innumerable time.

"Landing zone," Tangeman enlightened.

"Bloody Christ," Niles blurted. "Surely we're not going to—"

"Looks like we are," Jake said. "I've got a couple of harnesses. We've just got to determine if the cable will hold."

"Oh God, you can't be serious," Falcone muttered feebly. "Why can't we stay right here and just keep trying to get Alberto on the radio?"

The noise of gunships overhead nearly drowned him out.

Shouting, Jake said, "That's why! Apparently we're not going to get a signal unless we get to a clearing. Look around!"—he swept his arm in a semi-circle—"Every other direction is jungle."

"But what if—"

"Eddie, I don't have time for this," Jake snapped. "Let's go!"

Petropoulos had dug out the harnesses and was stepping into one, attaching the sling. "I'll go first," he said. "I think I weigh the most."

"Okay, bro," Jake said. He knelt on the platform to take a closer look at the cable. It was made of twisted steel, thickness the circumference of a dime. He knew that most zip line cables had a test strength of about twelve thousand pounds. In optimal, well-maintained condition. Properly anchored and regularly tightened. This was no zip line and there was no telling how, or if, it was maintained. A single pulley hung near the platform edge, but it did not look particularly sturdy. In fact, it looked ancient. Jake tested the line with a series of hard jerks and though it seemed secure, he had his doubts. He came away with a handful of rust, which meant corrosion.

Petropoulos clipped onto the cable and carefully eased his bulk over the rim of the bank. Holding onto Tangeman and Falcone, he let his legs dangle, bounced in the harness to test the pull of his weight. The cable held.

"Let 'er rip!" he said, giving a thumbs-up. Tangeman and Falcone reluctantly let go and watched in open-mouthed awe as the big man slid across, dipped at the far side and worked his way up to the bank. Jake had rigged the carabiner with parachute cord, and drew it back over.

A horrified Falcone and Niles were sent second and third. Both made it cleanly, if not without some shrill outbursts as they completed their crossings.

As he slipped into a harness, Jake asked Tangeman, "How much do you think Petrie weighs?"

"Gee, I don't know…210? 225?"

"Yeah, that's what I thought." Jake looked down at Callie, unconscious on the ground at his feet. "Thing is, there's no way I'm going to send Callie across by herself. She's a little thing, but if we go together—I mean, I'm 165, she's what, 100…105?—that would be pushing 270."

Tangeman whistled. "Damn, Jake. I don't know. Are you sure you want to take that chance? We've had three go across and we have no idea what that old cable will bear. We could rig something and pull her across. She's out of it, she'd never even know."

Jake flashed back to Callie's terror of the zip line in Costa Rica. "No," he said firmly. "I can't do that. I'll have to take the chance."

An explosion hit close by with such force it rocked them off their feet. Callie regained consciousness in a frightened wail. Jake bent down and began fitting the harness around her, taking extra care. "It's okay, love. It's almost over. Callie, we're going to do something right now that's going to be a little scary, and I know you're hurting but we have to do this. I want you to trust me and just hold on. Okay? Will you do that?"

Her eyes were glassy with fear, but he could also see she was shocky and did not grasp what he was saying.

Jake was clipping a sling to the carabiner when his fingers rubbed over rough places in the metal. Examining it more closely, he saw that the initial crossings by Petropoulos, Falcone, and Niles had worn deep grooves in the metal. Carabiners that he typically used were steel and therefore much more durable, but the ones carried as part of field gear were aluminum and had a tendency to wear after a handful of uses. This one had already been used a couple of times; he tried to remember how many but could not be sure. He ran his fingertip back and forth over the ruts, wondering if the metal would hold up for the remaining crossings. The carabiner appeared to be worn 20 to 30 percent through, which might have still been okay were it not for the questionable condition of the cable itself. He decided to tie it into the old pulley as added insurance, cutting a yard of parachute cord from the ball he always carried, knotting the ends and tying the cord through both his and Callie's harness rings. He then brought the cord up to the pulley, tightening it to distribute the weight evenly between pulley and carabiner, making a second sling. Jake really did not like the condition of the pulley or the wear on the carabiner, but he couldn't think of another option. He hoped the cord would do the trick. He slipped on a pair of gloves and cautiously maneuvered over the edge, holding onto Callie as he did. It was a struggle, but he managed by encircling her waist with one arm and using his other arm to maneuver. He knew he needed to keep the pressure on her lower torso to a minimum.

In his arm, Callie was trembling violently. Holding her tight and close, he put his chin on her neck and said, "I've got you, angel." And pushed off the ridge.

They slid over the canyon, with night blowing past and artillery lighting up the sky in bursts. Not even half of the way, the line seemed to sag—much too soon—and Jake felt his heart lurch and his throat close up. Was the cable giving out? The cord? Had the pulley or the carabiner deteriorated? He thought he could detect some instability, some increased drag. Instants later, the answer came as he felt the weight of Callie's body shift in his arm, grow slightly heavier. At the same time, he was aware of a change in the balance of his own weight. Pulling her tighter against him, his gloved hand closed around the pulley. It was holding, for now. He reached behind and checked the carabiner, also still intact. But for how much longer?

The cable sagged again, swayed, vibrated. The pulley screeched. He felt their weight sink. And drop, as something snapped.

For one horrible moment he thought they were plummeting to the bottom of the river basin, felt the momentum change. Even through the NVGs, he was disoriented in the weightless wide open, could not tell whether they were moving or hanging. There was a forceful jolt that sent them wheeling for several feet, and suddenly...suddenly his feet were hitting something uneven.

They must have dropped lower, caught on something. Even with the NVGs, he couldn't see what it was, possibly a tree branch. He felt Callie clutching his arm even as he held her tighter, felt her shaking, felt her chest heaving. Looking up, he saw the pulley dangling freely.

The cord had severed.

God in heaven, the carabiner was the only thing holding them—the only thing keeping them from falling into the canyon. The cable swayed but they were still caught by whatever had snagged them. He could see the river rushing below, felt nothing around them. They were just hanging.

His arm held her solidly, muscles straining not so much from her weight as from the tension exerted in the desperation of the embrace. He couldn't let go of her, couldn't work free of the impasse. And he felt as if the corroded cable, the remaining cord, or the worn carabiner—maybe all three—were on the verge of giving way and releasing them into the dark abyss.

He kicked out at the obstruction, finally breaking free. The line jerked again and they went sprawling.

But the ascent was incredibly steep and would require full hands-on maneuvering. Which meant letting go of Callie. In her ear, he said, "Love, I need you to hold onto my legs now. Okay? I have to let go, but it's all right. You're connected to me and we're both connected to the cable." The instant he released his arm from her waist, she wailed, but her hands grabbed his legs as he stretched them out and leaned back in his harness.

Hand over hand, Jake pulled them along the cable toward the other side of the gorge, straining as the carabiner slid inches at a time. Once, near the top, Callie lost her grip and fell free of him. She cried out, dangling beside him from her sling, and he quickly reached for her. He squinted up through his NVGs, trying to see if the cord and the carabiner were still intact. He couldn't tell. Wrapping her arms around him, he said, "Hold tight now," and grabbed the cable, going hand over hand again. And again. Pulled by inches, by feet, muscles working, tendons cramping. Straining, sweat streaking his face, he willed the cable to hold.

It did, and he pulled up to the top of the bank. Seconds later, they were being helped the rest of the way by Petropoulos and Falcone. He expelled a lungful of breath.

Using the combination of the weakened carabiner and pulley, Tangeman made it across and ran for the clearing.

Jake was holding Callie across his knee, and saw that she had lost consciousness again. Frantically, he felt for a pulse in her wrist, in her neck, anywhere. Barely palpable. He squeezed her to him, pressing his face against hers. "Oh baby, stay with me," he pleaded, "stay with me, love. Come on, Callie…please, stay with me, love. Oh God…oh God."

The sound of a helicopter could be heard closing in. The rotors whirred louder and louder, converging, but before the chopper was directly overhead, Jake was startled by the crackle of his radio headset.

"Jake, this is Alberto…repeating, Jake this is Alberto. Come in, over."

Jake keyed his mic in disbelief. "Where the hell have you been? Over."

"Right here, Jake. I have been right here, and we are right above you now. The interdiction is underway, but I see that you have made it to safety. Over."

"Thank God," Jake said. Then, "I've been trying to reach you for hours. How did you find us? Over."

"Apparently, I could hear you but you could not hear me. I copied everything you sent. I have been with you all along. Over."

Choked, Jake looked down at Callie's motionless form in his arms. "Get down here," he commanded. "Goddammit, get down here." Drawing Callie closer, rocking her against him, he whispered, "Callie…love…" The two words, uttered like a prayer, and an affirmation, as the helicopter descended.

47

JAKE STOOD LISTENING TO the soft thunder of the waves as the pitch picked up and their reach came closer, rolling and spreading a little farther with each pass. Dusk was flavoring the sky with a palette of ice-cream colors, the more muted shades of the richer ones to come. A light breeze rippled through the palms and stirred salt through the warm air. Jake listened to the sounds of tranquility, such a dramatic departure from those they had experienced in the Colombian jungle just a few days ago, and wondered what Callie was thinking and feeling. As a war-torn warrior, he knew what it was like to emerge from the hell of battle, and what Callie had been through was nothing short of that. But he was wired to deal with the destruction, cope with the losses, reconstruct and resume life. Callie was not.

She was sitting on the sand a few feet in front of him, a small figure in a pale pink dress. The breeze was lifting the hem of the dress and blowing her long blond curls back from her bruised and battered face. One hand was scooping sand, releasing it slowly, and scooping it again as she stared out at the ocean. The other hand worried with the dress hem, pushing it down each time the breeze blew it up.

Like a flash-bang, Jake saw the photograph from Valentín's house—Callie on the beach, this very beach.

Minutes ago, he had helped her from the Toyota 4x4 after a two-hour drive from the Quepos airport. He had taken his time, navigating with more care than usual over the rough stretch of road, mindful of her hurting. While he had removed his bags from the truck, she'd stood gazing trancelike toward the dunes. And then, unexpectedly, made her way to the beach. He had followed her, watching achingly as she lowered herself to the sand with obvious discomfort.

After being medevaced to Tres Esquinas for emergency treatment, Callie had been flown to Bogotá where she spent two days in the Fundacion hospital. Fully assessing the extent of her ravaged condition for the first time—exhaustion and dehydration, infection from bites and lacerations, not to mention the physical, emotional, and psychological toll of Valentín's brutality—and realizing for the first time just how close he'd come to losing her—Jake finally broke down. All the emotion he'd managed to constrain came rushing forth with a force and depth and intensity that overwhelmed him. The first evening in the hospital, as she finally slept peacefully, he had leaned over her and softly brushed a soiled and sweaty strand of her beautiful hair back from pallid skin that had been bludgeoned and bloodied, now blistered and bruised. Touched the fine brush of eyelashes with his fingertip. Felt their fragility. Just looked at her with more hurt than he had ever felt for anyone, anything, in his life. Hurt and something more, something that possessed every part of his being. He'd held one of her small hands in his, put his head down on the bed, and felt tears bleed from him. Like she had bled. Gutturally, from the soul.

After the third day, at Hernandez's house, even though he knew it was really too soon for her to travel, they flew back to Costa Rica. He wanted to get them both out of Colombia.

Forty-eight hours after their steamy night in the Colombian jungle, Operation Dark Sun had been officially wrapped up and deemed a success, depending on which version one subscribed to. According to the US State Department, NAS, the DEA, the Colombian police and military, several tons of cocaine were destroyed, as well as two-dozen or more processing labs and, perhaps most importantly of all, a half-dozen FARC encampments—along with their guerrilla troops—were wiped out. All, according to the official government press releases, without any loss of life on the counternarcotics side. However, information broadcast by the FARC, which played to the media's more aberrant side, told an entirely different story. In their version, several aircraft were shot down, at least thirty agents or soldiers were killed in action, as many as seventy-five hostages taken. Much was also made of the great loss of civilian lives, pegged by the FARC spokesmen as a "senseless political slaughter." Both the State Department and the Colombian government vehemently denied all of these claims. In reality, on the night of the interdiction operation, the agents and operatives were outnumbered and outgunned; the group comprised a scant twenty-four, and their aircraft was the target of aggressive firepower, including Cuban-made surface-to-air missiles. By comparison, the FARC guerrillas in the interdiction area exceeded three hundred. It had clearly been a disaster in the making. Even so, Hernandez related that all involved were satisfied with their efforts and felt that another significant dent had been made in the Drug War. The operation was heralded as a major coup for the "new" Andean Counterdrug Initiative.

While the demise of the Valentín patriarch and brothers had not been made public, privately both the US and Colombian governments were ecstatic. No explanation for the cause of their deaths had been given, nor was any investigation likely to ensue. Rumors of the cartel's successful reorganization and business continuity were already in wide circulation.

Subsequent to the completion of Operation Dark Sun, Vince McCauley had been promoted while Alberto Hernandez was swamped with the follow-up paperwork and reports. He was already being pushed to plan the next operation.

While at the hospital with Callie, Jake had told Hernandez that he might want to check out an old schoolhouse near Valentín's ranch. When Hernandez dropped them at the airport two days later, he asked Jake what he was supposed to find. "We passed it," Jake told him, "and thought it might be of interest." Hernandez had shrugged and said, "Nothing there but some desks and chairs falling apart...oh, and a deep musty cellar." An empty one. Except, he'd added, for some papers scattered across the cellar floor. Printed in Arabic and Somali.

Something so mind-blowing and heinous, Delaney had said in his letter. All those crates of arms...maybe not smuggled *in* by the FARC but on their way *out*. To arm terrorists, to kill American soldiers.

A few times prior to departing, Jake had tried to radio Raúl Aguilar.

Also made some general inquiries that yielded nothing. The paramilitary had slipped back across the ambiguous borderland where he lived and operated in pursuit of what Jake fervently hoped was, at least, a good and noble cause. Despite what had happened between them in the schoolhouse, he still believed Aguilar was a decent man and, he hoped, still a friend.

The money Jake had used during the ransom ploy was now back in the Bahamian bank account. He had no idea, no idea at all, what to do about it or with it—or the rest of the million-odd dollars. *So my challenge to you, Jake, is make it count for something,* Delaney had imparted from the grave. What was he supposed to do with money that didn't belong to him? It was not something he really wanted to think about right now.

Quincy Tangeman and Steve Petropoulos had returned to the States and respective military-related projects, promising to be ready for the next call.

Eddie Falcone and Curran Niles had also headed back to the US, to meet with their executive producers and discuss the future of the reality show they'd been dispatched to evaluate. It seemed the head of the production company was reconsidering the theme but was waiting for a full report from Falcone and Niles. When Jake bid them goodbye, they were undecided as to what their recommendation might be, but Jake had a feeling he'd be seeing them again before long—whether they went forward with the show or not. The experience they had shared with Jake had been, clearly, life altering, and it would take some time before they'd know exactly how. But for now, they reveled in even the most mundane things. Like the creaminess of butter on bread, the solid feel of a wooden chair, the cool and comfortable fit of coins in hand. The New York streets were reassuringly solid, free of tangling vines and hissing snakes, the sky above abundantly and sincerely blue—even if occasionally sooty. And they were very much alive.

Prior to parting, sporting new SpecOps activewear, Niles had quipped, "Almost got ourselves killed and all we got were these bloody t-shirts?" To which Jake responded with a smile that said more than words could have.

Falcone had then looked into Jake's dark eyes and asked, "How do you do it? How do you go back to a regular life after what we've been through?"

"I don't know," Jake had replied solemnly. "That's my problem...I can't. I ask myself that question a lot, Eddie. I'm still not sure what the answer is, which is why I think I keep doing what I do. Seems like no matter what battles I fight, there's always another war looming beyond the horizon."

"And this is how you *live*?"

With a wry smile, Jake had said, "Yeah. Hell of a life, ain't it?" As he watched the retreating backs of Falcone and Niles, heading for their taxi, Jake remembered what Falcone had asked him that night on the Amazon River. *And do you know? What you need?*

Did he?

Now, as Jake stood behind Callie, gazing at the welted skin of her shoulders, some of the deeper scratches still visible, he wondered—truly wondered for the first time in his life—what came next. It occurred to him that he had lived and worked in the dark for so long, it had almost become a comfortable place. Light was something new, something he was not accustomed to. He wasn't sure he was ready for it, if he even deserved to be in it. But his heart was telling him different things. Maybe it was time to let the warrior rest for a while. To heal. To need and be needed. Not just to lust, but to love and be loved.

Looking back toward the dunes, he spotted a hawk and watched it in idle fascination. Gliding, circling...circling, circling. The happy, heroic image of Haskell filled his mind and his eyes misted.

As much as he yearned for and needed the excitement, stimulation, and ultimate satisfaction of venturing and discovering, of extending his skills and expertise to help others and broaden the definition of himself...as much as he thrived in the independence of a life with no boundaries, of a destination with no destiny...maybe there were some other depths of himself that he should explore. But that thought was more frightening to him than any of the risks he took as a warrior.

Watching the hawk again, he thought: *Yes, Haskell, my brother, coming down is always the hardest thing.*

Jake stepped over to Callie, startling her as he knelt on the sand. "It's okay, love," he said gently. "It's just me."

She looked up at him and the pain pooling in her eyes, still so close to the surface, pierced his heart. Because he had been part of what caused that pain. Seeing her that day in San José, taking care of her, getting to know her—and then letting her get close to him—had almost cost her life. It was something that would live with him always, in a whole other realm of the dark place. So maybe he needed to be brave now, braver than he'd ever been, do the best thing, the right thing. Let his heart break and bleed, let her hurt for a while…but let her mend and be safe. Live a nice, peaceful life with a good man, somewhere. She looked up at him, he looked down at her. The sand beneath his feet felt warm, close; the sky was high and wide but pulling down as it darkened and deepened.

After a few moments, her breathing eased but her shoulders remained tense. Her head dropped. With his finger, he tipped her chin up, looking into the moist brown eyes, the hardness in his own replaced by a warm and soulful incandescence that only she seemed to evoke. He held the gaze for a long time, poised precariously and uneasily on the edge of wanting. Felt the sand under his feet, heard the surf.

And said, "I won't let anyone hurt you ever again."

She shuddered, closed her eyes. From the time she'd spent at the Bogotá hospital, during the time at Hernandez's house, and through the hours on the flights to Costa Rica, she had barely spoken. She had clung to him, desperately—clutched his arm, burrowed into him, but barely spoken. And she did not now.

"Callie," he said tenderly, "it's going to be all right. It is. Look at me, love."

Looking into his face, his eyes, trust began to reluctantly replace wariness and hurt. A single tear trickled down her cheek. He brushed it with his fingertip, put it to his lips. Touched a bruise on her cheekbone, traced a laceration along her forehead. Then he leaned in and softly kissed her. Drew her into his arms and just held her, without words, letting the tears come for a while. He would get her to talk about it, but not now.

Holding her, feeling her heartbeat against his own, he caught sight of the hawk in flight again, watched it sailing serenely against the maturing evening sky. And then, in a graceful and confident loop, it dropped down into the trees. His day was done, the night had come, and the sun was growing dark.

Jake stood, extending his hand. "Come on, love"—he paused, felt something shift inside him and then break like the flutter of giant wings—"let's go home."

Callie took his hand and they walked together to the beach house. Jake slipped his arm around her, pulled her close. As they stepped onto the front porch, a breeze scented with ylang ylang and Guayaba de Mono crossed the threshold. The fragrance was delicate but exquisite. Above them, the chimes tinkled as the last light of day fell behind the ocean and down below the trees where the hawk had landed.